*Insurrection
Resurrection*

Insurrection
Resurrection

A NOVEL OF POLITICAL AND RELIGIOUS SATIRE

James R. Keena

Copyright © 2001 by James R. Keena.
Cover Art by Maureen Carmody

Library of Congress Number:	2001116472
ISBN #: Hardcover	0-7388-6593-1
Softcover	0-7388-6594-X

All rights reserved. No part of this book may be reproduced or transmitted in any form or by any means, electronic or mechanical, including photocopying, recording, or by any information storage and retrieval system, without permission in writing from the copyright owner.

This is a work of fiction. Names, characters, places and incidents either are the product of the author's imagination or are used fictitiously, and any resemblance to any actual persons, living or dead, events, or locales is entirely coincidental.

This book was printed in the United States of America.
To order additional copies of this book, contact:
Xlibris Corporation
1-888-7-XLIBRIS
www.Xlibris.com
Orders@Xlibris.com

To Aristotle, for "A is A"

To Thomas Jefferson,
for the right to life, liberty,
and the pursuit of happiness

To Ayn Rand, for objective volitional consciousness

And to all other brave pioneers who think fearlessly and
independently

Contents

Prologue 9

Chapter One:
   "The Ball and Chain" 11
Chapter Two:
   "The Man Who Died Once" 36
Chapter Three:
   "The St. Patrick's Day Charade" 65
Chapter Four:
   "Who Will Guard the Guardians?" 88
Chapter Five:
   "Et Tu, Brute?" 116
Chapter Six:
   "Pandora's Coffin" 158
Chapter Seven:
   "The Human Bologna Grinder" 193
Chapter Eight:
   "The Juggernaut" 239
Chapter Nine:
   "Honchogate" 281
Chapter Ten:
   "The Insurrection Act" 328
Chapter Eleven:
   "Revolution Redux" 376
Chapter Twelve:
   "The Man Who Died Twice" 430
Chapter Thirteen:
   "The Man Who Lived" 476

Prologue

"To be free, not only from nationalism but also from all the conclusions of organized religions and political systems, is essential if the mind is to be young, fresh, innocent, that is, in a state of revolution; and it is only such a mind that can create a new world—not the politicians, who are dead, nor the priests, who are caught in their own religious systems."

J. Krishnamurti

Chapter One:
"The Ball and Chain"

> "To myself, I seem to have been only like a boy playing on the seashore, and diverting myself in now and then finding a smoother pebble or a prettier shell than ordinary, whilst the great ocean of truth lay all undiscovered before me."
>
> —Isaac Newton

Freeman's alarm went off, just like it always did. He dressed, ate, and sped off to work, just like he always did. He cursed the traffic, his job, and his pointless life, just like he always did. Then he saw something bizarre along the highway.

"Maybe it was a mirage," he thought, as his car was sucked along the freeway into the giant black hole called Washington, D.C. He worked for a politician, so he was accustomed to mirages.

Today's mirage was a strange woman that looked older than death, waving him to stop. Her fleeting image evaporated as quickly as it appeared. He mused to himself that nothing was certain anymore except uncertainty. Everything is nothing, and nothing is everything. At least for today.

Tomorrow, it will be just the opposite. Reality in one moment becomes illusion in the next, like a croquet game hosted by Wonderland's Red Queen, where the hoops move about the field and the balls are live hedgehogs. He gripped the steering wheel harder to counter the instability of his universe.

His heart skipped a beat when he saw the hunched old woman again. At least, he thought he saw her. The fog and twilight rendered everything nearly indistinguishable. He flicked his wipers on. He cranked the defroster and anxiously rubbed the windshield. Then he saw her again, much closer now. He slowed and stared intently out the passenger window through the haze. The bewildering figure subtly withdrew into the fog, as if teasing him. Driven by apocalyptic curiosity, he steered onto the shoulder of the freeway and screeched to a halt. Cars whooshed by, their headlights tracing eerie images against the backdrop of fog. He dully pondered the meaninglessness of this particular moment. It was the same meaninglessness that suffocated his whole life. Deviating from the numbing routine of his daily commute changed nothing.

A sharp knock on the passenger window startled Freeman. He recoiled as a gnarled hand with talonic fingers repeatedly rapped the glass. A draft of frigid air washed over him from nowhere. Shivering, he slumped lower into his seat. The knocking on the window continued. A car sped around the bend. Its headlights briefly illuminated the mysterious visitor and momentarily hypnotized Freeman.

Suddenly, the shadowy figure opened the door and lunged into his car. Freeman instinctively lurched toward the opposite door. He was stunned when the intruder pulled back an oversized hood to reveal herself as an enchantingly beautiful young woman. He puzzled over this instantaneous transformation from the ugliness of old age to the beauty of youth, but then he was lost in the magic of her eyes, which were green as molten emeralds and deep as all eternity. The pale luster of her cheeks, her deliciously flowing red hair, and her full, sensuous lips created an aura of womanly perfection that could only have been crafted by the great sculptors of ancient Greece. He was spellbound.

The enchanting beauty said softly, "I am Cassandra, the daughter of Priam, the last great King of Troy." Freeman sat mute, hypnotized by her emerald eyes, while she continued. "When I was young, the god Apollo fell in love with me. I did not reciprocate, so in order to buy my love, he offered me a most extraordinary gift, which I had the great misfortune to accept. As the sands of time passed, I found it impossible to love him and bestow my womanly favors upon him. Angry at my rejection, Apollo turned my gift into an abhorrent curse. I have lived in misery ever since."

Freeman's uncomprehending stare encouraged Cassandra to elaborate. "Apollo gave me the gift of prophecy, the ability to foretell events that haven't yet occurred." Warm teardrops formed in her eyes and slowly trickled down her alabaster face. "When I denied him romance, he sought revenge by decreeing to the universe that none of my prophecies were ever to be believed. Thus, I can see all of mankind's impending horrors, but no one believes what I foretell. It is an endless, terrifying nightmare. Apollo cursed not only me but also all of humanity. My curse is to know, yet to be ignored. The curse on the rest of you is to hear, yet to choose ignorance."

Freeman was bewildered. Why was this unbalanced woman in his car? What in hell was she talking about? And how should he react to a distraught woman who claimed to have lived thousands of years ago? "Aren't you dead . . . ?", he asked lamely.

"If I am dead, why do I suffer so?", she abruptly snarled, her emerald eyes blazing fiercely. "It's true that I was killed in one dimension of existence, after I abandoned Apollo and fell in love with Agamemnon. But in another dimension, I will live as long as there is at least one other consciousness in the universe. Although my murdered corpse is buried near the Corinthian Gulf, something uniquely 'me' lives on, does it not? History is always and everywhere, along with the men and women who lived it passionately. History surrounds us and compels us. It is lived and relived, in unending cycles. The past becomes present, which then becomes future. The deeper you look into the past, the more of the future you see. I am both dead and alive, and woefully ignored in either state." Cassandra sighed. "Oh, how I want to help!", she cried. "I want so badly to stop what's happening to us all!"

"What *is* happening to us all?", asked Freeman.

"Can't you see?", pleaded Cassandra. "We are all in chains. Just as the god Apollo put me into eternal bondage with his curse, the rest of you are chained to gods and kings and myths. I was born free, but Apollo couldn't tolerate my freedom. He is now my mortal enemy, and I have dedicated my tortured existence to destroying him and his aliases. All of you were born free too, but now your lives are but playthings to gods and kings, to be toyed with, abused, and ultimately discarded."

Freeman struggled to comprehend. He knew that things were screwed up, but he had no idea why. To him, the universe was simply a random collection of mysteries, riddles, and enigmas. He was, however, silently enraptured by Cassandra's sad, wistful smile, which would have been Leonardo da Vinci's masterpiece of paradox had he brushed it upon canvas. Joy and sorrow were captured in one simple expression of essential humanness, a timeless and unchanging legacy shared across the millennia, winding down through countless generations.

"Would you like to hear what will happen to you in the rest of your existence?", Cassandra asked, trying to tease Freeman out of his silence.

He nodded, and then fought back a surge of apprehension, fearing that his future would contain unwelcome revelations. She folded her arms across her chest and fell strangely still. She stared into the distance, as if bringing into focus something no one else could see. She rocked gently back and forth, transfixed like a child seeing a bonfire for the first time. In a throaty whisper that sounded like a faint echo from another realm, she began to prophesy.

"The forces of Good and Evil will confront Freeman directly. He will experience the worst hatred and abuse that mankind is capable of. He will see war, oppression, murder, fraud, slavery, and greed. He will remain confused for a long time. But then one day he will undergo a personal epiphany and discover his purpose in life. He will then expose the insidious schemes and deceptions of other men and dispel myths and conspiracies, leading us out of bondage to our gods and kings. But, this will not come without doubt, trial, and suffering beyond human imagination. And, there will be a man full of essential goodness and wisdom to help him. More than this cannot be told, for his is still a life to be lived."

Freeman was convinced now that this woman was insane. Her revelations implied his life had colossal import that he couldn't see the potential for. Perhaps she had revealed the biography of a much more competent ancestor or progeny. There must be countless Freemans to choose from. The Freeman sitting next to this uninvited lunatic was just an ordinary grunt who worked a day job in the government and spent his nights regretting his day job.

Frankly, he didn't believe one word of the bizarre woman with the burning emerald eyes. He was going to tell her that when she awoke from the entranced slumber she had fallen into. Without her hypnotic eyes boring into him, the absurdity of his situation struck him. He sat up higher, abandoning his fetal crouch. Traffic was much heavier on the freeway now. As if waking from an exotic dream, Freeman felt the dismal shock of what his life was really like.

He was a public relations stooge for a despotic senator in Washington. He detested this job, which was part of its appeal. He spent his time issuing dishonest press releases that put a positive spin on the unholy antics of his boss. His role was to counter the negative perceptions of voters, who despised the shenanigans in Washington. He rationalized this dishonesty as necessary to prevent the universe from becoming unbalanced and spinning helplessly out of control. He didn't actually believe this, but he didn't believe in anything else either, so he was comfortably self-deceived.

Freeman was among thousands of public relations specialists hired by politicians. Wayward congressmen employ these ventriloquist dummies because they know that the first rule in politics is to look like an owl after you've behaved like a jackass. For example, if you've legislated a national debt of a trillion dollars, don't point out to voters that this can be visualized as a stack of $1000 bills 67 miles high. Instead, hire an army of Freemans to cleverly mask the horrible truth of it, which is that our children will involuntarily inherit crushing obligations spawned by the spendthrift government of their parents.

The Senator who employed Freeman for the past twenty years was known simply as the Head Honcho. He had been re-elected with that nickname for so many terms that no one remembered his real name. He was the most powerful man in Washington. Even presidents depended on his support for their political livelihoods. His inordinate power was due to his tenure, the important committee chairmanships he held, and the unconscionable graft and corruption he wallowed in. He was pretentious, arrogant, and brutal. Getting re-elected forever was his reason for being. He invested every ounce of his legislative energy campaigning for the next election, which he pursued with the barbaric fervor of jackals devouring a dead antelope. He believed in government of the politicians, for the politicians, and by the politicians. Unadulterated power was his ideology, his concubine, his passion, and his narcotic.

Freeman's job as the Head Honcho's public relations stooge should have been impossible, given the Senator's constant moral and legal transgressions. But, no one paid attention to his illicit behavior, because in Washington, they not only ignore the arsonist who starts the fire, they ignore the alarm bells and sometimes even the fire itself, as if ignorance can keep human flesh from being incinerated. People naively accepted the Honcho's public relations disguise as the ardent defender of their sacred welfare and inalienable rights. Protected by this media smokescreen, he was a power-mongering juggernaut.

Freeman was indifferent to it all, because his job paid him well and because it was absurd enough to make sense, as long as he didn't think about it. His hibernating conscience was swept along by the Senator's momentum. He was the Head Honcho's unquestioning paid shill, which earned him the nickname "Yessir!". This didn't offend him, because it fit his desired state of being, which was to have no enemies who hated him, and no friends who liked him.

Despite his general apathy, Freeman was unhappy with the unconscious woman in his car. His irritation grew when he realized he was late for work. He brusquely placed his hand on Cassandra's disconcertingly cold shoulder and shook her awake. Her once-fiery emerald eyes were clouded by the incomplete transition from a dream filled slumber, but she felt the same pain that happened after each of her cursed prophecies. It was like the heart-rending anguish of a bride jilted by her lover while she apprehensively waits at the wedding altar, scorned in a moment meant to be gloriously triumphant, but instead is abysmally disappointing. Worse still, that moment of terrible grief is repeated throughout eternity. Such was the accumulated pain that constricted Cassandra's heart. Another of her prophecies was disdained. The curse had struck another of an infinite series of blows.

She couldn't blame Freeman, for this was the result of her rejection of Apollo's desire to own her, but she also knew that his unheeding reaction would become his folly. She wept for herself and for the procession of men and women who had ignored her prophecies and met their fates wholly unprepared. She wept for the German Jews, the Russian peasants, the Chinese proles, and everyone else who had been warned but chose ignorance instead. She wept because Apollo's spiteful curse was indeed a curse upon everyone. There were others who could foresee the impending disasters mankind frequently wrought upon itself at the behest of its leaders, but they too were ignored by the apathetic masses and were often judged to be insane. Humanity's curse manifested itself as a communal brainwashing, an abdication of the responsibility for critically and morally evaluating events.

Cassandra summoned the courage to offer another prophecy. "Freeman, I swear upon all that is sacred that your life will be as I have foretold. You don't believe me, and I know why. But there's one more thing I must tell you. One day, you will fall into an irresistible slumber, such as I did this morning. We who have the power of prophecy call it an incubation. It will occur during the moment of your greatest distress. When you fear that the universe has lost all of its meaning, I will bring you sleep. When you awaken, everything will be clear to you. It will be like awakening in the morning with your head so cleansed that ideas enter into it with startling clarity, only magnified a thousand times. You will bask in the glorious sunshine of refreshed innocence and a magnificent new life."

Freeman returned Cassandra's prophecy with a stare of uncompromising disbelief.

"So, again you don't believe me," she sighed, the words floating from her sensuous mouth like baby's breath. "I have done all that I can for you. Now, I must depart immediately, since today is the Seventh Day of the sacred Delphic Month. This is the only day I can reveal my divinations to mortals on earth, and you are but the first of many with whom I must consult. But, before I recede into the realm known only to those who live eternally, I leave with you two souvenirs of my prophecies. One of them is a gift, the other a curse. Please hold out your hand."

A passing truck sent a rumbling shudder through Freeman's parked car. He obediently held his palm open as Cassandra gently placed an unfamiliar green leaf in his shaking hand. He feared that it was the curse and would suddenly turn into a serpent or a deadly spider. "No thank you," he croaked, clumsily handing it back to her.

"Keep it, you fool," she laughed. "That laurel leaf is the gift, not the curse. It's a potent catalyst for bringing on the incubation that I just described. When you reach your greatest distress, chew it. The acrid taste will quickly dissipate. You will be overcome by euphoria, and then all will be revealed to you as you drift into a deep slumber."

Freeman reluctantly accepted the leaf. "And the curse?" he asked timidly.

Cassandra's emerald green eyes sparkled with the fire of delicious revenge, radiating an inner rage to inflict punishment on yet another mortal whose disbelief rent her heart and continued her eternal purgatory. Freeman was stunned by the acrimonious assault that lunged from her snarling lips and lashing tongue. "You, unbeliever, will suffer excruciating torment! You, to whom I have prophesied from the depths of my suffering soul, are separated from the Truth only by the obstinacy of your unthinking mind! You are ignorant because you choose to be! For years you will be nothing but cannon fodder for the myths, religions, and political propaganda that other men dazzle your self-neutered mind with!"

The enchantress suppressed the welling emotion spilling out of her like lava from a volcano. More gently, she said, "One day, you will be ready to know the truth, after you can no longer stand the torment of constant illusion. Then you will call out to me to release you from the bondage of your own mind. I hope that you will become the first mortal to cast aside the spell of ignorance with which Apollo has chained you and everyone else to horrible governments and misguided religions. But until that time . . . "

A searing flash of light punctuated Cassandra's last haunting words. Freeman instinctively recoiled and covered his face. He remained that way, shivering, until he realized he wasn't being incinerated. His eyes gradually recovered from the burst of intense light. The bizarre woman had vanished, leaving him alone in the dismal grayness.

Unfortunately, Cassandra left behind her promised curse. Freeman was astonished to find a rusted iron ball and chain clasped to his left ankle. This encounter may have seemed like a dream, but he stared at the contraption strapped to his ankle long enough to be convinced it was a coldly concrete fact, not an illusion. He even pinched himself several times. Alas, he was quite awake. He shivered again as he pondered his eerie predicament.

Then something even more extraordinary happened. Freeman's addled mind summoned it's best defense mechanisms, one of which was to convince itself that the bizarre distortion of reality it was experiencing was actually quite normal. "Is this really so unusual?", his brain mused to itself. "Everyone, in some manner or other, is burdened with balls and chains. Most people aren't aware of them or have become comfortably resigned to them." He subconsciously knew that few people challenge the historical, cultural, and religious dogmas that enslave them and stifle their spirits.

Everyone learns to endure their psychological balls and chains with great courage and fortitude. Minute by minute, he grew accustomed to his physical burden, just as he had grown habituated to his lifelong psychological and spiritual burdens. Freeman was actually well prepared to carry the burden of his ball and chain, being both Irish and Catholic, which is one of humankind's most insidious contradictions. The Irish are naturally romantic, witty, and poetic people who are intensely fond of wine, song, and life. Catholics, on the other hand, are deadly serious, with a profound propensity for guilt, self-immolation, and dogged hope that the afterlife will hold more joy and meaning than this life. Freeman's dichotomous birthrights caused him to be neither insightful nor naive, neither happy nor sad, but rather apathetically omniscient. He was aloof and apolitical, blasphemous but not rebellious, disdainful of tradition but willing to wallow in it anyway. He just didn't care.

He warmed to the comforting madness of his familiar apathy. He started his car and accelerated onto the freeway. The morning fog still lingered, like the scent of a mysterious woman. "Ha! A mysterious woman!", he chided himself. He was back in control of his psychological mayhem, which meant that his psychological mayhem was back in control of him.

He passed an opulent neighborhood infested with lawyers, lobbyists, and consultants who gravitate to the federal government like bees to honey. Their salaries make Washington the wealthiest domain in the world. It is the quintessential brothel, in which the oldest and second oldest professions are inextricably commingled. The medium of exchange is not only money, but also human souls. And the commodity bought and sold is more often power than sex, although the urges feel much the same.

Suddenly, his car careened headlong into nothing. He barreled into an unexpected absence of resistance, much like missing a stair step. He hurtled through space at a frightening speed, dizzily downward rather than forward, into a black, soundless void. He was startled to see that his car had vanished from around him. He helplessly spiraled lower. His body bounced like a ragamuffin doll, although he bumped against nothing. Not knowing how long his plummet would continue terrified him. Wondering if his descent would end abruptly terrified him even more.

The void he was falling into came alive and assaulted his starved senses, as if a giant curtain was suddenly opened in a darkened theater. A hot, dry wind blew in from nowhere, like the back draft from an immense inferno. He felt like a charcoal being fanned by the giant bellows of a mad blacksmith. The rancid smell of burning flesh stormed his nostrils. An unholy wailing in the distance rose to a screeching cacophony of inhuman anguish. Fear filled his soul.

He landed with a jolt. He expected an onslaught of pain, but felt nothing. He perspired heavily from the oppressive heat. The unholy cacophony continued, but something deep inside warned him that he didn't want to discover the meaning of the screams. In the impenetrable darkness, his fingers probed a rocky surface with a pitted texture like hardened lava. It was warm to the touch, as though just recently molten. He couldn't tell if his rock was floating in space or connected to something bigger.

He heard something rough sliding across the pitted rock above him. The sound was getting louder and closer. He followed its progress with trepidation, until whatever was making the ominous scraping noise was poised directly above him. He waited, his breathing now rapid and shallow. His instinct was to flee, but running in the absolute darkness seemed as dangerous as confrontation.

Without warning, a writhing, scaly, spineless mass of flesh fell on his shoulders. A sound that universally frightens all mammals came from the beast. It was the sinister "hisssss" of a snake. In the unending darkness, Freeman fiercely battled the slithering reptile. His muscles cramped from fatigue and paroxysms of fear.

Just as he was about to surrender his soul, the serpent unexpectedly released its chokehold. The loathsome reptile fell to the ground, although it was no longer a snake when it landed. It metamorphosed into a humanoid with an eerie green aura. The creature slowly moved forward. Freeman was transfixed by its fiery red eyes, which glowed like flaming embers against the obsidian background, boring through him as though he was a thin pane of glass.

"Welcome to my nightmare," hissed the glowing creature in a deep, inhospitable voice.

Freeman swallowed, but no saliva flowed in his constricted throat. "Who are you?" he croaked, although he really wanted to ask, "What are you?"

"Mephistopheles," the humanoid whispered fiercely and ominously. "Satan. The Evil Incarnate. Lucifer. I am known by a thousand aliases in your myths. Surely you recognized my disguise."

"Disguise?" squeaked Freeman, hovering somewhere between fear and morbid curiosity.

"The serpent disguise, you mindless slug. It got my career off to a fabulous start," Satan said indignantly. "Remember the slut Eve? The apple? The Garden of Eden?"

A chill ran up Freeman's spine and made him shudder, despite the oppressive heat. There was only one reason why he would be in Satan's den of iniquity. "Am I dead?"

Lucifer laughed fiendishly. "You tell me. I've observed humans for millennia, but sometimes not even I can tell the difference between living and dead ones. I just wait until the corpseless souls plummet down here. Most of them are surprised at the Final Judgment rendered upon them.

"I don't understand," confessed Freeman.

"Of course you don't, because you've chosen not to think! That's precisely why I can't distinguish between living and dead humans. Fortunately, the propensity of your species to avoid thinking makes my job embarrassingly easy."

"I don't understand," repeated Freeman, trying to avoid thinking about the Devil's riddled words.

"Humans suffer from a stifling tribal instinct", explained Satan. "They behave like the mindless herds of animals that they haughtily profess superiority over. When the chief bull veers to the right, the rest of the cattle do likewise, without considering the consequence or the purpose. And so it is with your species. When the Head Humans veer to the left, the rest of you trudge behind like automatons, unaware that you are more likely heading for oblivion than the glory they promise. This means I don't have to waste valuable time corrupting every human soul, which would be an impossible task. I simply have to corrupt your philosophical, political, and religious leaders. You uncalculating slugs will follow them into the eternal abyss, brainwashed through the media and willfully ignorant of the impending disaster until it has swallowed you whole."

Mephistopheles drew a long, hot breath, and then continued. "An excellent example is when I led the 20th Century Germans into mass eternal damnation. I tempted a few powerful men like Albert Spear, Adolph Hitler, and Heinrich Himmler with polished apples. Predictably, they devoured them like frothing children eating gingerbread from the witch's house. The German herd surrendered their guns and followed along behind them, their souls corrupted by default and their tickets to my nightmare purchased with moral apathy. They fell into my abyss because of unquestioning subservience to vile and murderous political ideas. This happens because people are so easily convinced that they are significant only as a group, not as individuals. The purpose of life is defined for them as a social movement or a collective ideological struggle. Each man's life is unimportant compared to the greater good. In this view of life, thinking is dangerously egoist, futile, and seditious.

"That horrendous cacophony is the screaming of millions of tormented human souls who chose not to think while they were alive, believing that this absolved them of guilt in subsequent moral catastrophes. Tragically, they didn't realize that mindless sheep are as guilty as the evil shepherd they choose to obey. Fortunately for me, humans don't understand that the most grievous sin is choosing not to think apart from the herd. Religions and governments abhor the questioning individual mind, demanding faithful conformity to their chosen gospel instead, as if spirituality and wisdom were no more complex than the children's game 'Simon Says'. They preach that understanding is achieved through mystery rather than reason. This preoccupation with faith not only makes your leaders' jobs easier, it makes my job easier too."

Freeman ignored Lucifer's confusing words and asked, "Why am I here?"

Lucifer's fiery red eyes narrowed into razor sharp slits. "You spoke with Cassandra today?"

"Yes," replied Freeman, who no longer knew the difference between dreams and reality.

"What did she tell you?" Satan demanded, his hot breath scorching Freeman's face and reeking like rotting refuse and decaying flesh.

"I . . . I don't know", muttered Freeman, stalling to fabricate a lie without understanding why. "I don't speak Greek."

Lucifer grabbed Freeman's throat violently. His slitted eyes torched into Freeman's naked inner self. "You can't lie to me! Have you forgotten who I am?" The Devil released his deadly grip and resumed his interrogation. "What did she tell you this morning?"

Freeman probed the blisters on his neck left by Satan's searing fingers. Intimidated, he retold the details of Cassandra's prophecy.

Satan chuckled menacingly. "So, the pathetic whore of mighty Apollo predicts that you will be a Messiah? Perhaps you too were born in Bethlehem, taking human form to save the rest from eternal damnation?" Another malevolent chuckle erupted from Lucifer. "Do you believe you are the great man the whoring bitch described?"

The Devil's firefly eyes glowed hypnotically in the darkness. Lost souls wailed forlornly in the infinite background, pleading for mercy in a merciless realm. Freeman was mortified and mute. He hoped against hope that this was a nightmare that just seemed frightfully real, although he suspected his lethargic imagination was incapable of conjuring such bizarre things.

Lucifer's scathing voice jolted Freeman from his enchanted daze. "Answer me, you mindless amoral slug! Do you believe her?"

"Why do you care about her and me?"

Satan exhaled a small fluke of flame. "Your ignorance appalls me. She's my mortal enemy, because she knows that unthinking faith is the secret weapon of all the kings, gods, and devils that ever existed. She knows that reason is the kryptonite that renders me and the gods and kings utterly powerless. Everyone has the potential to think, so those who believe her must be obliterated. Do you believe the lying slut?"

"I . . . I . . . no, I don't," Freeman mumbled, capitulating to the maniacal cretin despite the mournful emerald green eyes of Cassandra pleading with him from inside his troubled memory.

Lucifer's eyes sparkled. "Of course you don't! Nobody does. They believe me instead, because the illusions I offer ease their pain and cover the tracks of their directionless lives." Satan extended an eerie green palm holding objects that were hard to distinguish in the faint glow of his iridescence. "I have two gifts for you."

Freeman, suddenly remembering the ball and chain padlocked to his ankle, was leery of gratuities from nightmarish beings. He struggled to identify the suspicious objects in the hellish darkness. One was a plant, and the other was a cardboard stub. "What are these?" he asked.

"One gift is marijuana", Satan replied. "It replaces what Cassandra gave you this morning."

"It replaces this?" Freeman asked hopefully, rattling his rusty iron ball and chain.

"No, mindless fool," snickered Lucifer. "That contraption is yours to keep or shed, as you choose. I meant the laurel leaf she gave you to someday consume and be enlightened. Since you don't believe her, it's useless. Marijuana, on the other hand, is widely used by mortals who have surrendered their lives to the meaningless. It numbs their minds from the pain of moral confusion and salves the festering wounds inflicted on them during their search for meaning in a world diseased with insanity. It will be more useful to you than the utopian hope offered by Cassandra. It's also free," said the Devil beguilingly.

Freeman had already cocooned inside enough painkilling illusions during his life and didn't need to chemically induce more. He nonchalantly pocketed the marijuana. "What's the cardboard stub for?"

"It's your ticket out of Hell and back to the swirling madness of your insignificant time and place. However, unlike the marijuana, it isn't free."

"Price is no object!" declared Freeman, desperate to end this apocalyptic nightmare and to return to his more familiar insanity in Washington. He reached for his wallet.

Lucifer's narrowed red slits focused intently on his prey. "The medium of exchange isn't in your wallet, you naive paean. Money can buy you sex and power, but it can't buy your way out of that ball and chain or out of this nightmare. The price is your soul." He rubbed his eerily glowing palms greedily.

Freeman's price-is-no-object bravado evaporated. "Why do you want my soul?"

"It's worthless under normal circumstances", Satan said derisively. "However, you heard a dangerous revelation today. That lying whore Cassandra attempted to recruit another soldier in her eternal battle against Apollo and the rest of the gods, kings, and other demons who are the rightful masters of you lowly serfs. You claim you don't believe her, and even if you knew the truth you would probably squander it by turning it into a useless religion. But, I can't take any chances. Her meddling in your life is another of her misguided attempts to foil my grand plans. I have the same mission as St. Paul, who vowed to destroy the wisdom of the wise. Our goal is to eradicate the Aristotles, Thomas Edisons, Jiddu Krishnamurtis, and Ayn Rands from the universe. The power we seek requires ignorance by the masses, which is made possible only by blind faith in someone else's mythologies.

"The blinders of ignorance that you humans willingly wear prevent you from seeing the progress of my plan. Some of my most successful clients were the Pharaohs, Caesar Augustus, Attila the Hun, King George, Napoleon, Karl Marx, Nicolai Lenin, Joe Stalin, Adolph Hitler, Mao Tse-Tung, the Khmer Rouge, Idi Amin, Moammar Khadaffi, and Saddam Hussein. I don't want you or that prevaricating bitch Cassandra mucking up my assault on mankind via their chosen leaders. Therefore, the only acceptable price for that ticket out of here is your soul, so that you will be rendered philosophically ignorant and morally neutered. Not that anyone will notice the difference. But at least I'll be sure you are incapable of exposing my gambit. To leave, you must accept my terms."

Freeman wasn't convinced he had a soul at all, but if he did, it was probably expendable. Besides, no one ever really lost a soul in a harmless dream, which is surely what this must be. "Deal," he said somberly, extending his hand to formally seal the pact.

"Fuck you, Mr. Morally Neutered," swore the sadistic satyr, ignoring the hand. "Who knows better than me not to trust anyone? Put it in writing." He handed Freeman a document and a small knife, with an unsettling instruction. "You must sign it in blood."

Freeman nervously fingered the knife blade, which was coagulated with human blood from eons of repeated use by others that had made the same apocalyptic decision. He made a mental note to get a tetanus shot when he awoke from this unhealthy dream, not realizing that no medicinal concoction could cure the virus he was about to infect himself with. Gritting his teeth, he slashed his right index finger and scrawled his name on the dotted line, leaving a macabre trail of blood across the unearthly document.

As Lucifer grabbed the paper, Freeman blurted, "Where's my copy?"

"What would you do with it? Present it to your lawyer? Hand it to your priest? Mail it to your mother? You idiot! I took your soul, not your brain. This document has no legal precedence on earth. But, it is eternally binding beyond the vale of death," Satan spat out in a foreboding voice.

Freeman acquiesced timidly. He fingered the ticket stub in his damp palm. It was soggy with blood from his injured finger. "What about your end of the bargain? How do I get out of here?"

"Follow me," instructed Lucifer.

"Yessir!" replied Freeman, true to his nickname and his newly reinforced amorality. He bounded obediently behind the eerily glowing Devil, like a puppy afraid of losing its Master, as they traversed the thick gloom of Hell. He occasionally stumbled blindly over lumps of pumice, while Satan floated over them like a ghostly hovercraft.

Suddenly, the ground underneath his feet leapt to life. Embedded in the pumice were large ruby nodules that radiated brilliantly. The dazzling jewels formed a sparkling path that stretched toward an unseen abyss, an astounding swath of splendor in an otherwise desultory realm. "What on earth is this?" he exclaimed.

"This isn't earth," Lucifer reminded caustically. "However, this luminous monument was constructed diligently by people from earth who didn't realize they were building a path to oblivion."

Freeman was bewildered and speechless.

"Your reaction is normal. Every lost soul tumbling down that radiant path looks equally confused. Each had the delusion that their life's work was accomplishing a more noble objective." Mephistopheles gingerly handed one of the shining jewels to Freeman. "Does it look familiar?"

"No," replied Freeman after studying it briefly.

"It should, because you've placed a few of these gems here yourself." Holding a gleaming jewel in his ghostly hand, Lucifer declared, "This, my soulless follower, is a Good Intention. The road to Hell is paved several feet deep with them. These ruby nodules were carefully crafted throughout history by well-intentioned humans who fatally assumed that a desirable 'end' justified an immoral 'means', often without realizing that the 'end' was evil too. Anyone who ever did 'good', without considering the consequences, has helped construct this monument to my unceasing efforts. Humanity has never learned that having good intentions as a motive is not an absolution of responsibility for any ensuing calamity, which has contributed to a population explosion in my fiery domain."

"History is littered with examples, such as the mass suicide in Jonestown, Guyana," drooled Satan. "At the behest of a frothing madman named Jim Jones, hundreds of Americans poisoned themselves and their children. Every one of those adults then tumbled down my gleaming Road of Good Intentions. If you listen carefully, you can hear them screaming.

"The Jonestown comedy was one of my easiest victories", continued Lucifer salaciously. "All I had to do was corrupt the soul of one lunatic. A surprising number of other humans willingly sacrificed their sanity and morality to follow this self-proclaimed god to oblivion. They worshipped him with the best of intentions via a wonderful evil called faith. Even as Jones' henchmen rolled a hundred-pound drum of potassium cyanide into their encampment, his followers still believed that his philosophy of self-sacrificial socialism was a good-intentioned end. They still believed when he instructed them to squirt a deadly mix of purple Kool-Aid and poison into the mouths of their helpless offspring. While parents were murdering their children, their mad spiritual leader shouted a quote from St. Paul into a microphone. 'Children, obey your parents in all things', he told them, 'for this is pleasing unto the Lord.'

"After much faith and good intentions, they were all dead. In their last seconds of existence, they discovered the root of my power over them. Unthinking faith is the deadliest disease a human can ever be infected with. When chaos erupted during the poisoning, Jones lied to them again. 'Stop these hysterics!' he bellowed into a scepter-like microphone. 'This is not the way for good socialists to die.' What an absurd, wonderful lie! This was the ideal way for socialists to die. Suicide is the ultimate form of faithful self-sacrifice. Jones called them insane for attempting to flee the encampment as death mushroomed all around. This was another brilliant lie. They were insane the moment they joined his Peoples Temple. That was the well-intentioned spiritual beginning of their eventual suicides."

The Devil's spine chilling explanation caused Freeman to recollect his own Good Intentions gone awry. The majestic ruby nodules now looked disconcertingly familiar. It was so easy, he concluded, to aid and abet evil through casual thoughtlessness. Hitler's followers weren't aboriginal savages. Third Reich Germany was arguably the world's most sophisticated civilization. Many of them were parents and grand parents of Americans living today. Some of Jones' followers were wealthy Americans, educated in American public schools. A tingling wave of self-doubt washed over him. He was losing touch with what was really good or evil. The religious institutions that had guided his development contradicted themselves in theory and trivialized their moral pretensions with banal rituals. Consequently, Freeman wallowed helplessly in moral ambiguity. He gloomily recalled the Ecclesiastical supposition that life is useless and edged closer to the brink of lost hope. He dropped the radiant Good Intention and tugged lamely at the ball and chain weighing him down. "Get me out of here," he moaned.

"Thy will be done". Mephistopheles waved a phosphorescent hand in a sweeping arc. Weightlessness unexpectedly overcame Freeman, as if the force of gravity had been magically suspended. He felt himself ascending at a dizzying pace. Lucifer's menacing eyes receded from view, as did the luminous Road of Good Intentions. Freeman was irresistibly drawn into a violent whirlpool that inhaled his body upward. The wailing of lost souls and the revolting stench of putrid flesh were left behind in the bowels of Hell.

The vortex sucking him upward subsided, leaving him once again seated in his car, which was spinning slowly in a cosmic eddy. Soon, the engulfing darkness surrendered to a dawn struggling against an earthly fog to illuminate the countryside. The centrifugal motion of his car became a bank turn on the freeway leading into Washington. He had escaped his hellish nightmare.

The suffocating fog draped a somber funeral shroud over Washington, transforming it into a dark, secretive, clandestine, cold, and lifeless town. The fog was an oddly welcome sight to Freeman, because it was more concrete than anything else he encountered as the Head Honcho's public relations liaison.

He exited the expressway. As he idled in traffic, he pondered the glut of "left turn only" signs. In Washington, a continuous leftward bearing is necessary to remain synchronized with the traffic flow. This automotive peer pressure is known as Vehicular Correctness.

Freeman gazed curiously at his mindless fellow commuters. They were all dutifully obeying the traffic signs. He recalled Churchill's observation that rules are made for the obedience of fools and the guidance of wise men. "Are we fools, or wise men?" he wondered. The intuitive answer depressed him. A few drivers rebelled in fits of automotive rage by making radical right-hand turns, invariably meeting their demises in spectacular collisions with the leftward-bearing juggernaut. Freeman, though, had no desire to die in a rebellious right-hand turn. He didn't desire anything beyond surviving until 5:00 each day.

Suddenly, he swerved violently to avoid colliding with another of Washington's oddities, the Sacred Cows. Massive herds of these corpulent beasts roamed the metropolis, wreaking havoc, butting pedestrians, impeding traffic, and discharging feces indiscriminately. Worse still, the legislative shepherds of the Sacred Cows required taxpayers to fund the feeding and upkeep of the alimentary monsters at all costs. The Sacred Cows were blissful, well fed, and secure in the knowledge that they were eternally protected from slaughter by the legislators who created them. They chewed their cud, ambled about aimlessly, and were sometimes mistaken for bureaucrats.

The Sacred Cows passed, leaving Freeman gratefully untrammeled. Shortly, he arrived at the Senatorial Office Building where he worked. He took an elevator deep inside the complex to a sterile hallway that stretched farther than the naked eye could see. Countless doors marked the entrances to innumerable offices, which housed incalculable bureaucrats and clerks, who labored immeasurable hours to achieve nothing.

The cavernous building housed hordes of staffers whose only known function was to telephone hordes of other staffers. There were hundreds of such massive steel and concrete enclaves of bureaucrats all over the city. The federal government was infected with an edifice complex by contagion from its second cousin, the Catholic Church. Like their religious counterparts, the glorious temples of the federal bureaucracy were constructed in exaltation of a deity, albeit a secular one.

One of Freeman's jobs was to explain the incomprehensible purpose of this to voters. He didn't know the purpose either, but the public didn't care. He often wondered if his services were needed at all. Fortunately, being needed wasn't a prerequisite for government employment.

Suddenly, he heard a gentle whisper, which wafted like smoke about his ears. The woman's singsong soprano was hauntingly familiar as her cryptic words replayed again and again inside his head, flowing across his consciousness like a revolving neon marquee. "These doors are the gates to hell . . . These doors are the gates to hell . . . These doors are the gates to hell . . . ", the mantric message flashed repeatedly.

Freeman's enchantment was snapped by the abrupt realization that the haunting voice was Cassandra's. Skepticism immediately clouded his mind. "Just another illusion," he scoffed. He opened the door to suite 1984 and silently cursed the oppressive heat that engulfed him as he entered the Head Honcho's office block. Dragging his ball and chain, he surmised the air conditioning was malfunctioning again.

Deep inside the caustic bowels of the universe, the sadistic laughter of Mephistopheles rumbled throughout his evil domain. The Devil turned up the thermostat controlling the furnace of human damnation. All was going according to plan.

Chapter Two: "The Man Who Died Once"

> "Law has ceased to be an antidote for chaos; it has become chaos."
>
> —Joseph Sobran

Freeman's ball and chain clattered across the marble floor as he trudged to his desk. Despite his noisy entrance, his catatonic office mates remained communally hypnotized by triplicate forms piled high in their "in" baskets. Feeling snubbed, he hefted his cast iron ball above his head and slammed it down onto his desk, shattering it into a thundering cascade of splinters that snapped everyone out of their comas. The room fell deathly still. They eyed Freeman with great suspicion, some because they didn't know him well enough to understand his behavior, and the rest because they did.

"What are you up to, Freeman?", someone blurted out.

"My left leg is too short, so my doctor prescribed this contraption", he mischievously replied.

They stared at him suspiciously. He was the Head Honcho's paid shill, so he was probably lying through his teeth.

"I'm not lying", said Freeman through tightly clenched teeth.

Suddenly, the mahogany door to the inner office crashed open and the Head Honcho loomed menacingly in the doorway. He was a massive, intimidating man, with a six and one half-foot frame blanketed by 350 pounds of leathery flesh. His ruddy face formed a constant scowl and suggested a trace of Neanderthal ancestry. His thinning glaze of peppered hair was cropped in military fashion. The nose protruding beneath his heavy brow had been broken in South Chicago when he pickpocketed a defensive tackle of the Bears. This violent facial rearrangement persuaded him to switch careers from thievery to politics. He soon discovered that a thief's sleight of hand was easily translated into a politician's sleight of words. Politics was far safer too, because the victims of his legislation were almost never aware that his hand was in their pockets. It was also more lucrative, since he could now pick millions of pockets with one stroke of his legislative pen. He gradually became that shadowy man behind the scenes controlling the puppet strings, that fiendish manipulator everyone suspects is there, but is too clever to be caught or revealed. He became the motive force behind the Presidency, Congress, the Supreme Court, the CIA, the Mafia, and the Teamsters Union. He learned from Lenin that a leader should have unlimited power resting on force, unrestrained by any laws or rules. His only weaknesses were alcohol, women, and paranoia.

Lurking timidly behind the menacing Senator was But Sir!, his frail yet resolute aide. But Sir! was everything that the Honcho wasn't, or conversely, he was nothing that the Honcho was. He was a small, tubercular man in his late forties, with undistinguished features and unpretentious demeanor. He wore delicate wire-rimmed spectacles, had permanently disheveled hair, and spoke in a high pitched voice that squeaked when he got excited. He was the Honcho's conscientious superego, with an unexplainable knack for reigning in the boorish senator just before he completely alienated his electorate. The world was better off for But Sir!'s surprising fortitude in this dangerous role.

But Sir! worked with the Honcho from the beginning of the Senator's political career. His relentless admonitions to the deviant legislator always began with the words "But sir!", which became a substitute for his long ago forgotten Christian name. The names of the Head Honcho's key staffers had evolved into reflections of their typical responses to him. Freeman was often called Yessir!. But Sir! was always called But Sir!. Occasionally, there were some Nosir!'s, but they mysteriously disappeared.

The Honcho eyed the remains of Freeman's exploded desk suspiciously. "Where's the homosexual communist militia lover of the religious right that did this? I want that sonofabitch in my office right now!" roared the giant. He stormed back into his inner sanctum, secure in the dictatorial delusion that the sonofabitch who perpetrated the destruction would confess his heinous crime. Unfortunately, the sonofabitch was Freeman, who didn't intend to confess anything to anybody. He knew that the Honcho was dangerously afraid of any seditious behavior that hinted of political uprisings and military coups.

Lately, the Head Honcho had spiraled into abject paranoia. Reports poured in about a mysterious rebel who was secretly inciting uprisings against the Federal Government. This avenging conspirator was known in popular lore as the Insurrectionist. The Insurrectionist was stirring up tax rebellions, urging voters to boycott elections, publishing exposes of corrupt political leaders, and imploring citizens to arm themselves. He was the perfect political counterpoint to the Honcho, since he was as rebellious as the Honcho was dictatorial. The existence of this mysterious rebel was intolerable to the Senator, so he was determined to find and destroy him.

The Honcho enlisted the FBI, the CIA, and even the Mafia to capture the Insurrectionist, but they all failed. The unremitting acts of sedition by the Insurrectionist tormented him. He sat glumly in his office contemplating the burgeoning lack of respect for his government. A whole new generation was thoroughly disenchanted with the political establishment. Somehow, the sacred had become the profane for most Americans.

But Sir! sneaked out of the Honcho's office when no homosexual communist militia lover of the religious right came forth to confess. He approached Freeman, who was sitting suspiciously close to the splintered desk. "What are you up to?" he asked.

"I dropped this," replied Freeman, hefting his ball and chain for But Sir! to inspect.

"Jesus Christ!" shrieked But Sir!. "Hide that thing! If the Honcho sees it, he'll think you're the Insurrectionist! He wants whoever perpetrated this destruction shot or transferred to Detroit!"

"Aw, just tell him the Mad Hatter rampaged through here like a tornado because he was late for tea with the Red Queen", Freeman replied calmly. Falsely accusing the Mad Hatter was a malicious attempt to frighten the Honcho. Freeman was privy to a little known idiosyncrasy of the senator. Whenever the Honcho drank himself into a stupor, he had visions of the Mad Hatter, whose terrifying illogic reduced the politician to a powerless, drunken wreck.

But Sir! walked away in frustration, knowing that it was foolish to argue with a man strapped to a ball and chain. Freeman knew But Sir! would lie to the Honcho and tell him there was no explanation for today's chaos, just as he knew the Honcho would assume the Insurrectionist was somehow responsible. Sensing imminent mayhem, he took a stroll outside.

He wandered into a dark alley deep inside Washington's dilapidated industrial zone. Ramshackle brick buildings lined the alley, like tired sentinels futilely defending a long since vanquished era of prosperity. Dented garbage cans were carelessly overturned, their rancid contents spilling out shamelessly. Dirt and soot blanketed the surrounding facades, but did not obscure the desperate graffiti bearing the telltale signature of lost hope.

Oddly, Freeman felt comfortable in this forsaken venue. A burned out shell of a once proud building made a statement to the world that was unambiguous. These urban carcasses held no pretensions and offered a truth unfiltered by the media and politicians. Something once right was now terribly wrong. Something once heroic had gone awry. This industrial district was now a barren ghost town, inhabited only by furry demon rats that were gleefully dividing up the slowly rotting remains of a vanished civilization. These scavenging rodents were a metaphor for the political and cultural dissolution that ate away the foundation of the businesses that had once prospered here. The stark reality of this struck a harmonious chord in him, like a tuning fork ringing out in perfect melancholy resonance.

A stray dog ambled up to him in the desolate alleyway and walked silently beside him for a while. Suddenly, a police car stormed up. Two burly cops leapt out, aimed revolvers at him, and accused him of owning a dog without a license. Freeman explained that he didn't own the dog, so they accused him of stealing the dog. He assured them he was on an innocent stroll from the Senatorial Office Building and knew nothing about the dog. Then the officers spotted his ball and chain.

Unfortunately, the Head Honcho, believing that the Insurrectionist had infiltrated his office this morning, had contacted the police, who issued an APB for the infamous rebel. Freeman's incriminating mention of the Senatorial Office Building and his suspicious ball and chain convinced the officers that the dognapper they were apprehending was actually the Insurrectionist. He was summarily jailed and guarded by elite security forces. The officers triumphantly faxed a report of his capture to the Honcho.

Fortunately, the report was intercepted by But Sir!, who read all of the Senator's correspondence. He recognized Freeman as the unnamed captive in the report because his ball and chain was mentioned, so he rushed to post bail for him. On the way back to the Senatorial Office Building, he listened patiently to Freeman's rambling discourse on the crazy events that led to his imprisonment. But Sir! was incredulous at the bizarre tale. "Owning a dog without a license? Have you no shame?"

"It was all so incomprehensible", Freeman moaned. "They manipulated every word I uttered. They were seeing a different reality than I was. Unfortunately, their version was the official one. Hysteria overwhelmed fact, and they seemed to prefer it that way. I was presumed guilty, and their only mission was to discover what I was guilty of. I felt like a Branch Dravidian in Waco. The FBI and the ATF are probably firebombing my home right now." He vigorously rubbed the ink stains on his fingers, as if to erase the humiliation of being fingerprinted. "Thanks for posting bail. How did you get that much money so quickly?"

But Sir! waved a hand to dismiss Freeman's gratitude. "Please . . . it was nothing. The Treasury Department won't miss the loose change I borrowed. The Federal Government doesn't have to worry about a money shortage, because unlike individuals and businesses, it lives in a fairy tale world where revenue shortfalls are magically remedied by fiscal sorcerers in Congress."

Freeman nodded in comprehension. He often wished that he could manage his personal budget like the feds handled their finances. He wanted to tax other poor fools to pay for his profligate spending. He wanted to call out the sheriff if those poor fools refused to give their money to him. Unfortunately, he had never found any fools willing to be taxed by him, nor a sheriff willing to back him. He wondered why so many fools were willing to be taxed by the Federal Government, which is staffed by ordinary people like him. Why would people refuse to be taxed by him personally, but accept being taxed by the collective group of Freemans in Washington?

"Maybe that's why the Insurrectionist is so successful organizing tax revolts", he said aloud. Tax revolts were sprouting up like dandelions in a subdivision. Some people were sending in blank returns, invoking the Fifth Amendment. Others declared themselves ministers of spurious churches and their income exempt. Some claimed that their salaries couldn't be considered real income because the dollars created by government alchemists were no better than play money. Still others harassed IRS auditors or refused to answer questions. Many were willing to go to jail, believing that if enough fellow tax protesters did too, the country's judicial and penal systems would be overwhelmed. What could the government do at that point? Shoot everyone? Over 1000 groups had formed to spread the tax protest, many of them pledging their allegiance to the Insurrectionist. Some of the groups were armed and prepared to defend their livelihoods from the government, believing that the Second Amendment was their last line of defense against slavery to bureaucrats and politicians in Washington. Freeman wondered if the government was ready to go to war with these citizens. He was also still uneasy about his recent imprisonment. "Has the Honcho heard about my arrest?"

"He doesn't even know you were gone", replied But Sir!. "No one noticed except me and the coffee account dues collector tracking down your delinquent payment."

Freeman squirmed nervously. Potential disasters loomed like guillotine blades above his neck. What if the Honcho read about his arrest in the newspaper? What if the FBI was really firebombing his house? What if the coffee account dues collector broke his kneecaps? He ran trembling hands through his thinning hair, caressing his endangered head. "I'm scared", he confessed.

"Don't worry", said But Sir!. "The Honcho is distracted by a far more dangerous crisis."

Freeman could think of no greater crisis than being mistaken for the Insurrectionist and getting his head lopped off. "What's the sonofabitch paranoid about now?"

But Sir! looked apprehensively over both shoulders before whispering furtively. "The computer that tracks the government's spending ran out of zeros and commas. The Honcho suspects it's a plot by the Insurrectionist to undermine the federal bureaucracy."

"Wow!" Freeman exclaimed. "What's being done?"

"Every other computer in the entire government has been scavenged. The few remaining zeros and commas that were found are hoarded under tight security at an undisclosed location. Also, the Honcho decreed that all official government reports be issued without zeros and commas until the shortages are rectified."

"Won't that make the reports meaningless?"

"They were already meaningless. Now they're just more difficult to read."

When they arrived at the Senatorial Office Building, the Honcho was purple with rage. "This is a right wing, gun toting, tax evading homosexual plot by the Insurrectionist!" he roared ferociously. The brute force of his invective nearly blew But Sir!'s frail body away.

"What is, sir?" But Sir! asked meekly.

The giant man's jugular veins bulged precariously in his muscled neck. "This!"

But Sir! scanned the document that the Honcho's kielbasa-sized finger pounded on. "This report is incomprehensible without zeros and commas", he said.

"Of course!" bellowed the behemoth. "Only the Insurrectionist could take a perfectly meaningless report and make it impossible to understand! My. . . . our. . . . government is on its knees without zeros and commas! How can the IRS confiscate wealth without zeros and commas? How can the Teamster's Union fund my re-election campaign without zeros and commas? How can we calculate the national debt without zeros and commas?" He pounded his desk with two massive hamhock fists. Tears of rage streamed down his bloated cheeks. But Sir! imagined Adolph Hitler must have looked like this when his generals informed him he couldn't push his toy cannons and soldiers past Stalingrad on the battlefield map. But Sir! concluded that a frustrated tyrant is mankind's most fearsome spectacle, not counting a Catholic confessional. A stymied tyrant throws a spastic fit like a spoiled child whenever reality intervenes into its egocentric world. A spastic child, however, can only damage walls and furniture, whereas a frustrated tyrant threatens the entire planet.

"I want whoever did this shot for destabilizing my government!", the Honcho roared.

"But Sir!" implored But Sir!. "Voters won't approve of shooting someone over a few missing zeros and commas. Put things into perspective. This crisis isn't as bad as the time a hacker programmed the computer to print every number in the national debt one-by-one, which consumed all the government's paper, which sucked up all of Oregon's trees, which killed the spotted owl, which funded the retirements of two thousand lawyers. This crisis isn't even as bad as the Great Vodka Drought."

"Oh my God!" blurted the Honcho tearfully, as he recalled the devastating potato blight that stopped the production of vodka and forced him to find another source of liquid sustenance. He believed the Insurrectionist caused the Great Vodka Drought to personally spite him.

But Sir! regretted mentioning the Great Vodka Drought. But, that wasn't as grievous as mentioning the unfortunate Cleaning Lady Episode. He silently congratulated himself for avoiding that horrendous mistake.

The Head Honcho's cavernous chest heaved in sobbing convulsions. "The Great Vodka Drought always reminds me of the unfortunate Cleaning Lady Episode." He began to wail and blubber incoherently. But Sir! left so that the distraught man could resolve his emotional duress in solitude.

But Sir! passed by Freeman, who was meticulously gluing the splinters of his desk back together. "What's the commotion in the Honcho's office?" he asked. "It sounds like a walrus bellowing in distress."

"He's reliving the agony of the unfortunate Cleaning Lady Episode", confided But Sir!.

"The sonofabitch deserves to suffer for that!" Freeman's mood brightened as he reminisced about the bizarre Cleaning Lady Episode. It began when the CIA launched another ill-fated mission to find the Insurrectionist, whom they suspected was a federal employee. Unfortunately, the CIA didn't brief the Head Honcho about the clandestine plan before launching it.

The scheme featured a special task force of CIA operatives disguised as illegal alien cleaning ladies. They wore kerchiefs, checkered aprons, and austere patch quilt dresses that hung unevenly above their ankles. They mingled with federal workers and surreptitiously observed them. For a short time, the strategy worked brilliantly. The disguised CIA operatives gathered lots of data about the work habits and personal idiosyncrasies of government employees. CIA officers anxiously sifted through the data for clues to identify the Insurrectionist.

One day, Freeman glimpsed the naked leg of a cleaning lady who was dusting an unreadable government report. His keen eyes observed that the muscular leg was blanketed with dark curly hair. He became suspicious about her real gender. His coworkers were also skeptical of the gender of the mysterious cleaning ladies, particularly the ones with bushy mustaches and tattoos of naked women in lurid poses. They nominated Freeman to warn the Honcho that cleaning ladies who looked like transsexual right-wing militiamen had infiltrated the building.

Freeman's ominous report infuriated the Honcho. Unaware of the CIA's plan, he suspected it was a plot by the Insurrectionist to recruit his employees. Inspired by Freeman's clever suggestion, the Honcho disguised himself as the Head Cleaning Lady in order to infiltrate the ranks of the suspicious transsexuals. He became a frumpy woman who spoke broken English and barked out orders to subordinate cleaning ladies like a Marine drill sergeant.

In the meantime, the government workers despised the constant surveillance by the transsexual cleaning ladies. Inspired by Freeman's clever suggestion, they also disguised themselves as cleaning ladies, in order to mingle with the original cleaning ladies and discover their intentions. They were particularly interested in spying on the homely woman with the imposing girth who had recently emerged as their leader.

Consequently, the Federal bureaucracy swarmed with surreptitious cleaning ladies. Every employee took mop in hand and was either surveilling or being surveilled. Their frenzied activity resulted in cleanliness that would have passed military muster. Normal government operations ceased, since all resources were diverted to mopping, polishing, and surveilling.

The nation prospered while its government wallowed in hygienic distraction. Now that the teeming hordes of federal workers were scrubbing latrines and polishing spittoons rather than regulating and lawmaking, American industry grew exponentially. Gone were the anchor-like deadweights of federal paperwork and antagonistic legislation. Tax collectors were now preoccupied with washing sinks and squeegeeing windows, rather than confiscating the productive results of the nation's labor force like insatiable piranhas. The resulting leap in disposable income led to greater demand for products and services, driving the unemployment rate to an historic low. As federal employees disinfected moldy crevices and ceased being bureaucratic monkey wrenches, America's market economy demonstrated its miraculous power.

But, America's halcyon days were short lived. The Head Honcho experienced a painful public humiliation that led to the disbanding of the cleaning lady corps. The obsessively promiscuous senator fell in love with a subordinate cleaning lady. The ensuing sexual liaison, however, was not what he expected from someone with such a seemingly ample bosom. His transvestite sexual partner revealed his true gender and the sordid details of the illicit liaison to the slimy nether world of salivating tabloid editors and sensationalist talk show hosts, to whom the Honcho's misfortune was like golden nectar.

The Honcho's political career would have suffered irreparable harm from the slings and arrows of outrageous journalism, if Freeman hadn't invoked the Political Immunity Clause on his behalf. The Political Immunity Clause stipulates that politicians are not constrained by moral considerations, legal restrictions, or cultural norms, and are therefore protected from censure or impeachment. The Clause is so powerful some legal scholars speculate that a drunken married senator could drive his car off a bridge and swim away from the vehicle like a coward while his consort drowns, with no retribution whatsoever to his political career, or that a President could have sex in the Oval Office with a young intern and lie about the cover-up he orchestrated, with nary a slap on the wrist. The Clause cradled the Honcho through the turbulent media waters broiling around him after his sexual encounter with the male CIA agent, although it didn't shelter him from the agonizing syphilis he contracted.

The unfortunate Cleaning Lady Episode ended unsuccessfully. Once news of the Honcho's homosexual encounter with a disease-laden agent reached the soon-to-be-unemployed director of the CIA, operatives were ordered to abandon their undercover stations. After the rotund Head Cleaning Lady and her suspicious transvestite crew disappeared, the federal employees discarded their own cleaning lady disguises and returned to their old positions in the government. The Insurrectionist remained at large. The only person actually apprehended was the unfortunate agent who infected the Honcho with syphilis. He quietly went the way of Vincent Foster.

When the bureaucrats returned to their normal jobs, the economy slid into a brutal recession. Tax collectors once again shook down the country. Laborers worked less, since half of their extra income went to governments again. Low skilled workers dropped out of the labor market altogether, because the welfare system offered more compensation with much less effort. Industrial producers were once again bogged down by labor, safety, and environmental regulations imposed by legislators who knew nothing about labor, safety, or the environment. Hordes of lawyers were hired to ensure that industries complied with the resurrected regulations. Armies of lobbyists were hired by businesses to prevent the imposition of even more regulations.

The U. S. Mint resumed cranking out truckloads of dollars that rekindled inflation, pushing wage earners into higher tax brackets. Politicians used the increased tax revenue to finance pointless but politically expedient projects. Inflation encouraged workers to be debtors rather than savers, since it is foolish to save dollars today when they will be worth less tomorrow, so they engorged themselves on consumer products. When savings dried up, no capital was available for businesses to invest in new plant and equipment. Future leaps in productivity and income consequently evaporated. The American economy, once a magnificent engine for improving the human condition, collapsed as the federal dreadnought plowed up the market's seeds and left only the weeds. It was all very rational, in an irrational way.

But Sir! jostled Freeman to disentangle him from the reverie that had cast a spell over him as he reminisced about the unfortunate Cleaning Lady Episode. "The Head Honcho wants to see you. But be careful. His secretary is on vacation, so he's in a foul mood from sexual deprivation."

Freeman slithered into the Honcho's inner sanctum and held his breath anxiously. "Sit down, Yessir!" barked the senator. "I've been reflecting on the unfortunate Cleaning Lady Episode. It reminded me of how you cleverly used the Political Immunity Clause to get the media off my ass after that faggot CIA agent kissed and told. It was almost as clever as the Warren Commission's single assassin deception that covered up the involvement of the CIA, Israel's Secret Service, and the Mafia in Kennedy's murder. But, I digress. Care for a cigar?"

Freeman declined, fidgeting nervously. He sensed that the Honcho was up to something besides expressing his gratitude.

"I need your help with a difficult situation", continued the Honcho, puffing on a cigar. "I've been trying to capture a man who's destabilizing my. . . . our. . . .government. He's known as The Insurrectionist. Despite the efforts of America's best agencies, this villain remains at large. The FBI, the Mafia, the CIA, and the DIA have all failed. I've thrown every acronym at my disposal into the fray, to no avail. Even the unemployed agents of Russia's KGB and East Germany's STASI failed miserably. I can't stand for the Insurrectionist to be free for another goddamn day! I want that right wing militia lover caught!" He pounded a massive fist on his mahogany desk.

"I can't help you, sir. I don't know who the Insurrectionist is."

"Of course you can help! You're a clever sonofabitch. You're the one who recommended borrowing the unused zeros and commas from the computer tracking the Social Security Fund to resolve the zero and comma shortage. It's your patriotic duty to think of a brilliant strategy for me!"

"How can I succeed when the spymasters have failed?"

"Those blindfolded idiots wouldn't recognize a suspicious character picking their pockets with a club fist in broad daylight! Hell, a CIA agent was selling the identities of other CIA agents to the Russians for years. Despite his million-dollar home and his luxury cars, they had no clue he was a traitor. Helen Keller would be more likely to find the Insurrectionist."

Freeman never fancied himself a spy catcher. He couldn't even operate his secret decoder ring as a kid. His only exposure to rebels came from his Irish ancestry. When he was young, his father frequently recounted the exploits of legendary Irish rebels who struggled to banish the hated British from the Emerald Isle before the redcoats swallowed their Irish prey whole. His father described these Irish insurrectionists to him with an unforgettable fire in his eyes. Unfortunately, the passion didn't pass from generation to generation, leaving Freeman spiritually unmoved by the tales. He did, however, miss his deceased father terribly. A spark flickered in his heart that he couldn't classify or quantify, but it pleased him. Warmed by the spark, he softly declared, "I'll help you find the Insurrectionist."

The Honcho beamed with gratitude and relief. "Great! Give me a clever idea."

"Hmmm. . . . what if we appoint an Insurrection Czar?", mused Freeman, struggling to think like the Honcho would. "He could have unbridled power to dictate policy, raise money, and interfere in state and local affairs to capture the Insurrectionist. If we ignore the Constitution, we can give this czar unlimited authority with no accountability. That's how we deal with education, illegal drugs, and tax collection, so it must be the American way."

"A czar?", wondered the Honcho with curiosity.

"It's perfect. It projects an image of immutable power. The Insurrectionist will quiver in his boots with an Insurrection Czar hot on his trail. What do you think?", Freeman asked anxiously.

"It's brilliant, except that I fancied the title 'czar' for myself", mused the Honcho. "But, I can wait. Let's do it!" He slapped Freeman heartily on the back.

While Freeman charged off to recruit an Insurrection Czar, another crisis began when the Honcho's personal secretary, Buxomus Blondus, announced that the government ran out of paper clips. Everyone ignored her, since the Honcho employed her solely for her impressive physical attributes. What she lacked in office skills was more than compensated for by magnificent breasts protruding from her chest like erotic missiles. Her firm, voluptuous ass wiggled below an impossibly narrow waist and above two impossibly long legs. The services she provided the Honcho were completely unrelated to office work. She didn't know how to turn on the computer, make copies, or take dictation, but she was the Honcho's sexual plaything. So, when she announced the paper clip shortage, no one noticed anything but her physique.

However, a homely secretary who was actually employed to do office work also noticed the paper clip shortage. In the past, this was easily remedied by a purchase requisition authorizing a buyer to procure more. Unfortunately, the Government Accounting Office had recently instituted severe purchasing controls to prevent fraud and abuse. The multi-volume Federal Acquisition Regulations were intended to safeguard against the reckless spending of federal funds.

The paper clip buyer took to heart the new regulations, which stipulated that a detailed specification was needed to avoid confusion about which paper clips were actually required. Should they be one or two inches long? Should they be blue, pink, or metallic? Should they be tin or copper? Should they be bare or plastic coated? The buyer dutifully notified the homely secretary that he couldn't proceed with her requisition without a comprehensive spec.

Unfortunately, she didn't know how to write detailed specifications, particularly for ordinary paper clips. Fortunately, a secretary who used to work in the Pentagon suggested consulting with military technocrats, who were adept at specifying intricate acquisitions such as nuclear weaponry and freeze dried beer.

The Pentagon technocrats were eager to develop the specifications for the government's paper clips. The mere mention of the Head Honcho, who chaired the Senate Ways and Means Committee, was sufficient to get design engineers immediately reassigned from the MX Missile Project to the Paper Clip Project. The Pentagon wanted to impress him with their technical wizardry to guarantee a continued torrent of funds to develop weapons capable of deterring any enemies contemplating attacking America, if such exist.

To fund the effort, a special appropriation was hustled through Congress, who assumed that when the Pentagon needed money for a project of vital strategic importance, it meant national security was at stake, as opposed to job security of the technocrats in the military-industrial complex. The code name Paper Clip Project also misled Congress into believing that a substantial "black budget" effort was behind this innocuous moniker.

With the $500 million dollar appropriation, the Pentagon assembled a crack team of engineers, who left no design consideration unexamined. For example, the paper clips needed to be durable, to avoid the expense of continually replacing them. Therefore, the engineers specified the rare metal Unobtanium, which has extraordinary tensile strength and resistance to corrosion. Unfortunately, its melting point is one million degrees centigrade, so the smelting process requires nuclear fusion.

Standard paper clips are either one or two inches long. However, the ergonomic engineers at the Pentagon determined that a paper clip 1 3/4 inches long provided the optimum balance between paper gripping surface and ease of handling. In order to prevent electro-static discharge near sensitive electronics, they had to be coated with conductive paint. They had to be magnetized to adhere to metals, and have a PH factor of 7 to prevent skin inflammation. According to OSHA standards, they also had to be weightless, to prevent back strain and carpal tunnel syndrome. Fortunately, weightlessness could be achieved by using the Pentagon's top-secret anti-gravity rays.

The paper clips had to be gray, to prevent eyestrain and to avoid discrimination lawsuits, since any other color would be construed by minority groups as a racial slur. They also had to be usable by physically challenged employees, so they were specified with miniature motors and rotors controlled by microcircuits that react to voice commands.

When the design effort was completed, the engineers applauded their accomplishment. In the grand tradition of the military industrial complex, another product had been developed that was going to cost 411 times its budget, be impossible to manufacture, and have a mean time between failures of 4.6 seconds. As colossal bundles of money fell into very deep pockets, the Pentagon delivered the paper clip specification to the secretaries in the Senatorial Office Building.

Now the procurement phase of the Paper Clip Project could begin. Three competitive bids had to be obtained from qualified manufacturers, with the contract awarded to the lowest bidder who met the specifications. However, the contract was actually awarded to the firm that enticed the purchasing agent with the best wine, prostitutes, and kickbacks. An unsuccessful bidder filed a lawsuit challenging the contract award, on the grounds that it was physically and morally impossible for paper clips to cost $3 billion per box, which was the winning bid. The lawsuit was thrown out because the secretary of the presiding judge had recently procured thumbtacks that cost even more. The judge concluded that this was the going price for government paper fasteners.

Despite being paid $3 billion per box, the winning bidder experienced staggering cost overruns because of the utterly unmanufacturable specification. Pre-production models kept failing the first article tests. The dust test, in which a paper clip was subjected to a desert sandstorm, was particularly troublesome. Sand kept gumming up the miniature motors and rotors, so it didn't respond to voice commands. Worse still, the handicapped people giving the voice commands got their vocal cords gummed up by the ferocious sandstorms. The manufacturer went through 26 prototype paper clips and 11 handicapped people before passing this test.

The environmental stress tests were also difficult. Since paper clips might be used in Alaska or Saudi Arabia, they had to survive temperatures ranging from -40 degrees to 150 degrees. The paper clips themselves had no trouble operating in these thermal extremes. Unfortunately, the test operators weren't quite as durable. The first tests resulted in 14 hypothermia victims and 17 heat stroke victims. This problem was corrected by using dummies from the Education Department as testers.

The final hurdle was the nuclear survivability test, in which a five-megaton warhead was dropped on a paper clip. Amazingly, the Unobtanium clip survived the explosion. However, technicians suspected the test was flawed, because no other product had ever survived. For a more controlled test, a human holding a paper clip was placed at a desk on the test range. Another warhead was detonated. The control group, which consisted of the human and the desk, was obliterated by the blast, while the Unobtanium paper clip was unscathed. After examining the results, the technicians agreed the paper clip had indeed survived a legitimate nuclear test.

The manufacturing process was sophisticated and expensive. The smelter for the raw Unobtanium was actually a nuclear fusion reactor, with a core temperature of 1 million degrees maintained by four million-volt lasers focused on a plasma concocted of quarks and mesons. The cost to train the production workers was astronomical, because the manufacturer was required by its UAW contract to train existing workers rather than hire nuclear experts to operate the smelter. Their learning curve led to many errors, including a meltdown during a pre-production run.

Mining the raw Unobtanium was even more difficult. Unobtanium is found in a single deposit deep within the earth's mantle, directly below a habitat of the extremely endangered reticulated aardvark. So, the manufacturer had to do an expensive environmental impact study before drilling for the Unobtanium ore. They simulated the drilling process in a laboratory cage containing male and female reticulated aardvarks, while the Endangered Species Commission carefully monitored vital signs and reproductive activity. The only appreciable effect the drilling had on the animals was to stimulate fornication by creating a suggestive thought in the erotic lobe of the male's brain. The ESC reluctantly approved full-scale mining, and then moved on to prosecute a beachcomber for leaving a footprint in a protected sand dune along Lake Michigan.

Despite these hardships, the manufacturer eventually produced the paper clips. After four train loads of regulatory paperwork, $16 billion dollars of cost overruns, and the deaths of 43 unwitting test administrators, the paper clips were delivered to the federal government. The secretaries were elated. They nominated Buxomus Blondus, who originally discovered the paper clip shortage, to present the first box to the Head Honcho. Brimming with pride, she slinked into the Honcho's inner office and purred alluringly, "Honcho dear, I have something for you!"

"I've got a headache," replied the Honcho.

"Silly boy! I just wanted you to see these." She leaned over the Honcho's desk to hand him the paper clips.

"They're amazing! But what's in that box you're holding?"

"Paper clips! You don't seem excited," she whined.

"Paper clips don't do it for me."

"But the government ran out of them and us girls bought more!"

"How much did they cost?"

"Three followed by nine zeros."

"That's three billion dollars!", he roared.

"Was that too much?" she squealed nervously.

"No, of course not! I just want to know how you did it. I bought rubber bands last month that cost me twenty billion!"

"The Pentagon did the specification for us", she purred.

"Why didn't I think of them? NASA did my rubber band specification. You had to be an alien living on Mars to use their design." He slammed his fist down in frustration. "Now I'm all worked up!"

"Does that mean your headache is gone?"

"On your knees, my little love toy!"

"Freeman, the Honcho wants to see you", Buxomus said while brushing off her knees.

"After seeing you?" he asked nervously while reflexively tightening his buns.

"He wants to go over the resumes for the Insurrection Czar position."

Freeman cautiously entered the Honcho's lair with an armload of resumes. The response to the classified ad was staggering. Unfortunately, he had found only one resume with the right experience, out of the thousands he evaluated. He expected his boss to be angry at the lack of qualified candidates.

The Honcho's scowl confirmed his fears. "Freeman, most of these candidates look like unemployable graduates of our public education system. I would have written this off as just another of your shithead ideas, until one resume caught my attention."

"I found only one worthwhile resume, too."

"Just for laughs, which one did you select? I want to know who a shithead would pick."

"I picked a fellow named Jefferson."

The Honcho dropped his massive head into his fleshy hands. A deep moan gurgled from his cavernous chest. When he looked up, his cheeks were crimson with genuine embarrassment. "I picked Jefferson, too."

"So, you knew all along who a shithead would pick."

The Honcho's head shot up and his fists clenched. The tyrant looked like a ravenous lion about to devour a zebra.

His jugular veins were swollen from torrents of blood rushing to his grimacing face. Suddenly, he leapt at Freeman.

Two things saved Freeman from mutilation. First, his knees buckled, so his body involuntarily plummeted to the floor with a resounding thud, which caused the Head Honcho to catapult completely over him. Second, Buxomus Blondus entered just as the airborne senator crashed into a glass etagere.

"Stop wrestling like monkeys!" she chastised. "If I was your mother, I'd spank you both."

This notion distracted the Honcho from his seething rage. Unfortunately, Buxomus continued on without fulfilling his fantasy. "Mr. Jefferson is on the phone to discuss a job opportunity. What should I tell him?"

"Tell him to be here tomorrow at 10:00 to see me and Shithead," the Honcho said, pointing menacingly toward Freeman, who wisely escaped from the Honcho's office as quickly as his shaky legs and cumbersome ball and chain allowed. Buxomus followed close on his heels.

"If your name is Shithead, why do we call you Yessir!?" she asked.

"Just because that madman calls me Shithead doesn't mean it's my name."

"If he calls you 'Shithead', then 'Shithead' is your name", she said. "If he says things are so, then things are so. Someone has to tell us what's true and what's false, and in this country, it's the Head Honcho." She paused to bask in the joy of saying something that didn't require a giggle at the end. "And you should get rid of that horrible chunk of metal strapped to your leg, Shithead. Are you a prisoner?"

"No," lied Freeman, who felt very much a captive of something he couldn't quite see or define. "I have one leg shorter than the other."

When Jefferson arrived for his interview the next day, he wasn't what Freeman expected. Instead of a debonair statesman in a snappy business suit, Jefferson was a weathered septuagenarian wearing an old brown coat on top of a red waistcoat, a white linen shirt with a ruffled collar, black silken knee breeches, red silk hose, and black patent leather shoes. A black felt bicorne hat, with delicate gold and red brocade, sat atop his head. Underneath the hat flowed an unruly mane of gray hair with a hint of orange, combed back toward the nape of his neck and matted with powder, giving it a theatrical look. Though worn by exposure to wind and sun, his face had an aristocratic cut that could be at home at both a state dinner and a casual chat around a cracker barrel in a country store. His smile was a confident expression of good nature and friendliness beneath hazel eyes that had just a hint of blue. His stare was uncommonly direct.

Jefferson interrupted Freeman's silent assessment by extending a hand in greeting. "Good day, sir. I'm grateful for this opportunity to converse, in the hope of finding mutual advantage in our situations."

Freeman winced at the unusual firmness of Jefferson's handshake. He had the rough, callused skin of a man who knew the rigors of strenuous manual labor. Odder still was how deathly cold and clammy his hand was, despite his vigorous appearance. A shiver knifed down Freeman's back. He was spooked, like a dog catching the first scent of an approaching predator. Unexplainably, the hair on the back of his neck prickled, and his nerve endings tingled with electricity. Rattled, he mumbled, "I'm coordinating the hiring of the Insurrection Czar."

"The position intrigues me. Let's discuss particulars."

"Have a seat," instructed Freeman, gesturing. "Let me take your hat. It certainly is. . . . unusual."

Jefferson handed over his bicorne hat. "It's not of unusual design. Mr. Madison acquired it for me on one of his journeys to Philadelphia."

"Oscar?"

"No, James."

"Don't know him," said Freeman. "Your resume says that you live in Albemarle County, Virginia. How was your trip to Washington?"

Jefferson chuckled lightly. "It was a study in curiosities. The weather, for example, is not as I remember it. Hanging over the city like an insuperable shroud is the densest fog I've ever seen."

"It must have been a while since you were last here, to not remember this fog."

Jefferson patted down his powdered hair. "Much time has indeed elapsed since my last visit. This was always a humid town in the summer, situated as it is near the ocean. To avoid the sicknesses that bred from such humidity, I adjourned to my home at Monticello during the summer months. But never have I seen such stifling fog! Its very weight addled my brains this morning, such that I must confess I saw things that couldn't be possible."

Freeman empathized with him, because he too had recently seen things that couldn't be possible, such as his strange encounters with Cassandra and Satan. "Please elaborate."

"You will think me a doddering old fool if I do."

"There is nothing you could observe about this city that would make me think you lost your mind."

"If you insist. First, multitudes of huge cattle wandered the city and delayed my journey many hours. They wouldn't move for all of my shouting and arm waving. More curious than the cattle, however, was the apathy of my fellow travelers. They appeared to accept being trampled and abused by these animals. I, on the other hand, took great offense at the arrogance and callousness of these dumb beasts and beat them with my riding crop to clear my path."

"Those are our Sacred Cows", said Freeman. "They're indestructible. We've got chemicals to get rid of roaches, wars to get rid of young Americans, and abortion clinics to get rid of unwanted babies. But, we have no way to rid ourselves of these creatures created by the government."

Jefferson scowled. "The government created those beasts? By what authority? The Constitution doesn't empower beast creation!"

"What does the Constitution have to do with what our government does? Americans are schizophrenic. At Sunday mass they worship Christianity, yet after mass few behave as Christians. Likewise, they worship the Constitution on July 4th, yet few abide by its principles the rest of the year. Our principles and our behavior have become disjoined." Freeman abruptly ended his inappropriate harangue. "What other curiosities did you encounter?"

"There weren't any 'left turn only' signs when I traveled these roads many years ago."

"I thought they were always there", mused Freeman. "We're used to turning leftward now."

"What happens when someone turns right?" asked Jefferson.

"They're branded as reactionaries and run out of town. Any other curiosities?"

"There are many enormous buildings in this city now. What industry requires so much space?"

"The federal government owns just about every building you can see from here", said Freeman. "Government is the biggest industry in this country."

"Government cannot be considered an industry, since it creates nothing useful. For what purpose, then, does it own such an extraordinary amount of office space?"

"Government employees need a place to work."

"How many government workers are there?"

"There are at least millions of us. I don't think we've gotten to the billions yet."

Jefferson slapped the knees of his breeches and laughed

boisterously. "Your humor is very droll. But please, tell me how many fellow employees you have."

"I wasn't joking. There are millions of us."

The color drained from Jefferson's cheeks. "Not even King George III, with his teeming royal court, could count his administrators in the millions! My philosophy is that government should be scarcely seen and rarely heard. What earthly good can millions of bureaucrats do?"

Freeman dug deep into his nearly forgotten civics lessons. "We do the greatest good for the greatest number of people."

"The greatest number would seem to be the millions of government employees", retorted Jefferson. "Are they themselves the beneficiaries of this 'greatest good' they claim to perform?"

"Are you suggesting our government is a self-serving, self-perpetuating bureaucracy?"

"Not necessarily. Having recently returned here, my inquiries are innocent."

"Too bad. I would've agreed with you. Let's proceed with your interview. Writing your resume longhand on a parchment was a stroke of marketing genius. It says here you graduated from William and Mary College. . . . studied law under George Wythe. . . . practiced law in Virginia. . . . Representative to Congress. . . . Governor of Virginia. . . . Foreign Trade and Commerce Minister. . . . Ambassador to France. . . . Secretary of State. . . . founded the University of Virginia. . . . your background is so impressive, I didn't even review the rest of it. What are you doing now?"

"I'm involved in unfinished business," he replied, averting his eyes.

"You'll need a better answer for the Honcho," Freeman advised. "Tell me, how much practical experience have you had with insurrectionists?"

"I have witnessed firsthand the boldest insurrectionists history has ever known", replied Jefferson confidently. "I was with Patrick Henry when he denounced the Stamp Act and equated King George with Julius Caesar, which incited shouts of treason in the Virginia House of Burgesses. Later, I observed rebellious Virginia legislators in the Raleigh Tavern denouncing the duties imposed by British Parliament and proclaiming a war cry of 'no taxation without representation'.

"I saw Rhode Islanders burn the tax-collecting schooner Gaspee, in the first violent act of the coming revolution. I was one of the first in Washington to hear that protesting patriots stormed three ships from the British East India Company and dumped their cargo into Boston Harbor. I was there in Williamsburg for the First Continental Congress, where Patrick Henry issued his immortal call for armed insurrection, 'give me liberty or give me death'. My blood ran cold when the ominous news of casualties came from Lexington and Concord, knowing that this committed the lives and fortunes of the revolutionaries to a bloody uprising.

"And I am intimately familiar with the person who drafted a declaration to state for the ages the causes that inspired these insurrectionists to rise up against the tyranny engulfing them. When signed by John Hancock and a host of other rebels, this epochal declaration became the banner for history's biggest insurrection.

"I submit, Mr. Freeman, that I, more than anyone else, know what kind of man would become an insurrectionist. I hereby rest my candidacy for the position of Insurrection Czar."

Freeman didn't know what to make of Jefferson's spirited affirmation of his experience with insurrectionists. Like most Americans, his unfamiliarity with history prevented him from assessing the validity of anything that occurred prior to the advent of CNN. "Mr. Jefferson, I don't recall the events you described, but our human resources department will do a thorough background check to verify your statements. I hope that this won't offend you."

"My object is to win this assignment. All else is secondary, and will be borne with a light heart. Investigate my statements as you deem necessary."

"That's good, because I was bluffing. Our people won't actually get around to investigating you until hell freezes over. He handed Jefferson his bicorne hat and shook his hand in farewell. The unearthly cold of the statesman's hand sent another deathly shiver up Freeman's spine. He was glad that Buxomus escorted the candidate to the Honcho, because his stomach was queasy and his head dizzy. To steady himself, he put his hand on a chair. This only heightened his uneasiness, though, because it was the chair that Jefferson had sat in, and on it he saw a thin layer of frost, shaped roughly in the outline of a human's buttocks, spread across the seat.

This bizarre manifestation reinforced a troubling thought Freeman was already wrestling with. Jefferson's remark that he was currently involved in unfinished business puzzled him. Given the man's extraordinary accomplishments, what could be unfinished? Why couldn't the old man just retire in serenity? This reminded him of a common superstition. People who have profoundly unfinished business when they die are condemned to wander the earth as spirits, until the unfinished business is resolved. He unconsciously crossed himself, and then took his ball and chain in tow toward the rest of his life, which was becoming more curious with each passing day.

Chapter Three: "The St. Patrick's Day Charade"

> "If a government is big enough to give you everything you want, it is big enough to take everything you have."
>
> —Ronald Reagan

Thomas Jefferson's appointment as Insurrection Czar didn't raise any eyebrows, since the number of government officials with unlimited authority but no accountability was already unlimited, with no accountability in sight. Besides, the world was weary of the Honcho's interminable schemes to capture the Insurrectionist.

Buxomus Blondus, But Sir!, and Freeman were quickly attracted to the eccentric Virginian, especially after city police impounded his carriage for blocking a Sacred Cow crossing. Jefferson embraced their friendship, particularly with the renegade Freeman, whom he saw as a kindred spirit, albeit a taciturn, complicated one with no respect for protocol. One day, he interrupted Freeman's fixation with a crossword puzzle. "Shouldn't you be working? 'A fair day's work for a fair day's pay' is one of my mottoes. If we work hard and respect the rights of others, life will return us many favors."

Freeman squinted with suspicion. "That's a dangerous notion. What other disruptive thoughts are you going to threaten our comfortable numbness with?"

"Never put off till tomorrow what you can do today."

"Yikes!" said Freeman with an expression of mock horror. "We're bureaucrats. We put off everything we can. What else is up your sleeve?"

"Never trouble another for what you can do yourself."

"Careful. That attitude would destroy our entitlement system and deprive our boss of the opportunity to buy millions of votes with someone else's dollars. What else?"

"Never spend your money before you have it."

"Holy shit, Jefferson! Government thrives on spending our children's money on politically expedient things our generation wants today. We're three trillion dollars in debt. What kind of lifestyle could we lead if we had to pay that off? We couldn't even afford the insecurity of our Social Security system, which is a giant Ponzi scheme of inter-generation IOU's built on IOU's. The government has so little faith in it that it's own employees have a different pension plan. What's your next alien thought?"

"We never repent of having eaten too little."

"A bureaucracy never repents from eating too much", countered Freeman. "Bureaucrats spend everything they can get their gluttonous paws on, in order to win bigger budgets next year. So now we have 300 years worth of cheese stored away in warehouses. The government owns 30% of the nation's land. We have two years worth of oil stashed in Louisiana mines. The military has amassed enough weapons to squash our enemies under the weight of our unexploded ordnance. Government swallows money by force, and spends it indiscriminately to further it's own ambitions. The bureaucratic blob will eat everything in sight, so watch your fingers and your wallet. What's your next outdated aphorism?"

"Much pain have cost us the evils which have never happened", replied Jefferson.

"I agree", said Freeman. "The Salem witch hunts became McCarthyism became Political Correctness. Tyrants live in fear, even though no one has ever completely removed them from power. When one tyrant is pushed off the throne, another inevitably takes his place."

Jefferson snickered. "I've observed that phenomenon, even after we threw off King George III."

"You should keep your contrary ideas quiet", counseled Freeman, "or else the PC Police will burn you at the stake."

"Your advice is useful only for those without a conscience", said Jefferson. "But, let's return to the subject of work, since that's why we are paid."

Freeman sighed. "Okay, Mr. Insurrection Czar. Speaking of witch hunts, how do you know there really is an Insurrectionist?"

"Just look about you! Sparks of insurrection are crackling everywhere. A massive tax revolt is underway against a modern version of taxation with representation. Citizens believe they can't influence the decisions of bureaucrats in a far away place called Washington. They feel like slaves to a master that is ostensibly a group of elected representatives, but in reality is just a runaway legislative juggernaut. Find the millions of people joining this tax revolt, and you will find the Insurrectionist.

"Look for the millions of people appalled by the scandals oozing from Washington. Sexual escapades, bribes, kickbacks, election fraud, perjury, nepotism, drug addiction, alcoholism, and banking scams are exposed daily. But, the Political Immunity Clause protects government criminals from being held accountable. Find the people who get nauseated reading about these travesties of justice, and you will find the Insurrectionist among them, retching in disgust into a toilet.

"Look for the 100 million adults who choose not to vote out of revulsion over second rate candidates cheating and pouring slime on each other in an orgy of yellow journalistic campaigning. They can't respect a process tainted by Watergate, ballot stuffing, pernicious media influence, and Mafia-rigged elections. Find these cynics who have elected not to elect, and you will find the Insurrectionist reminding them that voting only encourages the scoundrels.

"Look for the entrepreneurs hounded out of business by a swarm of bureaucrats eroding their substance with costly regulations and impossible guidelines. If General Motors must employ 25,000 people to comply with federal regulations, how can a small business possibly survive? Alleged violators are punished unilaterally without a constitutionally guaranteed trial by jury. Find these disenfranchised proprietors waiting in line for a handout from the same bureaucrats who put them there, and you will find the Insurrectionist inciting them to rise up.

"Every American is a law breaker. Pick a square in an office football pool, and you've broken the law. Go too fast in a car, and you've broken the law. Win two dollars in the lottery without claiming it on your taxes, and you've broken the law. Sleep with a woman in a bordello, and you've broken the law. Smoke a joint, and you've broken the law. And those are just the laws we know about. The legislature cranks out laws faster than we can take note of them. Law has been transformed from expression of the general will into oppression of the general public. Find these lawbreakers, whose numbers are uncountable, and you will inevitably find the Insurrectionist.

"Look for the parents being taxed to fund a public education system that has succeeded only in continually lowering the general wisdom of its graduates by devolving into day care centers, psychology wards, and breeding grounds for politically correct propaganda. Look for the families who are forced to pay for a government that no longer considers the family to be the fundamental element of society. Their earnings are confiscated to fund a welfare system that encourages millions of single parents to have even more millions of illegitimate children. Find these families struggling to survive in this inimical environment, and you will find among them the Insurrectionist with a hand on their weary shoulders.

"Look for those citizens harassed by Political Correctness, the new state religion that suppresses all dissent that doesn't conform to its mythological dogma. Find the people held in contempt by the faithful cadres of this secular creed, and you will find the Insurrectionist rescuing them from being burned at the stake of heresy by today's political and moral high priests.

"If you open your eyes and ignore the media, you'll see that rebellion is in the air everywhere."

Freeman frowned. "I can't tell whether you want to apprehend the Insurrectionist or enshrine him. But, at least you're enthused about your job. Mine's a pain in the ass. I have to plan the Head Honcho's annual St. Patrick's Day fund raisers."

Jefferson raised an eyebrow. "Fund raisers?"

"Yes. Campaigns require millions of dollars to get our alleged leaders re-elected so they can continue misrepresenting us."

"When I ran for office, I spent no more than a few dollars to publish pamphlets documenting my positions on key issues", observed Jefferson. "How many position papers do you publish with these millions of dollars?"

"None."

"Then how do voters know where the Honcho stands?"

"Politicians religiously avoid taking positions on issues. It merely gives opponents the rope with which to publicly hang them and makes them a target for special interest groups who disagree. The ensuing carnage isn't pretty. If a candidate takes positions and still miraculously gets elected, the voters will inevitably remember his positions. Then when he fails to deliver on his campaign promises, they will not re-elect him. Sometimes, not taking a position is manifested by actually taking both positions. With sufficient bullshit, a candidate can successfully advocate both sides of an issue, switching back and forth between audiences."

"If candidates do not take clearly stated positions on the issues, how then do voters determine whom to cast their ballot for?"

"That's where the millions of dollars come in. Much of it is spent on ads discrediting opposing candidates by alarming people with scare tactics and hobgoblins, so that the voters clamor to be led to safety by you. It's a brutal process of elimination. The objective is to be the only survivor. Of course, a lot is spent denying the innuendo and scare tactics your opponents aim at you. So, millions are spent slinging mud, and millions are spent ducking mud. Most of this mud gets splattered on the voters."

Jefferson pursed his lips tightly. "How is the rest of the money spent?"

"Candidates star in TV ads with red, white, and blue bunting in the background, kissing babies, waving flags, leading victorious troops in ticker-tape parades, embracing celebrities, and advocating motherhood and apple pie. The goal is to be associated with more patriotic and popular icons than your opponents, which is usually a function of who has the most money."

"Is any money left after that?"

Freeman laughed. "We haven't talked about graft and corruption yet. Dirty tricks must be played, ballots must be rigged, the allegiance of the Teamsters, the Mafia, and the CIA must be bought, homeless people must be lured into voting booths with free cigarettes, retarded people must be escorted to precincts, dead people must be resurrected, illegal aliens must be legalized, and scurrilous people must be bribed to instigate damning innuendo. Trollops who are willing to claim they slept with the opposing candidate aren't cheap, so to speak."

"Does this consume the remaining funds?"

"Nope. Candidates use the rest of the money for personal pleasure. Trips to resorts, prostitutes, drugs . . . that sort of thing."

"From where do these incredulous funds come?"

"Have you been caught in a time warp? Are you that naïve?"

Jefferson's face tightened and his body became rigid. "I'm not naive. I have traveled the world and I've led many people through terrible times. In my own estimation, I have favorably influenced the course of human events. However, I am dumbfounded by your description of a process that should be recognizable to me, but is instead wholly unfamiliar and distasteful."

"I didn't mean to piss you off. I thought all this was common knowledge."

"It's not, but please proceed," said Jefferson stiffly.

"Okay. Most of the money flows from Political Action Committees, which exchange campaign contributions for favorable influence on future legislation. PAC's represent big labor, big business, and single issue special interest groups, such as the NAACP and NOW. As Woodrow Wilson put it, 'The U.S. government is a foster child of special interests. It is not allowed to have a will of it's own.'"

"Why do people allow such transparent chicanery?"

"You can't stop special interest politics," replied Freeman. "A PAC seeking a $2 billion subsidy from the government will lobby intensively for it and invest heavily with campaign contributions. The taxpayers won't actively protest, because the phone call to their congressman will cost more than the extra $10 in individual taxes to cover the spurious subsidy. The special interests therefore win by default."

Jefferson cringed. "Where does the rest of the money come from?"

"Fund-raising activities, like the Honcho's St. Patrick's Day parade, golf tournament, and banquet. Also, individual voters contribute a few insignificant dollars to candidates."

"Since individual contributions pale in comparison to the huge donations made by special interest groups, does the donation of a single voter gain him any recognizable benefit?"

"I don't understand the question. Are voters supposed to benefit from this?"

"That was indeed the original intent of our democratic process," sighed Jefferson.

"How passé", said Freeman. "Individual voters contributing to politicians are no more likely to influence political events than are people contributing to TV evangelists likely to influence cosmic events. The charades propagated by podium pounding politicians and by pulpit pounding evangelists are nearly identical, as are their motives. And the naiveté of voters and evangelical faithful is the same."

Thousands of people lined the streets of Washington to applaud celebrities lazily passing by on floats and convertible cars in the Honcho's St. Patrick's Day parade. Green bunting draped the parade route and green balloons danced arrhythmically in the light breeze. Leprechauns pranced about, and if you squinted your eyes a wee bit, the shimmering sea of green worn by the spectators looked like the rolling hills of the Emerald Isle. High school bands marched in choreographed symmetry, playing a litany of charming Irish-American tunes like "When Irish Eyes are Smiling" and "Danny Boy".

The lead vehicle in the parade was an ominous black Suburban ferrying National Security Administration agents to secure the route for the trailing dignitaries. Next was the Honcho's convertible. He was riding high on the back seat with Buxomus, who frequently appeared in public with him. Observers often assumed the voluptuous blond was his wife. He waved broadly with one arm to the citizens lining the streets, while his other arm was draped around her lithe torso. She served her purpose well, particularly on the bumpy streets.

Twenty of the nation's finest Sacred Cows ambled behind the Honcho's car. No one dared get in their path, for fear of being trampled by their merciless hooves. One of the behemoths had a five-sided geometric brand on its rump, while another was branded with the initials "SSA". Plowing through Sacred Cow feces was a car carrying Jefferson. The Honcho wanted to show the world his new Insurrection Czar. Freeman and But Sir! rode with him. Freeman reveled in the adoration of thousands of people who wrongly assumed that he was either famous, dangerous, or Politically Correct. He waved, blew kisses to the crowd, and executed stately bows. But Sir! was quietly embarrassed.

The parade snaked up Independence Avenue past the Library of Congress and the House Office Buildings. As the Washington Monument loomed ahead, Freeman noticed a peculiar phenomenon. Unenthusiastic cheers went up from the crowd when the Honcho passed by them. This subdued reception was surprising, because his reelection campaign was the reason for the parade. In contrast, when the car behind Jefferson's passed by the onlookers, enthusiastic roars shook the pavement. Freeman pointed this curiosity out to But Sir!, who had already surmised it's cause.

"It's because of him," said But Sir!, pointing at a man sitting in the vehicle behind them.

"Him who?" persisted Freeman.

"The Golfer."

"Palmer?"

"Nah. He's more famous than Palmer."

"Tiger Woods?"

"More famous than him."

"Who could be more famous than Palmer and Woods?" asked Freeman. "God?"

"Almost. It's the Safari Golfer!"

Freeman looked blankly at Jefferson, who countered with an equally uncomprehending stare. In unison, they asked, "Who???"

"Come on, you guys!" shrieked But Sir!. "You've never heard of the Safari Golfer?"

"Can't say that I have," murmured Freeman shamefully.

"I've not even heard of golf," confessed Jefferson. "Who is this man, and why does he elicit such insane adoration?"

They turned to stare at the Safari Golfer, who was a fragile wisp of a man sitting in the lotus position, entranced in meditation. He wore faded khaki overalls with no shirt underneath, and scruffy tennis shoes with no socks. Straggly brown hair hung past his shoulders. He wore a gold earring in one lobe, and a gold necklace with strange talismans. His face was colorless and his lips were thin. Small round wire-rimmed glasses obscured pale blue eyes. Nothing about him suggested fame or notoriety.

"He's the most famous man alive", But Sir! began. "Women get hysterical at the mere sight of him. His public appearances cause pandemonium. Crazed groupies tear off their clothes and offer him sexual favors. His golfing fame transformed him into a cult figure through media overkill and a cultural hunger for secular deification. He can go by just a single name, the Golfer, and get immediate recognition, like Madonna, Magic, Oprah, and Cher. He drives a Rolls Royce, has a thousand-acre ranch in Southern California, and has cornered the diamond and pork belly markets.

He makes millions of royalty dollars on the sale of T-shirts, posters, videos, and bubble gum cards bearing his likeness. Everything he touches turns to commercial gold, including products that he endorses.

"His words are gospel to legions of believers, who quote his surrealistic conundrums as if they have compelling cosmic significance, although no one can decipher their meaning, because none is intended. Ten of his followers died after meditating for three weeks on the question 'Who am I?' Most of his confusing incantations involve mysticism, sex, money, and drugs, but that's as much coherence as you'll find in them. His abstruse pronouncements are replicated on bumper stickers, T-shirts, and in the slang of the underclass as an indecipherable sub-language that everyone parrots in a frenzy of political correctness. The hysteria surrounding him is called 'Golfermania'.

"He completed his transformation into a cult figure by marrying an Asian mystic named Ohno, who added transcendental meditation, mind expanding drugs, and the eroticism of the Kama Sutra to his repertoire. He says the earth is flat and was created in 4004 BC, and that the sun revolves around it. He says you don't have to do anything good or bad to achieve nirvana except contribute to his causes. Finally, he says he's more famous than Jesus Christ and that the end of the world is coming soon. That's who the Safari Golfer is!"

"I want to hear more about the Kama Sutra thing," said Freeman.

"I cannot fathom the public's infatuation with him," observed Jefferson. "George Washington was first in war, first in peace, and first in the hearts of his countrymen, yet he didn't wear an earring, have millions of idolaters, or be infatuated with sex. How did this Safari Golfer get to be so famous? Did he win a war? Did he lead a nation? Did he cultivate a revolution?"

"None of the above," replied But Sir!. "It's no longer necessary to do anything significant to become famous. His notoriety began during a Masters Golf Tournament years ago. Up till then, he was a journeyman golfer on the fringe of the PGA tour. He might have faded into oblivion, except he had a gimmick that set him apart from the other marginal professionals. He was terribly inaccurate off the tee, so to survive on the tour, he nurtured a remarkable ability to recover from wooded predicaments and make par. Because of his frequent excursions into the underbrush, he wore khaki fatigues and knee high leather boots, with a safari hat on his head and a Bowie knife strapped to his waist.

"He removed certain clubs from his golf bag to make room for tools better suited to his style of play. He discarded his two iron, because not even God can hit one well. He discarded his fairway woods because his drives never landed there. And finally, because his putter was adding three strokes to his score each hole, he threw the damn thing away, which kept him competitive on the tour despite his habitual forays beyond the course confines.

"He loaded more useful paraphernalia into his bag. A machete replaced the two iron, so that he could cut a swath wide enough to address his ball in the bramble. Hip waders, a snorkel, and a diving mask replaced the fairway woods, because when there isn't jungle adjacent to a fairway, there is usually water. A Khalishnakov rifle replaced the putter. There are dangerous animals in the woods, and you can't win a golf tournament if one eats you. Besides, he wasn't winning any tournaments, so he fed himself by shooting wild game between errant golf shots.

"His eccentric play was generally ignored because he rarely survived the cut after the first two rounds, so he trudged through tournaments in obscurity. The few fans that appreciated his antics nicknamed him the Safari Golfer. Then, during a fateful Masters Tournament years ago, he played the best golf of his life. His recoveries from impossible lies were stunning, and as Saturday merged into Sunday, he not only survived the cut, he was among the leaders.

"The weather turned in his favor on the final day. The wind picked up and the greens became lightning fast. With TV cameras finally focused on him, thousands of fans and journalists got their first real glimpse of him. He cut a resplendent figure, with perspiration from the hot sun staining his khaki shirt, and with the Bowie knife dangling rakishly from his belt. As he made one fabulous recovery from the woods after another, the crowd abandoned Palmer and Nicklaus to follow the eccentric golfer they were suddenly infatuated with.

"The TV commentators were unprepared for his emergence. They hadn't studied his biographical information or his history on the tour. They didn't even know his name. They did know that everyone was calling him the Safari Golfer and that today he was the darling of the gallery. The cameras immortalized his bizarre exploits turning Augusta National's hallowed "Amen Corner", where he snorkeled across the pond at number eleven, tunneled under the azaleas at number twelve, and pole-vaulted over Rae's Creek at number thirteen.

"The contest came down to the final hole. Nicklaus, Palmer, and the Safari Golfer were tied at 13 under par. Jack and Arnie laced perfect drives down the fairway, while the Golfer sliced his tee shot into the magnolias. The crowd surged into the trail he blazed with his machete. He astounded them by launching a perfect four iron shot from a lie that wasn't on any map. He strode in unexpected glory up to the 18th green, which was surrounded by fanatics who had gone bonkers. His second shot had hit the fringe, hopped twice, and rolled into the cup for a tournament-winning eagle. Jack and Arnie shook his hand seconds before the gallery converged on him. He donned the fabled green jacket and was thrust onto the shoulders of adulating fans while firing wild shots from his Khalishnakov into the azure Georgia heavens. America's love affair with him had begun.

"His fame grew exponentially after that Masters victory, even though he never won another tournament. America was eager for a fresh new cultural icon, so he was magically transformed from mere golfing hero into a public persona that transcended sport into the realm of the mythic. The rest is history."

As But Sir! finished speaking, the head of the serpentine procession reached it's destination near the Lincoln Memorial. Dark suited security agents led the Head Honcho through a roiling mass of humanity to an elevated dais at the foot of the memorial, where he would make his campaign speech. The ocean of citizens parted for the famous Senator. Sycophants slapped him on the back and shook his hands as he bulldozed toward the dais.

The Honcho waved to the cheering throng and clasped his hands above his head in a gesture suggesting inevitable victory in the upcoming election. Then he extended his arms to the audience. "My friends, I'm humbled by your warm reception today. I am but a servant of this great nation. The honor of legislating on your behalf is all that sustains me during my most difficult hours." He paused, so the crowd belatedly applauded. In the shadows at the rear of the dais, Freeman remarked to But Sir!, "Who's he kidding? It's Buxomus that sustains him during his most difficult hours."

When the applause dwindled, the Honcho resumed. "Let me spell out the key planks in my campaign platform. The problems troubling our great nation demand unselfish, compassionate action. For instance, racial inequality is a terrible scourge. The gap in mortality rates is widening between blacks and whites. In Detroit alone, blacks are three times as likely to die prematurely than whites. After the election, I will unveil a detailed plan to equalize the death rates between the races. This genocidal disparity cannot continue!" He pounded both fists on the lectern for emphasis. The crowd applauded vigorously. But Sir! whispered to Freeman, "How is he going to solve this ugly problem?"

Freeman snickered loudly then whispered, "He's going to order the military to draft only whites. Then he'll instigate policing actions that won't end until enough whites have been killed to balance the death rates between the races. The body bags are already on order."

But Sir! Inhaled sharply. "That's barbaric!"

"Maybe so. But, the vague promise of equalizing death rates gets him re-elected, given the majority of blacks in his congressional district. Worsening the condition of whites to force equality with blacks is an American tradition. Bussing, progressive taxes, and affirmative action are examples. His new proposal is just a harsher variation on the theme."

"It's still barbaric."

"Shhhhhh," admonished Freeman. "It's time for our leader to lie again."

The Honcho continued his eloquent charade. "The responsibility to aid our downtrodden brethren does not end at the U.S. borders. Wherever there is suffering and despair on earth, we must respond with our limitless resources. If elected, I will help the third world country Vhaicam rise out of poverty. Vhaicam is ravaged by starvation, civil unrest, monsoons, floods, earthquakes, malaria, AIDS, and homosexuality. If we can put a man on the moon, we can rescue Vhaicam. Ask not what your country can do for you, but what can you do for Vhaicam!" Although no one in the audience felt a compelling need to personally help Vhaicam, they roared their approval anyway, due to mass contagion of Political Correctness. Alone, most of these citizens would not choose to give their own money to a mysterious Asian country. However, these were public funds being discussed today, and the crowd was driven by a Pavlovian public compulsion for altruism.

Jefferson leaned toward Freeman and asked, "Why is it so important to funnel our dear resources to Vhaicam?"

Freeman looked at him suspiciously. "Did you just get off the boat? It's important for two reasons. First, if we don't rescue the Vhaicamese, the communists will. Then we'll have to fight the communists. Either we give bushels of money to the Vhaicamese to keep them in the capitalist sphere, or we lob missiles at them, which will cost bushels of money anyway. Second, politicians get elected by making compassionate appeals, and no country is more desperate than Vhaicam. The Honcho's campaign ads will show photographs of starving Vhaicamese children with brutally distended bellies and maggot-infested sores. Promising to save them will hook half the electorate."

"How does any of that preserve the life, liberty, and happiness of Americans?" Jefferson asked.

Before Freeman could reply, the Honcho resumed his speech. "Fellow citizens, my campaign is based on hatred for the domestic and foreign social injustices that corner the downtrodden into inescapable traps of despair and lost hope. Unfortunately, running for Congress is expensive. But, like manna from the heavens, I know that I can count on your financial support. The Great Satan known as the Insurrectionist is sucking our nation into anarchy. Join hands with me to combat this evil terror. With your pennies and my power, we will slaughter this anti-social enemy.

"As my campaign volunteers make their rounds, please dig deep into your pockets and support this ultimate struggle. My campaign is financed with your individual contributions, so that I am beholden only to you. In closing, remember to ask not what your country can do for you, but what you can do for Vhaicam!" The crowd roared as his crew pickpocketed a throng that was emotionally intoxicated by mass psychosis. He had elevated petty thievery to an elegant art form on a canvas as broad as a nation.

Jefferson whispered to Freeman, "You told me there was no purpose for these citizens to contribute their individual dollars."

"There isn't, other than to maintain the illusion that their paltry contributions will actually influence something. The Honcho already has plenty of money from his Political Action Committees. Besides, he's extremely wealthy, despite being on the public payroll his entire career. He and many other congressmen are billionaires. He could finance his campaign with his own personal fortune, if he wanted to."

"I was unaware that Congressmen had filled their personal treasuries with billions of dollars," remarked Jefferson. "The only man I knew with such Midas-like wealth was King George III, and we certainly had no use for him or his gold."

Freeman squinted at Jefferson for a moment, then continued. "Even without his own fortune or his PAC money, the Honcho has other financing options. For example, he and his CIA buddies sell high tech weapons to enemies, such as the Chinese and despotic Middle East governments. The profits from these illicit sales are then used to finance other spurious activities, such as supporting insurgents in Latin America or political campaigns in the U.S. But, these deals are dangerous, because the perpetrators sometimes get caught. It's far easier to walk up to the teller window at the Congressional Bank and write a rubber check for cash."

"There is a bank that permits congressman to exchange bogus drafts for real money?"

"Sure! It's a special bank that doesn't make any profits, extend any loans, or charge any interest. It cashes personal checks for congressmen, whether or not they have sufficient funds in their accounts. So, when a senator is short on cash, a bad check written to the House Bank remedies the problem.

Without this convenience, some couldn't afford their lovers, their drug habits, or the high life of Washington, not to mention their re-election campaigns."

"The Honcho must have a formidable opponent in this election", observed Jefferson, "if such extraordinary funding measures must be undertaken."

"Actually, he's running unopposed."

Jefferson was flabbergasted. "Unopposed?"

"Virtually. There are a few quixotic opponents on the lunatic fringe, but no serious candidate would waste time and money trying to unseat the Head Honcho. He's held his office for countless years, and incumbents are virtually impossible to beat. Their media visibility and their ability to funnel pork barrel projects toward their districts makes their reelection almost a foregone conclusion. Also, PAC's are more likely to support candidates who have already demonstrated a willingness to legislate favorably. With this institutional inertia, democracy is just a dispiriting illusion, as office holders effectively latch on to lifetime appointments. This electoral aristocracy is difficult for commoners to join."

"It's worse than an aristocracy!" said Jefferson. "It sounds like the monarchy that my compatriots committed their lives and fortunes to toss off. These politicians are no different than the princes and dukes who dominated imperial England."

"There's a difference. Our political aristocracy is much subtler. At least a serf in England knew he was a serf. A serf in America thinks he's a free man."

"There was a time", said Jefferson, "when free men had relegated the serfs and overlords to the dungeon of history. Why do American voters participate in this charade?"

"Because they're like lemmings, which have a primordial compulsion to charge across frozen tundra in groups of thousands right off the continental shelf to drown in the ocean below. Lemmings can be excused for irrational behavior, though, because they have pea-sized brains."

After the Honcho's hypocritical charade, the crowd began the traditional march across the Potomac to Arlington National Cemetery to pay their respects to the remains of John F. Kennedy and the Unknown Soldier. Stoic secret service agents guided the dignitaries on the dais to waiting limousines. The vehicles headed slowly across Arlington Memorial Bridge, alongside thousands of strolling people.

Freeman gazed out the window at the Pentagon across the water as his limousine passed a Girl Scout troop marching in formation across the bridge. The innocent young girls bounded merrily against the imposing backdrop of the headquarters of history's deadliest arsenal. With cheerful, prepubescent voices, they sang the children's ditty "It's a Small, Small World", painting a vibrant portrait of the freshness of youth. For just a moment, Freeman was a young boy again. Joy filled his heart, the carefree joy that makes a little boy throw a ball in the air and chase it, or toss a stick for his dog to fetch, the fearless joy blissfully ignorant of toil and mortality. It was the joy that gives meaning to life.

His youthful flashback was short-lived. The juxtaposition of the pixyish girls against the morbid silhouette of the Pentagon made joy an alien emotion. "They're wrong", he sadly thought to himself. "It's not a small, small world. It's a big, bad world with big, ugly adults waiting lasciviously in the shadows to swallow up the trusting children of their own species. The Big Bad Wolf is not a fairy tale myth, and there are millions of Little Red Riding Hoods destined for the Beast's insatiable jaws. Today, the young girls of the world are sugar and spice and everything nice, but some of them will eventually die in a senseless Asian war and others will grow up to die from starvation in a desolate Russian gulag. A generation ago, young Jewish girls were playing stickball one day, and the next day they were floating up as ashes belched from Nazi furnaces. The wolves ruling the world have deceived children into believing there are guardian angels protecting them, and that these guardian angels work in their governments."

The somber ceremonies at Arlington National Cemetery depressed Freeman. He was glad when helicopters from Andrews Air Force Base landed near the Iwo Jima War Memorial to airlift the Honcho's entourage to the country club where the Fed Classic Golf Tournament was being staged. He was eager to rub elbows with former Presidents Ronald Reagan, Gerry Ford, Jimmy Carter, and Bill Clinton, and tour professionals Tiger Woods, Jack Nicklaus, and the Safari Golfer.

The Honcho always won the Fed Classic tournament, despite his ineptitude, because golfers sandbagged their games in deference to the powerful Senator. If they didn't, the Honcho's personal security forces created unplayable lies for them with a discrete kick here and an unnoticed stomp there. Occasionally, more drastic measures were used to ensure victory for the Honcho. Years ago, Jimmy Hoffa led the event by three strokes after seventeen holes. He didn't show up at the eighteenth tee, and hasn't been seen since. Rumors still circulate that his corpse lies at the bottom of a water hazard with his feet encased in quick setting hydraulic cement.

Today, the weather was perfectly suited for the Safari Golfer's game. Thunderstorms loomed ominously on the horizon and the wind kicked up to thirty knots. He took advantage of his ability to play under the harshest conditions and led the Fed Classic tournament after fifteen holes. The Honcho was the nearest challenger at five stokes back. Gerry Ford was near the lead for a while, until one of his errant drives struck a spectator in the forehead and killed him.

Ford made light of the situation by casually remarking, "Pardon me, as I have pardoned my fellow president," but this jest infuriated the spectators gathered around the fallen fan.

Jimmy Carter rushed to Ford's aid by declaring that everyone in the gallery was simply suffering from a spiritual malaise. He threatened to ration gasoline, to leave the hostages in Iran for four more years, and to lust in his heart after every female spectator if the fans didn't leave Gerry alone. Unfortunately, Jimmy was frightened off by a spectator who did an imitation of a killer rabbit. As Carter scurried after Ford in a run for his life, he shouted the word "stagflation" at his pursuers. This curse stopped most of them dead in their tracks, because it reminded them of how much suffering he could inflict. Reagan was unable to say anything to stop the angry spectators, because Nancy and his cue cards were back at the ranch. Clinton zipped up his pants and declared he had no controlling legal authority over the situation.

The Safari Golfer shocked everyone with an audacious, resourceful victory over the Head Honcho. No one had ever beaten the Senator in his own Fed Classic tournament before. This time it was the Honcho's personal security guards that disappeared on the back nine, so they couldn't influence the outcome. The number of missing security guards coincidentally matched the quantity of skinned pelts hanging on the Golfer's four-wheel drive golf cart. When tournament officials suspiciously examined the pelts, the Golfer pointed out that he had taken the requisite two-stroke penalty for slow play while obtaining them. This satisfied the officials, who then formally declared him the victor.

Enraged, the Honcho roared that it was impossible for anyone to have beaten him. After all, the tournament was being held in his honor, he had placed security guards at strategic points on the course, and he had subtracted one stroke from his score on each hole. Although this was a clear violation of USGA rules, he avoided disqualification by attaching a copy of the Political Immunity Clause to his scorecard. Despite these tactics, he came in second. As a sickly film of white foam formed around his mouth, he ranted about this travesty of justice.

Then he remembered that there were TV cameras filming his childish diatribe, so he subdued his remonstrations. But, as hordes of fans and journalists crowded around the beaming Safari Golfer, he seethed internally. This was the second time today he had been upstaged. During his own parade, the Golfer had drawn louder applause from the gallery than he had. He stared in disbelief as the Safari Golfer told the microphones that yes, he did indeed have momentum now, because his astral being had entered certain zodiacal houses which augmented his karma to favorably influence the yin and yang of the universe such that he would metamorphose into another plane of existence wherein he would become a supernatural god no other golfer could vanquish.

As journalists reverently jotted down these surrealistic words from the mystical leader of the free world, the political leader of the free world took a mental note. He recognized a good charade when he saw one, and this particular charade he was witnessing had potential far beyond any ruse he had ever conjured up himself. He resolved to tap into this powerful tool for harnessing the unthinking masses. He had always implicitly understood that the ultimate source of his power was his ability to convince people to substitute his own thoughts for theirs, but he was suddenly enamored with the Golfer's method for turning people into mindless followers. While he warmed to this prolific connection between mysticism and power, a rumbling, unearthly noise cascaded over Washington, which might have been just another roll of thunder from the approaching storm.

There was a storm of a different sort brewing in the nether world of humanity, where Mephistopheles smiled like the Cheshire Cat. He knew very clearly what the Honcho was just beginning to understand. The yearning for an almighty god was very much the same as the yearning for a powerful government. Each promised protection for the weak, incontrovertible laws, arbitration of outcomes, dogmatic views of life, and manna from on high. More importantly, each operated in a mystery-shrouded cocoon of non-objective reality, which was the prolific breeding ground for Satan's greatest triumphs. He was exhilarated that the Honcho was becoming aware of the awesome power of linking mysticism and power together.

Chapter Four: "Who Will Guard the Guardians?"

> "Contradictions do not exist. If you perceive one, check your premises. One of them is wrong."
>
> —Ayn Rand

The President's Marine One helicopter ferried the Honcho's entourage to the White House for a fundraising dinner after the Fed Classic golf tournament. The Honcho enjoyed the surge of power from the chopper's throbbing engine as they rose above the golf course. "Look at the thousands of cockroaches flitting about down there," he said to But Sir!, referring to Lilliputian people who were shrinking to the size of insects. "They're scurrying helter skelter, like someone just turned on the kitchen light and is about to squish them." He chuckled at his own metaphor. But Sir! turned his head away. He wanted to say, "But Sir!, those are real people, not bugs", but he suspected the Honcho no longer knew the difference, due to a mental affliction common to long term office holders.

Meanwhile, Jefferson shouted to Freeman above the heart stomping Whump! Whump! Whump! of the prop, "This flying carriage is amazing!"

Freeman chuckled. "If this helicopter amazes you, you'd be astounded by the President's Air Force One jet. It has accommodations fit for a king, including a master bedroom with a shower, an office, a conference room, encoding and decoding equipment, 85 telephones, a medical operating room, Secret Service agents, stenographers, and a flight crew of 23. It even has a steward to oversee meal preparation and check for poison. Keeping Air Force One aloft costs taxpayers $41,000 per hour, not including the C-20 cargo plane that trails behind to ferry the President's limousine and helicopter wherever he goes."

"Such extravagance flabbergasts me!" exclaimed Jefferson. "We got after Mr. Washington just for having new leather installed in his carriage. Your President should fear angry mobs of citizens threatening to tar and feather him for plundering the public till on such imperial luxury. Are people shaking their fists in righteous indignation at this expensive flying contraption?"

Freeman shook his head. "They're too busy bending over."

The introduction of Jefferson to the President didn't go well when they arrived at the White House. The Honcho hoped the President would be impressed with the new Insurrection Czar. Instead, the two men were unexpectedly cool toward each other. The sight of the rough-hewn Jefferson, who was dressed in a black wool jacket, red waistcoat, knee length pants, silk hose, and black leather shoes, made the President uneasy. Jefferson didn't help matters by strolling around like he owned the place.

Freeman avoided the President, fearing that he would be evicted from the White House if his ball and chain were spotted. Unfortunately, he stumbled over a discarded stained blue dress, causing his ball and chain to clang loudly against the marble floor of the entrance hall. The President rushed over to him, shook his hand vigorously, and whispered that it was unusual to see a criminal in the White House who had actually been convicted.

The Honcho invited an impressive line-up of America's most prolific campaign contributors to the White House for dinner. This $10,000 per plate fund-raising extravaganza would fill his campaign coffers nicely. Sammy Gioncarlo was there, representing America's most politically influential family, La Cosa Nostra. Ms. Elizabeth Bennington represented the National Teacher's Organization, which was responsible for the current condition of America's educational system. Big Jim, President of the Teamsters Union, showed up wearing six pounds of gold jewelry. An androgynous person named Terry represented the National Organization of Women, Gays, Lesbians, and other Oppressed Peoples with Narrow Political Agendas Raiding the Treasury and Imposing their Viewpoints on America through Government (NOWGLOPNPARTIVAG). And, surprisingly, the Safari Golfer came. The Head Honcho invited him at the last minute, having gotten over his humiliating defeat on the golf course earlier that day. Fifty other representatives of entrenched special interests were there to break bread with the Honcho and buy a piece of the American political pie.

The five White House chefs conjured a steady stream of tantalizing appetizers, aromatic entrees, and haute cuisine. Clams on the half-shell were served first, with caviar as an alternative for the squeamish. Next came piping hot French onion soup, followed by radishes, celery, olives, and salted almonds. The fourth course featured lake trout decorated with fanciful shaped potatoes and cucumbers. Warm sweet breads followed, and then came artichokes, asparagus, and spinach in pastry. The seventh and main course was a large roast brought to the huge mahogany table by two ravishing maids dressed in short black frilly dresses and white aprons. Frozen roman punch was proffered to clear palates for the remaining six courses. Custard pudding and an assortment of creamed sweets followed wild duck with tossed salad. Fine cheeses were then served with warm biscuits and fresh dairy butter. To finish the culinary orgy, crystallized fruits were served with bonbons, and a variety of coffees, liqueurs and sparkling waters were dispensed to wash down the last morsels.

At meal's end, the satiated dinner guests slumped in their velvet-upholstered chairs to contentedly digest food fit for kings. The Head Honcho asked a butler clearing the table if there was another course on the way. Buxomus Blondus slapped his massive shoulder and scolded him for being such a pig. He grunted a very passable "oink!", just like when divvying up the budget in Congress.

Jefferson asked where the cow was pastured that had been slaughtered for this feast. But Sir! whispered that cattle were not customarily pastured on the White House lawns or in any major metropolis. Jefferson insisted that someone named Mr. Harrison raised cattle here. He also insisted that raising cattle in a major metropolis wasn't unusual, since Washington was swarming with Sacred Cows, one of which he accidentally killed two days ago when his carriage turned left too sharply and crashed into a concrete curb. It's wooden wheels shattered, launching splintered spokes like arrows into the vulnerable flank of a Sacred Cow. The dead beast slumped into a bloated pile of useless flesh, just like before it was killed.

A horrified gasp went up when Jefferson mentioned this deadly encounter. Faces went pale and voice boxes became paralyzed. "Those who witnessed the skewering of the Sacred

Cow were similarly stupefied", observed Jefferson. "Is it so unusual for man and beast to collide, and for the beast to get the worst of it?"

No one answered. They looked as if he had just reported slaying the Pope. Finally, But Sir! regained his voice. "Mr. Jefferson! No one has ever been foolish enough to kill one of Washington's Sacred Cows! Other guests found their voices. "Jesus Christ, Jefferson! How did you survive?" "Holy shit! Did you get struck by lightning afterward?" "You're a marked man, my friend." "Something horrible is sure to happen to you."

"No courage was required to slay this beast", said Jefferson. "And I assure you, no evil has befallen me since. In fact, I fancy the world to be a better place with one less of those disrespectful animals defecating on sidewalks and butting pedestrians."

The guests cut short the after-dinner chitchat to take a guided tour of America's palatial First Home. The marathon tour took them through 132 full rooms, 20 bathrooms, and up and down five elevators. They soaked up the opulence of the ornate structure, which housed thirty thousand pieces of period furniture, fine china, bronze-dore utensils, exquisite glassware, and delicate linens. The ceilings showered dozens of gold chandeliers. The walls were decorated with intricately formed plaster facade. The windows were treated with beautiful velvet and gold lame drapes. Skillfully woven and fabulously dyed rugs carpeted the floors. The movie theater, bowling alley, Olympic swimming pool, tennis courts, perfectly manicured putting green, and basketball court were equally impressive. In between running the country, running for re-election, and running from scandals, the President did not lack diversion from matters of state and conscience that were undoubtedly pressing on him.

A menagerie of aides, doormen, butlers, maids, and curators maintained a regal environment for the First Family. The tour guide announced that the White House employed

91 people, including a barber, five florists for decking out the estate in luxuriant flora, five calligraphers for endorsing complimentary parchments, a military nurse for giving the President nightly rubdowns, and a staffer to continuously maintain a roaring fire, which was occasionally fueled by incriminating documents from foreign and domestic intrigues gone awry. Secret service agents lurked in strategic nooks, ready to apply deadly force to threatening intruders. These agents follow the president wherever he goes, making sure that he never opens a door, never gets stuck in a traffic jam, never waits for take-off clearance at an airport, or never gets shot by someone he double-crossed in the Mafia or the CIA.

The tour guide described the President's helicopter waiting at the National Naval Medical Center to respond in seconds to any medical emergency. The guests drooled over his door-to-door limousine service. They gasped when they heard that a Marine band is assigned full time to play music for state dinners and soirees at the White House. Their jaws dropped in amazement after hearing that Air Force One is maintained in a constant state of readiness at Andrews Air Force Base, in order to jet the President and his favorite bed to summit meetings, campaign events, or family vacations.

The tour concluded outside the Situation Room, which is the command and control center where the President and his staff hunker down during nuclear wars or natural disasters. It is deep underground and girded by thick layers of reinforced concrete. Secure encoding and decoding devices enable the Chief to maintain contact with his field commanders during crises. The Situation Room also houses the controls that only the President can access for arming the nation's nuclear arsenal. It is stocked with years worth of preserved food and bottled water, so that the President, his family, and his essential aides can survive the radioactive fallout after an exchange of hydrogen bombs with an irate foe. Some guests were disturbed that the man with his finger on The Button was so assured of survival if it was pushed.

The dinner guests, convening in the great entrance hall for farewells, brimmed with observations from the tour. Jefferson remarked that the abode was big enough for two emperors, a pope, and a grand lama, and that the President couldn't help but to lose touch with the rest of America in such ostentatious accommodations. He was also intrigued by the statue of George Washington that they spotted in the basement. The statue, depicting Washington semi-nude wearing a toga, was mothballed after its inaugural showing because it portrayed the leader of the world's first democracy too much like a Roman Emperor. Jefferson suggested cynically that it was time to resurrect the statue.

But Sir! did a sign of the cross as if the White House was a monument to a secular religion or a cult. Freeman said the experience made him proud to be an American, but inside he was angry at how many of his tax dollars were being spent on an otherworldly lifestyle for the man who was allegedly leading a government of the people, for the people, and by the people. His ball and chain seemed to get heavier in proportion to his silent anger.

The Head Honcho lagged behind the group to slip into the Lincoln Bedroom with Buxomus for a few lascivious moments, after a startled Barbara Streisand fled in dismay. In the room where Abraham Lincoln signed the Emancipation Proclamation, he emancipated his sperm into her warm depths, and the only proclamation heard today was her breathless squeal. Lincoln would have returned to the living to slay such a blasphemer, had he an inkling from the world beyond the grave. Unfortunately, he would have quickly discovered that the Honcho's blasphemy in his bedroom was but the tip of an enormous iceberg bobbing in the turgid waters of modern American politics.

* * *

The Honcho's St. Patrick's Day celebration culminated at a secret retreat frequented by a closed brotherhood of the nation's most powerful men. This mecca of sin and debauchery was called the Bavarian Forest, an adjunct of the Order of Illuminati formed in 1776 by international power brokers as an unintended antithesis to a separate group of men convening that same year in Philadelphia. The Order was dedicated to destroying all religions and political institutions, and to subverting human freedom. The whereabouts of the present-day Bavarian Forest is a secret tenaciously guarded by the members. Jefferson, Freeman, and But Sir! were invited to attend by the Head Honcho, despite the general prohibition against outsiders visiting the Forest. They were blindfolded during the trip to the infamous den of iniquity to preserve confidentiality.

The Bavarian Forest lies in a secluded wilderness deep inside heavily wooded mountains. It is accessible only by helicopter or canoe. The influential men who convalesce there seek refuge from prying paparazzi, because their behavior would shock the civilized world if reported. At the Forest, men take on the hearts of boys, the souls of Satyrs, and the minds of the pathologically unbalanced. The Forest sits on land owned by a wealthy magnate who insists on anonymity. Security is thorough and impenetrable. No cameras or tape recorders are permitted, since leakage of their damning escapades would destroy the public lives of Forest members. Private militia and hungry Dobermans constantly patrol the perimeter of the redoubt. The militia has standing orders to shoot trespassers. The dogs do not require any orders.

The Bavarian Forest has 125 luxurious bungalows outfitted with Jacuzzis, waterbeds, wine cellars, pornographic video rooms, expensive liqueurs, masseuses, and prostitutes. Nothing is illegal in the Forest, except theft and violence against other members. Local cops are bribed with enough cash, drugs, and women to have amnesia about the Forest's existence, leaving the members free to indulge in every pleasurable vice conjured up by men who never completely transitioned from adolescence to adulthood.

Membership in the Bavarian Forest is by invitation and must be blessed by at least 75% of the Brotherhood. Applicants must be white, male, obscenely wealthy or powerful, and able to stare directly into the naked souls of other men hell bent on exploring every nuance of their ids. Thus, the club is rather exclusive. It also has an unstructured, mysterious organization without a permanent leader. Responsibility for leading each Gathering of the Brotherhood is passed from member to member. The presiding leader is addressed as the Emperor, and is adorned with a jeweled crown and a Roman toga.

By tradition, the Head Honcho reigns as the Emperor on St. Patrick's Day. After arriving by helicopter, he donned the jeweled crown and the purple and gold toga, which exaggerated his usual imperiousness and created the illusion that Julius Caesar had somehow been reincarnated. He relished this authoritarian role.

When darkness fell and a bonfire in the campsite commons was roaring and crackling, the Honcho called the Gathering to order and initiated the Burning of Effigies, which is the opening ceremony. All members dress in white druidic robes, surround the fire, and bring effigies of their heaviest burdens. As a chorus of members sings eerie songs, they toss their effigies into the blazing inferno to symbolically vanquish their worries in the civilization beyond the Forest. They are then free to party with uninhibited Dionysian vigor.

As hypnotic reflections of firelight danced on robed bodies, the Honcho began the Burning of Effigies. He and his fellow Congressmen had been struggling for months to balance the Federal budget. They were torn between the desire to spend extra billions of dollars on pork barrel projects to entice citizens to vote for them, and the conflicting desire to avoid raising taxes to pay for it all, so as not to offend those very same voters. They were hopelessly stalemated, because none of them had big enough testicles to confront this budgetary disconnect. The result was a trillion-dollar deficit, which would be fatal to the nation's economy in the long run, but in the short run was politically expedient. To lift this weight from his sagging shoulders, the Honcho tossed a forty-pound copy of the Federal Budget into the licking flames of the inferno. "Fuck the budget", he announced solemnly to the Gathering. His flagging spirits brightened. The ritual cleansed him.

The Mayor of Washington went next. He was embroiled in a Grand Jury investigation into contracts he had awarded to procure fuel significantly above the market price for the city's bus fleet from a middleman, who turned out to be his brother and who had coincidentally made a hefty campaign contribution. The effigy that the Mayor offered up for immolation was a copy of the U.S. Constitution. "Fuck the legal system", he declared. He suddenly felt much better.

The President was next. He was having marital problems with the First Lady, who despised him for sleeping with every floozy who loosened her skirt. He had no recourse against her anger, since it was not politically correct to get divorced while in office, although it appeared to be okay to screw around. He ceremoniously tossed his marriage license into the hungry flames and said, "Fuck the whoring bitch!" In the background, the druidic chorus intoned haunting, mystical chants. Gnarled trees stood like dark sentinels around the Gathering, and the night sky hung like a solemn shroud over the quasi-religious ceremony.

The chief executive officer of a major American manufacturing company took his turn next. His worldly albatross was incessant competition from industrious, quality-minded foreigners. He was waging a life and death struggle to get Congress to ban them from doing business in America. He tossed a copy of Adam Smith's "Wealth of Nations" into the fire. "We can't compete with those slant-eyed yellow hordes, so we'll outlaw them", he muttered. "Fuck the consumers if they don't like it."

The Archbishop of the Washington Diocese took his turn paying homage to the Fire God. The aging defender of Catholic tradition was weary of his two millennia old conglomeration of myths that were really extrapolations of three millennia old Babylonian, Assyrian, and Egyptian myths borrowed and homogenized by the nomadic Israelites. He was tired of substituting dogma for metaphysics, moralistic stories for debate, and anachronistic rituals for a real intercourse between his flock and his god. He heaved his tattered Baltimore Catechism into the conflagration and declared, "The cosmology of two thousand years ago is of no use today." He wanted to declare, "Fuck something or other," just like everyone else, but his vow of celibacy had neutered that concept in his brain.

On and on went the Burning of Effigies. Freeman tossed in a wooden replica of his ball and chain, declaring "Fuck human nature." Unfortunately, the effigy didn't catch fire. "The wood must be green," he rationalized, unaware of how difficult his spiritual albatross would be to shed. Jefferson quietly tossed hastily made wooden stick figures covered by small swatches of white sheet into the bonfire. No one noticed the glistening tear drop sliding down his cheek. But Sir! stood silently without offering an effigy to the voracious Fire God. His conscience did not require him to participate.

When they had burnt their effigies and allayed the pressing concerns of the outside world, they proceeded to the Altar. The Altar was a huge slab of granite atop two smaller slabs. It was used for initiating new members and occasionally for bizarre sexual acts or human sacrifices to the Barley and Opium Gods. The only new initiate this evening was the Safari Golfer, which surprised everyone, given the Golfer's humiliation of the Head Honcho during the Fed Classic golf tournament. When Freeman pressed the Honcho for an explanation, his devious smile suggested an unseemly ulterior motive for influencing the Forest membership to invite the eccentric pop figure into the Gathering.

As the robed men circled around the granite Altar, the Safari Golfer climbed atop for his initiation. His faded khaki overalls and dingy tennis shoes were removed, leaving the wispy man buck naked before the phalanx of powerful men smiling bemusedly at his degradation. Nakedness reduces even the most confident of men into humble insecurity. His wire-rimmed glasses, his gold earring, and his necklace with the strange talismans were removed. When hair clippers began lopping off his brown curly tresses, the Golfer looked like a man who deeply regretted his predicament.

Shorn of his hair and his dignity, the most famous man in the world stood meekly before the Gathering. He was covered with a slimy concoction of honey, lard, and molasses as two men crashed through the ranks of the Gathering with a furiously bleating goat barely in their grasp. The goat broke free near the altar, which was okay, because the Golfer was required to chase and recapture the wayward animal.

He scampered after the bounding goat as the Gathering roared with laughter and spread out to contain the chase within a circle of humanity. After a few unsuccessful lunges at the elusive critter, the Golfer absorbed enough dirt to turn the gooey concoction covering his body into a muddy plaster. The spectators slapped their thighs with unrestrained mirth as the comic figure with the flopping genitals scrambled after the agile goat under the flickering torches ringing the Forest commons. A dramatic lunge by the Golfer ensnared the goat, to the disappointment of the wildly entertained men. He wrestled the bucking animal to the ground, and laid on it to subdue it.

His travails were just beginning, however. Following the dictates of the ritual, he dragged the twitching goat to the Altar and hefted it onto the granite slab. He deftly slit the throat of the bleating beast with a knife someone handed him. Brilliant red blood gurgled out of the mortal wound. Fighting a wave of revulsion, he put his mouth to the quivering animal's throat and sucked the warm fluid. A gold chalice was handed to him, which he held against the gashed throat and filled with blood. The limp corpse fell heavily onto the granite slab as he held the chalice triumphantly above his head. The Gathering roared its approval of his conquest. The chalice was passed around so each member could sip the blood of the vanquished animal to gruesomely cement their bond with the initiate. They shouted three "hurrahs!" to their new brother.

The Golfer's first official act was to recite the Bavarian Forest's unwritten anthem. Ringed by the robed Gathering, he stood proudly atop the Altar, his naked body coated with a macabre mask of blood and mud. Like a Marine recruit fresh from Paris Island, he shouted:

"No laws constrain me
No social mores bind me
No inhibitions limit me
I dance to a tune only my soul knows
The Bavarian Forest is now my home
Fuck everyone but my soul brothers"

The rituals were finished, so the Gathering fragmented into smaller cloisters to pursue a wide range of earthly pleasures, many of which involved sexual gratification in varying degrees of abnormality. Pornographic movies and magazines abounded. Women were allowed into the encampment solely for sexual exploitation. Many of the members spirited in prostitutes, groupies, and girlfriends. Bungalows were soon awash in naked bodies, groping and penetrating each other. Some men performed homosexual acts, while others mooned, streaked, and ball walked with their genitals protruding through their togas. Still others masturbated while watching lesbian women make love.

Drugs proliferated in the encampment. Anything that created an artificial high could be had from the Police Chief of Washington, a member of the Forest who regularly shared the narcotics scavenged from drug busts. The pungent aroma of marijuana and the nauseating smell of free-based cocaine wafted through the air. Crack, Ecstasy, Angel Dust, heroin, meth, and LSD were available in the Police Chief's bungalow. Before long, disoriented robed figures stumbled around in the throes of chemical intoxication.

A panoply of brands, vintages, and proofs of alcohol were heavily consumed during the Gatherings. In one bungalow, a fake penis jutting from a large poster of a rhinoceros dispensed alcohol directly into mouths. Women were forced to please the rhino when it wasn't dispensing drinks. Drinking was considered a religion in the Bavarian Forest, and the Honcho was its Supreme Deity. His massive body could absorb prodigious volumes of alcohol before stupefaction set in, because his metabolism had developed a partial immunity after years of being awash in it. But, he still always out drank the limits of his unusual tolerance.

The Honcho was the center of attention near the bonfire, partly because he was the Emperor tonight, partly because he was the most powerful man in America, and partly because he commanded an entertaining repertoire of ribald stories that flowed freely from his tongue as the alcohol took effect. Arrayed around the Emperor were the Archbishop, the Mayor, the Police Chief, the President, media moguls, several Congressmen, the Safari Golfer, a Mafia Don, and other nefarious characters. Jefferson, Freeman, and But Sir! joined these revelers.

While his drunken and stoned compatriots lounged on the ground around him, the Head Honcho unsteadily positioned himself on a rock. He recounted humorous drinking stories garnished during many years of imbibing excessively with a rogue's gallery of famous alcoholics. As a steady stream of glib anecdotes rolled off his tingling tongue, the audience reacted with back pounding mirth. He recounted the tale about Winston Churchill, who had drunk to excess at a formal affair that included Bessie Braddock, an MP in the British Parliament. Bessie scolded Churchill with a haughty, "You're drunk!" Churchill responded with an equally haughty, "And you, madam are ugly. But I shall be sober in the morning."

Before they stopped laughing, he told another Churchill classic. Churchill, who was behaving boorishly in a stuffy formal soiree, was confronted by Nancy Astor, another MP in the British Parliament. "If you were my husband, I'd poison your coffee," declared the frustrated woman, who was tired of his alcohol-inspired antics. Churchill quickly replied, "If you were my wife, I'd drink it!" The Gathering guffawed loudly as the Honcho segued into an anecdote about Oscar Wilde, the rakish Irishman noted for his dark humor. During a dinner party in France, Mr. Wilde was introduced to a famous, though unattractive, French actress. "Mr. Wilde, you're looking at the ugliest woman in Paris," she said. With as much flattery as he could muster, Oscar responded, "In the world, madam. In the world!"

The Honcho reeled off many more tales of social irreverence involving powerful men who drank liquor in stupendous volumes, which is exactly what the men in the Forest were doing. They goaded him on with toasts and frequent invitations to tip his bottle. As he neared the end of his repertoire, his speech became slurred and occasionally incoherent. The last few of his anecdotes sounded like they were spoken by a man with a tongue stung by a thousand bees. He told of Brendan Behan, who jested, "I saw an advertisement that said 'drink Canada Dry', and I've just started." He quoted the poet Dylan Thomas, who once declared, "An alcoholic is someone you don't like who drinks as much as you do." He closed his ribald monologue with a tribute to Murad IV, a Sultan of Turkey in the 17th Century, who forbade the use of alcohol, on penalty of death. After executing 100,000 violators, he died of alcoholism.

Deep into the night they drank, caroused, and practiced gynecology on comatose women. An ebony blanket enveloped the encampment as clouds blocked the twinkling starlight and the silvery lunar radiance. The entombing darkness left the encampment seemingly adrift in a cosmic void. As the night air became heavy and still, the heat from the bonfire made the Bavarian Forest a sweltering sauna. The smell of burning wood, the aroma of narcotics, and the sickly odors of drunken humanity created a rancid composite smell like burning brimstone or decaying flesh. Tortured voices pierced the anonymous darkness. The agonized wailing of crashing dopers, the gut-wrenching moans of vomiting drinkers, and the screams of victims being sexually abused blended into a macabre cacophony of sound that would have made sober men cringe with horror.

Freeman wrestled with an uneasy deja vu feeling. The disharmonic sounds, the putrid smells, and the searing heat evoked vague imagery of a terrible place he tried mightily to remember and to forget at the same time. Meanwhile, Thomas Jefferson wrestled with a different uneasy feeling. He approached the Mayor of Washington to get some puzzling questions answered.

"Membership in this elite fraternity must be very expensive," Jefferson observed, as the mayor took a long pull on his half-empty bottle.

"Damn shtraight, ol timer," confirmed the Mayor, whose numbed tongue was nearly dysfunctional. "The men in the Vabarian Foresht are among (hiccup) the richess in the world."

"Then I should conclude that salaries of civil servants like yourself have mushroomed into the realm of luxurious royalty?"

"No, of coursh not," chuckled Hizzoner, who looked suspiciously at Jefferson from behind the translucent vale of whiskey-clouded consciousness. "The shalaries of ush shivil shervants aren't even high 'nuff to attrack qualified cannidates for the job."

"Then the Brotherhood let you into the Forest for free?"

"Absholuly not!", declared the Mayor, pounding his whiskey bottle into the dirt for emphasis. "I paid evry damn penny of the memmership fee!"

"Then you must have fallen into a vast inheritance?"

At this point in such a conversation, a sober Mayor would have cut off the discussion and expressed indignation at this personal finance probe. Unfortunately, his judgment was impaired, so he answered Jefferson with disarming honesty after taking another pull on his liquid crutch. "Inheritanshe Shmeritanshe. I use my campaign fund to pay for pershonal espenshes. I've had this job sho long, no one ever sherioushly challenges me, sho I don' have to waste the money donated to me acshually campaignin'. An if that don' cover my espenshes, then I award city contracts to cronies who greash my palms with lots of long green. My shalary don' mean shit when money like that rolls in. An if that aint enough, I do some extortin'. If a developer wants to build a hotel on city proppity, it'll cost him big to get a buildin' permit from me. Nobody makes a buck in my city without me gettin' a share. I got ladies to shupport. I got whishkey to buy. I got a condo in . . . in . . . in shomeplace. I got to pay for this memmership. An 'nother good thing about bein' Mayor is that you never haff to pay for nuttin. Like, to get here tonight, we took the city hel'copter over...."

The Mayor abruptly stopped, because a warning signal finally plowed through his numbed neural network to the brain lobe responsible for concealing his indiscretions. Jefferson turned his attention to the Police Chief, who sat in bemused silence as the Mayor rambled down the heavily traveled path to incoherence. The stoic Police Chief was not as far down this road as the Mayor, although he had wetted his lips often enough to loosen his tongue. "Aren't you uncomfortable," Jefferson asked the burly Top Cop, "amid such unabashed disdain for the law?"

"No," responded the Chief, after a brief introspection. "Doesn't bother me a bit."

"Aren't you the Chief of Police?"

"Sure, which means I carry the burden of being a public servant."

"What do you mean?"

The Police Chief smiled. "It's very simple. Most of the guys here are responsible for making or enforcing the law. Those toga-clad bodies in drunken stupors are judges, congressmen, lawyers, and policemen. It would be unreasonable to expect them to have sufficient energy to actually obey the laws they create. You civilians don't have the heavy burden of creating and enforcing laws. You have only half the struggle, which is obeying them."

"Perhaps I'm naive," observed Jefferson, "but is not observance of the law the responsibility of all citizens, be they public servants or civilians?"

"You are indeed naive."

Jefferson ignored the jab. "How are you able to finance your membership in the Bavarian Forest? Do you partake in the same kickback and extortion schemes as the Mayor?"

"Nah, it's too risky. Someday Hizzoner will get caught, and then he'll have to give half of his ill-gotten fortune to dishonest lawyers to find clever loopholes created by mercenary lawmakers."

"Then how do you finance your membership?" wondered Jefferson with thinly veiled suspicion.

"Washington has a Secret Police Fund to finance covert interdiction of drug traffic and organized crime. It's called Project 82-1."

"You don't use much of this fund for those purposes?" surmised Jefferson.

"Do I look like I'm stupid?" said the Police Chief indignantly. "If we actually executed widespread drug busts, we would inadvertently snatch up some of our distinguished guests here this evening, which would limit my career. And only a masochistic fool fond of broken legs, concrete boots, and assassinated relatives would interfere with the Mafia."

"What does Project 82-1 have to do with financing your Forest membership?"

"Everything. This fund is a secret 'Black Budget' with little administrative oversight, so no one knows where the cash is going, even if I use it for my own financial obligations. Getting money from Project 82-1 is as easy as ordering a sandwich at the police commissary. I just tell the cashier that I need 50 G's for a covert operation, and soon a stack of cash magically appears on my desk. Then I go to the nearest mall to buy trinkets for my wife and three girlfriends. Or, I wire money to my daughter, who's attending Stanford on an '82-1 Scholarship'. Or, I make payments on my Porsche 928 and my vacation home in Boca Raton. Or, I pay my Forest membership fee. Or, if I'm feeling really arrogant, I do this. . . ." The Chief lit a cigar with a curled wad of cash that he ignited from a flaming bonfire ember.

Jefferson cringed. "Do you use any of the money for real covert operations?"

"Sure," said the Chief through a cloud of cigar smoke. "I occasionally do drug busts, if only to keep the Bavarian Forest stocked with narcotics. I also use 82-1 money to pay undercover police to protect the mayor's daughter, since she's in love with a notorious drug kingpin. And sometimes the Mayor asks me to use 82-1 money to surreptitiously do horrible things to opposition mayoral candidates."

"Why do you assist the mayor in this manner?"

"He's my boss. I follow orders well. Besides, if an honest person got elected in his place, I'd be in deep shit. The only bond stronger than blood is honor among thieves. Also, on a few unfortunate occasions, my boys have inadvertently ensnared Hizzoner taking illicit drugs in dingy hotels with exotic prostitutes. I do dirty tricks for him to redeem myself. I scratch his back and he scratches mine."

Jefferson fell silent. He couldn't bear to hear any more. Unfortunately, the Police Chief continued the conversation. "What do you think of our clever financial arrangements?"

Jefferson looked at him coldly. "I participated in the civil service myself, but when I served my country many years ago, we weren't tempted by overflowing campaign treasuries, undocumented covert funds, or huge city contracts to award to cronies in exchange for kickbacks. The government I served didn't even have that much money at its disposal. King George's government did, but we dispensed with it. The men serving their country alongside of me were of impeccable honor, with rare exceptions, like Burr, Hamilton, and Arnold. Today, however, the rare exceptions are honorable men."

The Chief frowned at his whiskey bottle as if it had just failed him somehow. "How are you associated with the Head Honcho?"

"I'm his new Insurrection Czar."

The Police Chief spat. "What the fuck is an Insurrection Czar?"

"My job is to prevent insurrections by American citizens, so that politicians like the Honcho won't be dethroned."

"Jesus Christ! How could a government as powerful as ours, led by politicians as ruthless as him, ever be overthrown?"

"It's been done before," said Jefferson. "And it could happen again. Men like the Honcho, who seek power as fervently as Parcival sought the Holy Grail, live in mortal fear of it slipping from their hands. Power is a manmade narcotic more addictive than any of Nature's chemical concoctions. Like other drugs, it is corruptive and destructive."

"Have you found any insurrectionists yet?"

Before Jefferson could reply, a hullabaloo erupted among the revelers near the Head Honcho. The inebriated Senator was gesticulating angrily toward the perimeter of the encampment. Apparently, a threatening visitor lurked where light from the bonfire melded with the dark of night. "I told you never to show your wrinkled face here again, you sonofabitch!" the Honcho bellowed into the darkness. "You didn't invite me to your last tea party, so I'll be goddamned if you'll get into my Gathering!"

"Whom is he addressing?" Jefferson wondered aloud.

"The Mad Hatter," said Freeman.

"That's very curious," observed Jefferson. "Does anyone else see this deranged hatter?"

"Of course not," said Freeman. "The Mad Hatter is one of the Honcho's frequent hallucinations when he's drunk."

This wasn't a hallucination to the Honcho. The Mad Hatter, the March Hare, and the Dormouse were ignoring his remonstrations. He clenched his fists and shouted louder, but Alice's three acquaintances continued toward him. "We are most certainly going to be late", reminded the March Hare. "The Queen shall have off with our heads."

"Nonsense! The Queen shall have off with *his* head," judged the Mad Hatter, pointing to the Honcho. "He's much too noisy. If he weren't such a large beast, I would say we should stuff him into the teapot. It's no longer good sport to do it to the Dormouse."

Presently, the Hatter, the Hare, and the Dormouse stood calmly in the Honcho's menacing shadow. The Hatter's pencil thin arms and legs sprouted from a small potbelly. He was dressed in a dinner jacket, high starched collar, a polka dotted bow tie, and a black top hat with a price tag indicating it could be had for 10 pounds, six pence. His disheveled gray hair receded from a wrinkled face with bulging eyes, thin lips, and a prominent nose. Large teeth dominated his mischievous smile. "Have some treacle," he offered to the Honcho. "It's six o'clock, and time for our party."

"It's not six o'clock. Your watch must be wrong."

"You must have eaten too many mushrooms," replied the Mad Hatter. "It's always precisely 6:00, ever since Time got angry and declared that it would always be so. I'd show you my watch to prove it, but it only tells the date, since the time of day is now rather fixed."

"That's nonsense!"

"It most certainly is not," corrected the Mad Hatter. "It is merely absurd. It would be nonsense only if I continued to use a watch that told the time of day."

"Regardless of the time, I don't want any treacle", said the Honcho.

"Which is just as well, since we didn't bring any with us", replied the Hatter with grating politeness.

"Then why did you offer?"

"Why do you care? You said you don't want any."

"Why are our conversations always so brutally confusing?" wailed the Honcho.

"Off with his head!" interjected the Dormouse.

"Be patient, my dear little rodent," admonished the Mad Hatter. "There'll be plenty of time for that after the croquet tournament. Which reminds me, I do believe we're going to be late." He grabbed the March Hare's umbrella and swatted the Dormouse. "The Dormouse is mad, you know. He thinks that everything begins with an 'm'."

"That doesn't seem like madness to me", said the Honcho, who had just recently weathered a devastating zero and comma shortage.

"Which doesn't surprise us, since you're mad, too."

"I'm not mad!" protested the most powerful man in America, teetering on the edge of dementia.

"Then why don't you want any treacle?"

The Honcho took a deep breath. "Because I don't like treacle."

"Then it's very rude to keep talking about it, especially since we don't have any."

"Please tell me why you're here", pleaded the Honcho pathetically.

"Very well. Alice has a message for you. She said you would understand. I don't, because it sounds very much like madness. It goes like this:

> *"How cheerfully the crocodile grins,*
> *how neatly spreads his claws,*
> *And welcomes little fishes in*
> *with gently smiling jaws!"*

The Honcho smiled nervously. "Alice's message is nonsense. It means nothing to me."

"That wasn't her message," said the Hatter mischievously. "I just made that up. She really said to push the button."

"What button?" asked the Senator.

"How should I know? Go ask Alice."

The Mad Hatter, the March Hare, and the Dormouse turned abruptly and disappeared just beyond the illuminating clutches of the bonfire. The Gathering stood in befuddled amusement around the Honcho, who was still trembling from his encounter with the apparitional viscera of his tortured mind. "You saw them, didn't you?" he pleaded. The group took a silent, synchronized step backward toward presumed safety. The frightened giant grabbed But Sir! by his toga and pulled his aide's face up to his own, suffocating him with a cloud of fetid breath and spraying him with spittle. "You saw him, didn't you? Tell me you heard Alice's message!"

"But . . . Sir! I . . . can't . . . breathe!" The Honcho's powerful arms had lifted his frail aide off the ground and constricted his diaphragm. Fortunately, the President stepped forward and put a comforting arm around the discombobulated Senator. "Calm down, big fella," he condescended. "I seen him too!"

"I knew it!", the Honcho shouted with glee to the nonbelievers encircling him. "I wasn't imagining it! The President saw the Hatter, too." Turning back to the Commander in Chief of the most powerful military in history, he said anxiously, "Alice wants me to press the button!"

"Aye, I heard", acknowledged the President, gamely.

"But what does she mean?" shouted the Honcho. "What button? And why should I press it?"

The President didn't know what to say. He had merely intended to reassure the Head Honcho that he wasn't the only inebriated fool hallucinating this evening. Unfortunately, he now had to interpret drunken visions, for which he wasn't well suited. The only button in the vicinity he knew of was the one that armed the nation's nuclear arsenal. This button, called the "football", was carried wherever the President went, so it was in the Bavarian Forest tonight. He pointed to an innocuous briefcase held by an agent next to him. "I think Alice is referring to the football", he confided quietly to the Honcho.

"That's it!" shouted the Honcho. "The Communists are about to attack us. Alice is warning us to attack first! She wants us to press the Button! Off with their heads! Let's go for it!"

"Hold on, Red Queen!" said the President nervously. "If we push that button, nuclear Armageddon will result. Once our missiles are in the air, the Communists will counterattack with everything they've got. The entire world could be obliterated!"

"So what?"

This momentarily stumped the President. Through a drunken haze, he tried to reason with the Honcho. "There are millions of people, myself included, who probably don't want to die tonight."

"We don't have to die. After I press the button, we can helicopter to the White House Situation Room and watch the blips on the maps light up. By the time the Communists shoot back, we'll be safely tucked away!"

"What about everyone else without the good fortune to be us?" asked the President, who deeply regretted what he had inadvertently started.

"Come on!" pleaded the Honcho. "Don't be maudlin. Let's have some sport tonight. Fix bayonets! All hands on deck! Sound General Quarters! Batten the hatches! DefCon One! DefCon Two! DefCon Three! Hut Hut!"

Chaos erupted in surreal slow motion, like a nightmare in which the dreamer is powerless to stop the horrible things that are happening and can't even shout a warning. The Honcho tackled the secret service agent who was holding the football. The agent fumbled it onto the ground as he crumpled into an unconscious heap. Nobody moved. The Honcho snatched the errant briefcase as his barrel chest heaved from exertion and rabid dementia. He stared fiercely at the President and growled, "Give me the launch code!"

No one expected the President to comply. Just then, Freeman saw his own madness-inspired apparition. A greenish glowing humanoid with two piercing red eyes appeared in the opaque darkness just beyond the pale of the Forest. His heart skipped several beats as the glowing figure moved with catlike fluidity. "Something evil is out there", he thought. He heard the rumbling laugh of Satan roll across the encampment like dull thunder.

"It's a two step process," said the President coldly, shocking the eerily transfixed men in the Forest. "First, you put the nation's nuclear triumvirate on red alert by keying in the proper defense condition code." The Honcho tore open the briefcase and turned on the COMSEC encoding device nestled inside. While the President coolly dictated the code, the Honcho keyed it into the transmitter.

"Now what?"

"Wait for our nuclear arsenal to be activated", instructed the President in a robotic monotone. "Missile silos in the Rocky Mountains are opening, and MIRV warheads are being armed on top of Inter-Continental Ballistic Missiles. NORAD is searching the heavens for incoming missiles or unfriendly aircraft. Pilots are scrambling into the cockpits of B1 and B2 bombers on American airbases throughout the world. Trident submarines are preparing to launch their deadly atomic cargo from every ocean. The command center at the Pentagon is trying to figure out where the hell I am." He glanced at his watch. "There, they should be ready. Now, key in the code for Operation RedDead, which authorizes our field commanders to launch a massive strike. Twenty minutes later, there will be nothing left of the Communists except the missiles they launch in retaliation." Freeman's apparition with the two piercing red eyes was now directly behind the President, who enunciated the code slowly in an otherworldly voice.

The Honcho's staccato tapping on the encrypting device rang out in nightmarish contrast to the absolute silence that entombed the Forest. Something primal stirred in Freeman's soul, stoking a nearly extinguished ember of essential humanity. He heard Cassandra's voice inside his head, pleading ferociously with him to prevent Lucifer, Apollo, and the other dark forces of naked power and aggression from triumphing. He suddenly plowed through a wall of frozen zombies toward the madman tapping a farewell tune for humanity on the keyboard. "Stop him!" he screamed with torrid passion. When the Honcho had three keys left to tap, Freeman had three steps left to reach him. The drunken Senator was typing keys at the same rate that Freeman was putting one step in front of the other.

With two steps to go, Freeman tripped over his ball and chain. He sprawled forward in one final lunge. As he landed on the turf, his clutching fingers fell six inches short of the Honcho's ankles. These six inches might as well have been six miles. The Honcho nonchalantly stepped backward and poised his finger to hit the final key to launch Operation RedDead.

Impossibly, a man in a white toga flew like a missile over Freeman's prone body, dramatically interrupting the slow motion reverie of the dreamlike scene. This blurry human projectile impaled itself on the Honcho's stupendous abdomen before he could type the last letter of the code. The impact compressed the air out of his lungs and drove him backward several staggering steps. He tumbled over a rock and dropped the briefcase, which fell beeping on the ground. The code entry that he had nearly completed was canceled by a fail-safe program designed to detect such violent disturbances. The terrified secret service agent responsible for the briefcase quickly scooped it up.

The Honcho writhed on the ground, struggling to fill his lungs with oxygen while retching the curdled contents of his stomach. Thomas Jefferson, the irresistible human projectile that sent the Honcho's immovable mass reeling, slowly picked himself up and brushed the dirt off his toga. Everyone was stunned by his seemingly impossible feat. The Archbishop nervously did a sign of the cross. The glowing green apparition Freeman saw receded back into the infinite darkness, and Satan's rumbling laughter faded into oblivion.

A welcome hint of dawn beckoned on the distant horizon. Freeman lay on the grass of the Forest commons staring up at the stars as they softly showered their timeless light onto him. He pondered man's relatively brief interlude in eternity, and became vividly aware of his own mortality, of the brevity of his existence. The Honcho's drunken flirtation with Armageddon had nearly exterminated his one brief lightning flash of life, as well as the brief and unfinished lives of billions of other humans.

There is an inherent contradiction in our social existence, Freeman eventually postulated, as he absorbed the therapeutic light from a billion stars on the dewy grass. Those who desire to rule are tainted and dangerous, and therefore shouldn't rule. Those who don't desire to rule could safely rule, but won't. This apparent contradiction reinforced his general distrust of people in power. His unguarded guardians had nearly annihilated him. Who will guard these tainted and dangerous guardians?

As he wrestled with this conundrum, the metallic band on his ankle loosened, not enough to free it, but enough to whet his appetite for more. He rolled onto his side and waved a greeting to Thomas Jefferson, who was carefully studying the same stars. And somewhere beyond the hills of the Bavarian Forest, innocent people in quiet villages slept peacefully, secure in the illusion that their precious lives were safely in the hands of their guardians.

Chapter Five: "Et Tu, Brute?"

> "The fault, dear Brutus, is not in the stars, but in ourselves, that we are underlings."
> —Cassius (William Shakespeare)

The Head Honcho's inebriated attempt to blow up the planet was leaked to the media. This violation of the secrecy sworn by Bavarian Forest members shocked the Honcho and stunned the world. An anonymous culprit, using the pseudonym Bottomless Esophagus, revealed the sordid details of the Senator's drinking binge, his nonsensical conversation with the Mad Hatter, and his brutish attempt to unleash the nation's nuclear arsenal. Desperate action was required to salvage his campaign from the ensuing public relations firestorm.

"Where are my plumbers?" he angrily demanded of his staff, which was gathered for an emergency damage control session. The smell of crisis was pungent as Cuban cigar smoke. "Where're my plumbers?" he screamed again. No one responded. Jefferson looked quizzically at Freeman, who looked rapaciously at Buxomus, who looked dumbly at But

Sir!, who said feebly, "But Sir! No one knows what you're talking about."

"No wonder I'm up to my ass in alligators! There isn't a resourceful person in this room . . . other than me", the Honcho hastily added. He glared menacingly at Freeman. "As my public relations liaison, you should've already figured out how to get my neck out of this noose. Do you know why I need a plumber?"

"Did you take a shit?", Freeman asked mindlessly.

The Honcho gave up on him and turned to Jefferson. "Bottomless Esophagus could be the Insurrectionist himself. Do you know why I want a plumber?"

"No, but take heart. The fickle scribes will soon forget these revelations in favor of some other scandalous muckraking."

"Bullshit!" The Honcho picked up a tattered newspaper. "Listen to the last sentence written by Bottomless Esophagus. I quote, '. . . Ye shall know the truth, and the truth shall make you free.' Unquote." He slammed the paper on his desk, stirring up a faint cloud of cocaine powder. "Do you realize the significance of that phrase?"

"It's from the Bible," But Sir! said.

"You shithead! It's much more significant than that. That phrase is inscribed above the entrance to the goddamn CIA! The plot to get me has thickened, if the bloody CIA is in cahoots with the Insurrectionist. That's why I need plumbers, and that's why I invited Sammy Gioncarlo to this meeting. Sammy, tell them why I need plumbers", he instructed with an air of solemn anticipation.

Everyone turned to stare at the heavyset gentlemen sitting unobtrusively behind them, smoking a Cuban cigar. They had taken little note of him, since sanguine Italians often hung around the Honcho. "It's lik'a dis," began the Sicilian. "Plumbers is'a what did'a dirty tricks for Nixon. Plumbers is'a what broke into da Watergate Hotel. Plumbers is'a what bugged Daniel Ellsberg's phone. Plumbers is'a what's required in situations lika dese." He punctuated his commentary with a prodigious puff on his cigar.

"That's goddamned right!" said the Honcho. "I've appointed Sammy to head my Committee to Re-Elect the Presiding Senator, or CREEPS. He's going to recruit plumbers, mechanics, electricians, and perhaps even some masons from his rather large family. His CREEPS will make secret tapes, delete expletives from secret tapes, distribute hush money, and obstruct the investigation of my Bavarian Forest behavior by those fucking journalists who think they're prosecutor, judge, and jury."

"But Sir! Isn't that illegal?" But Sir! interjected.

"Of course it is! Journalists have no right to investigate me like this!"

"But Sir, I meant isn't it illegal to obstruct justice and do dirty tricks?"

"I'm a goddamned U. S. Senator! Can't I do those things?" the behemoth roared.

"I found it hard to believe myself, Sir"

"No matter. Sammy says I can cover up all my indiscretions with Unlimited Executive Privilege, which is a derivative of the Political Immunity Clause. It's an impenetrable shield of legal obfuscation like nolo contendere, habeas corpus, and ex post facto invented by lawyers and unemployed Latin scholars. So, while Sammy is doing the dirty work, I need some brilliant public relations strategies to negate my negative press. Freeman, that's your fucking job."

Freeman hated his fucking job during times like these. Justifying, rationalizing, and glorifying the Head Honcho's misdeeds was an odious task that required him to subvert his peace of mind to get a paycheck. Fortunately, he had recently surrendered his conscience to the Devil, which made this prostitution more palatable.

One day, while dreaming up ways to salvage the Head Honcho's campaign, Freeman noticed that a co-worker named Doolittle was doing absolutely nothing. He wasn't even doing a crossword puzzle, making personal phone calls, stealing office supplies, or masturbating in the lavatory. Freeman brought the situation to But Sir!'s attention. "Why is Doolittle doing absolutely nothing? Is he a homosexual militia lover of the religious right?"

"No", replied But Sir!. "I checked on it earlier today. It turns out he has a note from his doctor that says he's recovering from an illness. He's nearly well, so he's been authorized to return to work. But, to aid his full recovery, he's not allowed to do anything. He can't lift, he can't be stressed, he can't move, and he can't even think. We have to treat him as if he joined a union."

"For how long?" asked Freeman, who was concerned that Doolittle might never do another thing as a government employee, which wouldn't be unprecedented.

"His doctor's note specifically says that it's just for today."

This placated Freeman until the very next day, when he observed that Doolittle was again doing nothing. "Why isn't Doolittle working today?" he asked But Sir!.

"He has a note. I already explained this to you."

"But that was for yesterday, not today", protested Freeman.

"It wasn't for yesterday. It's for today. The note is clear."

"But, if he shouldn't work today, then he should've worked yesterday, since yesterday isn't today."

But Sir! shook his head solemnly. "Unfortunately, yesterday was indeed today, when it was yesterday."

Freeman tried a new approach. "Will Doolittle work tomorrow?"

"He should work tomorrow, unless tomorrow becomes today. Then he should be excused."

Freeman gave up and immersed himself again in his own work. A few hours of brainstorming yielded two public relations strategies to repair the Senator's tarnished image. Amazingly, neither strategy required the Honcho to resign.

The first strategy was to hire a celebrity spokesperson to extol the Honcho's virtuous character according to a script written by high-powered copywriters with no consciences. The mindless horde would then associate the celebrity's worshipful qualities with the Honcho, as though he had absorbed the celebrity's charisma by telemagical osmosis.

The Honcho wanted the Safari Golfer to be his celebrity spokesperson, because he was clearly the most charismatic and wildly popular person alive. His fame skyrocketed after his victory in the Fed Classic golf tournament. He traveled the world, wowing adoring crowds with a unique blend of cosmic philosophy and arcane mysticism. He healed the sick, gave sight to the blind, raised the dead, and made the Cubs World Series champions. Of course, these miracles were playful illusions that contradicted common sense. Everyone knows it's really impossible to make the Cubs champions. But, the public lusted for miracles, so he facilitated their delusions.

Everywhere the Golfer spoke, uproarious audiences applauded continuously, leaving him only a few chance moments to utter "thank you's". If he tried to say anything more substantive than "thank you", the crowds cheered louder. He learned the precise moment to open his mouth and yet be unable to make a sound, due to the redoubled remonstrations of his audience. Using this technique, he could speak for hours without uttering a single word, which guaranteed acceptance of whatever views he would have professed if he had been allowed to articulate them. The Golfer thus became the preeminent cultural and spiritual leader. He was stupendously famous simply because he had previously been remarkably famous. He was now a mythic figurehead everyone worshipped, yet really knew little about, much like Jesus Christ.

This fanaticism surrounding the Golfer fit perfectly into the Honcho's plans. He had an epiphany during the dark moments after his stunning loss at the Fed Classic tournament. A politician seeking power could use the support of a stupendously famous cult figure, because politicians need millions of followers to accomplish their goals. Also, the Honcho didn't want his power grab to be judged rationally, so he needed someone to convince the masses to empower him on the basis of some elusive zephyr like the "common good" or "a higher authority". He needed a man who could fabricate a mystical reality steeped in illusion, steeped in the unknowable, and steeped in the undefinable. He needed the Safari Golfer.

Coincidentally, the Golfer needed the Honcho. His meaningless words of wisdom that nobody could interpret had evolved into a pseudo-religion that captivated millions of worshippers. Unfortunately, he was the leader of a flock going nowhere. These millions of bleating sheep were useless to him. They were spiritual captives, following him merely for the sake of following. He could herd them off the edge of a cliff, if he so desired. But if he was going to lead them over a cliff, it should be a meaningful cliff. A cliff with purpose and direction. A cliff with a campaign platform. Heaven requires no political activism, but on earth there are plenty of opportunities.

The most unadulterated politician on earth was the Head Honcho, whose lust for power was unrivaled. The Golfer wanted to attach his millions of worshippers to that lustful purpose. He and the Honcho fit hand in glove. Power and mysticism are inextricably linked, much like the chicken and egg, although the Golfer and the Honcho as yet only vaguely understood this. The Golfer's millions of followers would enable the power that the Honcho fervently sought.

Then, the Honcho's power would ensure that the Golfer's mystical influence would never wane. The Egyptian "god-king" pharaohs exemplified this kind of symbiotic relationship.

Once the Golfer was contracted as the Senator's celebrity spokesperson, a defining "ism" was needed as a name for the Golfer's mystical, unknowable, and therefore religious movement that the Honcho was adopting. For this critical task, Freeman sought the assistance of the Federal Ismological Czar to wade through the existing isms to find one that fit the Golfer's secular religion. This would be much easier than developing a completely new ism, because it takes the Food, Drug, and Ism Administration ten years to approve one.

So, Freeman and the Ismological Czar sorted through the existing isms. Communism, Marxism, and Socialism belonged to the enemy, so they were rejected. Capitalism wouldn't do, since the Honcho was it's bureaucratic anti-Christ. Anarchism would only make the Honcho nervous. Monarchism would evoke pathetic images of sappy British royalty. Existentialism had no future. Even the more esoteric isms were found wanting. Speciesism, scientism, sexism, androcentrism, chauvinism, phallicism, elitism, fascism, colonialism, Zionism, militarism, totalitarianism, cynicism, stoicism, Catholicism, monogamism, ageism, rightism, and even rapism didn't seem to fit.

They evaluated the entire six-volume catalog of the world's existing isms, yet didn't find an appropriate one. Thus, they had to invent a new ism, which would be subject to FDIA review to ensure it was safe for public consumption. This would involve many years of laboratory analysis and carefully controlled exposure of the experimental ism to test mammals.

Since there was no time for such a lengthy approval process, the Ismological Czar mentioned a loophole in the FDIA's rules. Generic substitutes for already approved commercial drugs require no testing by the FDIA, so why not develop a generic ism? Freeman seized this opportunity and invented "Ismism", which was the most generic ism he could think of. The Ismological Czar formally registered Ismism with the FDIA.

Initially, the Honcho disapproved of Ismism, because it was generic and therefore described nothing specific and could mean anything to anybody. Freeman argued that it was a philosophy that simply left its options open. If the masses rallied behind Ismism, it didn't matter what it stood for, or that it actually stood for nothing at all. After all, most adherents of other isms have long since forgotten the substantive tenets that originally inspired their worship. They worship their particular ism because it's their particular ism. Most likely, it was handed down from parent to child, and is simply a conditioned family tradition.

Freeman also argued that Ismism doesn't require any laborious memorization of dogma or commandments. It simply requires devotion to whatever the leader of Ismism declares important. Being completely unstructured, Ismism also avoids a clash between its tenets and the facts, since it has no tenets, which matched the Golfer's philosophy exactly. More precisely, it matched the philosophy that he had never really professed, since audiences kept cheering whenever he tried to speak.

Eventually, the Honcho embraced Ismism with great enthusiasm. The Golfer embraced Ismism too, because it gave structure and purpose to his movement, even though that structure and purpose was completely undefined. So, with great fanfare, the Safari Golfer launched a whirlwind evangelical tour to describe to his enthralled followers the wondrous beauty of Ismism and what it would do for them when they re-elected the Head Honcho, even though there was nothing to describe. Phase One of the Honcho's political resurrection was successfully under way.

Phase Two of the Honcho's resurrection was a diversionary tactic. One of the favorite ruses of demagogues in domestic trouble is to divert attention to the international scene. Normally, this comes in the form of a war. However, Freeman knew that a war initiated by the Head Honcho after his intemperate attempt to blow up the planet would be very unpopular. He therefore advised the Honcho to overplay his ringing campaign cry, "Ask not what your country can do for you, but what can you do for Vhaicam". Initiating the Vhaicam relief effort before the election would impress the voters with his humanitarianism and the altruistic beauty of Ismism, even though altruism wasn't specifically one of its tenets. But, while the voters were busy making their own inferences about Ismism, they would be distracted from the media hullabaloo regarding his Bavarian Forest escapades.

Politics aside, Vhaicam desperately needed help. The recently formed nation in Southeast Asia had no meaningful social or political infrastructure, and its 500 citizens experienced an unending cycle of calamities, including civil unrest, torrential monsoons, earthquakes, diphtheria, malaria, AIDS, and homosexuality. Creative suffering was their only natural talent. To make matters worse, the Vhaicamese had two peculiar physical features. Their noticeably extended ears and pinkish noses led foreign xenophobes to call them the "Rabbit People". Fortunately, Ismism wasn't xenophobic. Unless, of course, it had to be.

The Honcho coerced Congress to create an agency called Food for Undernourished Nations. F.U.N.'s mission was to provide the 500 Vhaicamese with the essentials of Western lifestyle, including food, medicine, shelter, clothing, education, VCR's, cable TV, and sofas. Congress funded F.U.N. with $1 million for actual relief to Vhaicam and $999 million for administrative overhead.

The Honcho produced TV ads to get the F.U.N. message out to the voters. These ads featured the Safari Golfer extolling Ismism and narrating vivid video images of the horrible conditions that existed in Vhaicam prior to F.U.N. These stomach churning clips of starving children with distended bellies, maggot infested sores, and gold rings in their left earlobes were an emotionally compelling backdrop for the altruistic beauty of F.U.N. The Honcho's approval rating rose and the media interest in his Bavarian Forest malfeasance waned.

The F.U.N. initiative succeeded brilliantly in feeding the starving Vhaicamese, quelling their civil unrest, abating the monsoons, stopping the floods, quieting the earthquakes, curing diphtheria, malaria, and AIDS, and eradicating homosexuality. Consequently, the Rabbit People doubled in population. With 500 more Vhaicamese mouths to feed, another $1 billion had to be appropriated for the relief effort, most of which went to cover the quadrupled administrative costs.

The increased cost of F.U.N. made the Honcho uneasy. He didn't want to raise taxes during an election year. Therefore, he rammed a bill through Congress lifting the ceiling on the national debt to an extraordinary number with more digits than could be counted on a normal human's fingers and toes. To keep track of this exploding debt, the Office of Management and Budget hired fifty more employees with degrees in Transcendental Accounting.

The Honcho was also uneasy about the unanticipated population explosion in Vhaicam. He dragged Freeman into his office to explain why it was happening. "How did those rabbit-eared bastards double in population overnight?" he demanded.

"Missionary style, sir."

The Honcho unconsciously snapped a pencil in half. "How did they learn to fornicate missionary style?"

"They learned from missionaries", Freeman answered calmly.

The Honcho snapped another pencil nervously. "Missionaries? That's not good, is it?"

"It's worse than you think. These were Catholic missionaries who wanted to get in on the F.U.N. They're arriving in droves to convert the Vhaicamese to Catholicism."

"My God!. . . Catholic missionaries. . . . That means no birth control!" The Honcho unconsciously snapped his umbrella in two.

"It also means the Vhaicamese need lots of offspring to propagate the Faith and fund the Vatican."

"Shit!" exclaimed the Honcho. "Maybe we shouldn't have been so quick to eradicate homosexuality from Vhaicam." He fretted over this thought for a moment, and then asked, "Does Ismism have any qualms about homosexuality?"

"Absolutely not", replied Freeman. "Unless qualms about homosexuality become expedient."

"I see. Now, get the hell outa here before I fire you for perverting the F.U.N. we were all having."

The door slammed behind Freeman's hasty retreat. Depression overcame the Honcho in his solitude. Ever since Bottomless Esophagus revealed his Bavarian Forest escapades, he was increasingly disillusioned with running for elective office. It used to be so simple. If you were an incumbent, you got re-elected, no matter what happened during your previous term. But after Nixon's Watergate mess, the voters became surly and self-righteous, and the media became skeptical and penetrating. Needing approval from voters was alien to him.

He tearfully reminisced about days gone by, when incumbents could count on the sheer weight of their office, party loyalty, and behind-the-scenes political chicanery to ensure election outcomes. He missed that old sense of power and self-determination that nowadays he only experienced as the honorary Emperor of the Bavarian Forest. Emperors don't have to worry about elections. They hold their office for life, no matter how sorry their performance is. He desperately desired that same omnipotence. Being dependent on voters to retain power was an intolerable crock of shit. It wasn't right for a man of his stature to grovel in front of ordinary peasants to get their blessing to tax, regulate, draft, and otherwise oppress them. It was unnatural. It therefore had to change.

His recent stint as Bavarian Forest Emperor planted a mental seed that sprouted into the beanstalk of a grandiose idea. He summoned Buxomus, Freeman, Jefferson, and But Sir! into his office and announced, "I'm going to become Emperor."

"But Sir!" exclaimed But Sir!. "You can't make yourself Emperor!"

"Why not?" asked the Honcho with genuine incredulity.

"I . . . I'm not sure", stammered But Sir!. "There must be some sort of approval you need to become Emperor."

"Hmmmm", mused the Honcho. "Freeman, does Ismism say I can't be Emperor?"

"Absolutely not."

"There. It's settled. I'm going to become Emperor, unless someone here thinks that would be a mistake." He scowled menacingly and slowly scanned the room, searching for expression of contrary opinions. His eyes arrested on Freeman, who was trying to blend into the office decor. "What say ye, my alleged public relations liaison?"

"Can I have my own Nubian slave women if you become Emperor?"

"You can have my leftovers."

"Then I say go for it", said Freeman, drooling at the prospect of a harem.

The Honcho turned to Jefferson. "What's your opinion, Insurrection Czar?"

"There is little difference between being an Emperor of yore and a politician of today", replied Jefferson. "You are not in need of greater power, which you already possess to an unconscionable degree. Rather, you need a populace that is more willing to submit itself to you completely and unquestionably. Americans have tasted the sweetness of liberty, and although they have forgotten much of what is required for liberty to flourish, they will never fully submit themselves to absolute tyranny again. If it was possible, it would be better for you to step backward in time, to an era when despotism was not only tolerated by citizens, it was expected. You would be happier as Emperor of Rome, for example, than as Emperor of America."

The Honcho stared quietly at Jefferson, trying to determine whether he was hearing the words of a genius or a scoundrel setting him up for acute embarrassment. While he pondered this, a strange recollection flashed into Freeman's brain. When he heard Jefferson's suggestion to go backward in time, the haunting words of Cassandra reverberated in his head . . . "Although my murdered corpse is buried near the Corinthian Gulf, something uniquely 'me' lives on, does it not? History is always and everywhere, along with the men and women who lived it passionately. History surrounds us and compels us. It is lived and relived, in an unending cycle. The past becomes present, which then becomes future . . . "

The Honcho broke the silence. "Jefferson, I'll take your suggestion and make myself Julius Caesar, Emperor of Rome!"

"But Sir!" interjected But Sir!. "How can you become an emperor who lived 2000 years ago! Time travel is impossible!"

The Honcho grinned like the Cheshire Cat. "You skeptics! Have you forgotten that I'm an U.S. Senator? Have you forgotten that I'm the most powerful man in America? Have you forgotten that I conquered the debilitating zero and comma shortage?"

As he launched these rhetorical questions, he rummaged in a drawer until he slowly and dramatically extricated a black leather-bound book. He blew a musty layer of dust from the tome and placed it gently on his desk. The four skeptics instinctively leaned forward for a better view of the mysterious book.

"Is that a book of black magic?" Freeman asked, half in jest and half in fear.

In a secretive voice, the Honcho revealed, "This is the 'Book of Liberal Policies, Marxist Economics, and other Occult Phenomena'."

His audience gasped. But Sir! did a sign of the cross. "What does it say about time travel?" asked Freeman breathlessly.

The Honcho frowned. "I don't know. It's been years since I've dared to open this book. Its tremendously powerful spells have proven to be unpredictable and often catastrophic. I'll check the table of contents. . . . let's see . . . Great Society . . . Welfare State . . . Progressive Taxation . . . Labor Theory of Value . . . Dialectic Materialism . . . ah, here it is . . . Time Travel!"

"Now what?" asked Freeman.

"I turn to page 317 and do as it says." The Honcho read the instructions aloud to his enraptured audience. "Compared to Marxism, Time Travel is relatively safe and understandable, and not nearly as improbable as creating wealth simply by redistributing it. All that's required to journey through time is a suspension of reason and a quotation from a dreamy fairy tale." He looked up at his staff. "Seems pretty simple. I suspend reason every day as a Congressman. And the book even provides a quote from a fairy tale, although it sounds like a concoction by the Mad Hatter." This caused him a momentary flash of doubt, but he quickly regained his courage. "What the hell! I'm going for it! See you all earlier."

He stood on his desk cradling the "Book of Liberal Policies, Marxist Economics, and other Occult Phenomena". He took a deep breath and then recited the fairy tale:

"Imperious Prima flashes forth
Her edict 'to begin it'
In gentler tone Secunda hopes
'There will be nonsense in it!'

"The dream-child moving through a land
Of wonders wild and new,
Lay it where Childhood's dreams are twined
In Memory's mystic band,
And half believe it is true.

"And ever, as the story drained
The wells of fancy dry,
And faintly strove that weary one
To put the subject by,
'The rest next time—it is next time . . ."

    The Honcho was drawn irresistibly into a churning vortex of millions of tiny lights that formed a brilliant funnel coiling mysteriously backward in time. He was sucked into the past like a speck of dust by a huge cosmic vacuum as the swirling lights blurred into streaks. He curiously noted that he felt no different, even though he was traversing deep into the past, decade by decade, century by century. He flirted with the realization that humans are the same, no matter what era or circumstance they're in.

    He was blinded by a ferocious blast of kaleidoscopic light a hundred fold more brilliant than the churning vortex. Then he was assaulted by an explosion that made thunder sound like a whisper. He stopped moving abruptly. He rubbed his stricken eyes vigorously to remove the fireflies flitting across his seared retinas while his other senses assessed his new world. A disgusting odor permeated the air. He smelled animals, feces, and filthy humans. He felt oppressive heat driven by a tropical breeze. Gritty dust filled his lungs. The thunder crashing in his ears subsided into a rolling rumble, like waves of hurrahs reverberating in a stadium full of spectators. Emotionally charged voices close by seemed to be addressing him. With trepidation, he opened his wounded eyes.

An astonishing vista greeted him. He was standing on a balcony jutting out from a massive coliseum with tiered expanses of stone, concrete, and marble. A crowd of 50,000 people generated the thundering sound that reverberated painfully in his stricken ears. A fishy-smelling tropical breeze swept out of a blue sky and wafted over the colonnaded peristyle of the stadium. Below him marched a motley assortment of misshapen dwarfs, loinclothed Negroes, and bearded Jewish men who looked starved and beaten. Suddenly, this procession of discarded humanity stopped and cried out in unison, "Hail Emperor! Those who are about to die salute you!" Musicians launched into a vigorous fanfare. The Honcho became acutely aware that all eyes were upon him.

Completely disoriented, he searched uncertainly for guidance. The first person he saw gave him a sudden surge of relief. He immediately recognized the wire-rimmed spectacles, the disheveled blond hair, and the tubercular face of the unpretentious little man beside him. "But Sir!", exclaimed the Honcho. "What in hell is going on here? And why are you wearing that ridiculous white sheet?"

The thin man's hollow face contorted with confusion. He glanced down at the woolen toga draped on him like a ridiculous sheet. "Has too much wine brought the wrath of Bacchus down upon you? Why did you call me But Sir!, my illustrious Consul?"

"Because that's who you are. Quit fooling around."

"I swear on the honor of the Vestal Virgins that I am not But Sir!," protested the anemic man, who was indeed a dead ringer for the Honcho's aide.

"Then who the fuck are you?"

"I am Justinius, your chief administrator. Are you okay, my glorious Consul?"

The Honcho rubbed his temples. It dawned on him that things weren't quite as they used to be, and would probably never be again. He thought up a ruse to explain his disorientation. "Forgive me, Justinius. I bumped my head in a chariot accident this morning and lost some memory. Help me out."

"Okay", replied Justinius. "The first thing you should know is that you owe me a hundred denarii for our bet on the chariot races at the Circus Maximus last night. How else can I help you?"

"Explain what's going on here."

"I'm not sure where to begin. You're Julius Caesar. This is the Coliseum. On the field are gladiators and in the stands are spectators. They're all waiting for your signal to start the contests."

"What contests?"

"The gladiator fights!" exclaimed Justinius. "How fast was your chariot going when you fell off?"

"Never mind," snarled the Honcho. "What happens at a gladiator fight?"

"Gladiators hack each other mercilessly with gruesome weapons. Severed appendages fall to the ground. Many men die. The crowd goes wild. Then animals fight. Lions versus bulls. Hippos versus panthers. Tigers versus rhinos. At the end, deranged followers of a Judean fool named Christus are fed to starving lions. It's great fun. They actually believe Christus rose from the dead!"

The Honcho was intrigued by the submissiveness of the gladiators standing at attention below his balcony. Every time he tried to send young men off to die in foreign skirmishes to entertain his electoral whims, all he ever got in return was protests, draft evasion, and moral outrage. These Roman gladiators, on the other hand, were willing to accept their unhappy fate without protest. They even saluted him, while acknowledging they are about to die. "Tell me", he said to Justinius, "Why are they so willing to forfeit their lives to entertain this stadium of more privileged people?"

"They know it's how things are ordained. It's in the stars. Gladiators die. Spectators cheer. Emperors drink ambrosia and smile contentedly during the carnage. If the great god Jupiter wanted them to be safely on this balcony, and you in the mouth of a voracious lion, surely he would have done so."

"And they never protest?"

"They did once, but you took care of it rather adroitly. Don't you remember?"

"Hmmm. Refresh my ailing memory, Justinius."

"Spartacus, the famous gladiator from Thessaly, led an uprising of 70,000 enraged slaves against the Empire. They held out for three years in the crater of Mount Vesuvius, and terrorized Rome with periodic raids. Your Praetorian Guard finally captured them and hung the six thousand remaining outlaws on wooden crosses along the Appian Way, from Capua to Brundisium, as a gruesome warning to anyone else considering rebelling against their ordained servitude to us."

The Honcho memorized this tidbit. Such a clever tactic could be useful in two thousand years, especially if he ever had to send in the National Guard to shoot renegade students on an Ohio college campus, or send in the BATF to incinerate a religious cult in Waco, or send in the FBI to murder the family of a tax protester in Ruby Ridge. But, he was still perplexed by the lull that had descended upon the Coliseum. Everyone was staring at him. "How do I start the festivities?" he asked Justinius.

"Just do this." Justinius held his arms outstretched toward the crowd, with thumbs upraised from clenched fists.

The Honcho clumsily extended his arms, clenched his fists, and stuck his thumbs out. Unfortunately, he mistakenly pointed them downward.

"What are you doing?!" cried Justinius, as he yanked the Honcho's arms down. He then frantically waved and shouted at the centurions, who had drawn their swords to slay the gladiators. He eventually got their attention and signaled to them that they had received a false command from the Emperor. Fortunately, only three gladiators were slain in error. "My good consul", he said in a shaking voice, "When you give the 'thumbs down' sign, gladiators die. The 'thumbs up' sign is for beginning these contests, and for acknowledging brave performances. Please try again."

The Honcho's upraised thumbs evoked a thunderous response from the 50,000 spectators. As the bloodletting commenced, he sat on a marble throne and absorbed his surroundings. He too was wearing a toga, which was pristine white bordered by a purple band, signifying his rank as Consul. A gray woolen tunic was under his toga, and leather sandals were strapped to his feet. Drinks were arrayed in pewter cups on a marble pedestal at his side. Another pedestal held a cornucopia of hors d'oeuvres, desserts, and entrees prepared by the royal epicure, Apicius. There were lobster, truffles, sow's udders stuffed with salted sea urchins, patina of brains, boiled tree fungi with peppered fish fat, Jericho dates, boiled ostrich, roasted parrot, dormice stuffed with pine kernels, and fricassee of roses.

A large retinue of people surrounded him. Slaves hustled hither and thither delivering wine and food. Beautiful Nubian women in long white belted stolas perpetually waved palm fronds at him. Several people carried themselves officiously. To his left was a tall man with a laconic smile who looked disturbingly like Freeman. Curious, he asked Justinius, "Who is that man?"

"That's Marcus Brutus, a city praetor. He publicly extols your virtues, although I often suspect he is condemning you with faint praise. You shouldn't trust him, my illustrious Consul. He's a renegade and prankster who knows no humility or respect."

The Honcho squirmed uncomfortably on his marble throne. The ominous similarities between Freeman and Marcus Brutus, who winked mischievously in his direction, bothered him. Not even two thousand years could erase Freeman's discomforting vibes. He looked away from Brutus, whereupon his eyes fell hungrily upon a vision of feminine loveliness. She was seated on a throne and wore a diamond studded golden tiara on a glorious mane of black hair. Her lustrous skin was a sensuous brown and her eyes were wide, dark, and mysterious. She wore a white stola with a luxurious purple saffron cloak draped over her slender shoulders. Her magnificent breasts rivaled the fabulous pair that Buxomus regularly nurtured him with. When the stately lady arose and slowly strolled across the balcony, the Honcho bit his hand to ease his unrequited lust. Her voluptuous ass moved back and forth in a scintillating rhythm duplicated by only one other woman in the universe. If not for her black hair and brown skin, the Honcho would have bet an emperor's ransom that she was Buxomus. "Who is that sexy, mysterious woman? I envy the sonofabitch who lays her every night."

Justinius laughed impolitely and nudged him knowingly. "That makes you a sonofabitch, my glorious Consul. She's your mistress, Cleopatra."

The Honcho's jaw dropped in disbelief at his good fortune. "My mistress?"

Just then, the captain of the Praetorian Guard charged up and begged for attention. "What is it?" the Honcho mumbled through his teeth, which were still embedded in his skin to ameliorate his insatiable lust.

"It's the Christians, your Highness."

"What Christians?" snarled the Honcho.

"That's exactly the point, your Highness. We've run out of them, and it's not even halftime."

The Honcho glanced up at the scoreboard, where freshly hung Roman Numerals showed the score as Lions IV, Christians 0, with three minutes left on the sundial before halftime. "How could you run out of Christians in such a low scoring massacre?" he asked.

"It is indeed inexcusable, your Highness. Many centurions will be put to death because of this miserable transgression. However, it's getting difficult to hunt down those clever Christians in the catacombs."

The Honcho was puzzled. "What should I do?" he asked Justinius.

Justinius whispered, "Forget the Christians. Tell him to round up some Gnostics and Essenes during halftime. The spectators won't know the difference, as long as they see religious fanatics of some sort devoured by lions."

"Forget the Christians," the Honcho advised the captain. "Take your best men and round up some Gnostics and Essenes during halftime. Be quick about it!"

"Yes, my eternal Emperor!" The captain saluted sprightly and evaporated from the balcony. The Honcho nervously asked Justinius, "Are you sure nobody will notice the difference between Christians and other religious fanatics?"

"As long as bones snap and blood flows, nobody will give a damn whose god failed to save the victims. Besides, since we drape the victims in animal skins to entice the lions to gobble them up, the spectators can't even see the zealots inside."

The first-half sundial expired. Halftime entertainment was a potpourri of odd spectacles. Trained elephants wrote Latin phrases in the sand with their agile trunks. Panthers harnessed to chariots raced around the stadium. Bears wrestled with buffaloes, and bulls collided mightily with rhinoceroses. The most intriguing spectacle was a band of dwarfs armed with daggers battling female Nubian archers. The women struggled to hit the diminutive dwarfs with arrows, and the dwarfs struggled to stab the taller women with their short arms. The battle was decided when the dwarfs cleverly hacked at the legs of the Nubian women until they were short enough to be stabbed in the heart. The Honcho, watching with bloodthirsty glee, gave a thumbs up verdict and bellowed excitedly, "This is barbaric!"

"No, this is civilized", corrected Justinius. "The Barbarians live outside the empire, which is something I should brief you on. Alaric the Visigoth, Attila the Hun, and Theodoric the Ostrogoth have deployed their barbarian armies along the Rhine and the Danube, which is currently our northern frontier. We are threatened by hordes of ragged Neanderthals who wouldn't appreciate the sophisticated culture we're experiencing here today."

"Sounds serious," said the Honcho, as a gladiator lopped off a foe's head. "But can the briefing wait? I want to see if the Gnostics and Essenes stage a comeback against the Lions."

"Sure. But you should take the Lions and give the points."

"Perhaps," said the Honcho. "The Lions seem overconfident. By the way, why do we feed Christians to the lions?"

"Because the lions are hungry."

"But why feed them Christians? Shouldn't we feed them something healthy?"

"We do it because Vergil told us to."

The Honcho felt like he was solving a riddle one clue at a time. "I'll bite. Who is Vergil?"

"Vergil is the most famous and popular Roman . . . besides you, of course. His poems bring tears to the eyes of heroes, courage to the hearts of cowards, laughter to the lips of the despondent, and nobility to the souls of infidels. His poetic acumen is revered throughout the empire, from Carthage in the south to Londinium in the north, from Olisipo in the west to Babylon in the east. He has grown in cultural lore to mythic legend and quasi-religious hero. You recognized that his fame could be harnessed to cement your grip on imperial power. You saw in Vergil an opportunity to transform popular mythology into another chain binding unthinking people to their leaders. You understood that the key to political power is being the one who interprets the unknowable and the unprovable for the masses.

"That's why Emperors and Kings usurp religion. He who controls the mythology rules the world. He who is accepted as the interpreter of reality becomes the master of everyone else. This has been true ever since Hammurabi claimed the god Shamash handed his famous Code to him. That's why you coerced Vergil to use his magnificent skills to write an epic poem venerating and deifying the secular heroes of Rome. It took him ten years to finish the 'Aeneid', and when he was done, he had such unsettling qualms about it that he wanted the manuscript burned. But, you ordered the 'Aeneid' published, and your deification began."

The Honcho was impressed with Caesar's grasp of the symbiotic relationship between mysticism and power. However, his original question remained unanswered. "You haven't yet explained why Vergil told us to feed Christians to the lions."

"Be patient, my Emperor. As I was saying, the mythology of Vergil and others transformed the Imperium into an extension of the will of the gods. Legend says that Romulus, the mythic founder of Rome, stood by the Tiber River as he christened the city and boldly shouted to all of Italy, 'It is heaven's will that my Rome shall be the Capital of the world.' Ovid retold the tales of classical mythology in Roman vernacular, beginning with creation and ending with your very own metamorphosis into a god alongside Jupiter and Juno. You cemented this claim to divinity by taking the title of Pontifex Maximus, the Chief Priest of the Romans."

A huge roar rocked the coliseum. The Honcho and Justinius turned toward the playing field to watch a voracious lion shred an unfortunate Essene clad in deerskin. Despite the terrified man's pleas for his god to save him, the lion methodically bit off his appendages and then disemboweled him completely, leaving only a few large bones on the sandy ground as evidence that he ever existed. The victim's god was apparently distracted today. A new roman numeral was hung next to "Lions" on the scoreboard.

When the hubbub subsided, Justinius continued. "The religion you preside over is a flexible amalgamation of faiths absorbed from the indigenous Italians and other nations that the Roman Empire swallowed. This spiritually generic religion has no specific dogma or set of principles. It can be anything you need it to be, as long as Romans continue to recognize you as their chief priest. Thus, you are the Pontifex Maximus of many gods and isms, including Jupiter, Venus, Mars, Mercury, Diana, Minerva, Apollo, the ancient Etruscan gods, the indigenous animist spirits, Mithraism, Stoicism, and Epicurianism. These are now an interlocked latticework of popular myths that have become Rome's universal religion, which has been distilled into a worship of Rome and of you as its Emperor."

"What does any of this have to do with feeding Christians to lions?"

"Be patient with your unworthy aide", entreated Justinius. "Rome absorbed many religions, and those religions equally absorbed Rome. Christianity, however, stands alone as the one religion that refused to absorb Rome. Christians chose rebellion, insisting that they alone possess the eternal truths. Christus even declared, "I am the Way, the Truth, and the Life." Such a declaration of independence from the Empire is treason, and must be dealt with accordingly. The first step was to crucify Christus for insurrection, which he committed by attacking our merchants in the temple.

"If religion gets separated from politics, it would cast away the moorings of your power, because he who controls the mythology rules the world. Christus knew this when he explained to the Pharisees how a Christian should deal with Roman taxation. He pointed to your likeness on the back of a Roman coin and said, 'Render unto Caesar what is Caesar's, and unto God what is God's.' The impudent upstart was contesting the lesson history has taught thus far, that God and Caesar are one and the same, and that the role of religion is to validate your power, not to repudiate it. Christians declared all other religions to be false, implicitly calling your title of Pontifex Maximus null and void. As this philosophical disease spread like an unstoppable plague throughout the Empire, it became imperative for us to attack."

The danger of the situation dawned on the Honcho. He had two thousand years of historical perspective to assess Justinius' explanation. He squirmed uneasily on his throne. Such heresy was indeed a threat to his livelihood, he realized with foreboding certainty, so it had to be dealt with firmly. He preempted the punch line of Justinius' rambling dissertation. "So that's why Vergil told us to feed Christians to the lions."

Justinius smiled. "Precisely! There's nothing particularly odious about the Christian dogma; they simply have an attitude problem. So now we persecute them. We blame them for every disaster. We burn their homes and churches. We incinerate their women and children in furnaces. We torture them to abdicate their beliefs and declare their allegiance to you and Rome. Of course, the true believers refuse and thus become martyrs, because worshipping Caesar would be worshipping a god other than their own, which is exactly the issue. So, we feed them to the lions, because the lions can stomach them, whereas you cannot. They are rebels and anarchists. They are insurrectionists. They must be exterminated. . . . "

The Honcho suddenly remembered the Insurrectionist that tormented him in modern America. He fought back tears of frustration. He couldn't even escape the looming shadow of insurrection across a gulf of two thousand years. Was there nowhere that he could find safe haven? Life wasn't fair, he concluded, as a lion ripped the flesh off a hapless Gnostic victim on the coliseum floor.

Despite his concern, the Honcho's biggest threat wouldn't be the rebellious creed of Christus. Christianity would eventually be conscripted into the profane service of worldly kings when history scrolled into the Middle Ages. Although Christianity was the harbinger of separation of church from state, a broader movement to separate mysticism from politics would ultimately be the greatest threat to the Head Honcho's spiritual archetype.

The Honcho awoke the next morning to the sound of squawking sea gulls and a growing certainty that he wasn't dreaming he had been transmogrified into Julius Caesar by the "Book of Liberal Policies, Marxist Economics, and Other Occult Phenomena". After a sumptuous breakfast served by Judean slaves, he asked Justinius what was on the day's agenda, besides sporting events featuring prolific dismemberment of various mammals.

Justinius perused a parchment scroll. "Recreation, mostly. You'll have to participate in a few pompous ceremonies, but we'll intertwine those yawners into your daily routine of hedonistic pleasure seeking. We start today at the bathhouse, Noble One."

The bathhouse was like a modern day shopping mall, with multi-storied shops, eateries, libraries, gymnasiums, and public gathering places, in addition to bathing facilities. The marble and stone structure covered 33 acres. Aqueducts from distant mountains funneled thousands of gallons of cold, pure water into the building. Aristocrats congregated there for social, business, and political interaction. Bathers splashed, singers crooned, confectioners hawked their wares, gossipers spread rumors, businessmen negotiated deals, and schemers plotted secret things.

A trumpeted fanfare announced Caesar's entrance into the huge bathhouse. The naked bathers immediately prostrated themselves on the concrete floor. The trumpeter bellowed mightily, "Enter Julius Caesar, Pontifex Maximus, Father of his Country, most powerful man in the universe, crowned by god, dictator for life, great and peaceful Emperor of Rome!"

The Honcho slid like a whale into a cold bath. "Now what?" he asked Justinius, who slid in alongside him.

"You either dispense patronage to unscrupulous agents and traders, or sentence insurrectionists to death. What are you in the mood for?"

"Tough choice", mused the Honcho. "Tell me more about dispensing patronage."

"In Rome, all things are for sale, and you have more to sell than anyone else. In exchange for bribes, you award business to traders, merchants, and other jackals bidding on imperial projects. You give cohorts lucrative positions in the bureaucracy, in exchange for their unwavering loyalty and handfuls of denarii in a tradition as old as government itself. One of your predecessors ascended to the throne simply by being the highest bidder for the vacant seat, which was auctioned off by the Praetorian Guard after the untimely death of the previous occupant. The furious bidding cost him thousands of sesterces to become the most powerful man in creation, but it was a worthwhile investment because of the Golden Guideline of Graft."

"What's that?"

"I'll explain", said Justinius. "It costs a fortune to capture a lucrative government office. The Golden Guideline of Graft determines how long it will take to recoup the investment. It takes one year of graft in office to recover the cost of the bribes used to get the appointment. It takes another year of graft to amass enough money to fend off inquisitions into the first year of graft. And it takes a third year of graft to amass a retirement nest egg for when shit hits the palm frond."

"Our government in the States was also a gold mine of pocket lining opportunities", said the Honcho. "How big is the Roman bureaucracy?"

"It's exceeded only by the greed of the men who profit from it. But what did you mean by 'in the States'? The chariot fall has addled your brain, I fear."

"I meant 'provinces'", recovered the Honcho. "I was referring to my stint as Governor of Gaul."

"That stint was a good example of the bureaucratic blob that has descended upon the empire with a sickening 'plop!'", said Justinius. "Even though Gaul is a small province, your staff included three secretaries, a doctor, twenty slaves, a valet, two chambermaids, two footmen, a bevy of cooks, four gardeners, ten security guards, an unscrupulous keeper of accounts, a Nubian girl whose duties can't be mentioned in polite company, and a flock of tax collectors. You also controlled a multi-tiered hierarchy of petty magistrates whose only purpose was to sufficiently fragment the civil government so that insurrection couldn't reach critical mass. The natural result was an onslaught of paperwork, regulations, and taxation, which gave you even more opportunities to fill your pockets from the provincial treasury."

The Honcho noted to himself that Julius Caesar had raised bureaucratic malfeasance to an art form many centuries before he had as an U.S. Senator. He concluded that only the names and faces have changed over the millennia, and sometimes the 'isms' used to rationalize it all, which made the philosophy of Ismism even more useful, since a generic 'ism' eliminates any semantic confusion about why some men have power over others. "Life is good for me, then", he summarized aloud.

"Absolutely. The whole world is your sandbox, with one exception", said Justinius, pointing to a tall, stately gentleman who had just entered the bathhouse and was headed directly toward them. When the visitor emerged into the light showered through the clerestory windows above, the Honcho shivered involuntarily. He immediately recognized the man's aristocratic face, his unruly mane of orange-tinged hair, his bluish hazel eyes, and his cracker-barrel grin. "Hello, Julius. I see that no one has drowned you yet," said the striking man.

"Jefferson . . . what are you doing here?!" the Honcho exclaimed confusedly.

"I am here because you are here", replied the tall man. "For every Caesar in the universe, there must also be a Cicero, or else the imbalance will cause the heavens to convulse with tyranny and oppression. We are like matter and antimatter." Cicero slid out of his toga and joined the Honcho and Justinius in the chilly waters. "But why did you address me as 'Jefferson'? It's a peculiar jest."

The Honcho now knew the tall man was Cicero, but he was still shaken by his uncanny resemblance to his Insurrection Czar in the 20th Century. Unfortunately, he didn't have a plausible explanation for calling Cicero 'Jefferson' that anyone in 66 AD would comprehend. Fortunately, Justinius rescued him. "Julius had a chariot accident yesterday. He's having trouble with names because of the blow to his head. Yesterday, he called me 'But Sir!'."

"My condolences", said Cicero congenially. "I am civilized enough to temporarily set aside our public differences to sympathize with your injury."

"Thank you," muttered the Honcho, who was puzzled by Cicero's remark. "What public differences do we have?"

"You have indeed taken quite a blow to the head. We disagree on almost every aspect of your administration of this

Empire. I am one of the few who is not afraid to speak out against you. What are you doing right now?"

"I am preparing to dispense patronage to unscrupulous piranhas who pay cash for illicit access to the imperial bureaucracy."

"Therein is just one of our many disagreements," replied Cicero. "I believe that civil authorities should not be bent by influence or spoiled by money."

"No one will resist those temptations once they are given authority. Power inevitably corrupts."

"True enough. The answer is to eliminate these positions altogether. There is no natural reason for such power to be institutionalized among rational men. I am continuously amazed at how willing my fellow citizens are to take on the yoke of evil tyrants and conniving clergy. The pestilential statutes you put in place no more deserve to be called laws than the rules a band of robbers might enact."

Justinius whispered to Caesar that it was time to leave for a scheduled appearance at the Circus Maximus. However, the Honcho wasn't ready to end this extemporaneous debate. "If you eliminate these positions, who will care for the Empire's downtrodden citizens?"

Cicero laughed. "If you are so benevolent, why are you surrounded by a belt of barbarous henchmen listening to me sword in hand? Is it not more noble to perish a thousand times than to be unable to move among your subjects without a guard? Let's go to lunch on the way to the Circus and continue this debate. While we're traveling, note how poorly the one million citizens of Rome are cared for under your administration. Most of them endure conditions animals wouldn't tolerate. They are jammed into foul smelling apartments that the mice have abandoned, if they can find rooms at all. Inflation is driving living costs out of reach. Crime is rampant, and unemployment is spreading like a contagion. Your massive civil service and its volumes of regulations create the illusion that your administration is solving these ills, but the reality is that your administration is the cause. Your army of tax collectors, policemen, building inspectors, and public health officials are a sham. Like doctors who prescribe boiled lard for broken bones, goat's hair for sleeplessness, and owl's toes for fevers, they've prescribed deadly poisons instead of healing drugs. You've conciliated the ignorant crowd with public works and handouts, instilling in them the habit of slavery and dependence. You've created a bureaucratic disaster!"

The Honcho rubbed his prodigious abdomen. "The only sensible thing you said was let's get lunch. Join us so we can finish this silly debate, Jefferson."

"There's nothing I'd rather do, since your existence is my reason for being. But please call me Cicero. Being Rome's head honcho doesn't empower you to change my name."

Justinius found the lunch time debate between Caesar and Cicero to be exquisite fare. Cicero was a master communicator. His oratories in the Senate and in the Forum Romanum were legendary. Caesar also had deft command of the language, having written his "Commentaries" about the Empire's campaign to absorb Gaul. The two great antagonists exchanged verbal incendiaries about liberty and government as the world swirled around them in the Forum. The Forum was closed to chariot traffic, and was encircled by stucco government buildings, temples, and shops. In the middle was the Golden Milestone, from which all roads fanned out of the city, thereby making it the centerpiece of the Roman universe. Businessmen, senators, priests, centurions, fishmongers, butchers, cooks, dancers, and prostitutes plied their trades here.

Justinius, whose attention had been distracted by the bustle in the Forum, returned his focus to a dissertation by Cicero. " . . . and those whom Nature has endowed with the capacity for administering public affairs honestly and with integrity should direct the government; for in no other way can public offices be administered with greatness of spirit."

"If it's greatness of spirit that you seek, then watch this." The Honcho signaled to the captain of his Praetorian Guard, who relayed the signal to centurions standing on a wooden platform looming high above the Forum floor. The centurions drew their daggers and slashed the ropes that were suspending three haggard men in the air. The men plummeted through openings in the wooden platform and came to an abrupt, sickening halt just above the ground. They hung there dying in the hot sun, with nooses about their necks and their heads jutting from their twitching bodies at awkward angles. When they ceased convulsing, Caesar raised his hands above his head and applauded slowly and deliberately, triggering lackadaisical applause throughout the Forum. People who he deemed insurrectionists were publicly executed every day at high noon to dissuade other revolutionaries from conspiring against the Imperium.

"Now there's greatness of spirit," remarked Caesar. "Did you see how long the one on the right kicked and swayed? It takes extraordinary spirit to stave off death that long with a broken neck and a crushed esophagus. I applaud his greatness. I applaud his spirit. And I applaud any other spirited sonofabitch that rebels against my right to rule over him. I'll applaud him until his amputated skull is delivered to me on a pike. Hell, I even applauded the spirit of that scoundrel Christus when Pilate's soldiers dragged him up the Via Dolorosa to his crucifixion."

Cicero spat on the ground. "What you call greatness of spirit, I call barbarism."

"You're wrong", said the Honcho haughtily. "The barbarians live outside the Empire."

"What is barbarism to some is civilization to others, and vice versa", countered Cicero. "History shall be the judge, in the long run."

"Piss on history. In the long run, we're all dead."

"Do not denigrate the value of history. Not to know what happened before birth is to remain perpetually a child. What is the worth of a human life, unless it is woven into the lives of our ancestors by the records of history?"

This retort silenced the Honcho. He wasn't certain whether he was history, is history, or would be history, due to the uncertainty of time travel. As they made their way to the Circus Maximus, a heavy fog descended over Rome. The suffocating vapor was familiar to him, as were the roaming herds of Sacred Sheep and the "Left Turn Only" signs along the chariot route. He concluded that life was good.

The Circus Maximus was an enormous structure that seated 260,000 spectators. Its featured attraction was the chariot races, in which daredevil drivers raced headlong around the narrow track for fame and glory. The charioteers were reckless and ruthless. Collisions were frequent and often fatal. Death was no stranger to the spectators, either. Roman leaders kept the unemployed from revolting by placating them with free attractions like chariot races. Consequently, huge crowds of disenchanted rabble with lost hope, energized by adrenaline and testosterone from the thrilling races, periodically stampeded wildly, resulting in crushed bodies and wildfire brawls. They had nothing to live for except bread from the dole and state sponsored spectacles, so dying was uneventful. The opportunities to be crushed to death in public gatherings were plentiful, because politicians promulgated an ever-increasing number of free events to mollify the ever increasing number of unemployed who were supercharged with ever increasing hopelessness and anger.

After the Honcho watched a chariot race end in a blazing charge across the finish line, he said to Justinius, "I want to try that."

"You've already tried it, my glorious Consul."

"How did I do?"

"Terrible. You have no athletic skills and you know nothing about horsemanship. You fell off your chariot three times during the race."

"Damn! I hate losing."

"Don't be silly! You won the race hands down. Your Praetorian Guards lining the track spooked the opposing charioteers. Every time you fell, they halted their chariots and waited patiently for you to regain your mount. So, you won the victory wreath, and they won the right to live for another day."

The Honcho noted to himself that Caesar won chariot races the same way that he won elections as an U.S. Senator. As a thunderous roar followed a brutal collision between chariots, the Honcho scanned the hundreds of thousands of rabble watching the race. "Don't these people have anything better to do than hang out here?" he asked Justinius.

"No, Rome is a welfare empire that's being overrun by people who have taken the government up on its offer to feed and house them. Hordes of idle workers intimidate public officials into placating them with handouts because it's easier to throw them crumbs than to stave off armed insurrection. It's a frighteningly contagious form of extortion that will eventually bankrupt Rome."

"This is starting to make sense," said the Honcho. "Cleopatra has been complaining about the terrible work ethic in Egypt. So it isn't because Moses told them not to do anything until he got back?"

"It has nothing to do with Moses. There is simply little incentive to work. People have lost their sense of personal responsibility, since the government guarantees their survival. It supports their unwanted children, systematically distributes medicine and money, and grants free access to all circuses and festivals. Supporting a few indigent citizens with taxed surplus from the many productive citizens was well intentioned. Unfortunately, the poor mysteriously multiplied like fishes and loaves, putting the government in a political catch-22.

"If aid was denied to the burgeoning welfare class, they would overturn the government, so these burdensome social programs grew. The empire resorted to increasingly clever tactics to replenish the draining treasury. Productive Romans became enslaved by enforced tributes to tax collectors. The Roman currency was frequently devalued to increase tax revenues through inflation. Excise taxes on hundreds of activities were levied. Property was confiscated from enemies. When that was no longer sufficient, property was confiscated from allies. Citizenship was granted to all men, not out of devotion to liberty, but simply to increase the number of taxpayers. The estates of rich men who died were confiscated. When that was no longer sufficient, rich men were forced to bequeath their estates to the government while still alive. Tax rates were doubled, tripled, and quadrupled, forcing many in the upper classes to forfeit their rank and retire to the lower classes where taxes were less severe. Unfortunately, this resulted in less revenue for the treasury, so taxes were increased on all classes.

"The government can no longer meet the social demands placed on it, and yet it will face armed insurrection if it doesn't. There is nothing left to tax, and there are more mouths to feed than ever before. Something has gone terribly wrong, even though it all began with good intentions."

"What's being done about this devilish situation?" the Honcho asked.

"We're fighting more and more wars", replied Justinius. "Isn't that the obvious solution?"

"Of course", muttered the Honcho, recalling a succession of 20th Century conflicts he instigated to focus attention on harmless international enemies so the restless domestic populace couldn't figure out who the real enemy was.

"'Enrich the soldiers, and scorn all other men' is now the Empire's anthem," continued Justinius. "The military has been heavily reinforced to protect the Imperium from enemies within and to capture more plunder and enslave more taxable foreigners. We've instigated spurious wars with the Phoenicians in Carthage, the Ptolemaics in Egypt, the Macedonians in Greece, the Visigoths in the North, and the Celts in Hibernia. The military has become our identity and our modus operandi. The legions of centurions are training grounds for officers to infiltrate the government bureaucracy when they retire from the military. Our productive capacity is being diverted to weapons and provisions for soldiers. The biggest source of employment for the indigent is as foot soldiers in our war machine. They prefer the risk of death to the certainty of squalor. We are on a permanent war footing to distract the hungry masses."

The Honcho smiled knowingly. The Romans had discovered the blessings of allying their political administration with a military-industrial complex. In fact, they had already invented many of the devious abuses of institutional power that he thought were the creative genius of despots who lived eons later. He realized how similar the machinations of men were, even across a gulf of two thousand years. "The situation is well in hand, then?"

"Perhaps not," retorted Justinius. "An insidious inflation has gripped our empire. We have been continuously devaluing the denarius by coining more. This transfers wealth from our subjects to us, since we create and possess the additional coins, while the coins they hold are worth less. Since there are no additional goods to purchase, but many more coins, prices go up. This doesn't concern us, but it greatly concerns the consumers.

"Unfortunately, when inflation sets in, people stop saving, because coins will be worth less tomorrow. It is better to go into debt, which can be paid back with devalued coins later. Romans are now so eager to spend money, even on unproductive assets, it is said that they would buy and sell themselves for the right price. Since little is being saved, little is being invested. Therefore, the economy has stagnated. Therefore, we have less income to tax. Therefore, we need to coin more money. Therefore, more inflation. Therefore, more stagnation. It's a vicious cycle we call stagflation. I hope future civilizations learn to avoid this ugly death spiral."

The Honcho turned crimson from embarrassment. "What are we doing about this?"

"We're distributing millions of 'Whip Inflation Now' buttons."

"That's ridiculous!" reacted the Honcho instinctively.

"I was joking", smiled Justinius. "No empire would do anything that silly."

The Honcho turned crimson again. "What are we really doing?"

"We've decreed that all prices and wages remain fixed forever. Nothing can change. Not even the price of wheat, bread, wine, or sex. Death is the punishment for violating this edict."

"Is it working?"

"There are a few problems. We overlooked the fact that markets use fluctuating prices to adjust for changing conditions. Tastes change. The number of workers entering occupations changes. The bounties of harvests vary from year to year. In order to deal with this volatility that freely floating prices took care of automatically, we had to not only freeze wages and prices, but all human activity as well."

"Everything?" asked the Honcho incredulously.

"Everything. People are required by law to perform the same jobs forever. If they grow wheat now, they must continue to grow wheat with the exact same yield each year. Their children must grow this same amount of wheat each year after their fathers die. Artisans must produce a steady output of art, merchants must sell the same volume of goods, prostitutes must perform the same number of obscene acts, politicians must solicit the same flow of bribes, and soldiers must slay the same number of enemies. It's the only way we can keep the economy in balance with frozen wages and prices."

"Very clever. Are people complying?"

"No. They resent producing primarily for the benefit of the empire, so they are ceasing to produce. Where once we were the most industrious people in the world, our wharves are now merely receptacles for loot and plunder. Since we no longer are a producing and trading nation, theft is all we have left. And who we steal from, be they friend or foe, alien or citizen, doesn't matter to us."

"Sounds good to me," said the Honcho. "As long as we bureaucrats are getting richer and more powerful with each passing day, then all is as it should be."

"Perhaps that is so, Julius. However, talk of insurrection is in the air everywhere, despite your daily executions. I don't trust anyone, and neither should you. I hear whispers in the halls of the Senate. I see conspiratorial looks quickly averted when you enter the room. How much longer can this go on? We are constantly at war, we have taxed the empire dry, teeming hordes of unemployed threaten us, inflation impoverishes us, and the bureaucracy has grown so large and unwieldy that it is out of control, even under your iron rule. Your life is in jeopardy. The end of our empire may be at hand."

The Honcho sneered. "Don't be maudlin. Our powerful empire will never flounder! Rome will rule the world forever, and I will rule Rome until I die!"

"Perhaps you are right, wise and glorious Consul. But when I hear the mysterious phrase 'beware the Ides of March' whispered seditiously in the Senate, I'm chilled to the marrow of my bones. Something unspeakably dangerous is afoot. And tomorrow is the Ides of March."

"Beware the Ides of March," Brutus whispered seditiously to Cassius, in a marble encrusted Senate chamber. He playfully punched Cassius in the arm.

"Where did you hear that?" asked Cassius suspiciously.

Brutus couldn't tell whether Cassius recoiled from the force of his punch or from the impact of his words. "Everyone who hates Julius Caesar is whispering it", he explained. "I wanted in on the fun."

"And you? Do you hate him?" asked Cassius, who was deadly serious.

Brutus looked long and hard at Cassius, whom he had known for many years and trusted wholeheartedly. "Truthfully, yes", he confided. "Caesar is a vile, murderous, loathsome, thieving, brutal, warmongering, lying, and obscene bastard. He grinds us all under his heel. He's a greater curse to Rome than any pestilence, famine, or disease. Why have the Fates condemned us to such unremitting servitude to that oppressive monster? Why have the stars ordained our condition thus?"

"The fault, dear Brutus, lies not in the stars, but in ourselves, that we are underlings", said Cassius. "Only by our own inaction in the face of Caesar's oppression has Fate bound us with such unyielding chains. It is our responsibility to throw off these chains and take possession again of our own fates. As Cicero told us many times, the right to pursue the aims of our own lives is derived from the laws of nature, and is not the gift of the emperor, the chief magistrate, or the high priest. Our tolerance of the balls and chains on our ankles is no one's fault but our own. The stars are silent on the matter."

"What should we do?"

"What do you think we should do, dear Brutus?"

"We could make a ringing declaration in the Senate decrying Caesar's infamous acts. Cicero has been working on some words...."

"Words will not unlock our chains", interrupted Cassius. "Freedom, like nobility, is achieved only by bravery. Bravery requires action."

"But what action?"

"'Beware the Ides of March' is the code phrase for a conspiracy. I'm surprised you've heard these dangerous words. They should not be repeated loosely. Caesar has eyes and ears everywhere."

"What's the conspiracy?" implored Brutus impatiently.

"We're going to kill Caesar", whispered Cassius. "It's the only way to rid ourselves of his pestilence, and to restore the exalted citizens of Rome to their proper status as free men. The time has come for insurrection!"

Brutus was suddenly dizzy. His heart pounded madly, thumping a drumbeat that began in the womb of humanity, in that place within us all where our essential spirits lie untrammeled by the machinations of other men and the onerous burden of myths and institutions. The drumbeat subtly transformed itself into the gentle voice of a woman calling from the depths of history's sordid experience and from the heights of tomorrow's nascent hopes and dreams. Cassandra's voice was irresistible, and Brutus had no choice but to heed her call. He grabbed Cassius by the arms and boldly declared, "I want to kill Caesar. I must strike the first deadly blow."

The sun didn't rise the following morning. The Ides of March were ushered in by an intense electrical storm that illuminated the fabled cityscape like a huge celestial strobe light. Rainwater rushed down Rome's filthy stone streets in unrelenting torrents. Thunder crashed ominously around the seven famous hills. The heavens were in such turmoil that those who paid heed to cosmic portents feared the forces of Good and Evil were locked in mortal combat.

The Honcho was at the Senate waiting to deliver a tedious speech defending another devaluation of the denarius. He paced heavily in his private chamber. He was so absorbed with the troubling fears of insurrection expressed by Justinius yesterday that he didn't hear the door open. As he perused a list of suspected insurrectionists for today's executions, he felt a tap on his shoulder. He whirled around, and came face to face with unexpected peril. The visitor had a dagger in his hand, hatred in his eyes, and destiny etched in every fiber of his body. In that instant, the Honcho knew that his list of insurrectionists was incomplete. "You too, Freeman?" he called out in shocked recognition.

The intruder was stunned that Caesar mistook his identity. "I am Brutus", he corrected, and then raised his dagger to strike. "I'm going to rid Rome of your scourge."

The Honcho was terrified and disoriented. A man who looked like Freeman but was really Brutus was about to stab a man who looked like Caesar but was really the Honcho. "Et tu, Brute?" he asked forlornly.

"Yes, me too, Julius. This blow comes from Cicero and Cassius and all of the others who hate you. May this be the end of tyranny for all eternity!"

Brutus wrapped both hands around the dagger and thrust it at the spot where Caesar's brutish neck met his fleshy left shoulder. As the glinting blade hurtled downward, the Honcho feared that his life was about to end ignominiously in the body of another tyrant, 4000 miles from home, and 2000 years from his rightful place in history. In the milliseconds it took the blade to reach his jugular, he wondered whether it would be he who would die when the dagger struck home, or Caesar, or both.

This question would be decided by a cosmic wrestling match being furiously waged while the dagger, nominally in the hands of Brutus, was plunging toward a body nominally inhabited by Caesar. This match had been repeated many times throughout history, and would be repeated many times henceforth. While Cassandra screamed into the ears of Brutus to hurry his downward thrust, Mephistopheles frantically worked to rescue the soul of Caesar and the Head Honcho, who were one and the same. Cassandra screamed louder. Satan evoked every nuance of his black magic. Something had to give. The dagger slammed into Caesar's body, severing his jugular. Brutus looked through Caesar's terrified eyes directly into the late emperor's soul. To his surprise, there was nothing there. His soul had already escaped.

Chapter Six:
"Pandora's Coffin"

"I don't make jokes—I just watch government and report the facts."

—Will Rogers

They heard an unforgettable scream, an all-encompassing emanation from the deepest, darkest corners of a terror stricken soul cowering in the Grim Reaper's shadow. The agonized screech reverberated in the Honcho's office, coming from everywhere and nowhere all at once, enveloping the people there with a cold, wet blanket of tormented human emotion.

A blinding flash of light erupted. Freeman, Jefferson, Buxomus Blondus, and But Sir! recoiled from the staggering brilliance of a luminous ball that materialized above the Honcho's desk. The screaming came from inside the luminous mass, where a human silhouette was writhing in an incongruously elegant ballet of pain. As the ball dimmed, they recognized the writhing screamer as the Head Honcho. His twisting body was draped in a bloodstained white sheet.

The Honcho's soul had narrowly escaped Brutus' plunging knife. It had been whisked from the jaws of death by the otherworldly force that powered the "Book of Liberal Policies, Marxist Economics, and other Occult Phenomena". Unfortunately, his soul had lingered long enough in Caesar's body to feel the knife stab and experience a brush with mortality that fueled his bellowing screams.

Oddly familiar people in an oddly familiar setting surrounded him, although the pain in his shoulder, the fear in his soul, and the blinding luminosity of the time warp disoriented him. When his eyes adjusted to the relative darkness of his office, the sight of Freeman enraged him. Freeman scrambled furiously to escape the clutches of the bloodied giant who had pinned him to the floor and was choking him. "I'll kill you, Brutus!" the Honcho screamed. "How dare you stab me? You impudent, insurrectionist bastard! I'm Julius Caesar, ruler of the world. I'll rip your fingers off one by one! I'll pull your arms and legs off one by . . ."

A tidal wave of humanity careening into him interrupted his murderous tirade. Jefferson, But Sir!, and Buxomus Blondus all grappled with the savage, frothing beast he had become. In the confused flailing of bodies, Freeman wriggled free. Jefferson and But Sir! tenuously pinned the Honcho's mammoth arms to his prodigious girth. Buxomus stared angrily at him. "What are you doing?" she cried.

"That sonofabitch traitor stabbed me!" shouted the Honcho.

"Did not!" shouted Freeman shakily.

"Look at the blood on my shoulder! This is treason! This is insurrection! This is . . ."

Jefferson slapped the delirious Senator. The torrent of vituperative spilling like lava from him abruptly stopped. "Gather your wits! This man is not Brutus, and he certainly didn't stab you. He has never left our sight!"

The Honcho was stunned by the slap and by the oddly familiar man who slapped him. "Cicero!" he cried out in sudden recognition. "You bastard! You were in on the conspiracy, too! Brutus implicated you and Cassius as he stabbed me!"

"I'm not surprised that Brutus implicated Cicero", said Jefferson. "All good men were guilty of conspiring to murder Caesar. Some had no plan, some had no courage, and some had no opportunity. But everyone had the desire." He now realized that the Honcho hadn't yet completed his transmogrification from Caesar back to his self in modern America. "But that's all ancient history. I'm not Cicero, he's not Brutus, and most importantly, you're not Caesar."

"Is this true, Justinius?" the Honcho asked But Sir!.

"But Sir!, I'm not Justinius!"

"And you aren't Cleopatra?" the Honcho asked Buxomus with disappointment.

"No, silly!" she giggled.

"My God", he moaned. His head dropped morosely into his hands. "It's coming back to me now . . . ." Sobbing shook his massive frame.

Buxomus embraced him. "There, there. You just had a bad dream, that's all."

"Yeah, just a bad dream", confirmed Freeman, who had a big stake in stabilizing the Honcho. "Remember me, your old pal Freeman?"

"And me, But Sir!?"

"And you couldn't forget my face, could you?" said Jefferson.

The Honcho struggled to sort out fact from fiction. "But . . . but it wasn't a dream . . . ", he murmured, to convince himself as much as to convince them. He stared at them intently, yet remained confused about their duality. "You were there! . . . and you! . . . and you! . . . and you!", he declared, pointing to each of them.

"We all dream lots of silly things", purred Buxomus.

"Doesn't anyone believe me?"

"Of course we do. You're a U.S. Senator", they all said in a subconsciously synchronized Pavlovian response.

"How long was I gone?" he asked warily. "It seemed like I was in Rome for days . . . and yet, you're all still sitting here in this room, as if I hadn't left at all . . ."

"But Sir!" exclaimed But Sir!. "We didn't leave. There was a lot of smoke and light when you uttered the incantation from the 'Book of Liberal Policies, Marxist Economics, and Other Occult Phenomena'. Then you seemingly disappeared. Seconds later, another blinding flash of light erupted inside the smoke. After the light diminished, we could see you again. Curiously, you were wearing that bloodstained sheet when you re-appeared."

"I had to have left here. I couldn't have just imagined it. Things were so terrible in Rome . . . there were conspiratorial whispers in Senate halls, Rome was constantly at war, the empire was taxed dry, teeming hordes of indigents threatened the government, inflation was rampant, and the huge bureaucracy was out of control, even under Caesar's iron rule . . . I mean, under my iron rule. I feared for my life . . ."

"Guess what's happening here and now?" interjected Freeman. "There are conspiratorial whispers in the halls of Congress. We are constantly at war. The country has been taxed dry. Teeming hordes of indigents are overwhelming the government. Inflation has rampaged a few times this century. Our huge bureaucracy is out of control, even under your iron rule. And, the Insurrectionist continues to threaten you."

"Oh shit!" the Honcho cursed. He threw up his hands in despair. "This staff meeting seems like it's been dragging on for thousands of years. Get the hell outa here!"

Everyone thankfully scurried toward the door. Freeman, with bruises on his neck from where the Beast had nearly strangled him, was particularly gratified to be exiting the Honcho's lair.

"Stick around, Freeman", ordered the Honcho. "We need to talk."

Freeman did a reluctant about-face and slid dejectedly into a chair. "What did I do now?"

The Honcho looked at him suspiciously. "I don't know. I just want a status report on our 1000 charity cases in Vhaicam."

Freeman breathed a sigh of relief. "Which 1000 do you want to hear about first?"

"What do you mean? The last I knew, there were 1000 Vhaicamese in total."

"Their population has doubled four times since your last update. Scientists who normally study the reproductive proclivities of fruit flies have been awarded a huge federal grant to study the Rabbit People. In related news, the Vhaicamese won the Vatican's prestigious Golden Cross of Fertility for propagating the Catholic faith at a more astounding rate than any other nation."

The Honcho turned white as a ghost. "How much is 1000 doubled four times?"

"Sixteen thousand", replied Freeman, who learned how to calculate enormous numbers from doing his income tax returns.

"Damn! What do I do now?"

"What the rest of us are doing. Place a wager on when their population will double again."

A pageboy charged into the Honcho's office and breathlessly announced that Vhaicam's population officially reached 32,000 at 2:34 PM. Freeman tore up a betting slip in disgust.

The Honcho wasn't interested in gambling. "How are these people surviving? Their economy can't possibly be growing fast enough to support them."

"Of course it's not. That wasn't part of our program. They're starving in the streets in wretched squalor again. If we don't send them another boat load of relief money, they'll die."

"We can't let them die!" wailed the Honcho. "I can't run on a campaign platform of compassion if I've caused mass starvation."

"Then send more money. No one will miss it. Besides, we need the exports."

"Okay, but it's an election year. I can't increase taxes. We'll raise the ceiling on the national debt again, so the next generation will have to raise taxes to pay themselves back what they thought they had already saved with government bonds."

"Good strategy. But what should we do about the Mormon missionaries?"

"I thought the missionaries in Vhaicam were Catholic."

"They were", confirmed Freeman. "And they still are. But Mormon missionaries followed them and convinced the natives that the Catholic notion of monogamy is passé, so the Vhaicamese men took multiple wives. Unfortunately, they retained the Catholic opposition to birth control, which means that each male has multiple opportunities to sire children under the Pope's watchful eye. NASA's super computers need only three more days to finish calculating the projected population growth from these combined lifestyles."

These revelations disturbed the Honcho, so he changed the subject. "What else is happening?"

"Militant radicals took over the United(?) Nations and rendered it impotent."

The Honcho sneered. "That's not news. The Soviet-organized block of third world countries took over the United(?) Nations years ago. It's been impotent ever since."

"But this time it wasn't the Russians and their cronies. It was fundamentalist Muslims. They're holding the General Assembly hostage until the Great Satan is vanquished."

"Who's the Great Satan?"

"Us", informed Freeman.

"That's ridiculous!"

"Not from their perspective. They believe that our foreign policy has violated their sovereign right of self determination by supporting secular dictatorships in their midst. They're also pissed off by our support of Israel, an antagonistic military power on their sacred soil. They want us to surrender our influence over the world body of nations."

"We haven't had any meaningful influence in the United(?) Nations for decades", said the Honcho. "Even though we fund 50% of the budget of those anti-Western demagogues, all we get in return is ingratitude, insult, and humiliation."

Freeman silently agreed that America's involvement in the U.(?) N. was dubious. The institution had long ago devolved into a farce, despite a noble beginning inspired by Roosevelt and Churchill. Even its name was an oxymoron. Why call a group "united", when their very association is in response to the nearly insurmountable barriers that separate them? These "united" nations had boundaries delineating huge divisions carved by religion, territorial disputes, historical atrocities, philosophical gulfs, and general xenophobia. Member nations disagreed over the nature of Man, the course of history, the role of government, human rights, and even truth and morality. The United(?) Nations quietly added the "?" to their official name shortly after the Soviet Union invaded Afghanistan, both of whom were members that had signed the U.(?) N.'s "Universal Declaration of Human Rights".

The only thing more ridiculous than calling the U.(?) N. "united" was that the United(?) States was paying for most of the charade, despite the likelihood that involvement with the U.(?) N. would lead to responsibility for all of the world's problems, and thus to a world tax and further erosion of individual rights in America, which would be a New World Order much like the Old World Order of chains and oppression, although on a larger and more creative scale.

"Fuck the U.(?) N.", declared the Honcho, interrupting Freeman's wandering thoughts. "What's next on my list of things to catch up on?"

"We have a civil rights issue to deal with."

The Honcho sighed mournfully. "Why do I need to get involved with these things? Everyone thinks I'm the watchdog of their rights or a professional guardian angel. Don't they realize what my job is?"

Freeman knew that the primary element of a senator's job was doing whatever it took to get reelected. "30% of your constituents are minorities. You need their votes."

"I'm glad someone understands my job. So, what's the issue?"

"One of your constituents claims his parents violated his civil rights by spanking him."

The Honcho yawned. "Why is that a civil rights violation?"

"He claims they spanked him just because he's black."

"Aren't his parents black too?"

"Coincidentally, they are. However, they've launched a separate lawsuit against America, claiming that the spanking of children is a practice they learned from their violent white oppressors, and that this acquired behavioral deficiency is a violation of their civil rights that wouldn't have occurred if their ancestors hadn't been forcibly removed from Africa by slave traders 300 years ago."

"What would Ismism say about this muddled mess?"

"I've already consulted the Safari Golfer", said Freeman. "He paused from filming his latest music video to make this pronouncement: 'When the yin and yang become one, when the universe is once again darkness and the void is once again light, when the poets are mute and the muses are deaf, when the looking glass reflects its own image, and when fairway bunkers turn into the finest of lawn, only then will unrelenting order emerge from the chaos of random kinetic occurrences that create the illusion of our divergent views of reality. May all your double bogeys be happy ones. Amen.'"

The Honcho was so impressed by Golfer's cosmic eloquence that he had only one reaction. "What the fuck does that mean?"

"I asked him that too, because I had no idea what the fuck it meant, either. He confessed it meant nothing, since that's the essence of Ismism."

"Then why did he say it?"

"He claims it doesn't matter what he says anymore. Since he's a stupendously famous leader of a worldwide cult, his proclamations automatically become infallible dogma, even if they're incomprehensible. To entertain himself, he randomly arranges arcane words into pronouncements. As long as he doesn't use the same combination of words twice, he picks up additional worshipers each time he opens his mouth. He also pointed out that the proclamations of the other major religions don't make any sense either. He used the example of the Trinity—three gods for the price of one."

"But what do I do about the black boy and his discriminating parents?"

"Why not pass a law permitting blacks to spank white people? That way, the boy's parents have an outlet for their acquired urge for corporal punishment, and the black boy won't bear the brunt of their beatings."

"That's brilliant, Freeman! But, will such a law help my campaign?"

"I'm not sure. Put the legislation into committee, so that it emerges as an anonymous bill that Congress can pass by voice vote. Thus, no one will actually be responsible for it, in case it turns out to be a tragic error. On the other hand, if the idea works fabulously, you can claim ownership of it. If you're quick enough, you can claim ownership before all the other senators do too. It's the same principle as giving the five men in a firing squad one blank and four live rounds of ammunition. The marksmen can then choose to believe they either fired the blank or the fatal shot."

"Bravo!" proclaimed the Honcho. "What's next?"

"Time for a break, boss. You've worked hard for fifteen minutes, now. Let's get some grub from the cafeteria. Along the way, we can check on the latest Vhaicam population statistics. Our crack analyst is downloading the data from NASA's super computers."

They approached the crack analyst, who was leaning back in his chair with his hands comfortably linked behind his head, his feet propped on the computer, and his eyelids closed. Freeman kicked his legs away from the terminal, jarring the government employee from his peaceful snooze. He instinctively reached for his coat. "Holy shit!" he squealed. "Is it quitting time already?"

"Sit down!" commanded Freeman. "Show us the data you've downloaded."

"I'd like to, but something's wrong with my machine."

"Perhaps it would work better if you plugged it in." Freeman dangled the offending plug for the blushing analyst to inspect. He plugged the machine in and it sprang to life with a torrent of data. "My God!" declared the analyst. "This thing actually works! Our repair department couldn't figure out how to fix it."

They resumed their trek to the cafeteria. "That man wasn't earning his paycheck. I want him shot", the Honcho said, without blinking or breaking stride.

Freeman blinked and broke stride. "We shouldn't do that, sir", he croaked.

"Why not?"

"Shooting unproductive government employees would set a dangerous precedent, for which we don't have enough bullets."

"Not enough bullets?" howled the Honcho. "The fucking Pentagon is just down the road!"

"You don't understand the numbers involved here."

"Perhaps. How many people work for the federal government?"

"The Office of Management and Budget began studying that question last year."

"And the answer was?"

"The answer isn't . . . at least not yet. They're still counting."

"The OMB is the world's largest collection of accountants. How can it take them so long?"

"The numbers are extraordinary", said Freeman. "It took six months just to count the departments, agencies, committees, administrations, services, divisions, and councils that comprise the federal government. They had to use CIA cryptologists to crack the bewildering acronyms hiding the shadowy legions of employees that the OMB was trying to count. To make things worse, their method for counting people was very inefficient."

"How so?"

"When counting employees, it's customary to count heads. Unfortunately, the computer geeks programming the counting software were spooked by rumors of bicephalic federal workers . . . "

"How does that compare to being homosexual?" the Honcho interrupted nervously.

"It doesn't. Bicephalics have two heads. Thus, if only heads were tallied, the complex software would have yielded a confusing fractional count of people, which is impossible, unless you're a statistician."

"It's possible to have fractions of statisticians?"

"No, statisticians believe it's possible to have fractions of humans."

"So what did the programmers do?"

"They told the counters to count fingers instead of heads. The software then divides by 9.7, since that's how many fingers the average person has."

"That's an odd average."

"It was 9.9, before the Vietnam War", said Freeman. "Some people allegedly only had one finger, which skewed the average downward. But the OMB is now theorizing that these were cases of unfriendly gestures."

They reached the cafeteria and stood in line to see which line to stand in. After filling their trays, the Honcho charged their food to his campaign account. As they sat down, he said, "I heard there was a big explosion in the National Archives. What happened?"

"They had a slight problem with a mouse. Crafty sonofabitch. Probably a communist. It routinely scared the secretaries. The janitors tried to catch it by setting a trap with a cracker on the trip wire. The mouse ate the cracker without setting off the trap. They put two traps out the next night, one with a cracker, the other with peanut butter."

"Did they catch the mouse?"

"No", replied Freeman. "The mouse not only ate the cracker, he covered it with peanut butter from the other trap without setting off either one! The janitors were humiliated. So, the very next night, they tied a cracker to the trip wire with twine."

"Then did they catch the mouse?"

"No, but the mouse left a thank you note, which gave them a handwriting sample to go on. With their reputations in jeopardy, the janitors called in the heavy artillery."

The Honcho chuckled. "They asked the Army Corp. of Engineers to blow the mouse to smithereens with a Howitzer?"

Freeman choked on his doughnut. "It's rude to let someone tell a funny story when you've already heard the punch line."

"I was joking."

"Maybe you were, but the janitors weren't. They wanted their mouse in the worst way, which is exactly how they went about it. The Army rolled a Howitzer up to the basement window of the Archives and fired a live shell. The subsequent explosion scattered paper and microfiche for blocks, covering the ground with four inches of Congressional Record fragments. The road crews mistook this confetti for snow and called in sick, so that they could plow the streets later on overtime."

"I'm really pissed off", growled the Honcho.

"You're emotionally attached to the Congressional Record?"

"No. I'm glad it was shredded. It's tedious enough legislating the drivel that it reports, much less reading about it afterward. I'm pissed because the Army Corp. of Engineers was supposed to be landscaping my private estate, rather than blowing up the Archives. So, did they finally get their mouse?"

"Negative", replied Freeman. "When they searched the rubble, they found no trace of a mouse carcass. Turns out someone from the SPCA tipped the rodent off about the janitors' plans. The feisty critter hid in the Smithsonian basement with his buddies, until the fire was snuffed out. Then he made a triumphal return."

"So they never got him?"

"Actually, they did."

"Did they go nuclear?"

"No. They used an even more devastating weapon. They turned our bureaucracy loose on it. They created a federal agency whose sole charter was to protect the life of this particular mouse at all costs. The agency had a ten million dollar budget, a staff of mouse protection experts, and the usual approval to violate the Constitution."

"What happened?"

"The plan was successful. The mouse died of unknown causes two days later."

"What happened to the agency created to protect the mouse?"

"The same thing that happens to all government agencies that fail. They doubled its budget, broadened its mission, and gave lifetime appointments to its senior administrators, who blamed their previous failures on someone named 'society'".

"Hmmm", mused the Honcho. "Perhaps I can use them to protect the Insurrectionist at all costs, so he'll wind up dead two days later too. Put them on my agenda for tomorrow."

"Can't do that, sir."

The Honcho was unaccustomed to this response. He glared through Freeman's eyes to the back of his skull and growled, "Why . . . the . . . fuck . . . not?"

"Tomorrow's a federal holiday. We have the day off."

"Oh! What holiday is it?"

"Don't remember. We're either celebrating an old war, a dead president, or a politically correct minority leader. Seems like we have a lot of holidays, nowadays. We must have an unnatural proclivity for waging war, assassinating leaders, and assuaging our national angst about slavery by deifying outspoken African Americans. If we keep up the momentum, we may never have to work again."

On their way back to the Honcho's office, they picked up Jefferson, But Sir!, and Buxomus to help work through the rest of the day's issues. They passed by the analyst gathering the Vhaicam population data. Over his sleeping body, Freeman saw on the computer terminal that the population had doubled again, to 64,000. This was ominous news that would have to be dealt with later.

The Honcho and his staff dug into their work. A letter from a concerned citizen asked why the government subsidized the tobacco industry, which causes thousands of deaths each year, while banning artificial sweeteners, which hadn't yet killed anyone. The Honcho instructed Freeman to ask the Safari Golfer to make a psychedelic announcement to the masses on this subject that would be so garbled it would be accepted as compelling wisdom and resolve the silly question.

An entrepreneur in Ohio filed a complaint because his application for a business permit consumed 16,000 pages, weighed 65 pounds, and cost $116.42 just to mail in. The Honcho directed Jefferson to find out why postage costs so much. An elderly homeowner in Minnesota asked the government to do something about the windfall profits that oil companies were presumably getting since the cost of home heating oil had skyrocketed. The Honcho instructed But Sir! to write a letter promising to slap a windfall profits tax on the oil companies, thereby making the government the beneficiary of the windfall and further increasing the price of oil.

A pastor in Alabama wrote a letter objecting to the poor example that the illicit sexual activities of Washington's leaders set for the rest of the citizens, who might be tempted to emulate their degeneracy. The Honcho's dictated response agreed that licentiousness was inappropriate for the masses, because sex is too good for the common people. He vowed that all of his fellow Washingtonians except Clinton would be more discrete in their sexual dalliances, to keep the public from getting jealous.

A community complained that the Civil Rights Commission was prosecuting them because they had no minorities living among them. The Honcho advised them to quit whining and create incentives for minority families to move into their neighborhoods, in order to avoid the pernicious prosecution of the CRC. He suggested creating a "black market", in which neighborhoods would bid on homeless minority families to come and live among them.

A schoolteacher in Peoria complained that the National Endowment for the Arts spent a million taxpayer dollars on an obscene sculpture in her town. The sculpture depicted an industrialist with a fistful of dollars urinating on a downtrodden proletarian family kneeling at his feet holding empty bowls. The artist entitled the work "Capitalism", and bought a mansion in Beverly Hills with his commission. Leftists came in droves to ritualistically urinate on the stainless steel industrialist, which presented a health hazard as well as a disgusting example for the town's children. The Honcho dictated a reply suggesting that the statue be secretly electrified, which would discourage public urination.

This went on for hours. The Honcho's staff neared exhaustion keeping pace with his ruination of the country by fiat. Fortunately, they got a reprieve when they stumbled upon the Great Tree Growing Incident. Actually, they stumbled over furniture in the Honcho's office when total darkness mysteriously descended upon Washington, causing everyone to wander about in sightless disarray.

Since it was unacceptable for America's leaders to stumble about in darkness rather than broad daylight, the Defense Intelligence Agency was ordered to find the source of the inky blackness that had swallowed Washington. The DIA's first working hypothesis was that Washington's ubiquitous fog had somehow congealed into an opaque substance. However, using sophisticated infrared night vision devices, DIA technicians discovered that a huge canopy of trees had blossomed above the city's skyline, blocking out any light that might otherwise have penetrated the fog.

Further DIA investigation revealed that the Great Tree Growing Incident began innocently enough when two intrepid employees at the Department of Agriculture planted trees in front of their office building to assuage their guilt about subsidizing people who grow things for a living to not grow things anymore. Unfortunately, other agencies in Washington suspected that this was a secret strategy by the Agriculture Department to get additional federal funds by subsidizing themselves to stop growing trees.

A remarkable contest of horticultural leapfrog ensued. Government agencies grew trees greater in size and number than each preceding attempt by their competitors, hoping for the federal government to step in and subsidize the non-growing of trees once the situation got out of hand. The Commerce Department imported fast growing bamboo from the Far East. The Interior Department transplanted Sequoias from California. The Labor Department conscripted labor unions to plant millions of seedlings. The Education Department banned textbook printing so that their trees wouldn't be needlessly sacrificed to pulp mills. The Justice Department declared Dutch Elm Disease to be unconstitutional.

The Department of Housing and Urban Development bulldozed huge tracts of apartment buildings to plant trees. The Energy Department developed a tree that grew so fast people got whiplash and radiation poisoning watching the iridescent mutants grow. The Defense Department produced invisible Stealth Trees that were undetectable by radar, in case a jealous adversary in these horticultural war games launched surface-to-foliage missiles. The CIA transplanted palm trees they had used for training Cuban exiles for the Bay of Pigs invasion. The Internal Revenue Service confiscated all the fruit trees from growers in Florida under the guise of an obscure tax law.

This tree-growing contest escalated, as a matter of greed, prestige, and bureaucratic momentum. Maples, elms, cedars, ashes, walnuts, pines, redwoods, birches, willows, and oaks transformed the landscape into an immense urban forest.

There were soon more trees in Washington than in the Amazon rain forests or in Poland's Bialowieza National Park, which the noted conservationist Hermann Goering had zealously protected while his Luftwaffe rained death on Europe's humans. Thousands of tree huggers flocked to this magnificent new forest, although they had trouble finding it because the trees blocked their view. As they embraced millions of insentient trunks, they chanted "Treat human beings as a tool, and Nature as the object", which helped explain the Hermann Goerings of the world.

Washington was suffocatingly dark under the canopy of this primordial forest. The Honcho sat alone in his blackened office after everyone left to find flashlights. He dreaded this bizarre arboreal manifestation, mostly because his constituents would expect him to conquer it. He began to moan aloud. He abruptly stopped moaning when other moans answered his. At first, he thought they were echoes in his cavernous office, but the other moans continued even after he stopped. He was clearly not alone. "Who's there?" he demanded.

"It's me again", a voice called from the darkness.

The Honcho couldn't place the nasally voice with a name or a face. "Who's me?"

"Who's you? You is the Honcho."

The Honcho still couldn't place the voice. "Why were you moaning? Are you okay?"

"How would I know?" said the disembodied voice. "I've never been okay before. And why shouldn't I moan? Is moaning fit for you, but not for me? At least I know who I am."

"But who are you? I can't see you!"

"That's a reasonable excuse for not knowing who I am, but why don't you know who you are?"

"I know who the fuck I am!" shouted the Honcho. "Who the fuck are you?"

The Honcho heard his humidor being opened, followed by the sound of a cigar being unwrapped. Suddenly, a struck match starkly illuminated the visitor's face, from which an expensive Cuban cigar dangled jauntily. The Honcho's heart sank to his toes. The pallid face floating eerily in the darkness was the Mad Hatter's. "Why do you torture me like this?" he asked.

"I'm not torturing you. You were moaning before I got here."

"But every time you show up, things get so fucking confusing."

"Things are indeed more confusing on your side of the looking glass than ours", agreed the Hatter haughtily. "Just the other day, we in Wonderland observed a ridiculous farce on your side of the glass. Somebody fired a Howitzer at the Dormouse. Missed him completely, although your nonsensical archives took a direct hit. Doesn't seem sporting to kill a dormouse with a Howitzer. Or to kill paperwork with a Howitzer either. Or worse still, to kill a dormouse with paperwork, which is what eventually happened. Care for some treacle?" he offered.

The Honcho ignored him. "Tell me why you're here", he begged.

"Care for some treacle?" the Hatter repeated emphatically.

The Honcho thought to himself, "Every time he offers treacle, I decline it. Then, he tells me he didn't have any anyway." He decided to cross the Hatter up. "Yes, I want some treacle", he said aloud with a self-satisfied chuckle. "Now, tell me why you're here."

"I'm here because other Mad Hatters mated. Why are you here? No . . . wait . . . It's silly of me to ask. You don't even know who you are. I withdraw the question."

An uneasy silence ensued. The Honcho waited for his treacle while the Mad Hatter puffed contentedly on a cigar, his face dimming and brightening intermittently as he inhaled and stoked the embers. The Honcho broke the maddening silence. "Where's my treacle?" he asked menacingly, suspecting that the Mad Hatter had been bluffing all these years about having some.

"Right in front of you", said the Hatter politely. "Should I have served it behind you?"

"But I can't see it!"

"Of course you can't. It's much too dark."

"Then why did you bother to give it to me?"

"Because you asked for it. It would have been rude to do otherwise."

"How do I know it's really here?"

"Reality is indeed very confusing in the dark . . . and in the light", said the Hatter. "Especially for Ismism followers. By the way, did I tell you why I was here?"

"No! And not because I didn't ask!"

"I would have told you sooner, if you hadn't already asked."

"That doesn't make any sense", said the Honcho, with intense anguish.

"That's why things are much clearer on my side of the looking glass. We are quite content to wallow in nonsense. It makes our world rather orderly, in a queer sort of way. Your world wallows in just as much nonsense, but you foolishly try to make sense of it. You should either stop wallowing in nonsense, or stop trying to make sense of it. Doing both is quite impossible. But that's not why I'm here."

The Honcho gritted his teeth. "Why…are…you…here?"

"To help you."

"I don't want your help", barked the Honcho. "Things will just get worse."

"You don't know who you are, you can't find your treacle, darkness has swallowed Washington, and your reelection campaign is floundering. Don't you want just a tad bit of help?"

"What kind of help?" the Honcho asked warily, edging closer to biting the hook.

"I can't help your reelection campaign. On our side of the looking glass, the Red Queen frowns on democracy, so we avoid it religiously. On your side of the glass, democracy is an elegant charade that you and your subjects perform with blind religious pomposity, which is another reason why things are much clearer for us. We don't put up with elegant charades or with blind religious pomposity. The Red Queen rules, and that's that. When she says off with our heads, it's off with our heads. However, I can help with this confounding darkness."

The Honcho felt madness coming on. "What can we do?" he pleaded.

"Let's use the Socratic method to unravel this. What's your problem?"

"The darkness."

"What's causing the darkness?"

"More trees than anyone can count."

"What must be done with the trees?"

"They must be destroyed", the Honcho concluded.

"What is the quickest, surest way to destroy a government creation?"

"Make it a low income housing project?"

"Precisely!" The Mad Hatter snuffed out his cigar embers in a handcrafted alabaster ashtray. The office fell completely dark and silent. The Honcho sat motionless for a while before surmising that the Hatter had vanished. He arose and moved around the darkened office, swinging his arms in empty space to assure himself that there were indeed no hatters present. Then he drafted an official announcement designating the huge forest entombing Washington to be a low-income housing project. In a flash of inspiration, he named the arboreal tenement "Wonderland".

The next morning, daylight magically bathed the cityscape. It only took one night as an officially designated low-income housing project to destroy Wonderland. Little remained of the towering groves of trees, thanks to the fearsome vandalism of nihilistic urban outcasts. When dawn came, the hooligans who wrought the devastation returned to their normal jobs spray painting forlorn graffiti on subway walls.

Unfortunately, one city block remained shrouded in darkness, even though no trees could be seen, which seemed like witchcraft. At first, the Honcho suspected someone had gotten unauthorized access to the "Book of Liberal Policies, Marxist Economics, and Other Occult Phenomena". But, the Defense Department eventually confessed that the eerie darkness came from stealth trees planted during the Great Tree Growing Incident. The nihilistic hooligans hadn't destroyed them because they were invisible. This city block seemed condemned to live in shadows forever.

Fortunately, the Safari Golfer came to the rescue. The world's foremost mystic recommended simply announcing that the shadows were no longer there. He pointed out that it was irrelevant whether the shadows were real or not. The only matter of substance was belief, and if people could be persuaded that the shadows weren't there, then they weren't real and would go away. It was, he argued, the natural role of government to brainwash citizens in this manner.

The Honcho loved this idea. He publicly announced that the stealth shadows left over from the Great Tree Growing Incident no longer existed, so people should stop believing in them. Unfortunately, the visual cognition of those living in the abysmal darkness defied the government's contradictory proclamation. To combat this pernicious objectivity, the Safari Golfer went on TV and declared the shadows to be non-existent. Since his legendary persuasiveness was more potent than that of even Lamont Cranston, "The Shadow" of radio fame, who could "cloud men's minds so that they cannot see him", he convinced everyone that the shadows weren't real. Thus, daylight returned to the stealth tree community, winning the Honcho critical voter support.

To celebrate his political triumph, the Honcho toured the newly illuminated stealth tree community. People lined up to greet the man who saved them from darkness. Along the way, a disheveled vagrant stepped out of the shadows that no longer existed and begged the Honcho for a small handout so he could stave off sobriety for another night. The Honcho sensed an opportunity to enhance his image in front of thousands of eligible voters. With news cameras focused on him, he boldly reached into Freeman's pocket, withdrew a wallet, pulled out a wad of currency, and dangled the money in front of the eager bum. He announced to the crowd and the cameras, "As a U.S. Senator, I'm honor-bound to ensure that every registered voter is provided with life's necessities." Then he ceremoniously handed Freeman's money to the derelict.

The vagrant was thrilled by the Senator's generosity and his brief notoriety. Turning his unshaven face toward a camera, he mumbled with alcohol laden breath, "Mr. Senator, how can I repay you?"

The Honcho cocked his head self-righteously. "No repayment is necessary. Just cast your ballot for the most worthy candidate on election day."

As the derelict stumbled off toward the brothels and bars, Freeman angrily pulled the Honcho away from the camera's probing eye. "How dare you grab my money and give it to some indigent to further your selfish political ambitions?" he growled venomously.

The Honcho smiled serenely, like a crocodile. "It's no different than when the government funnels your tax money to special interests in exchange for votes. You've always passively accepted the formal version of this gambit. Why do you object so strenuously now?"

"Does Ismism approve of this charade?"

"Of course", bluffed the Honcho.

"I'm not sure I like Ismism, then."

"Jesus Christ, Freeman. It's far better than alternatives like communism, where man exploits his fellow man. Under Ismism, it's just the opposite, so we're much better off."

Freeman just shook his head. The ball and chain strapped to his ankle was getting heavier with each passing day. "Let's get back to the tour", he mumbled.

Suddenly, a gun barrel protruded menacingly from a stealth shadow that was no longer there. Within the unexplainable darkness lurked the Man from Nebraska. The Honcho's secret service agents thought it was the Man from Detroit because of the gun, so they edged back toward safety.

This left the Head Honcho dangerously exposed to the double-barreled shotgun pointed at his stomach by a stranger lurking under invisible trees in a stealth shadow that was oblivious to the Safari Golfer's reality-bending proclamation. Unfortunately, the Man from Nebraska had never heard of the Honcho, the Golfer, nor the thousands of acronym-laden agencies that ran the country from fog-bound Washington. He had faith in none of these alien institutions. He had faith in nothing at all, other than his ability to transform sunlight, water, and seed into amber waves of grain, which fed his family and many others.

Freeman mustered enough courage to interrogate the armed man. "What do you want?" he asked timidly.

"I want my money back", was the unhesitating answer from the shadow that didn't exist.

"I don't have any money", said Freeman, who had just been relieved of it. "But he has plenty", he offered, pointing at the Honcho. "He's a U. S. Senator."

The Honcho shot Freeman a murderous glance, as the sound of a double-barreled shotgun being cocked echoed against his prodigious abdomen. "Perfect", declared the voice from the shadow. "Then you're the one I came to see. I want my gol'darned money back. Now!"

"I don't have your money", lied the Honcho, who, as chairman of the Appropriations Committee, had everyone's money.

"The hell you don't!" pounced the Man from Nebraska. "I been paying taxes for 35 long years. I did it patriotic like, even though they took more'n more every year. I did it, even though I felt like a plow horse with a saddle on my back. I did it, even though my son never came back from fightin' in Asia, and even though the Missus ain't been the same since losin' her youngun. I did it, even though my neighbor got paid more'n me to grow nothin'. I did it even when I learnt our leaders were busy breakin' laws, when they weren't busy fornicatin'. But I ain't doin' it any more!" He jammed his gun deeper into the Honcho's flabby belly.

The Honcho gulped. "Why not?"

"'Cuz my eyes have been opened."

"By whom?" asked the Honcho nervously.

"By a man who calls hisself the Insurrectionist. Us folks in Nebraska have taken a likin' to him."

These were ominous words to the Honcho. A gun jabbed in his belly was one thing, but hearing that his nemesis was still corrupting Americans caused nervous sweat to sprout on his forehead. "What did the Insurrectionist tell you?"

"First off, he said we wasn't born with saddles on our backs, so a favored few with boots and spurs could ride us. He tol' us that to have more self respect than a plow horse, we had to buck the booted and spurred sons-of-bitches off."

"What else did he tell you?"

"He tol' us that only lies need the support of gov'ment. Truth doesn't need force to enter our minds, so we don't need a gov'ment to know the truth. We should just open our eyes and judge for ourselves, or else become slaves to those who claim they know truths the rest of us can't see. That's why I'm standing in this shadow that really does exist, despite you folks pretendin' it don't."

This perplexed the Honcho, who believed that truth was whatever Ismism declared it to be. He took a mental note to ask the Golfer about this. "What else did the Insurrectionist say?"

"He tol' us whether Man's nature is good or bad doesn't change how much gov'ment we need. If Man's nature is good, then a powerful gov'ment ain't ne'ssary. If Man's nature is bad, then a powerful gov'ment should be avoided at all costs.'"

Blood vacated the Honcho's face and sank to his toes. The Insurrectionist's poisonous words threatened to crumble the foundations of his world. "What else did he say?" he croaked through pallid lips.

"The sheep are happier of themselves than under the care of wolves."

"Who are the wolves?" interjected Freeman.

The Man from Nebraska scowled. "The wolves pay my neighbor to let fertile ground sit idle while I work my ass off growing crops 12 hours a day, earning calluses, back aches, and not much else. The wolves pay my other neighbor welfare money, so they can eat the food that the first neighbor gets paid not to grow. The wolves plucked my only boy from behind the plow, shaved his head, and then stuck him in front of some angry Asians who shot him dead for no reason the wolves could ever explain. On top of all that, the wolves tell me I gotta keep payin' more taxes. The wolves tell me it's for the common good, and that I must have faith in things I can't see or unnerstand. I'm tired of wolves that care for me like this. I want my money back, or I'll shoot your ass off!" He angrily jabbed the shotgun into the Honcho's belly.

"Easy, big fella", said the Honcho. "You'll be in deep shit if that thing goes off."

"I'll be in less shit than you. What've I got to lose? My son? He's already dead. My farm? I can't pay the taxes I owe on it anyway. My wife? She went crazy when she got the death notice from the Marines. My neighbors? I can't tell if they're friend or foe anymore—we've all been set one against the other by our gov'ment. My faith? Faith is what got me into this mess. My self respect? That's what I'm here to salvage. Hand me back my money. All 35 years of it." The shotgun plowed deeper into the Honcho's abdomen.

Fortunately, the Honcho had an inherited Machiavellian survival instinct that had been genetically reinforced through millennia of such confrontations. He motioned for the Man from Nebraska to move closer. The man hesitatingly stepped out of his concealing shadow. The sunlight revealed a tall, lanky farmer with an honest, weathered face, a plaid shirt, denim overalls, cowhide boots, and a rumpled straw hat. His callused hands gripped his shotgun resolutely. His jaw was square, solid, and clenched. The Honcho whispered something to him. The Man from Nebraska listened with increasing interest, nodding several times. When the Honcho finished, the lanky man said, "Much obliged", and headed off at a brisk pace toward Capitol Hill with his shotgun leading the way.

"What did you tell him?" Freeman asked breathlessly.

"I told him I agreed with everything he said, and that I had voted for or against everything that he was for or against. Then I told him that Senator Smetzenbaum from Oklahoma was really responsible for all of this, and that he deserves to get his ass shot off after he refunds the 35 years of taxes."

"Do you think Smetzenbaum will crack under the pressure and refund the money?"

"That's impossible!"

"Wow! Smetzenbaum must be one tough hombre!"

"Actually, he's a mealy mouthed weasel with no intestinal fortitude", said the Honcho. "The bastard has made a career out of filibustering my best legislation just because I screwed his wife and daughter at the same time in his own bed. He won't be able to refund the money, simply because there isn't any. We're a godzillion dollars in debt."

Freeman pulled the empty pockets out of his pants. "How could I forget that?" he said facetiously. "I'm surprised he fell for your gambit. Luckily, he wasn't here to get his social security contributions back. He'd have been in for a real shock!"

"Why the hell shouldn't he fall for my gambit? He's just a hick cornhusker from Nebraska. We've fooled him for 35 years. What's one more day and one more ruse?"

"We should get back to the office", advised Freeman. "I heard buzzing in the street that Vhaicam's population doubled again, to 128,000. We'll have to lift the ceiling on the godzillion dollar national debt again so we can have more F.U.N."

The buzzing in the street was wrong. Vhaicam's population had actually quadrupled to 256,000. Worse still, the national debt had already rocketed through its previous ceiling, simply because the Treasury had made the quarterly interest payment. The national debt is like a thermonuclear explosion, in which intense heat generated by fusion leads to more fusion, which leads to more heat, which leads to more fusion, which leads to more heat, and so on, until all available fuel is consumed and the reaction dies. The sun is an example of a natural reactor that feeds on itself until it no longer exists. Likewise, as the national debt gets bigger, it requires more interest payments, which makes it even bigger, which leads to still more interest payments, and so on, until all available capital is eventually consumed, and then the nation dies in a calamitous implosion. Then, in a faraway galaxy, alien beings staring at their nighttime sky will witness a beautiful supernova. They might even form a new religion based on this mysterious cosmic event.

Fortunately, the thermonuclear debt hadn't yet fusioned the nation into oblivion. So, the Honcho threw more fuel into the fiscal reactor by raising the ceiling on the debt so the Treasury could borrow more money to keep the F.U.N. going. Unfortunately, he didn't realize that additional funding for F.U.N. was the least of his concerns. Vhaicam's social fabric was melting down, much like the meltdown percolating beneath the exploding national debt.

Before F.U.N., Vhaicam was a loose collection of primitive tribes living tenuously on the edge of starvation. When aid arrived from America, life was good, at least for a while. The Vhaicamese ate, they procreated, they ate some more, and they procreated some more. Unfortunately, no one told them there was more to Western style life than eating and procreating. They were unaware of the nutritional, educational, and economic infrastructures required to support their burgeoning numbers. So, whenever the Vhaicamese population outgrew F.U.N.'s resources, the people sank back into squalor, which required more F.U.N., which led to a larger population plummeting into squalor, and so on.

To make matters worse, certain Vhaicamese discovered they could use force to avoid starvation during the periods of squalor. Thus, armed gangs expropriated food shipments coming from F.U.N. Other Vhaicamese had to beg for food from the armed elite and promise their fidelity to the gang with the most guns. Rival gangs aligned themselves according to old tribal animosities, so a bloody civil war erupted. Now, death not only came from starvation, but also from a bullet or a slit throat. As the conflicts escalated, the fragile social and economic infrastructure disintegrated. Wretched sanitary conditions, grinding poverty, rampaging disease, anarchic lawlessness, and astonishing cruelty overwhelmed Vhaicam.

Even when America periodically increased F.U.N.'s funding, none of the food got to the starving hordes inside Vhaicam. What wasn't pilfered by roving gangs on the docks rotted in warehouses for lack of a safe distribution channel. Vhaicamese died in droves as the world watched in horror. The situation was so grim that the United(?) Nations issued a terse statement condemning the wanton violence in Vhaicam, and they threatened to issue an even harsher condemnation if the warring factions didn't cease and desist.

Catholic missionaries made the situation even worse. Not only were they committed to propagating their faith through wildfire population growth, they were also Jesuits, so they were equally committed to propagating Marxism. Marxist Jesuit missionaries are extraordinary beings. Born of wealthy families in capitalist nations, they devote their lives to sending food earned and produced by their parents to people in starving countries. Then they tell the starving natives that communism is their only salvation, even though communism was incapable of adequately feeding them. Paradoxically, the Jesuits also convince them to hate American capitalism, even though food produced there is the only sustenance for both the missionaries and the natives.

As the Marxist Jesuit missionaries proselytized the Vhaicamese, communism became an energetic force. Once communism gained a foothold, other communist countries aided their Vhaicamese comrades with firearms, artillery, advisers, and divisions of soldiers. Soon the northern half of Vhaicam was under the polished jackboots of a proletarian dictatorship. So now not only was there tribal warfare for control of food, the tribes and the communists were killing each other for control of Vhaicam. Extraordinary numbers of people were dying from starvation and armed conflict. And whenever lots of people die, someone must be blamed.

* * *

"Murderer!"

The Honcho looked up suspiciously from the Wall Street Journal. Freeman had just stormed into his office shouting something that hadn't yet penetrated the barriers his brain had erected to filter out the things that Freeman stormed into his office shouting. "What did you say?" he snarled.

"Murderer!" repeated Freeman.

No one ever dared call him a murderer before, despite many legitimate opportunities, including his support for the Vietnam conflict, his backing of abortion rights, his Mafia entanglement that led to several political assassinations, his legislation to make nutritional supplements illegal, his support of the Waco and Ruby Ridge assaults, his backing of genocidal right wing dictators in Latin America, and his complicity in Senator Smetzenbaum's death at the hands of the Man from Nebraska. "What the fuck are you talking about?" he barked.

"It's in all the papers!" Freeman waved a rolled-up newspaper under the Honcho's crooked nose. "Blame must be assigned whenever lots of people die. The press says you're the culprit. They're calling you a murderer!"

The Honcho's face turned crimson with rage. "That's preposterous!"

"But sir!" said But Sir!, who had followed Freeman. "People believe even preposterous things when the talk show hosts broadcast them."

The Honcho stomped his feet in frustration. "Damn Oprah and her cronies! What started them on my trail?"

"The communists in Vhaicam, sir", said Freeman.

"Those homosexual sonsofbitches! Why did they single me out?"

"Communists blame every evil on American capitalist imperialism. Since lots of Vhaicamese are dying, they're blaming you as the preeminent agent of American capitalist imperialism because of your F.U.N. initiative. So now the papers are proclaiming you a murderer."

"Damn! I was hoping they'd blame Bill Gates."

"Take this seriously, sir", advised Freeman. "The purpose of F.U.N. in Vhaicam was to divert attention from your embarrassing attempt to annihilate the planet in the Bavarian Forest. Unfortunately, the newspapers are calling the Vhaicam relief effort a complete disaster. They're also resurrecting the Bavarian Forest fiasco again. It's a public relations nightmare. We've opened Pandora's Box."

"Pandora's Box hell!" exclaimed the Honcho. "We've opened Pandora's Coffin."

"Because so many Vhaicamese are dying from your F.U.N. idea?"

"No, because my re-election campaign is becoming a cadaver that will fit nicely in it. Right next to your cadaver, since you thought up this absurd F.U.N. idea. You have exactly thirty seconds to solve this mess for me!" screamed the Honcho, waving a clenched fist under Freeman's nose.

"Thirty seconds?" croaked Freeman.

"Twenty-nine, twenty-eight, twenty-seven . . ."

Freeman fainted under the pressure, dropping impolitely to the carpet in an inanimate pile. The Honcho put his size 14 shoe on Freeman's prone body and rolled him over with a violent kick, causing his ball and chain to clatter loudly. Giving up on his comatose liaison, he turned to But Sir! for help. "What do I do now?"

"Sir, the Vhaicamese believe you're an archetypal American capitalist imperialist, because that's what the communists tell them to think. We need to convince them that you're really not an imperialist."

"Shit, that's easy", said the Honcho. "To change the mythology of a nation, you take over its mass media, you set up mandatory public schooling to propagate a rewritten history that favorably depicts your hegemony, you infiltrate their government with secret service operatives, you fund a beholden military, and you establish a vicious police force that terrorizes renegades who don't worship the new mythology. We do it all the time."

"But Sir!" squealed But Sir!. "Are you suggesting that we convince the Vhaicamese we're not imperialistic by being even more imperialistic?"

"There's no other way to do it", said the Honcho solemnly.

"Why don't we just leave them alone?"

"Don't be foolish. They'd think we were up to something, if we weren't up to something."

"But Sir! That doesn't make any sense."

"Maybe not on our side of the looking glass," said the Honcho. "Look at it this way. If we don't surreptitiously dominate their culture, their politics, and their very lives, just think what those godless communists will do to them."

"Forget about what the godless communists will do to the Vhaicamese", said But Sir!. "Worry about what the American voters will do to you."

"How did it end up like this?" moaned the Head Honcho. "It began with good intentions."

Freeman's ball and chain rattled as he slowly regained consciousness. He sat up and rubbed his bruised skull. His eyes were still glassy, and his mind was clouded. "I had a vision", he mumbled.

"A vision? Of what?" demanded the Honcho.

"It was very strange", said Freeman uncertainly. "When you counted down my thirty seconds, I slipped away to a dark, terrifying place. Someone . . . or something . . . was counting there, too. It was so hot there that I feared my flesh would melt. The stench was so horrible that I wished I had no sense of smell. It smelled like thousands of rotting corpses, as if all the dead Vhaicamese were tossed in a big compost pile. I heard tortured screams in the distance. Despite the darkness, I could see the ghostly green Beast that was counting. Curious, I moved toward it. Then it spun around and skewered me with scorching red eyes that tore through me like laser beams...."

"The Beast didn't say anything?" interrupted But Sir!.

Freeman hesitated. "He said he was glad to see I still had Cassandra's ball and chain."

"Who is Cassandra, and why was she in this vision?" demanded the Honcho.

"You wouldn't understand."

"What else did the Beast say?" snarled the Honcho impatiently.

"He was counting the Good Intentions he had collected for the construction of his road."

"What road?" asked the Honcho suspiciously.

"He didn't say. But I suspect it's not a pleasant road, because of the screams that made my skin crawl and my hair stand on end."

The Honcho became uneasy as Freeman's vision unfolded. "Did the Beast mention the F.U.N. disaster in Vhaicam?"

"He said he unearthed a particularly magnificent Good Intention today. I asked him if it was the F.U.N. Good Intention. He said he'd embedded that one into his road a few weeks ago."

"Which one was it, then?" asked the Honcho.

"He said I'd find out soon enough."

"And then what?"

"And then nothing", said Freeman. "The next thing I knew, I was sitting here rubbing my head."

The Head Honcho smiled and said nothing. His alcohol-reddened eyes were compressed into piercing slits by his Cheshire Cat grin. Freeman shuddered and resisted a chilling urge to do a sign of the cross. He guessed that the

Honcho knew what Good Intention the Devil was so proud of.

In the meantime, Satan's slitted red eyes glowed with carnivorous excitement. Among the menagerie of Good Intentions that spilled his way today through the portals of hell was the one he desperately yearned for. It was the Mother of all Good Intentions, wherein some humans gird themselves to defend all that's Good on their side of the looking glass, against other humans who gird themselves to defend all that's Good on their side of the glass. Out of this impending clash of good-intentioned humans, Lucifer anticipated millions of souls plummeting down the brilliant ruby Road to Hell.

Satan stroked this Good Intention lovingly, admiring its phosphorescent magnificence with the soulless joy of a vampire at dusk.

War was the name of this Mother of all Good Intentions. And in time of war, the Devil makes more room in hell, according to an old German proverb. Satan silently congratulated himself on the progress of his macabre plans.

Chapter Seven:
"The Human Bologna Grinder"

> "No one is so senseless as to choose of his own will war rather than peace, since in peace sons bury their fathers, and in war, fathers bury their sons."
> —Croesus (According to Herodotus)

"The answer is simple", said the Safari Golfer. "Kill them at both ends."

The Head Honcho had come to the Golfer's newly erected Temple of Ismism, Political Correctness, and other Will O' the Wisps for advice on how to quell Vhaicam's exploding population, which had quadrupled another four times to a staggering 65 million. "How do you kill them at both ends? By lopping off their head and feet simultaneously?" He salivated, because this would make the Red Queen green with envy. He couldn't wait to boast to the Mad Hatter about it.

The Golfer sighed. "You don't kill people at both ends. You kill the population at both ends."

"What's the difference?"

"Lopping off heads and feet at the same time is very difficult, especially with fidgety folks. It's far easier to kill the population at both ends, which merely involves killing babies and old people."

"That sounds un-American."

"Absolutely not!" declared the world's spiritual leader. "Most Americans are comfortably between those two demographic extremes. They kill unwanted babies by the millions in government funded abortion clinics. And they're warming to the idea of euthanasia, since old people are also such a burden."

"But there're no old Vhaicamese. Their population explosion is a recent phenomenon, so they're all still in the primes of their lives."

"We can't have an unbalanced slaughter", mused the Safari Golfer. "Is there a legitimate reason to kill people in their primes?"

"We can send them off to war to defend us against every other Ism but our own."

"What would you do without me?" beamed the Golfer. He retired to his private chapel to practice putting, leaving the Honcho alone in the cavernous Temple of Ismism, Political Correctness, and other Will O' the Wisps. He did a sign of the cross and rushed out.

The Senator summoned his staff for an announcement. "I've spoken to the Golfer", he declared solemnly. "He recommends reducing the Vhaicamese population by killing them at both ends."

"Does he mean we should lop off their heads and feet?" asked Freeman.

"Don't be stupid!" said the Honcho haughtily. "He

means we should kill their old people and their young people. It's the American way."

"But Sir!" exclaimed But Sir! "Vhaicam doesn't have any old people. Their population explosion is relatively new."

"Exactly! So we'll have to send them off to war to defend themselves against every other Ism except their own, in order to kill those in the prime of their lives."

"But who would they declare war against?" asked But Sir!.

"A poor, underdeveloped, third world country nobody gives a damn about."

"Like Detroit?" suggested Freeman.

The Honcho scowled. "No, you ass hole. Detroit's too close to our borders."

"Maybe so, but they solved their own population problem. In twenty years, they went from two million residents to one million, without killing their population at both ends."

"So I should appoint the ghost of Coleman Young as mayor of Vhaicam?"

"No", conceded Freeman. "It would cause a mad rush for the suburbs. Since oceans rather than suburbs surround Vhaicam, millions of Vhaicamese would drown. Better stick with the war idea. It's wholesome entertainment for CNN nightly news. Mass drowning isn't."

"Precisely." The Honcho turned to Jefferson. "What do you think, Insurrection Czar? Should we coerce Vhaicam's government to declare war on somebody?"

Jefferson met the Honcho's inquiring stare. "Wars fill the pages of history with momentous events. Blessed is the nation that furnishes nothing for history to say. The protection of human life, and not its destruction, is the only legitimate object of government. Why would the Vhaicamese want to commence a war? Unless coerced by their governments, most people aren't naturally combative."

"Holy shit!" the Honcho exclaimed. "I had no idea people might think like that. What do we do if that happens?"

"Not a problem", declared Freeman. "If the Vhaicamese won't declare war on a poor underdeveloped third world nation, then we'll declare war on Vhaicam, which is a poor underdeveloped third world nation itself."

"Attaboy!" The Head Honcho slapped Freeman heartily on the back. "Goddamn! It's great when a plan comes together."

"But Sir!" interjected But Sir!. "Don't we need to do some things before declaring war?"

The Honcho was puzzled. "Like what?"

"Like rescuing our POW's from the last war."

"Is that a rule?"

"Rules can't be constructed by any reasonable person to codify the horrible protocol of war", replied But Sir! resolutely. "But my conscience squirms when I hear reports of Americans sighted in prison camps in Son Tay or in concentration camps near Ho Chi Minh's tomb in Hanoi. I can't sleep when I hear of satellites sighting the letter "K", the Air Force symbol for 'pilot in distress', scrawled in Morse Code on prison rooftops in North Vietnam. My heart cramps when seeing grainy photographs of aging American GIs behind bars and fences in Haiphong and Da Nang. I served in Vietnam. I came back with fewer friends than I went there with. A lot fewer. Deep down in my soul I believe some are still alive there." He wiped a tear from his pale cheek. "I'm sorry. I'm getting maudlin."

"Tell someone who gives a damn", said the Honcho. "What else do we need to do?"

"We need a reason for going to war", But Sir! replied through tight lips.

"We already have one. We need to kill the Vhaicamese at both ends to reduce their population so I can avoid the political embarrassment of thousands of them dying from starvation instead."

"Is that what you really want historians to write about this war?" persisted But Sir!.

The Honcho silently evaluated the potential reasons for going to war that historians might look favorably upon. One was that Vhaicam had split into two separate nations, the northern one a communist dictatorship. Whenever an Asian nation splits in two, America must go to war, especially if communists run the northern half. This precedent started with North Korea and continued with North Vietnam, because it's America's duty to do everything the opposite of the communists, even if it means dying alongside them in an Asian rice paddy.

It would be easy to convince America that communists intended to systematically overrun Asian states until they had circled the globe and arrived at the White House. He could simply reveal that CIA agents had captured secret documents revealing China's malevolent ambitions. The "captured secret documents" ploy is useful for producing evidence to justify an action, without having to actually produce evidence. It's sufficient to merely allude to the existence of secret documents, which can't be publicly revealed. The CIA has a four-story warehouse containing 200 million classified documents, including 800 manuals that specify what else should be classified. The only way to see these documents is to become a CIA agent, after which you're forbidden to reveal their contents. It's the bureaucratic equivalent of a celestial black hole. Frequently, the authors of classified documents aren't permitted to ever see them again, because they lack proper clearance. The oldest document in the warehouse is a report on World War I troop movements, which is still considered confidential by a bureaucrat who is apparently unaware of the Treaty at Versailles.

If communist xenophobia isn't enough justification for war, the glory and sanctity of U.S. military bands is. The bands are a magnificent American military tradition descended from the fife and drum corps that led revolutionary soldiers in battle against the British. Today's bands are polished extravaganzas costing $200 million annually. An investment of this magnitude begs to be used for leading gallant troops to die to the beat of a John Phillip Sousa march. The military not only invests heavily in musical instruments, it also invests heavily in bullets, rockets, and guns. These beg to be used too. Using the stockpiled military bands and associated armaments boosts the economy as replenishments are built for the instruments and ordnance consumed by warfare, which is why George Orwell predicted that the East and the West would maintain continuing military confrontation. As the economies of both hemispheres produce weapons, the national leaders of the combatants entrench their power.

If that isn't sufficient for going to war, there's the Mother of all Reasons. The Honcho could announce that oil was discovered in North Vhaicam, and that the Vhaicamese might form a cartel and slap an embargo on us, thereby devastating our economy and idling the citizens who would otherwise be building band instruments and bullets. The Mother of all Reasons had never failed to justify a military conflict.

After the Honcho shared these thoughts, his staff agreed that America should declare war on North Vhaicam, except for Jefferson, who sat quietly with a furrowed brow and a dumbfounded expression. The Honcho ignored Jefferson's silent veto. "It's settled! We'll save my re-election campaign by declaring war and killing Vhaicam's population at both ends!"

"But Sir!" interjected But Sir!. "None of us have the authority to declare war. We need to involve other people."

The Honcho glared at him. "Like who? Jane Fonda?"

But Sir! sighed. "No, but what about the President? He's the Commander in Chief."

"He'll cooperate", smiled the Senator. "If not, he'll get a visit from Sammy Gioncarlo, my Sicilian golfing buddy who knows a lot of good stories. There's one in particular about an Irish Catholic President and his Attorney General brother who attacked organized crime. Whenever Sammy tells the punchline to this story, the President is suddenly agreeable to anything."

"What about Congress?" persisted But Sir!. "They have the sole authority for declaring war, no matter what stories Sammy tells the President."

"Have you forgotten I'm the Chairman of every significant congressional committee? What's good for me is good for the Armed Services Committee, and what's good for them is good for the Senate, and what's good for the Senate is therefore good for the country. But, we don't actually have to declare war in order to declare war."

"But Sir!" protested But Sir!. "How can you declare war without declaring war?"

"It's a cherished tradition in Congress. It enables us to engage in the violence of war without the political baggage of having declared war, so that when our constituents complain their children are being killed in the war, we can honesty argue that they aren't being killed in the war, because we haven't declared war."

"But if you don't declare war, how will your enemies know you're fighting them?"

"Their first clue is usually the smart bombs dropped down their chimneys by stealth bombers flying unseen over their sleepy heads. If that doesn't make our intentions clear, we pass a resolution in Congress defining our non-declaration of war. During the Vietnam non-war, we passed the Gulf of Tonkin Resolution, which empowered President Johnson to 'take all necessary measures to repel any armed attack against U.S. forces.' This somehow authorized us to attack North Vietnam, even though they had never actually attacked us. It eased the minds of parents whose children were dying in Vietnam jungles, since it wasn't a declared war that was devouring their offspring. We need a resolution like the Gulf of Tonkin one", said the Honcho abruptly. "Are there any gulfs in Vhaicam?"

"How about the Gulf of Credibility?" volunteered Jefferson.

"Attaboy! I'll have one of my golfing buddy admirals stage a skirmish in the Gulf of Credibility with a North Vhaicamese fishing boat allegedly disguised as a Chinese trawler. Then Congress can pass a Gulf of Credibility Resolution authorizing our military to launch a defensive attack. The non-war will then unfold of its own accord. In the mean time, we'll initiate a grain embargo against the Vhaicamese."

"But Sir!" exclaimed But Sir!. "Won't the Vhaicamese starve if we do that?"

"Yes, but we need to kill the Vhaicamese at both ends to stop their population explosion and salvage my campaign. The non-war will only kill them at one end. The grain embargo will kill them at the other end as children die from malnutrition."

"But Sir! Won't American farmers lose valuable markets if we embargo?"

"They should be willing to make any sacrifice to stop the onrushing tide of communism."

"But Sir!" objected But Sir!. "We fight communists because they're ruthless authoritarian rulers. Your grain embargo is just another form of authoritarianism. Why should our farmers acquiesce to your authoritarianism, just to fend off communist authoritarianism? What's the difference to the farmer?"

"The difference is, I'm doing it for their own good. If

they understood Ismism's tenets, they wouldn't worry about such petty things."

"I thought Ismism didn't have any tenets", said Freeman.

"It all depends on circumstances, such as poll results", explained the Honcho. "That's why clear understanding is required, and that's why we have the Safari Golfer to give us clear understanding in the most divinely incomprehensible terms possible."

"But Sir!" exclaimed But Sir!, "The Vhaicam disaster started with your Food for Undernourished Nations effort. Now you're going to starve the beneficiaries of F.U.N. with a grain embargo. How will you explain this policy paradox to the voters?"

"I won't", said the Honcho haughtily. "Freeman will. He's my public relations liaison."

Freeman choked on the phlegm in his throat. "How in hell am I going to explain that paradox?"

"Quit your bitching!" commanded the Honcho. "If your job was easy, we'd get somebody else to do it. Besides, you didn't get the nickname 'Yessir!' for nothing."

Thus began the Vhaicam non-war. The staged confrontation in the Gulf of Credibility between American destroyers and the Vhaicamese fishing boat that was alleged to be a Chinese trawler by captured secret documents nobody was permitted to see, went off with only a minor glitch. The glitch was that the Gulf of Credibility was not a real geographical entity, but merely a sarcastic jest by Jefferson. This confused naval planners for several days, until an enterprising lieutenant, who had tired of vainly searching maps for a Gulf named Credibility, picked an anonymous inlet and penned in the name Credibility, so the operation could finally commence.

America lurched energetically into full-scale non-war. Thousands of troops were airlifted to South Vhaicam.

Armadas of ships loaded with tanks, missile launchers, machine guns, helicopters, bombers, fighter planes, torpedoes, defoliant chemicals, and band instruments steamed overseas. Generals and admirals feverishly developed strategies. Corporals and sergeants feverishly readied their men for the battles ahead. The most powerful military in the universe mobilized as the world trembled.

The home front also mobilized. Tearful wives and mothers waved goodbye as their husbands and sons boarded military transports, and then took their places on the assembly lines of the defense industry. The media continually broadcast the unfolding non-war in Asia, including detailed maps of Vhaicam with large arrows indicating important activity. Retired military experts analyzed the battles on TV as if doing play-by-play at the Super Bowl.

The omnipresence of these TV maps was mesmerizing. If you squint enough at Vhaicam's shape and used a little imagination, an old-fashioned bologna grinder appears in your mind's eye. The island is long and narrow, with a funnel-shaped promontory to the North, and a discharge-shaped promontory to the West. A narrow L-shaped peninsula juts out perpendicularly from the east coast of the island like the handle of this imaginary bologna grinder. This "handle" was an extension of the line separating American troops from enemy troops. The line moved to and fro daily, depending on the outcome of each battle. The swooshing arrows depicting this daily activity created the illusion that the peninsular "handle" was actually spinning. Other arrows, depicting American troop ships steaming toward Vhaicam, were being sucked into the funnel at the top of the bologna grinder. This flesh-grinding imagery didn't dampen the patriotic fervor sweeping America like an epidemic.

The Safari Golfer fueled this patriotic fervor by selling non-war bonds to the public, in order to finance the massive military spending required to defeat the communists threatening the American way of life on the other side of the planet. The Head Honcho appeared on TV each night shouting his battle cry of "speak loudly and carry a big stick." He often punctuated this statement, when the cameras were off, by pointing to his groin and declaring "and I got your big stick right here".

The non-war effort was so massive that the Pentagon ran out of room, so Congress authorized funding for expansion. Since the pentagonal designation no longer described the newly remodeled eight-sided gargantuan edifice, its name was changed to the Octagon. This geometric reconfiguration followed precedent set by previous American military build-ups. The Defense Department headquarters was originally a small rectangular structure in Arlington County, Virginia. However, World War I military growth necessitated expansion of the building. The east and west sides were flared out, such that the oddly shaped military headquarters came to be called the Trapezoid.

World War II, the second in a long-running series of wars to end all wars, caused history's largest military mobilization. This necessitated another expansion and reshaping of America's military headquarters, so in 1943 the Pentagon was christened. At the time, it was the world's largest office building, providing generals and admirals with 34 million square feet to house countless colonels, captains, and lieutenants, whose calling in this life was to efficiently send on to the next life as many people as possible.

So when the Vhaicam conflict came along, expansion of the Pentagon into the Octagon was inevitable, if only by precedent. The facility now sprawled out of Arlington County into Fairfax County and was bigger than several small nations. It had twenty mailing addresses in three different zip codes. The northern half had one telephone area code, the southern another. The complex was so big that the sun set fifteen minutes earlier on the eastern perimeter than on the western. Huge buildings like the Octagon invite hordes of workers to fill available office space, so it was soon brimming with legions of military personnel.

Senior officers nurtured by the Octagon eventually became leaders in government and private industry. This incestuous menage-a-trois insulated the Octagon from downsizing. Private industry eagerly employed retired military officers to get the inside track on contracts fueling the Octagonal juggernaut. Military officers moved easily into politics too, as companies feeding at the military trough eagerly provided campaign financing. From this beachhead on Capitol Hill, a steady flow of defense spending was ensured to private firms with umbilical cords attached to the Octagon. This business, military, and political alliance is called the Military Industrial Complex.

Riding his horse to work one day, Jefferson inadvertently crashed into the Octagon, which overflowed the night before across his usual route through the woods near Washington. The unexpected collision sent him sprawling. Unhurt, he remounted his steed and galloped around the perimeter of the mysterious monolith, expecting only a brief detour. Unfortunately, the building went on and on for miles. He eventually got to work, where he asked Freeman about the gigantic, continent-sized structure that had suddenly sprouted in the woods of Fairfax County.

"The only mysterious continent-sized structure in the area is the Octagon", said Freeman. "But I thought it was still in Arlington County."

Jefferson scratched his head. "It was definitely octagonal. I traversed its entire perimeter on my steed. It not only occupies Fairfax County, but also Montgomery and Prince Georges Counties."

"Hmmm", mused Freeman. "The Octagon may have overflowed into neighboring counties because its mission was expanded to include not only making the world safe for democracy, but also getting the Head Honcho re-elected. Were there any military personnel around?"

"Aye! The earth trembled under thousands of polished jackboots."

"I'll be damned!"

"We will all be damned", agreed Jefferson.

"No, I mean that proves it was the Octagon! Were you hurt by the collision?"

"Fortunately, I was unharmed."

"That's unusual", said Freeman. "Most people die when they encounter the Octagon. Why don't you get a car so that your horse doesn't gallop into continent-sized octagonal structures anymore?"

"I prefer my horse", said Jefferson. "It at least has the sense to ignore 'left turn only' signs."

"Suit yourself, but people are beginning to think you're nuts."

"Oh? Tell me, what do they think of a man who drags around an iron ball and chain every step of his miserable life?"

"We all have crosses to bear", Freeman said quietly.

"Indeed", concurred Jefferson. "The biggest cross is the blood-stained military cruciform that has been lain on our backs. Sound principles do not justify taxing ourselves for wars that might not happen but for the temptations offered by the very existence of that military horde. A huge military machine is dangerous to a nation's rights, because it places citizens totally at the mercy of their leaders. People cannot tamely look on and see their representatives violate, instead of protect, their inalienable right to life.

"This cross lain upon our shoulders not only burdens our every step and our every productive effort, it grinds our children like grist under an irresistible stone. The innate spirit of this country is totally adverse to a large military force. It should be said of us that our people are so wise that they will not hire themselves out to be shot at for a few dollars a day, that a standing army is inconceivable here in America, because we have no fools to furnish the flesh for the hellish bologna grinder. What inducement has the farmer to lay aside his plow and go to war with the farmer of another country?

"Standing armies are inconsistent with freedom. Better to make every man a civilian soldier, and trust him to voluntarily defend his country whenever his own good sense of self-preservation dictates. Distrust leaders who seek to disarm you personally, and to put in place instead an omnipotent military machine beholden to no civilian control. For a people who desire to remain free, a well-organized and well-armed civilian militia is their best security. This supremacy of civil over military authority I deem an essential principle of the government founded on these shores many years ago. To permit anything else is to deliver your children into the jaws of an insatiable wolf over which you have no control, a wolf whose hunger grows with each succeeding repast.

"Let the rest of the world be the cannibals eating one another. A war between Russia and Germany, for instance, would be like a battle between the kite hawk and the snake. Whichever destroys the other leaves one less destroyer in the world. This pugnacious strain of mankind we should restrain and starve, rather than unleash and fuel. The cocks of the hen yard kill one another. Bears, bulls, and rams do the same. I've always hoped that our nation would prove how much happier is the life of the feeder than the fighter, that we would milk the proverbial cow, while the Russians held her by the horns, and the Germans by the tail, pulling with all of their belligerent might, expending prodigious amounts of national energy, only to suffer their demise in battle without having tasted the fruit of their struggle. On the useful pursuits of peace alone can a stable prosperity be found."

"Wow!" said Freeman. "I haven't heard words like that since we captured a pamphlet distributed by the

Insurrectionist last month. Hey, are you somehow involved....?"

Jefferson interrupted abruptly. "My friend, ask not of me such questions. Things are never what they seem in this city. I have pledged my sacred honor to accomplish a mission that gives meaning to my entire existence, a mission that won't allow me to rest peacefully until it is completed. There is much danger everywhere. Take heed." Freeman instinctively looked over his shoulder. When he looked back, Jefferson was gone. In his stead was a rush of cold, damp air that chilled Freeman to the core of his being. He looked around anxiously, but saw no sign of Jefferson, who seemed to have simply vanished. He returned to his desk, dragging his ball and chain along with morbid thoughts that were heavy as rusted iron with troubling questions.

Meanwhile, the Vhaicamese non-war was being escalated with murderously efficient vigor. America pursued a righteous defensive struggle against the communist hordes with staggering offensive military might. As the casualties mounted, even the United(?) Nations shied away from stepping between the combatants, explaining to the world that the situation was too dangerous for peacemakers to be loitering about. Into this vacuum of U.(?) N. cowardice rushed the Orwellian philosophy of maintaining peace in the world through eternal conflict.

The North and South Vhaicamese tore into each other with all of the sophisticated military technology that their Chinese and American surrogates could muster. Backfire bombers and SS-20 missiles were countered by B-1 bombers and Tomahawk cruise missiles. C47 transports with Quad-50 machine guns strafed hidden enemies in rain forests. Beehive bombs fired from Howitzers sent thousands of small darts ripping through the jungle underbrush. Harrier jump jets hovered over the battlefield, launching laser-guided bombs and Maverick air-to-surface missiles. Cluster bombs, containing hundreds of tiny bomblets packed with anti-personnel shards, were dropped on enemy troops. Aden cannons fired 2600 armor piercing rounds per minute into hostile convoys. Sidewinder heat seeking missiles honed in on the engines of combat vehicles. MIG and Tomcat jets engaged in spectacular dogfights in the smoke-filled sky. NAVSTAR satellites scanned the earth below for enemy movements. Infrared night vision devices allowed the killing to continue with deadly efficiency even after the sun set on the broiling conflagration consuming the landscape and its occupants.

As these technological marvels were deployed, thousands of real humans died in the killing fields. Many of the native Vhaicamese didn't know why they were being killed or who was commanding such mystifying weaponry. They didn't understand things like blood drives for wounded soldiers, so they feared that the medicos sucking plasma out of healthy soldiers were really vampires. As a precaution, some Vhaicamese drove stakes into the hearts of sleeping doctors.

Some observers were disturbed by the American military strategy. Despite heroic thrusts and parries, the North and South Vhaicamese armies remained stalemated along the 33rd diagonal. The North Vhaicamese couldn't penetrate the Southern defenses due to the superior technology of their American protectors. American forces were unwilling to attack North Vhaicam in full force, since they were there to defend South Vhaicam, not to invade North Vhaicam. Day after day, thousands upon thousands of troops were hurled against each other, with neither army gaining an advantage.

Normally, the sheer volume of troops being killed would have eventually exhausted the supply of human cannon fodder, and the non-war would have ended for lack of raw material. But, the Rabbit People were extraordinary breeders, so there was an inexhaustible supply of Vhaicamese gristle to feed the human bologna grinder creating a river of blood all along the 33rd diagonal. Unfortunately, Americans were being fed into this bologna grinder as fast as the Vhaicamese. This troubled the Head Honcho because the boys being ground into hamburger could only vote for him if they survived to reach voting age. He became acutely despondent over this dilemma.

"I've backed myself into a corner", he moaned to Freeman. "I thought this non-war would be a tremendous political feather in my cap by slaughtering the population explosion that your stupid F.U.N. idea created. Unfortunately, the brutal carnage of war isn't the political windfall I expected. I've discovered that dead people can't vote, except in Chicago."

"We should just bomb the hell of North Vhaicam and end it quickly", said Freeman. We've spent trillions of dollars amassing history's deadliest arsenal. Why not fully utilize it and spare thousands of potential voters?"

"Because we haven't actually declared war on the Gooks. Remember, we intentionally made this conflict a non-war, because parents get unhappy when their children die in declared wars. Our mission is to defend South Vhaicam."

"How about if we pull out and let the South Vhaicamese determine their own fate?"

"What?! And lose the war? No American leader ever got re-elected after losing a war!" The Honcho stared at Freeman suspiciously. "Are you a homosexual communist pacifist?"

"I like girls! I'm just concerned about the thousands of young men that we're forcing to fight on the other side of the world in a war that isn't a war, and in which the only outcomes for them are death, injury, or psychological trauma."

"They're performing a noble patriotic service for their nation", said the Honcho, "which is primarily to ensure that I get re-elected."

"Suicide isn't patriotism. Death isn't the purpose of life. A nation that drives its youth to death without a purpose can't claim nobility."

"Bullshit!" cursed the Honcho. "Everything is relative. Sure, maybe a few of our boys are taking flesh wounds, but look at what other dictators did. Hitler killed 6 million Jews because they were money-grubbing capitalists who were polluting the genetic purity of the Aryan race. Stalin killed 16 million people with a man-made famine while he collectivized his farmlands. And when the world pointed accusatory fingers at him, he killed his census takers, because they couldn't 'find' the population that he'd murdered. I may not be pure as the driven snow, but I'm purer than some of the alternatives. I don't want your smarmy moralizing. I just want a way out of this mess."

"I don't have any ideas", confessed Freeman.

"Then get your ass over to Vhaicam, and don't come back until you do!" The Honcho stood up summarily as Freeman's cue to leave. Freeman ignored his leader's unspoken command. He was paralyzed by the frightening prospect of being dumped amidst rampant mayhem and murder. "Get your leaden ass to Vhaicam now!" roared the Honcho, who looked eager to strangle him.

"All right! I'm going!" Freeman shouted. "But I'll be pissed if I get killed over there! And I'll be even madder if I get the clap."

"If you're concerned about dying, see the Safari Golfer on your way to the airport. He'll hear your confession and pray for you, but only if you buy a non-war savings bond from him."

"But the Golfer is a secular mystic, not a religious one."

"What difference does it make? The important thing to remember is that whoever controls the mythology rules the world. It doesn't matter whether the mythology is divine or secular."

* * *

A day later, Freeman was wearing camouflage khaki inside a foxhole just 600 yards from the 33rd diagonal in Vhaicam, where the non-war was being ruthlessly waged. It was a ghoulishly dark moonless and starless night. Occasional muzzle flashes from blurting machine guns and lightning flashes of exploding ordnance on the horizon made the return to darkness even more suffocating and terrifying. A constant, inescapable rain soaked his ill-fitting uniform. Muddy rivulets ran down the foxhole walls and turned the soil into slimy goo that seeped into every bodily crevice.

A panoply of noises froze his heart. A nearby mortar blast rattled his nervous system. A cannon shot screamed overhead at mach three, arriving and passing in an unearthly rising and descending crescendo. Bullets whizzed by like buzzing insects with skull-crushing bites. A jet thundered by, spewing 130-decibel cacophony. The rapid whump! whump! whump! of a helicopter gun ship reverberated against the night like the heartbeat of a tortured universe.

Human sounds were the most disturbing. Pain-filled screeches announced a direct hit. Agonized moans heralded long waits for exhausted medics. Soldiers cursed malfunctioning equipment and the bad karma causing their miserable predicament. A rifleman wept over a compatriot lost to the Grim Reaper. Disoriented squadron leaders barked out terse commands. But the most maddening human sound was the arcane chatter pouring from the other fellow in Freeman's foxhole, who apparently was convincing himself he was still alive by delivering an unending monologue with machine gun rapidity.

Freeman, in his effort to find a solution for the non-war devouring the Honcho's potential voters, was asking the poor sonsofbitches who were getting shot at for ideas, figuring that these front line troops had the most vested interest in thinking of clever ways out of this mess. Unfortunately, most of their ideas involved killing various American leaders for condemning them to this hellish existence for no reason that any of them could understand. The Head Honcho was at the top of their hit lists.

Freeman's foxhole hopping to interview soldiers had deposited him with the lad who wouldn't stop talking. He was eager to escape the mind-numbing drivel cascading out of the youth's mouth. Unfortunately, the raging battle had intensified, making a sprint to another subterranean refuge exceptionally dangerous. He had two choices. He could endure the maddening monologue of his temporary companion, or he could stand up and take a bullet in the head. He stood up.

No bullets slammed into his skull. Instead, he saw an amazing sight. Garishly silhouetted by strobe flashes of exploding ammo was a man running a life-or-death sprint across the 33rd diagonal, dodging bullets and bombs that miraculously had not yet obliterated him. Freeman stood transfixed, watching this desperate enemy skate and slide across the muddy Vhaicamese soil. Freeman's suspense mounted. The suicidal figure was heading directly his way. A moment later, the mud-soaked man collided brutally with him. They plummeted heavily to the slimy bottom of the foxhole and became entangled with the verbose youth that had never stopped talking.

All three of them laid in the muck intertwined like snakes. Freeman cleared his mouth of mud and shouted, "Who the fuck are you?"

The other two responded with a stereophonic "Who the fuck are you?"

"I'm Freeman", he offered as they extricated themselves from each other. "I'm a public relations liaison for the federal government. I don't belong in this foxhole."

"I'm Sam Winters", said the youth that had talked Freeman to the brink of insanity. "I'm a private in the U.S. Army. I'm pretty sure I don't belong in this foxhole either."

"I'm Aiden Tyler Smith III", said the mysterious man who had made the death-defying battlefield dash. Reeking of prep school arrogance, he added, "I'm a Jesuit Marxist missionary. I'm absolutely certain I don't belong in this foxhole, since my dad is a wealthy American industrialist."

Freeman shook his head. "This is too weird. None of us belong in this foxhole, which is the most god-forsaken spot on earth, yet here we are."

After an uncomfortable moment of silence, Sam Winters asked, "Why _are_ we here, then?"

"The Head Honcho sent me here to figure out how to end this non-war, which was supposed to stop the population explosion created by our F.U.N. program and the communist scourge started by the Jesuit Marxists", replied Freeman.

"I'm here because I was too fucking stupid to go to college or be born of rich parents", said Winters. "The army was the only decent job I could get after squandering my teens smoking dope, drinking beer, and screwing ugly but willing girls. Unfortunately, I got sent to Vhaicam by the Head Honcho and his generals to be killed. Seems too harsh of a punishment for drinking a few beers and screwing some pimpled girls."

Winters and Freeman turned to Aiden Tyler Smith III. "I came to Vhaicam, he began, "to convert the natives to Catholicism and Communism. I was a missionary propagating ism's in a world that I hadn't lived in long enough to know anything about, which just makes me a pest. I was an ideologue intent on installing the dictatorship of the proletariat everywhere, to fulfill a youthful urge for rebellion against the establishment represented by my wealthy father. I was jealous of his success, which I interpreted as exploitation of the working class and as an inordinate focus on the accumulation of worldly goods. The Jesuit Marxists attracted me because they had added Catholic mysticism to the dialectic materialism of Marxism. Christian maxims such as 'the meek shall inherit the earth', 'the first shall be last', and 'the Lord's Kingdom is not of this world' justified my Marxist tendency to despise my father's wealth, and also eased my fear of being unable to achieve all that he did, simply by convincing myself that his achievements were immoral. These Christian maxims spiritually excoriated the wealth-creating dynamics of capitalism, which made it easier for me and the Vhaicamese to accept the wealth-deteriorating philosophy of communism. There was a better life waiting for us in heaven, so there was no reason to value a high living standard on earth.

"We were wildly successful converting the Vhaicamese to Marxism and Catholicism. They were eager to embrace any ism that absolved them of responsibility for their own actions and that refocused their lives on heaven rather than on earth's demanding environment. People are frightfully willing to blame their destitute conditions on someone else, and to believe that the only purpose of life is to somehow tolerate this existence until the postmortem rewards of heaven can be reaped.

"We made North Vhaicam a model proletarian state. We gave the means of production to the workers. We took from each according to his ability, and gave to each according to his need. We encouraged the workers to unite and to shed their chains. We created the Communist Party to oversee this final glorious stage in human evolution. Unfortunately, it all collapsed into a hellish nightmare. We felt like Jacob, who labored seven years to win Rachel as his bride, only to discover in his darkened tent that he had won the ugly Leah instead."

"That's too bad", said Freeman, who didn't give a damn. He was more concerned about dodging bullets targeted for his cranium. "How did that happen?"

"We all fervently believed in communism", replied Aiden Tyler Smith III. "Unfortunately, Communism didn't believe in us. It requires inhuman creatures to live it successfully. We could never fully convince the Vhaicamese to discard their own individuality and to subsume their lives into the great proletarian collective. They wanted to live, love, and create, but the collective wanted them to sacrifice, obey, and conform. They each had magnificent dreams distinct from the magnificent dreams of all other individuals. But communism requires a communal dream, which never seemed magnificent or even interesting to the millions who were forced to abandon their individual yearnings and accept tasteless socialistic pabulum.

"Communism, like all isms, is a dogmatic mythology propagated and subverted by people who lust for power. Communist party leaders oppress just like monarchs, czars, and emperors. The monarch invents the mythology of divine right of kings to bind his subjects. The Master invents the mythology of class and caste distinction over his slaves. The pharaoh and the emperor invent the mythology that they are earthly incarnations of gods, to which the peasants must kneel in submission. Government bureaucrats invent the mythology of the common good to chain taxpayers to a black hole of spending that does nothing but enhance the lifestyles of these bureaucrats. The Communist Party preaches the mythology of the Species Being, and the proles kowtow in worshipful bondage. Fundamentally, each ism is substitutable for any other, because they are all merely psychological tools some people use to assume power over the rest, under the protective cloak of their uniquely 'true' mythology. When Marx invited the workers of the world to unite, they didn't realize it meant they would be chained together in servitude to a master even more abusive than the one they sought refuge from.

"The workers' paradise became a nightmarish quagmire of corruption, ineptitude, and destroyed ambition. 'From each to his ability and to each according to his need' was contorted into 'from each according to the state's five year plan, and to each according to whatever is left after party officials skim the cream off the meager production the disenfranchised workers eke out'. Haggard families clothed in rags are now begging for food from a system that never knew how to produce. Shoes and soap are a long forgotten luxury. Ration cards allocate every essential commodity. Long lines wait for scant supplies. Housing is one vast slum, because what everybody owns, nobody takes care of. Meanwhile, Party operatives confiscate the best of everything, including land, homes, and possessions. Power has been concentrated into a small caste of corrupt bureaucrats protected by mercenary security forces who pick through whatever the bureaucrats don't want. The liberation of the workers cast them adrift from everything they had known or loved or been. Psychologically, they're now all refugees, since the North Vhaicamese state has become an omnipresent monolith that nobody can muster the emotional energy to call 'home'.

"Yes, we liberated the Vhaicamese", sighed Aiden Tyler Smith III. "They are now free to consume the fruits of their socialist economic system, but there are none. They are now free from the exploitative bourgeois class, but their hunger belies the joy of their emancipation. They are now free to revel in the equality of their new society, which mysteriously doesn't apply to privileged party members. We credit-card socialists promised equality, liberty, and prosperity. But what we actually delivered to them was corruption, servitude, and destitution. Communism is a sham, the same sham that has been repeated many times throughout history, disguised by many different isms.

"Death by starvation, disease, or the silent bullets of secret police were the inevitable fates of workers in this paradise. I had to get the hell out of there. It reminded me of an old joke about a shipwrecked sailor who floated for days on flotsam until a rope was thrown to him from out of the darkness. He called out, 'What country is this?' 'The Soviet Union', voices answered. 'I'll float a little further', said the shipwrecked sailor.

"Unfortunately, I discovered I couldn't leave. I was told I was property of the state, that I was an inseparable, though insignificant, element of the proletariat. I was forbade to do anything of my own free will, since I didn't have a free will, according to their dogma which I had given them in my youthful naiveté. It was either escape and live, or stay and die. So I ran. Right into this foxhole, where I now sit with mud up my asshole, and my soul filled with dirty shame."

"Wow!" exclaimed Freeman. "It's a good thing we're fighting the communists here in Vhaicam, so they don't take over the rest of the world."

"Bullshit", spat Aiden Tyler Smith III. "Communists are paper tigers. There's no need to fight them, unless they attack you directly. They will eventually kill themselves. Their proletarian time bomb will implode inward. Humans won't tolerate that environment forever. They will inevitably discover that communism is just another facade for generic oppression that has existed since the dawn of civilization, manifesting itself in varying forms and isms, but always of the same essence—some men clinging to power over the others behind a protective shield of mythology."

This retort silenced the three men. Overhead, a war raged furiously, oblivious to their introspections and impervious to their wishes and dreams. Men were killing one another, as they had since the first spark of mysticism twinkled in a primitive tribe. Nobody in the foxhole wanted to be a part of that killing. Nor did anyone else in any of the other foxholes, on either side of the 33rd diagonal. But the bombs continued to drop, the bullets continued to fly, and the casualties continued to mount. The three men in the foxhole were mystified by the absurdity of it all. The absurdity wasn't attributable to Communism or Capitalism or any other mythology ending with an ism. The absurdity was simply that presumably intelligent individuals were allowing themselves to be slaughtered.

Proverbial light bulbs flashed on in the heads of the three men. They each had only one life to live, and to sacrifice it as pointlessly as this was obscene. They each had one golden opportunity on earth to grow, love, and prosper. Fate awarded them one heart, one soul, one brain, and one body with which to take one solitary crack at living life to its fullest. This wasn't a gift to be squandered or carelessly discarded. They discovered that the preciousness of life is its scarcity and brevity. Sacrificing this one priceless opportunity to flesh-devouring warfare or spirit-devouring mythology was unforgivable.

It was fortuitous that this revelation dawned on Freeman, Sam Winters, and Aiden Tyler Smith III when it did. Hurtling through the blackened sky was a missile. It was nominally a North Vhaicamese missile, but that would be insignificant to the poor souls it obliterated. Corpses don't care who fired the weapon that killed them. Death renders all implications of life irrelevant. Death destroys all personal perspectives. Death unmasks all mythologies and all social conditioning. Sometimes it is death's approach that finally reveals the naked truth of life.

The North Vhaicamese missile continued its deadly flight toward the front lines. The three men looked skyward in reaction to the eerie screeching that was getting louder by the millisecond. During their fleeting glimpse of the nighttime sky, the missile skewered their foxhole. Their bodies were brutally scattered about the battlefield in a shower of blood and shredded limbs. Fragments of their flesh sprinkled soldiers in other foxholes, mingling with the rain into an unrecognizable pink goo that was an apt byproduct of the pointless effort to prove the superiority of one ism over another, which was of no consequence to those sent by the purveyors of their ism to die for it.

The casualties in Vhaicam disturbed the Honcho. It wasn't remorse over personal loss, since he hadn't yet heard of Freeman's fate. Nor was it grief for the anonymous troops that were dying. Rather, he was pissed off about the dwindling supply of soldiers. Americans had stopped volunteering for the military, apparently because they had better things to do than go to Asia and die. This shocked the Honcho, who fervently believed that it was every American's duty to be shot at whenever the government wished. It infuriated him that North Vhaicam had an endless supply of bodies to funnel into the bologna grinder, while America was short on human flesh volunteering for disposal. The Vhaicamese had a superior willingness to die selflessly for their ism. America's pride was now at stake, in addition to his re-election. Something had to be done!

So, the Honcho did what all spineless leaders do when citizens stop volunteering to be killed. He forced them to enlist and die anyway by re-instituting the draft. Horribly efficient Selective Service computers distributed dreaded draft notices to young Americans, who were herded through processing centers that removed hair, lice, and egos. They were issued uniforms, weapons, and dog tags, and were taught how to kill effectively and to die respectably. This ruthless cattle-herding machinery spewed out torrents of cannon fodder for shipment across the ocean into the yawing funnel of the Vhaicamese bologna grinder. The Honcho was pleased. His forced conscription proved that America could sacrifice its youth as callously as any backward Asian country.

The draft went well until the Selective Service reluctantly reported that an entire generation of draft-age Americans disappeared. Millions of youths fled across the Canadian border to evade conscription, so there was no one left to draft. These draft dodgers now had to live apart from their loved ones, but at least they were still alive.

When the Honcho saw TV images of the graffiti that escaping Americans spray-painted on rocks near the Canadian border, he erupted into wall-pounding fury. Phrases such as "war is a good indication you picked the wrong leaders", and "the American Government violates, rather than protects, the right to life" enraged him. With so many people disrespectfully fleeing the draft, who would be left to pay the taxes, kneel in supplication to the regulations, or die in the non-wars? He had to stop the seditious exodus.

A humane leader would have done this by ending the pointless non-war in Vhaicam and welcoming back the evaders from Canada. Instead, the Honcho diverted six army divisions from Vhaicam, stationed them along the entire U.S. border, and ordered them to shoot anyone fleeing the country, since it was un-American to evade being killed for or by the government. If Americans wanted to leave their country, they'd have to do it in Government Issue body bags, not by sneaking across the border like unpatriotic cowards

This strategy worked for seven minutes, which was how long it took the first draft dodger approaching the border to silently challenge his uniformed fellow Americans to shoot him. The soldiers dutifully leveled their rifles, but as the escaping rebel strode resolutely across the international line, none of them pulled the trigger. Instead, they dropped their weapons, tore off their uniforms, and followed the brave youth into Canada. The torrent of evaders fleeing America resumed.

The Honcho ruminated over this dark manifestation of human nature. He paced his ornate office, nursing the foulest mood of his life. He desperately needed Freeman's help to resolve this dilemma, but hadn't heard from him for days. Freeman was his most trustworthy and productive employee, even though the Honcho secretly suspected him of being a seditious traitor who seldom accomplished anything. He subconsciously rubbed the scar near his neck where Brutus had stabbed Caesar. His funk deepened. He feared that his world was about to implode, that the walls were closing in on him, inch by innocuous inch, slowly but inexorably. Claustrophobia assailed him. He was certain now that the walls were moving toward him. He neurotically positioned himself in the center of his office to buy time before the walls crushed him. He was consumed by fear of the walls.

Suddenly, his morbid fixation with walls gave birth to an idea. Walls are effective barriers to movement. Since his principal problem was disloyal Americans moving across the Canadian border, perhaps a transcontinental wall would stem the flow. The Berlin Wall had already proven successful at keeping disgruntled East Germans from fleeing their government. He wasn't troubled that the Berlin Wall was a Communist manifestation, because Ismism is flexible enough to embrace pragmatic concepts of other isms, even if they're abhorrent.

The Honcho twisted arms on Capitol Hill to get congressional approval for construction of the Wall. Thousands of Americans were conscripted to contribute two years of national service to their country to build it. The completed structure was a monumental testimony to Ismism, which was quite extraordinary, since Ismism remained completely undefined. It was all things to all people, unless this became inconvenient, at which point it became nothing to no one. It was a philosophy ideally suited for modern American politics, and the wall was its ideal manifestation, since it too was monstrous, it too consumed huge amounts of national resources, and everyone lied about its real purpose.

The wall became known as the Bemidji Barrier because its construction began in Bemidji, Minnesota. The Bemidji Barrier was a hostile impediment to border crossings. It was twelve feet high, six feet wide, and was made of impregnable concrete imbedded with flesh-shredding glass shards and scrap metal. It was intertwined with enough barbed wire to encircle the world, or at least to imprison 270 million inhabitants. Turrets were interspersed along its 3,000 mile length, which was patrolled by former East German soldiers who were available because the Berlin Wall had been dismantled after the East Germans cleverly exiled their government rather than themselves. These soldiers were hired because they had no consciences and didn't speak English, so when fleeing Americans pleaded with them, they sprayed the outlaws with machine gun fire and collected their bonuses for each corpse.

Vegetation was napalmed on both sides of the wall so searchlights could scan for escapees and give machine gunners a clear view. Between rows of high voltage barbed wire were thousands of land mines. Fragmented body parts were splayed around mines that had already been detonated. Canals filled with putrid water lined the wall. The splashing of swimming escapees made marksmanship easy for the guards. Sensitive seismic monitors continuously scanned the earth for tunneling. Even if the seismic monitors didn't notice you, the Dobermans would catch your scent long before you tired of shoveling. Steel bars and rats prevented escape through the sewers.

The Bemidji Barrier cut an unholy swath across the continent, splitting small towns in two, carving through cemeteries, displacing churches and schools, despoiling millions of arable acres, and defiling the natural beauty of the countryside. The Barrier also cut an unholy swath through the fabric of American families. The East Germans brought with them the philosophy of "Sippenschaft", which meant that the families of escapees were held equally accountable for the actions of their wayward members. Thus, parents and siblings were also riddled with bullets.

Despite the Bemidji Barrier, a few intrepid Americans still escaped to Canada. Some hopped the wall in hot-air balloons or homemade aircraft. Others fled in small boats running up the coast of Maine or out of Puget Sound, braving tempestuous ocean swells. This extraordinary persistence by the draft dodgers tormented the Honcho, particularly after he heard reports that the mysterious Insurrectionist was assisting them. The seditious rebel was an increasingly painful thorn in his side, and he wasn't going to tolerate it any longer. He summoned Jefferson to his office.

Jefferson removed his bicorne hat, eased his lanky frame into an expensive chair, and adjusted the stockings under his breeches. "Where has Miss Buxomus gone off to?" he asked.

"She joined the USO to entertain the troops in Vhaicam", the Honcho said gruffly. "It was irresponsible of her to abandon me."

"Indeed", said Jefferson. "Governments thrive on paperwork. You must sorely miss her administrative assistance."

"Administrative assistance, hell! I've got lots of people to handle paper. 'A person for every piece of paper, and two pieces of paper for every person' is our credo. I meant it was irresponsible of her to leave without... hugging... me...." His voice trailed off uneasily because Jefferson probably wasn't attuned to the services she was paid to provide. "Have you tracked down the ring leader of these cursed draft dodgers yet?"

"It's difficult", replied Jefferson. "Not only is the Insurrectionist very elusive, he has widespread popular support. Your policy of impressment has fomented an enduring hatred of government."

"What the fuck is impressment?"

"Impressment is the term we used in Virginia to describe forced servitude to the government. We found it particularly odious when King George impressed our sailors to serve in His Majesty's Navy. It was one of the compelling reasons we threw off the shackles of his monarchical tyranny."

"King George . . . ?" The Honcho's question trailed off into confused silence. After an uneasy moment, he continued. "Why do people hate being forced into military service? Don't they love their country? Why do they lap up the Insurrectionist's subversive rhetoric and risk their lives to dodge the draft?"

Jefferson smiled coyly. "Perhaps it's because they understand why Hemingway said, 'the first panacea for a mismanaged nation is inflation of the currency; the second is war'. In Virginia, the draft was considered the most severe of all oppressions and was the most unpopular thing ever attempted. The evils encompassing the life of man are sufficiently numerous. Why add to these evils by pressing men forcibly to destroy one another?"

"But it's everyone's duty to defend my country!"

"Protagoras said, 'Man is the measure of all things'. He didn't mean Man's government was the measure. The first and only duty of every citizen is to protect the life and liberty of himself, his family, and his community. As citizens, we must energetically defend against every hostile agent. When our own government is the hostile agent, resistance is a moral response. If someone threatens to enslave or kill me, what difference does it make if he is a king or a common man, my countryman or my enemy, an individual villain or an army of them? The most grievous hostility is the impressment of citizens through the draft. We must sacrifice our last dollar and drop of blood to shed that badge of slavery."

"How can a state function if it can't forcibly harness its citizens?" the Honcho challenged. "If they object to being forced to die for the state, perhaps they could substitute a few years of national service toward a more peaceful objective."

"If a state can only function by forcibly impressing its citizens, the question is not how can this state function, but rather, why should it be permitted to function? Nothing will so quickly divest us of liberty as giving the state a perpetual right to our services. This would annihilate the blessings of existence, and contradict the nature of life itself, which was given for happiness and not for wretchedness and subjugation. To substitute mandatory national service for the military draft is tantamount to slavery, and this concept would soon expand to include not only two years of everyone's lives, but their entire existence as well. As Cicero put it, 'slavery is the worst of all evils—to be repelled, if need be, not only by war, but even by death.' Repelling slavery includes resistance to your government's unholy policies of the draft and national service. The draft evaders are not answerable to your god or your ism, and they should not submit to enslaving themselves or destroying their fellow man at the behest of tyrants in Washington."

The Honcho was stunned by these words laden with threatening images of sedition and insurrection. Even more disturbing was the mention of Cicero, which reminded him of his brutal sojourn to the Roman Empire, where Cicero led the resistance against him. He sullenly recalled his abject fear when Marcus Brutus drove a dagger into his jugular. Strangely, this reminded him of Freeman, from whom he had received no reports for days. He nervously rubbed the scar where Brutus' dagger had stabbed Caesar's body.

Freeman carefully adjusted his mutilated body in a M.A.S.H. tent where he had spent the past 48 hours recuperating from extensive surgery. He reveled in his head-to-toe agony, because it confirmed he was still alive. Life was suddenly very precious to him, but not for his ex-foxhole mates, Aiden Tyler Smith III and Sam Winters, who had been sliced and diced by a North Vhaicamese missile while still in the preamble of their lives.

Freeman's miraculous survival of the missile was ironic. It had detonated next to his ball and chain, which deflected most of the concussion and shrapnel, so he escaped the explosion with only life-threatening wounds. Cassandra's gift, given to him as a continual reminder of his self-inflicted bondage, gave him a second lease on life. As he lay near death, he whispered words of thanks to Cassandra into the ethos, hoping to somehow reach her and give her a brief emotional respite from Apollo's curse.

When the dulling effects of morphine subsided, he noticed a heavily bandaged youth laying in a cot next to him, staring into space. "I see you tried to die for your country as unsuccessfully as I did", said Freeman wryly.

The Youth on the Cot slowly turned his blood-splotched face. "You can't die for your country", he replied. "You can't die for anything. Dying for something is a contradiction in terms. The minute you die, the thing you died for simultaneously ceases to exist, at least from your perspective. You can only live for something."

Freeman couldn't argue with the Youth on the Cot, although he disliked the implicit burden to find something valuable to live for. "How did you get so mangled?"

"NV soldiers assaulted our position near the 33rd diagonal. Most of our regiment was killed. I took bullets in the leg and the stomach, but I managed to crawl to our machine gun emplacement. I mowed the attackers down, and then I blacked out."

"Geez, that makes you a hero!"

The Youth on the Cot shook his head. "If you kill one person, you're a murderer. If you kill hundreds, you're a hero, especially if you scratch 'Semper Fi' in the dirt before you die. To save my own life I killed NV youths that didn't want to fight in this non-war either. Oh, I'll get a ticker tape parade back home, but I won't smile during it. When I see politicians heaping praises and confetti on me, I will be thinking of how Jesus described the Pharisees as 'hypocrites, all white and shining on the outside, and inside filled with dead men's bones.' True heroes are those working to achieve universal emancipation from warfare, which will only come from an enormous undercurrent of people forsaking national and religious chauvinism. As Thomas Jefferson put it, 'It is strangely absurd to suppose that a million human beings, collected together, are not under the same moral laws which bind each of them separately. Moral duties are as obligatory on nations as on individuals.'"

Freeman thought it rather odd that the Youth on the Cot quoted Jefferson, whom just recently had been appointed Insurrection Czar. "Yes, it is absurd", he murmured.

"This non-war has sired many absurdities", said the Youth on the Cot. "One day, our regiment was ordered to capture and destroy a munitions factory while video cameras rolled, so that our general could relay heroic images back to the top brass in the Octagon. Everything went according to plan. We crossed into enemy territory and captured the factory. Unfortunately, there were no munitions in there, because they had already been distributed to the front lines. The general was furious, but he wasn't deterred by our bad luck. He ordered the captured factory workers back to the production lines until they produced enough munitions to make an explosion big enough to make a video spectacular enough to get our general his third star. So, we blew up the factory, sent the video to the Octagon, and applauded when our general got promoted."

"That is absurd", agreed Freeman.

"There's more. Another general ordered us to invade a NV village to liberate it from Communism. We attacked and drove out the enemy soldiers. Unfortunately, they counterattacked the next day. After absorbing horrendous losses, we retreated. But, in order to complete the general's mission to save the villagers from communism, we were ordered to shoot them before we left. We objected, of course. But our commander gave us three choices: shoot the villagers, get court martialled and be shot, or shoot our leaders. We shot the villagers. Every last one of them. And so the villagers were liberated from communism simply by being liberated from life."

"That's really absurd", said Freeman. "But, I can top your story. Back in Washington, the Head Honcho was pissed about the high cost of the non-war. It's expensive to transport troops, provisions, and weaponry around the world. He feared that these exorbitant costs would force him to raise taxes, an unpalatable election-year tactic. He hired consultants to find a cheaper alternative. They recommended killing the American soldiers in America, because it's cheaper than sending them to Vhaicam to be killed. So, the Honcho organized a program to kill our troops before they even boarded the transport planes, which would be a big political feather in his cap, because it would save taxpayers millions of transportation dollars. Unfortunately, he overlooked one detail."

"What was that?" asked the Youth on the Cot.

"The Honcho forgot he was accumulating frequent flier miles for every troop transport flight to Vhaicam. Killing the troops in America would cost him a lucrative perk. So, the plan was scrapped."

"That tops my story", said the Youth on the Cot. "Jefferson was right when he said 'never was so much false arithmetic employed as that used to persuade nations it's in their interest to go to war. Were the money that it cost to wage war expended in making roads, opening rivers, building ports, improving the arts, and fostering industry, it would render nations much stronger, wealthier, and happier. These false arithmetics have led me to abhor war and to view it as the greatest scourge of mankind.'"

Another quote from Jefferson, thought Freeman. He pondered this strange coincidence, then asked, "What leads us into these absurd situations?"

"Religion", snapped the Youth on the Cot unhesitatingly.

Freeman was beginning to think that the Youth was a lunatic operating on the heretical assumption that life was just a bizarre farce along the way to some other more reasonable existence, which is what Freeman emphatically believed. "Religion?"

"Yes, religion", confirmed the Youth on the Cot. "You know, 'Praise the Safari Golfer, and pass the ammunition.' I think it was Dean Swift who observed, 'We have just enough religion to make us hate one another, but not enough to make us love one another'".

"My adult experience confirms that, but it still seems unfair to attribute all of this bloodshed to religion."

The Youth on the Cot exhaled a cackling laugh. "Unfair? Communion, which is the heart of Catholic religious experience, is a vicarious cannibalization of the deity being worshipped. It's a throwback to the nightmarish beginnings of mankind's conceptual consciousness, a celebration of flesh-eating and blood-drinking made palatable only through the suspension of critical thought and the activation of dogmatic faith. Communion plagiarizes pagan rituals that deified the forces of nature supporting the agricultural efforts of primitive tribes. Virgins and virile youths were sacrificed to the gods of nature in exchange for favorable weather or crop growth. These sacrifices were usually followed by a ceremonial feast in which the tribal members ate the victims in order to ally themselves with their deities. The wise men convinced the others that this bloody human sacrifice would ultimately benefit the whole tribe, as long as they believed the myths. They created a mythical pact with the gods, who gave mankind their best fruit and crop in exchange for bloodletting. This tradition of religious cannibalism and human sacrifice is entrenched in every primitive culture. It has been passed down to modernity in familiar rituals like the Catholic practice of consuming their savior's flesh and blood."

Freeman wondered what Christ would think if he saw a modern assemblage of Catholics making pious ceremony out of symbolically eating him. Meanwhile, the Youth on the Cot continued. "Man has always used mythology to justify killing friend and foe. Primitive myths were rooted in worship of nature and inanimate objects, giving rise to a class of priests. The priests translated these myths and signs from the natural world into commandments to enslave and kill other humans, ostensibly for the benefit of the tribe, but more likely for the benefit of the priestly class itself or the tribal ruling elite that had expropriated the priestly class as its shill.

"Eventually, these gods of nature took on anthropomorphic characteristics, and the historically familiar religious deities evolved and became inextricably intertwined with every emerging civilization's ruling elite, who claimed to represent these deities. In this light, all wars were instigated by mythology, because deities were the ultimate authority of the earthly leaders, as interpreted by the dogmas and myths of the realm. Behind every battle lurks a myth, such as the divinity of the Pharaoh, the divine right of the European Kings, control over the Holy Land, or propagation of the Aryan Race, to name a few. We kill each other for the sake of myths, burying objective truth under an avalanche of corpses.

"Do you know that Pope Pius IX issued a declaration called 'Syllabus of Errors', which contained 80 sweeping points condemning principles such as freedom of speech and religion, and disavowing the separation of church and state? He then confined 19th-Century Jews in Rome to a dehumanizing ghetto, in an eerie precursor to Nazi initiatives less than a century later. When Pius died in 1878, some incensed Italians tried to dump his body in the Tiber River.

"As our mythologies evolved, they became less divine and more secularly humanistic. But, these newer myths demanded as much uncritical faith as their deistic predecessors. Myths like Hegel's Species Being, Manifest Destiny, the Dictatorship of the Proletariat, the Common Good, the Cultural Revolution, Political Correctness, or even Ismism itself, have served as the war cry for man's organized conflicts. 'Deutschland Uber Alles' is mankind's most horrific metaphysical nightmare. Skeletons littered on the battlefields of history attest to the deadliness of faith in myths. All mythologies glorify sacrifice, and death is the ultimate sacrifice, particularly if it comes with sword drawn on behalf of a deity or earthly representative thereof.

"Myths devalue individual lives and life on earth in general, making absorption into the collective, and even death itself, life's compelling objectives. When Jim Jones instructed his followers of the Peoples Temple in Guyana to commit suicide, they willingly complied, since the meaning of their individual lives had been neutered. The Spartans memorialized their fallen warriors by inscribing 'Having done what men could, they suffered what men must', on their graves as the ultimate summation of the pervasiveness of duty, suffering, war, and death in man's experience with mythology and power. When primitive tribes believed the myths of their priests, they consigned themselves to slavery and the threat of death. The root of man's oppression at the hands of other men is the sacrifice of individual rational interpretation of the world in deference to mythology. As Thomas Paine said, 'All churches, whether Jewish, Christian, or Turkish, appear to be human inventions set up to terrify and enslave mankind and monopolize power and profit.'"

The Youth's words defied Freeman's cultural conditioning. "You're slandering religion by making it responsible for such pervasive misery and cruelty", he protested.

The Youth on the Cot cackled again. "Look at you! Full of shrapnel and bleeding from head to toe, and yet you persist in defending the mythologies that caused it. Did you choose to come here and risk death? Is this what you envisioned as the purpose of your life when you were a child? What good will come from dying in this fucking Asian hellhole? Have I done religion an injustice? No, secular and divine religions have done the injustice to us."

While Freeman and the Youth on the Cot philosophized in their M.A.S.H. tent, the war outside consumed a steady flow of believers. The line separating the two armies hadn't moved more than two hundred yards in either direction since the battles began, but a generation of humans had been sacrificed to the war god's gluttony for flesh. The irresistible force of the communist armies grinded against the immovable American and South Vhaicamese armies, yielding nothing but death. The wafting stench of slaughter intermingled with the stink of feces and urine in hastily dug outhouses. Millions of casualties blanketed the muddy landscape several layers deep. Artillery barrages churned fractured bones, jumbled limbs, and vivisectioned bodies like a grotesque tossed salad. It was impossible to dig a new trench without disinterring a jigsaw puzzle of cadavers. A dismembered arm jutted out from the muddy walls of one trench. Passing soldiers routinely shook its lifeless hand, hoping the dark absurdity would ward off insanity.

No one had time to bury the dead, but Nature worked heroically to remove the evidence. Millions of flies engorged themselves on decaying corpses, creating an eerie background hum with their massed wings. Jackals, buzzards, and vultures scavenged mercilessly, dragging around corpses in a surreal image that no Hollywood director could ever sculpt on celluloid. The air vibrated heavily with mosquitoes that were so voracious some men slept immersed in marshes, risking snakebites and drowning rather than the torture of a thousand insect bites.

Blood ran from the wounded in a crimson river that lapped incessantly against the consciousness of every soldier. Injured men wept and screamed and cursed, coughing up lung residue from their scrambled innards. Other men vomited at the sight of brains and eyes running together in a sticky goo inside the helmet of a fragmentation bomb victim. When men saw appendages laying about, they involuntary checked to make sure their own hadn't been unknowingly severed by scything shrapnel. Incapacitated soldiers stumbled about on footless legs and gesticulated madly with handless arms.

Men were dying in more ways than a sane observer could catalogue. They were hung, scalped, mutilated, impaled, suffocated, speared, drowned, burned, gassed, decapitated, dissected, disemboweled, bayoneted, machine gunned, infected, injected, and irradiated. Ten soldiers per second were killed, making the beachhead battles at Iwo Jima look like training exercises. The slaughter rivaled the cudgeling and disembowelment of cattle in a Chicago meat processing plant, except that cattle are mindless beings with no choice in their demise. The end result, however, is still hamburger and bologna, ground out by ruthlessly efficient flesh-churning machinery.

But the soldiers continued to charge, goaded on by commanders who were goaded on by generals and politicians safely tucked away somewhere else. Military obedience, social conditioning, and religious self-sacrifice had broken their spirits. As they plodded toward enemy trenches, they fell rhythmically, like clay ducks targeted at a carnival sideshow. They rushed forward with élan and died with élan, falling atop one another like toy soldiers swatted by a hyperactive child. They careened into the yawing jaws of certain death numbed by opiates. They smoked marijuana, injected heroin, and swallowed LSD. They drank gallons of alcohol, sniffed cleaning fluids, and read arcane Biblical passages. But these merely cloaked the dark dangers of the battlefield with sugar coated psychedelic illusion. Death was still invincible and unavoidable. For them, the Wolf was no longer at the door. It was inside the door.

Nitrate-laced smoke hung like a dark thundercloud over desecrated land that was more moonscape than earthscape. The terrain was lacerated with tunnels, trenches, gun emplacements, and bomb craters. The incessant rain turned the soft soil into a gooey quagmire that swallowed soldiers up to their waists. Latticed pontoon bridges lined the undulating surface of the battlefront like huge treadmills designed for the goalless exercise of giant rodents. Anything that used to bloom was devoured by napalm, flame throwers, Agent Orange, and explosions. Forests were reduced to a haunting composition of charred tree stumps jutting out from the muddy earth like ghostly wooden sentinels. Foliage shredded by volleys of projectiles was strewn about the battlefield, as if a horrible supernatural force had ripped through the area and annihilated everything.

Hidden in this scarred venue were frightened men who had survived the human bologna grinder yesterday and today, but probably not tomorrow. For them, hope and dignity had already expired, leaving behind only vague recollections of what it meant to be civil. If they miraculously survived the slaughter and regained some semblance of humanity, their lives would still forever be tainted by this soul-wrenching glimpse of the Apocalypse.

Back in America, the nation's mood turned distinctly somber. A whole generation of youths had either circumnavigated the Bemidji Barrier to Canada or had been abducted from their teenage hangouts into a Southeast Asian inferno, for reasons no one understood. A funeral pall descended over America as it mourned for it's missing generation in a communal requiem.

To assuage this angst, a memorial for the non-war in Asia was constructed. It was an enormous black granite wall with the names of all that had died in Vhaicam etched into dark stone. People came to touch it, to place flowered wreathes, and to somberly remember lost loved ones. But the monument didn't sufficiently salve America's accumulated grief. The victims of other wars also deserved remembrance. So, additional miles of black granite walls were constructed with millions of names etched into their seemingly endless obsidian surfaces, memorializing the victims of Kosovo, Somalia, Beirut, the Gulf War, Vietnam, Korea, World War II, World War I, the Civil War, and the Spanish American War.

But even this massive granite commemoration was insufficient. The urge to remember inspired an eruption of monuments dedicated to all governmental and religious violence throughout history. The Jews incinerated by Hitler got their monument. The Russian peasants murdered by Stalin got theirs. The Irish farmers starved to death by the British landowners got theirs. The native Americans got theirs. The victims of the Spanish Inquisition got theirs. The men who fell on both sides during the Crusades got theirs. The Mayans sacrificed to their gods in mass burials got theirs. The blacks that starved in African Marxist dictatorships got theirs. The slaves who died in coffin ships got theirs. The victims of the SS, the KGB, the CIA, and other secret polices of the world got theirs.

This urge to construct monuments to memorialize man's organized inhumanity would have exhausted the country's granite quarries, if an anonymous person hadn't cleverly suggested building a generic monument to commemorate all victims of organized atrocity. The monument served the same purpose as the Tomb of the Unknown Soldier in Arlington National Cemetery, so it became known as the Tomb of the

Unknown Victim. It was built on the tidal basin near East Potomac Park, and featured a shimmering reflection of the Jefferson Memorial. It bore a tantalizing epitaph: "If people universally pursue peace, perhaps governments and religions will get out of their way and let them have it. If they beat their swords into plowshares, their spears into pruning hooks, and their chains into tinsel, perhaps organized oppression will vanish and nations will no longer wield arms against each other or their own citizens."

The Unknown Victim had no name or place of birth. But, despite its silent anonymity, the Unknown Victim had a Message of incalculable importance for the rest of humanity. Its tale wasn't told by words, but rather by the unyielding finality of the black-as-death tombstone marking its figurative resting-place. This unwritten Message was very simple: "Here lies a man slain by believers of myths".

The Message from the Unknown Victim would be ignored for a long time. More victims would follow, with more woeful tales to tell. However, a few people understood the message, such as the ancient Croesus, who said, "No one is so senseless as to choose of his own will war rather than peace, since in peace sons bury their fathers, and in war, fathers bury their sons."

One woman in particular learned the common sense of the Message. Late on a wintry night in the heartland of America, with an icy wind knifing through the darkness, she rocked herself slowly in front of a dying fire. She was not alone, although no one was with her. Her company that evening was a memory, represented by a Teddy Bear cradled tenderly in her arms, a stuffed effigy of something very dear lost. With the bear hugged tightly against her bosom, she heard the faint voice of a little boy saying "Mommy, I love you". The gentle echo of this refrain kept time with the rocking chair as her mind's eye watched her son do little boy things. He climbed and he jumped and he ran, with the abandon of a youth that knows no mortality. He pretended and he imagined and he dreamed, with the creativity of a child to whom life is an endless panorama of potential. Large tears squirted out of his innocent round eyes and ran swiftly down his pristine cheeks, from the pain of scrapes and bruises earned as badges of childhood daring and exploration. His lip quivered as he explained how the neighborhood bully stole his snack and pushed him down. His faced beamed like a lighthouse as he described the home run he hit at the ballpark.

These images unfurled through her mind like a poorly produced home video. Tears ran from her reddened eyes down care worn cheeks and dripped quietly onto the Teddy Bear's mottled fur. She wanted desperately to see that little boy again, to run her fingers through his disheveled hair, to wipe the tear from his cheek, to comfort him, to hug him, to feel the love flowing through his tiny arms embracing her torso. She wanted so badly to rock him in that chair, as she had so many years ago, feeling his tiny heart lightly thumping against her bosom as her own heart thumped out a passionate response of pure love. She yearned to place his tiny mouth against her bare breast again, to pass on her life giving milk as his marsh mallow hand instinctively caressed her face. She yearned to sing a gentle lullaby to him while his frail body drifted into peaceful sleep, with pleasantly pungent baby breath wafting noiselessly from his lips. She yearned to look deep into his infinitely trusting eyes to understand the meaning of joy again.

But it was never to be. She had received the Message sent vicariously by the Unknown Victim. A military officer delivered an impersonal telegram announcing that her son had been killed in Vhaicam. It proclaimed that he died bravely defending Ismism, and that she and the entire nation should be proud. But those were just the written words. She locked onto the unwritten words passed on telepathically from the Unknown Victim. Her son didn't die in glorious defense of Ismism. He died for no reason at all. The meaning of life wasn't to be found in the self-sacrificial defense of any mythological ism. The meaning of life was to be found in the love between mother and child, which was now lost forever for this woman.

After the military officer uncomfortably dismissed himself, the woman slowly tore up the telegram and collapsed to the floor in abject grief from which she would never fully recover. At the funeral of her son, she placed flowers on his tombstone. Attached to the bouquet was a tear-stained note, written in shaky cursive. The note was an emotional echo of the ethereal Message from the Unknown Victim. It said simply, "To my son. Since your eyes were closed, mine have never ceased to cry."

If Croesus were still alive, he would have acknowledged that there is only one thing worse in this existence than a father burying his son. It is a mother burying her son.

Chapter Eight: "The Juggernaut"

"Power tends to corrupt, and absolute power corrupts absolutely."

—Lord Acton

Freeman unexpectedly reappeared in his Washington office, sporting bandages, crutches, and a case of clap. His return put an end to the rancorous tug-of-war over his office furniture that had been waged fiercely since he disappeared, and everyone assured him that any scandalous rumors he might hear about himself were totally untrue and of unknown origin. Generally, though, they ignored him, except for the Coffee Account Dues Collector. "Your account is two months in arrears", said the coffee account enforcer, who wore a green visor and spoke in the same morbid voice as actuaries, tax collectors, and morticians.

"That's impossible!" protested Freeman.

"I've never been wrong before."

Freeman knew that this was true. "Still, there must be some mistake," he persisted. "I didn't drink any coffee during the last two months. I was gone! Look at my wounds!"

He admired Freeman's traumatized body with an appreciative eye unique to debt collectors. "Hmmm. Did I do that?"

"No, I was struck by a missile in Vhaicam", said Freeman.

"That's most unfortunate. Was it friendly or enemy fire?"

"I'm told it doesn't matter."

"Yes, I suppose that's true", conceded the Coffee Account Dues Collector. "It also doesn't matter whether you drank any coffee or not. You still owe the dues."

"Why?" cried Freeman, his voice rising half an octave in frustration. "Paying for a service I didn't use doesn't make any sense."

"I didn't say it made sense. I said you still owe the dues. You're on the wrong side of the looking glass if you expect things to make sense."

Freeman indeed suspected he was in the wrong plane of existence, but there was little he could do about it, except make one last valiant effort to dodge the caffeine-dispensing cretin. "Paying for a service I didn't use is unfair."

"Demanding fairness is rather antisocial", said the Coffee Account Dues Collector. "Our government would collapse if everyone thought like you."

Freeman wondered if it was actually the Coffee Account Dues Collector that the Honcho saw during his inebriated encounters with the Mad Hatter. He pushed his ball and chain out of the way, opened a desk drawer, and extracted an envelope stuffed with money that had been given to him by an Italian golfing buddy of the Honcho for no apparent reason. "How much do I owe?"

"How much do you have?"

"Quit kidding around. You sound like an IRS auditor."

The Collector didn't look like he was kidding. "$150 will settle your account."

Freeman shook his head in disbelief. "How can it be that expensive? Did the world's coffee crop fail while I was in Vhaicam?"

"Of course not. The coffee only cost me $2.37", said the Collector with annoying precision.

"Then what's the rest of the money for?"

"Administrative overhead. And it's a bargain compared to the overhead of the Octagon's coffee klatch."

Mention of the Octagon made Freeman despondent and eager to end the conversation. He handed a wad of bills to the morbid man in the green visor. "This should cover it. I'll see you later."

"Not so fast", said the Collector, as he meticulously counted and rearranged the money.

"It's all there!"

"Of course it is. But you haven't paid your delinquent Office Birthday Cake dues yet."

"I don't participate in a Office Birthday Cake fund!"

"Of course you do. We all do. You have no choice, even if you don't eat cake or have birthdays."

Freeman stamped his feet and stumbled over his ball and chain. "That's not fair!"

The Coffee Account Dues Collector sighed heavily. "We've been through this already. You don't want to be labeled antisocial, do you?"

Freeman shook his head in quiet submission. He paid his delinquent birthday cake dues. And then he paid his delinquent funeral flowers dues. By the time he finished paying delinquent dues for services he never used or even knew existed, he was broke. But, he endured the shakedown to avoid being labeled antisocial. That's one thing that would never happen to him.

"That antisocial sonofabitch!" bellowed the Head Honcho. "Freeman's been in Washington for four hours, and he hasn't even stopped by to tell me he's alive."

"But Sir!" said But Sir!. "He wasn't being antisocial. The Coffee Account Dues Collector was raping him."

Just then, Freeman made his delayed appearance. "Sorry I'm late, Chief. I'd have been here sooner, but I was getting raped."

"So I heard", said the Honcho, who secretly feared the Coffee Account Dues Collector because he looked like the Mad Hatter. "I'm glad to see you're still alive. Now I won't have to fabricate all that damnable paperwork proving your suicide mission was voluntary so the government won't owe your estate anything for a wrongful death. But, enough sentimental claptrap. My re-election campaign is floundering because of the F.U.N. fiasco and the mounting casualties in Vhaicam. I need to abandon these foreign policy quagmires and focus on domestic issues. While you were feigning death and screwing nurses in Vhaicam, I came up with a brilliant idea. I'm going to campaign against the unconscionable power and scope of the federal bureaucracy."

Freeman looked surprised. "That's uncharacteristic of you."

"Not really. My proposal increases my staff tenfold and doubles my powers."

Freeman looked confused. "Isn't it a contradiction to publicly oppose big government while your own power and administration grow exponentially?"

"No. For me to effectively diminish the power and influence of the federal government, I must acquire enough power and influence to order myself and my fellow bureaucrats to stop being so powerful and influential."

"When will you be powerful and influential enough to curtail your power and influence?"

"Never", said the Honcho matter-of-factly. "The more powerful and influential I become, the more power and influence I will further need to prevent myself from being so powerful and influential. I'll never catch up with myself."

"Then what's the point?"

"There is no point. This is a question of politics, not logic."

"Okay, but why would your proposal compel people to vote for you?"

"It's all about advocacy. Voters want to believe someone in the bureaucracy is on their side. It doesn't matter whether my proposal makes sense or even has a chance of succeeding. As long as they believe I'm campaigning to protect their interests, everything else is irrelevant."

"So what happens if you win the election?"

"The same thing that happens after every election I win", said the Honcho. "I start campaigning for the next election."

"Won't people feel betrayed when they eventually realize that you will never achieve enough power and influence to squelch your power and influence?"

"Nah. Voters are like sheep. Once the election is over, they'll go back to nibbling grass and surrendering their wool. Occasionally one of them will bleat out a protest, but other sheep will nudge the recalcitrant one until he eventually shuts up and rejoins the flock. German Nazis understood this very clearly. In 1920, they ran on a platform that many Americans would still call decent and reasonable. They advocated full employment, profit sharing with big business, expanded care for the aged, broadened public education, public health programs, and placing the common good above individual concerns. When the Nazis got elected, they abandoned every campaign promise. Instead, they built a fearsome war machine, attacked nations on all sides, and committed racial genocide. They demonstrated that the object of all politics, no matter what the venue or era, is to get elected. There are no rules governing what happens after that. Just ask Clinton."

"Doesn't that make democracy a sham?" protested Freeman. "What about the Constitution?"

The Honcho chuckled ominously. "Our Constitution is safely tucked away in a museum. It says that the powers of the federal government should be few and defined, but the reality is that the people who get elected make the rules. Just like water always runs downhill, governments always seize more power. I don't think that makes democracy a sham, but I'm in power looking down, not a subject looking up."

The idea of looking down intrigued Freeman. It was the only direction he hadn't yet looked for enlightenment. His driving instructor taught him to look straight ahead. His parish priest taught him to look up. His father taught him to look to the right. His college professors taught him to look to the left. He distrusted them all, and consequently spent his life looking backward. So, he stared down at the floor, waiting for something enlightening to happen.

Something did happen. The Honcho's office door swung open violently as the Safari Golfer made an extravagant entrance that Freeman didn't see because he was staring at the carpet. Nor did he see the swinging door that slammed heavily into his body and sent him sprawling onto the floor he had been staring at.

"You shouldn't look down", said the Golfer. He extended a hand to Freeman, who gratefully reached for it to pull himself up from the floor.

The Golfer angrily pulled back his hand. Freeman grabbed nothing but air and fell on his face again. "I wanted you to kiss my hand, not to grab it", he growled disdainfully.

As Freeman arose, he noticed that the stupendously famous celebrity wasn't wearing his usual psychedelic khaki. Instead, he was somberly dressed in black pants, black shirt, black shoes, and a contrasting white collar. "Don't you have to be a priest to wear that outfit?" he asked suspiciously.

The Golfer looked down at his attire serenely. "These are the only God clothes I could find. I found them in a brothel. There's a very embarrassed priest running around in nothing but skivvies."

"Why do you need God clothes?"

"Because I'm God", said the Golfer piously.

"Why are you God?" interjected the Honcho.

"Somebody has to be. I stumbled across an old New York Times headline that declared 'God is Dead'. That was like a Help Wanted ad, since it's unnatural for there to be no God. Besides, I was bored with being merely stupendously famous."

"Why are you here, then?" asked the Honcho. "If I was God, I'd be in a room full of lissome blond nymphets who just overdosed on aphrodisiacs."

"If you were God, we'd all be atheists", jeered the Golfer. "I'm here because you and I have an arrangement. Don't you remember? Whoever controls the mythology rule the world. I deliver the mythology, and you deliver the political acumen. Our religion is Ismism."

Freeman wanted to know more about this new religion, particularly since he had the attention of its God. "Tell me about Ismism."

The Safari Golfer placed a benevolent hand on Freeman's forehead. "Ismism is a worship of the Common Good. It transcends all other isms."

"How will I know Ismism?"

"You cannot know it."

"Where is it?"

"It is no where."

"Of what value is it?"

"It is the reason for being."

"Why do we worship Ismism?"

The Golfer glanced over at the Honcho, who winked mischievously. "Some people need to find meaning in their lives, and others need to wield power over everyone else. Ismism fulfills both needs."

Freeman struggled with God's identity, as he had since he was a child. "Aside from your God clothes, how will people know you're God?"

"How would anyone recognize God? Do you know what God looks like?"

Freeman had no idea, other than a vague recollection of a painting by Michelangelo, who he suspected also had no idea. "I suppose you look as much like God as anyone else. But shouldn't there be outward signs of your godliness, like miracles, speaking in tongues, or calamitous events?"

"I've rendered a miracle", said the Golfer haughtily. "I holed out a four iron from deep within the magnolias at the Masters for a tournament-winning eagle. But, the sign of true faith is to eschew miracles. Dostoevski said, 'Do not seek miracles, for miracles kill faith'. St. Augustine told us 'faith is to believe what we do not see, and the reward of this faith is to see what we believe.' Therefore, it would be profane for me to dazzle you with a shower of manna or some burning bushes."

"What about speaking in tongues?"

"I suppose I could recite Latin verses for you. Latin was the tongue used by Catholic priests to make the liturgy seem deep, sophisticated, and hypnotic rather than like vapid dogma that had been incanted unthinkingly millions of times for two thousand years. It's much like the game of Deep Out, which was a ruse parlayed by the poet laureates of the Hippie movement, such as Dylan and McLuhan, who wrote things so profoundly meaningless that they garnered millions of followers and became inordinately famous, simply by confusing people into finding meaning in words that had none. However, incanting dogma in strange tongues makes it difficult for meaningless phraseology to be understood, since the meaninglessness often gets overlooked in the translation. I prefer my meaningless pronouncements to be clearly understood as such. That's what Ismism is all about."

Freeman shrugged helplessly, because he found no meaning in the Golfer's words. "What about calamities, like the Four Horsemen of the Apocalypse?"

"Calamities are my forte", boasted the Safari Golfer. "I've had more triple bogeys than the original God. Also, as the Honcho's associate, I can take vicarious credit for the F.U.N. fiasco and the Vhaicam disaster, which are bigger calamities than the biblical death, famine, pestilence, and destruction."

"What about the Unfortunate Cleaning Lady Episode, the Great Tree Growing Incident, and the Debilitating Zero and Comma Shortage?"

"If blame for those calamities is still available, I'll take it", said the Golfer graciously. "Then people will fear me. I can't be the Prime Orchestrator of the universe if no one fears me. Once Dorothy and her friends learned that the Great and Powerful Oz was really just a paranoid old man frantically manipulating a mechanical illusion, his power over them vanished. Ironically, it was the dog Toto who revealed the charlatan by pulling aside the curtain."

Freeman understood the fear of God. As a youth, he once peeked up a schoolgirl's skirt and ogled her lily-white panties. Having sinned, he feared that he was going to be struck dead by lightning if he didn't hurry off to confession. Unfortunately, on the way to church, he was sidetracked by a sandlot baseball game. Later that evening, as he lay in bed, he remembered with a start that he had forgotten to confess. He waited apprehensively in the darkness for the lightning bolt. He wondered what his mother would think when she found his corpse in the morning. He briefly considered leaving a note, but abandoned this notion because putting his sinful thoughts into writing would probably just increase the voltage of God's death strike.

When morning came, he was still alive. There had been no lightning bolt or any other violence by an angry Supreme Being lurking somewhere in the universe. After this sleepless yet uneventful night, Freeman concluded that either there was no God, or he didn't care if boys ogled the underwear of young girls. "What happens after you create an aura of fear?" he asked the Golfer.

"Oscar Wilde said the greatest service that could be rendered to Christians would be to convert them to Christianity. Likewise, the greatest service that I can render to Americans is to convert them to Ismism. It would be a shame for Ismism to be the national religion if no one actually practiced it. It would also be a shame if the Honcho didn't get re-elected, which is more to the point."

"That doesn't sound very religious," said Freeman.

"I'm not religious. I am God. Organized religions and God have little in common."

"How are you going to convert Americans to Ismism?"

"I am the Word, according to the gospel of John", explained the Golfer. "I am the Truth. If I say it, it therefore is. My words become the myths and beliefs of other men. I see and think for the masses, which then act on my behalf. We are one. We are me. Like the biblical Yahweh, 'I Am'. Once the masses understand this, their conversion to Ismism will follow. Since I'm going convert Christians to Ismism first, I've founded a group called 'Sincere Christians Righteously Engaged in the Abolition of Morality'. S.C.R.E.A.M. will subtly bastardize Christian principles into the contrary tenets of the new secular state religion, so that the antitheses of the Ten Commandments become the American credo without anyone noticing."

"How is Ismism the antitheses of the Ten Commandments?"

The Safari Golfer patiently enlightened his pagan postulant. "For example, the fifth commandment tells Christians 'Thou shalt not kill'. Ismism exalts killing, through abortion, war, CIA plots, Mafia collaboration, support of right and left wing dictatorships, genocide of native populations, testing of nuclear and biological weapons, subsidies for the tobacco industry, limits on medical aid imposed by national health insurance regulations, and banning of alternative health approaches to protect the doctors' monopoly.

"The fourth commandment admonishes Christians to honor their parents. Ismism seeks to destroy the nuclear family and make parenting irrelevant. The state is the parent in Ismism, which advocates welfare, government funded day care centers, homosexuality, and militant feminism as the means to obsolete families and make the state an enormous orphanage.

"The seventh commandment instructs Christians not to steal. Theft is a trademark of Ismism. It's followers confiscate money through income taxes, excise taxes, surtaxes, sales taxes, tariffs, licensing fees, estate taxes, value added taxes, use taxes, property taxes, and any other form of institutionalized theft they can get away with.

"The tenth commandment tells the Christian not to covet his neighbor's house or belongings. Ismism is an orgy of covetousness. Ismists covet everything that isn't theirs, and if they can't confiscate what they covet, they outlaw it or declare it to be environmentally dangerous.

"The eighth commandment compels Christians not to bear false witness. Ismism is a proponent of the Big Lie, also known as Political Correctness, which is used to squelch dissenting opinions from the Unbelievers. Ismists abandon truth in favor of slogans that dogmatically defend the Faith, rather than illuminate the masses.

"It's amazing how many Christians have unwittingly abandoned Christ's philosophy and adopted Ismism", the Golfer concluded. "They have unconsciously repudiated their faith and accepted ours. Most Christians are no longer Christians. They just don't realize it."

A bizarre rush of frigid air into the Honcho's office suddenly distracted the three men. When they wheeled around to find its source, they were surprised to see Thomas Jefferson, who had somehow entered without catching anyone's attention. A shiver instinctively snaked down Freeman's spine. Jefferson had an unholy habit of appearing and disappearing in ways that defied the laws of physics.

"Mr. Freeman", said Jefferson, "Please do not fall under the spell of that charlatan. It is degrading for any human to do so."

Freeman was momentarily torn between fear of God and respect for Jefferson. "But . . . but he's a priest! He claims he's God!"

"I'm not afraid of priests, and neither should you be. They've tried upon me their pious whining, hypocritical canting, and deceitful slandering, without giving me one moment of pain. In every country and in every age, the priest has been hostile to liberty. He's always in alliance with the despot, abetting his abuses in return for protection of his own. As Pascal noted, 'Men never do evil so completely and cheerfully as when they do it from religious conviction.' And whenever those with religious conviction cast a longing eye on public office, a rottenness begins in their conduct."

"Careful, Jefferson", said the Honcho. "The Safari Golfer is now the Prime Orchestrator of the universe. He has dominion over life, death, and sand traps. Some reverence is in order."

"Nay, heresy is in order", retorted Jefferson. "Civil and ecclesiastical rulers, who are themselves but fallible and uninspired men, have set up their own opinions as true and infallible and imposed them on others in order to establish and maintain false religions over all the world and throughout all time. The Safari Golfer knows no more of the way to heaven than I do, and is less concerned to direct me right than I am to go right of my own inclination. I have no need of him to understand what God means to Thomas Jefferson. No man should abandon the care of his salvation to another, because it is a matter that lies solely between him and his god. Even less involved should be the government, because it can't impose opinions. Therefore, I revere the American revolutionaries who built a wall of separation between church and state.

"Separating church from state was the most profoundly courageous and momentous act ever executed on this planet. The American revolutionaries recognized that the Holy Spirit and the Common Good are simply different manifestations of the same desire—to coerce people into accepting a non-reality through which they can be manipulated, because this non-reality is outside the realm of logical discussion and therefore unchallangeable. There is very little difference in style, substance, and purpose between a pulpit pounding reverend and a podium-pounding politician. It is immeasurably important to remove mysticism from the realm of politics, leaving it flooded in the cold harsh light of reason. This was the quintessence of the American Revolution. State must be separated from church, or more precisely, from secular and divine mysticism. Our lives depend on it."

"Government without either secular or divine religion is inconceivable", sniffed the Safari Golfer haughtily. "How will people know what to believe without religion?"

"How will they know what to believe with religion?" Jefferson retorted. "The Inquisition was established by Pope Gregory IX of the Catholic Church to stop people from thinking. At one point, the Inquisition included the Bible on its infamous Index of Forbidden Books to keep common folks from reading it without ecclesiastical guidance. True understanding doesn't require religion, it abhors religion. When Napoleon asked the astronomer Laplace where God fit into his view of the universe, he replied, 'I have no need of that hypothesis.' Laplace's message was that the universe can function without God, just as men can flourish without the dogmas, faiths, and myths that have marched in lockstep with the organized oppressors of mankind from civilization's dawn. Those who claim mythical knowledge while suppressing free thought inevitably seek to oppress. As Dostoevski's Cardinal Inquisitor put it, 'In return for salvation, the church takes our freedom.'"

Freeman wallowed in confusion as two enormous polarities pulled on his malleable soul. On his left was the imposing presence of God, who had for some unknowable reason manifested himself as the Safari Golfer. On his right was the unyielding rational presence of Thomas Jefferson, who more and more frequently spoke out in opposition to the religious and political dogmas suffocating the nation.

While these two metaphysical polarities tugged on his uncertain soul, Freeman sensed that his ball and chain was not only a physical deadweight, it was a spiritual albatross. As he sunk deeper and deeper into his subconscious inner self, disembodied voices haunted his mind. Cassandra, who herself paid an enormous price for bravely defying the gods, pleaded mournfully for him to stand tall and defy the mystics and power mongers. Then Mephistopheles beguilingly teased him to surrender his mind and kneel in supplication to the greater Common Good as defined by priests and kings.

The tempestuous forces that had battled for mankind's spiritual allegiance for millennia assailed him. The ball and chain binding his ankle and choking his soul felt heavier and tighter. He wasn't yet prepared for the enormous psychological struggle to choose a path toward one of these polarities. He succumbed to the safer haven of unconsciousness, which was merely a more acute state of the apathy that characterized his conscious existence. His body, following the lead of his unconscious mind, slumped to the floor. He laid in a dead faint between the feet of Jefferson and the Safari Golfer.

* * *

Several days later, the Head Honcho and his entourage climbed aboard the Juggernaut, which was a train he used for whistle-stop tours of his constituency. This campaign swing would give him opportunities to feed his people innocuous slogans and to promise them wonderful things that had no earthly chance of happening. The Juggernaut whisked him to a steady stream of fund raising dinners where lobbyists tendered large campaign donations in exchange for future legislative largesse. The tour also permitted him to shmooze labor union representatives, to wave flags and kiss babies in public, and to screw the breath out of Buxomus in the privacy of his luxurious coach car. The Juggernaut was a runaway political orgy on wheels that trampled everything wholesome in its unstoppable path.

The Juggernaut's 100 cars housed assorted aides, secretaries, spin doctors, policy wonks, consorts, butlers, cooks, reporters, ghost writers, masseuses, pollsters, secret service agents, and Italian golfing buddies. The opulent caboose, which trailed behind this political paraphernalia, housed the Honcho and his close associates, including Buxomus Blondus, Jefferson, Freeman, But Sir!, the Safari Golfer, and Sammy Gioncarlo.

The train also carried a menagerie of token minorities. There were token blacks, Hispanics, Eskimos, native Americans, and representatives of all other oppressed races and nationalities. There were token feminists, rape victims, gays, and lesbians. There were token fat people, anorexics, midgets, ugly people, and quadriplegics. There were token veterans of foreign wars, senior citizens, and environmentalists. Every human classification was represented except healthy WASP males. These token minorities were kept constantly ready for display with the Head Honcho whenever photo opportunities arose.

The first stop on the Juggernaut's itinerary was a liberal college town full of idealistic youths that would eventually make careers out of spending someone else's money. To an exuberant gathering at the train station, the Honcho promised wage and price controls, progressive taxation, nationalization of industry, improved relations with communist and socialist regimes, expanded welfare programs, free college education for all, government-funded abortion, affirmative action for everyone except WASP males, unilateral disarmament, and free sex with Bill Clinton. The youthful crowd surged forward to embrace their new champion and to collect their free sex vouchers. The Senator played them like a master violinist strumming a Stradivarius. Through a bullhorn, he shouted arcane quotations from George McGovern, John Anderson, and Al Gore as the Juggernaut pulled away.

The next whistle stop was a bastion of conservatism. To address these constituents, the Honcho donned a suit and tie, spoke in a grave businesslike monotone, and paid homage to Herbert Hoover and Ronald Reagan in his opening remarks. He promised them subsidies for failing businesses, government loans for colossal agribusinesses, and increased tariffs to protect American industries from fiendish Pacific Rim competitors. He also promised regressive taxes, improved relations with right wing dictatorships, elimination of student loan programs and welfare, a ban on abortion, more defense spending, and an end to affirmative action. Finally, he promised to draft into the armed services the irresponsible college students in the town he had just visited. The conservatives surged forward and hungrily grabbed for copies of his 100-point plan to lull American business into a false sense of security.

At the next stop, angry Asian immigrants confronted the Honcho because of the mayhem and death in Vhaicam and because of his xenophobic plan to slap tariffs on Pacific Rim nations. Banners and posters virulently condemned him and the federal government. As the unruly crowd chanted irate slogans, he reached deep into his bottomless bag of political chicanery. He held aloft a large picture of a Japanese child and declared to the Asians that he was one of them, since this was a picture of himself as a young boy. He explained that he acquired his Caucasian features and white pigmentation in a high school gene-splicing experiment gone awry.

The hostile crowd, unconvinced that the Honcho was Japanese, demanded more proof, which put him in a serious bind. The most compelling proofs of Japanese ancestry are compulsions to become a kamikaze pilot, to commit hari kari, or to build electronics and automobiles with better value than anyone else. Unfortunately, since he was really an American, he couldn't build electronics and automobiles cheaper and better than anyone else. And being a kamikaze pilot or committing hari kari would perhaps gain him enough respect to win the election, but he would be unable to savor the victory.

As perspiration stained his armpits, he looked anxiously to But Sir! for a way out of this political mess. But Sir! handed him a razor-sharp machete and apologetically whispered that there was really no choice, since thousands of critical votes were at stake. However, the Honcho wasn't ready for suicide, even if it ensured his re-election. He stared past But Sir! to Freeman with a deeply beseeching look. Freeman paused to decide whether he preferred the Head Honcho alive or dead. He pragmatically chose the "alive" option, because the senator signed his paychecks.

Freeman rushed into the bowels of the train. Moments later, he reappeared on the podium with a confused Japanese youth that had been borrowed from the stash of token Asians. He whispered instructions to the Honcho. The crowd grew louder and more impatient. The Honcho smiled as Freeman's words sunk in. He embraced the confused Japanese boy and declared boldly, "This is my son!" The audience gasped. The boy looked up at the Honcho with astonishment. "Would you all agree that if my son is Japanese, then I too must be Japanese?"

The crowd murmured momentarily before nodding their collective assent. The Honcho declared, "I will now prove that my son is Japanese!" He handed the machete to the young child, who instinctively wrapped his pudgy hands around its handle. The Honcho told him that the Emperor wished him to commit hari kari for the sake of the Motherland. The child wasn't certain which emperor or motherland wanted this, but he had so much faith that he vigorously thrust the weapon into his midsection. Blood and viscera spurted from his lacerated innards as he churned the blade. He fell lifelessly to the podium floor with his face contorted in a horribly brave and faithful grimace.

The grisly suicide immediately effected the crowd. They surged forward toward the train's podium in an unrestrained frenzy to acclaim their newfound Japanese candidate for Congress. While the Honcho handed out campaign literature, Freeman summoned two token Hispanics from inside the train to clean up the bloody carnage that used to be a Japanese boy.

Freeman wondered why his idea ended tragically. He assumed that God would intervene to save the faithful child, just as God had intervened when the biblical Abraham offered to sacrifice his son. Unfortunately, God had failed to save the Japanese boy, so Freeman sought him out. After scurrying from car to car, he finally found the Safari Golfer studying stock quotations in the Wall Street Journal. Freeman recognized the greedy look on the Golfer's face. It was the same look that he had seen as a young acolyte on his pastor's face every time he emptied the wicker basket containing the weekly tithes donated by parishioners. "If you're God, why are so preoccupied with money?" he challenged.

"You can't run a religion without money", preached the Safari Golfer. "If the Catholic Church wasn't so well endowed, Christ would have been just another statistic, lost amongst the thousands of other anonymous criminals and rebels hung on crosses by the Romans in 33 AD"

"Perhaps, but because of your preoccupation with money, you missed your cue to rescue the Japanese boy."

"What was his religion?" the Golfer asked calmly.

"I suppose he was a Bhuddist."

"He'll understand then. Shit happens, and there's nothing we can do about it. The Golfer resumed tabulating his riches.

Back on the podium at the rear of the caboose, the Honcho shouted farewell promises to his newly hooked Asian worshippers, including a commitment to tear down the trade barriers he had promised to erect at an earlier whistle stop, so that cheaper Oriental goods could flow into American markets. The crowd celebrated wildly until the Juggernaut drew out of sight.

The Honcho met with his staff to prepare for the remaining whistle stops. Freeman, who had inventoried the token minorities and disadvantaged people stashed in the train in case the Honcho got into another embarrassing bind, read off his tally of the politically correct menagerie, until his brow furrowed with concern. "What's troubling you, Yessir!?" asked the Honcho as he caressed the bare thigh of Buxomus Blondus, who was pretending to take shorthand minutes.

"One of our politically correct tokens is missing."

"Of course! We consumed a Japanese boy at the last stop."

"No, I already took him into account. We're missing a Jew."

"That's exactly what the Romans said when they found an empty sepulcher on the first Easter."

"This is serious", scolded Freeman. "What if we need to circumcise your Jewish son to prove you're not a gentile?"

"Then I'll slap a yarmulke on your head, hand you a copy of the Old Testament, and circumcise you, my son."

Freeman shivered and subconsciously slid his hand down over his genitals. He glumly recalled Lyndon Johnson's observation that the only difference between a cannibal and a politician is that the cannibal eats only his enemies. "I've already been circumcised", he bluffed.

"Damn! I wonder if castration is a traditional Jewish ritual….Oh well, there aren't any Jews in my district anyway. I already checked the Registry of Politically Correct Demographics. Therefore, I'm adding anti-Semitism to my campaign platform."

"But Sir!" interjected But Sir!. "How can you run a campaign of anti-Semitism if there aren't any Jews in your district?"

"The same way I can run a campaign of honesty and integrity on Capitol Hill. It's all just vapid slogans and silly posturing. Nobody gives a damn."

"But Sir! Even if there are no Jews in your district, a campaign of anti-Semitism will repulse reasonable people and remind them of the Holocaust."

The Honcho raised his eyebrows sharply. "The Holocaust? What was that?"

"Adolph Hitler and his National Socialist government gassed and burned two Jews per minute for seven years to purify the Aryan race and rid the world of money-grubbing capitalists."

"Who says governments aren't efficient?" gloated the Honcho. "Speaking of which, how many people have we killed in Vhaicam so far?"

"Not enough", said Freeman. "Even though four million have died on both sides, the Rabbit People bred eight million more since the non-war started."

"That's no fun."

"No sir, that *is* F.U.N.", corrected Freeman, as the Juggernaut pulled into another station. Hearing the whistle's loud lament, the Honcho reluctantly removed his giant paw from Buxomus' milky white thigh and readied himself for another pro forma performance for his constituents. But when an aide announced their arrival at Middletown, he angrily confronted Freeman. "I told you to leave Middletown off the itinerary, you insubordinate imbecile!"

Freeman gulped and took two steps backward. "Yessir, you did. But, I thought we should stop here anyway, because Middletown is the only American city that doesn't receive any federal assistance. Middletowners have an exceptional work ethic, and they're intensely proud of their self-sufficiency. You can use them to illustrate what the American dream is all about."

"Freeman, you're the stupidest goddamned public relations liaison in political history!"

"I . . . I don't understand", he croaked.

"Why waste time campaigning in a town that needs nothing? How in the Safari Golfer's name can I buy their votes, if I can't offer them any federal grants, programs, or loans? Not only would they realize they don't need me, they'd realize they're paying for all of the grants, programs, and loans I've already promised to the other cities on the Juggernaut's itinerary! That would be a disaster!"

"I'm beginning to understand", said Freeman. "You refuse to see them because they pay your salary and for the electoral bribes promised to everyone else who's not as self-sufficient, so that you can remain in office and continue to ignore them until the next election, at which point you will ignore them even more."

"Exactly. Not only will I refuse to see them, I'm going to officially condemn them, just so no one thinks the self-sufficient bastards have contaminated me. Hell, give me a town full of helpless people any day. Not only will I get re-elected by promising to help, us professional bureaucrats will get rich administering spurious programs for them. Our jobs depend on ignoring the anti-social renegades in villages like Middletown. Get us out of here immediately!" He fumed until the Juggernaut's engines rumbled to life.

The next whistle stop was a press conference. The Head Honcho ascended the train's podium and planted his imposing body in front of a bank of microphones. The hands of several reporters shot in the air. The Honcho acknowledged one who asked, "Mr. Senator, what will you do about the recent spate of shootings at post offices by disgruntled employees?"

The Honcho leaned forward with his jaw set and his steely eyes charged with passion. "Nothing. Is there a follow up question?"

The reporter was astonished by the Honcho's terseness. "How can you just do nothing?"

"We considered taking measures to protect postal workers from each other. But during our investigation, we actually stood in line at a postal retail window with some commoners, which was a rare experience for those of us endowed with the franking privilege, which shouldn't be confused with other congressional privileges that begin with the letter 'f'. The service was so slow and the truculent workers were so rude I was tempted to shoot them myself. We concluded that it's better for postal employees to shoot each other than for customers to do it." He summarily waved his arm. "Next question."

Arms shot up. He pointed to a Washington Post reporter. "Mr. Honcho, you fought vigorously for the bussing bill Congress just ratified. How would you feel if your child was bused to an inner city school full of poor minorities?"

The Honcho smiled warmly. "This bussing bill is one of the crowning achievements of my humble public service career. The only things I'm prouder of are saluting the Stars and Stripes, eating apple pie, buying Chevrolets, and supporting Major League Baseball's exemption from anti-trust regulations, which reminds me of the legislation I sponsored declaring Willie Mays the greatest baseball player of all time. Willie Mays is black, you know. Include that in your story." He paused briefly to admire his own political finesse. "Do you have a follow up question?"

"You haven't answered my first question. Would you be apprehensive if your own child was bussed to an urban school full of poor minorities?"

"No, because my child would be safely tucked away in an exclusive private school, and would therefore be exempt from my bussing legislation."

"Here's my follow up question. Isn't the contradiction between your public position and your private behavior a clear example of your cynical abuse of democracy?"

"Hell no! I'm not going to let a Prima Donna bureaucrat in Washington bus my kid to a ghetto school, even if that Prima Donna bureaucrat is me! What's good for the Head Honcho is good for America, but that doesn't necessarily imply that what's good for America is good for the Head Honcho." He snorted his disgust and pointed to another reporter. "Next question."

"Mr. Honcho, as a college student, you were arrested several times for instigating anti-war demonstrations, and you authored vitriolic letters in the campus newspaper condemning Johnson's escalation of the Vietnam conflict. How do you now justify your support of the brutal non-war in Vhaicam?"

The Honcho paused to rearrange history in his head. "Years of public service taught me that defending the American way is the noblest sacrifice one can make."

"Sir, what *really* caused your flip-flop on this issue?"

The Honcho chuckled. "When I was in college, my draft number was 16, so I was guaranteed to get my ass shot off. My situation is completely different today. Not only am I exempt from the draft, my ass is safely protected by secret service agents. Next question."

"Senator, at the end of each year, the government wastefully expends its remaining funds to avoid budget cuts in the next fiscal year. Usually, one quarter of the government's annual budget is spent in the last month of the year. Former Secretary of the Treasury Blumenthal described this as 'pushing money out the door with a wheelbarrow'. Do you plan to fix this?"

"Absolutely!" said the Honcho. "We're installing motorized conveyers to automatically suck money out of the Treasury in the final month of the year. Conveyers are ten times more efficient than wheelbarrows, which will enable the government to squander money more effectively than ever, making us all proud to be Americans."

"Sir, won't that wasteful practice worsen the oppressive burden borne by taxpayers? Currently, the average American must work until May 17 to pay his taxes for the year."

"American taxpayers have the wrong mindset", countered the Honcho. "Third Reich Germans had a better attitude. They simply said, 'Work makes you free'. They were so enamored with this concept they put these words above the entrances of their concentration camps. Next question."

"Mr. Honcho, the budget of every federal government department was increased by Congress this year, yet none of them achieved their objectives last year. Why is such chronic ineffectiveness rewarded with more money?"

"Everyone involved is simply being rational", the Senator replied calmly.

"Could you please explain how it's rational?"

"Sure. A department foolish enough to achieve its objectives gets disbanded and it's employees get thrown into the brutal private sector, where they are woefully unprepared for adding value to a product or service. Look at what happened to NASA. When Kennedy challenged them to put a man on the moon, those imbecilic rocket scientists actually did it! It was an unprecedented bureaucratic snafu. Consequently, their budget was slashed, and many people involved in mankind's noblest achievement were laid off. NASA would have been better off if they had missed the moon by a wider margin with each succeeding attempt. If they had launched a moon shot and mistakenly landed on Pluto, Congress would have doubled their appropriation the next year. Likewise, it's foolish for the Welfare Department to eliminate poverty, for the Defense Department to eliminate wars, and for the Education Department to cultivate a generation of intelligent children. They're paid by the hour, with guaranteed cost of living increases, to be inept. If you were paid by the hour to battle an inferior opponent, would you slay him with the first blow? Of course not!"

"Sir, you've explained why bureaucrats rationally fail, but not why it's rational for Congress to reward the failures with more money."

"It's extortion through incompetence", said the Head Honcho. "Politicians who cut expenditures on welfare, defense, and education, even if those bureaucracies have failed in their missions, will not be re-elected. Americans want something done, even if it's just throwing more dollars and bureaucrats at problems each year. The politician wants to keep his job as much as the bureaucrats want to keep theirs. The only way he can keep his job is to advocate spending more extravagantly than his opponent. Once he gets elected, there's no other place to spend these extravagant funds than with the bureaucracies that have already failed, because the federal government is a monopoly, and that's the American Way. Next question."

"Mr. Honcho, is it true that you almost blew up the planet during a drunken reverie at a secret encampment where unspeakable acts of debauchery are performed?"

The Honcho knew there were two ways to dodge such a question. He could deflect attention toward another scurrilous senator by pointing out that more people died at Chappaquidick than died at the Bavarian Forest. Or, he could use the technique Ronald Reagan made famous by pretending to be urgently summoned and abruptly ending the press conference. Who could forget those endless images of Reagan, with his hand cupped around his hearing aid, struggling to hear imaginary aides while reporters fired ruthless questions at him?

The Honcho chose the second method. He cupped his hand to his ear, craned his head toward a nonexistent aide, and apologetically advised his audience that he had to leave immediately to avoid inconveniencing the good citizens at his next whistle stop.

The press conference was actually the day's last event. Freed from the media's clutching tentacles, the Honcho settled into his opulent railway car to drown in liquor, which he had consumed moderately thus far to give his constituents the mistaken impression that he was a sober, temperate, and disciplined leader. But now he yearned to get indecently drunk. His hands shook as he poured a double blast of Old Bushmills over ice. He dumped the mind-numbing ambrosia past his dry lips. His stomach lurched and his throat burned, but he craved more. As the Juggernaut rumbled down the tracks, shots of Old Bushmills streamed into his cavernous innards.

Soon, he was so drunk that he didn't see Buxomus Blondus enter. The liquor even blinded him to the sensuous strip tease she did in anticipation of his traditional coup de grace after an exhausting campaign performance. Fucking her brought completeness to his universe, because she was usually the only person whom he hadn't yet screwed in some manner while politicking. Today, however, he was more enthralled with his liquor than his secretary, so he was oblivious to her captivating gyrations.

After a few minutes of teasing the libido of her boss in vain, Buxomus flopped onto a leather couch, clad only in pink panties. She indolently twirled her brassiere on her finger while the Honcho emptied a bottle directly down his throat in order to more efficiently drink himself into a stupor.

Suddenly, the caboose door swung open. But Sir! thrust his uninvited face into the Honcho's lair. Buxomus screamed as her delicate hands inadequately covered her corpulent breasts. The Honcho spun around angrily. He noticed Buxomus for the first time, tossed an afghan over her, and then confronted his intrusive aide. "What the fuck do you want? Can't you see that I'm busy?"

"But Sir!" squealed But Sir!. "Look outside! The tracks are lined with thousands of people who're preparing to lynch somebody. You're the guest of honor, judging from their banners."

The Honcho slammed his empty bottle down, rushed to a window, pulled aside the drapes, and saw the mob. The Juggernaut was moving too fast for him to read their signs, and he couldn't hear their shouts. But he could see the contorted anger in the faces whizzing by his window, and the intent of their clenched fists was unmistakable. "It's a goddamn insurrection!" he cursed. He grabbed But Sir! by the shirtsleeve and rushed through crowded cars toward the lead engine of the Juggernaut to better assess his predicament. They brushed past astonished secret service agents. They flew by stunned spin doctors and policy wonks. They clambered over politically correct token minorities. When they finally arrived at the lead engine, they found Freeman and the Safari Golfer already there.

The Honcho forced his way closer to the cab's windshield, where he could now read the signs being held aloft by the insurrectionists. The crowd's political and emotional disposition was ominous. "The time for action is now!" blared one sign. "We're reclaiming our inalienable rights to life, liberty, and the pursuit of happiness", asserted another sign. "Governments derive their power from the consent of the governed", contended a third banner. "Whenever government becomes destructive, it is the right of the people to abolish it", threatened a fourth. "No taxation without representation", demanded a fifth. "No more Vhaicams", pleaded a sixth. "It's time for a new Declaration of Independence!" declared a seventh. "The Juggernaut stops here", said an eighth placard, which elicited a self-assured chuckle from the Honcho. "Idealistic fools! They can't possibly stop my Juggernaut!"

"They're going to try anyway", said Freeman, pointing toward the horizon. The sinuous crowd lining the tracks curved up and over the steep embankment. Barely visible from the cab of the onrushing Juggernaut was a phalanx of insurrectionists who had mounted the rails and formed a dense human barrier directly in the locomotive's path. The Honcho stopped smiling, and everyone else fell stonily silent as three massive diesel engines hurled them toward the human blockade. All eyes turned to the engineer, expecting him to engage the rampaging train's emergency brakes. Unfortunately, he was paralyzed by confusion. He looked helplessly toward the Head Honcho for direction. The people on the tracks were now in immediate danger of being vivisected by the slicing wheels of the projectile hurtling toward them.

The Honcho's face was alive with beads of nervous sweat. He was locked into a sophomoric game of chicken, pitting his stubborn ego against the dogged determination of the insurrectionists. To make matters worse, his judgment was severely impaired by whiskey. A few more seconds slipped away. The crowd on the tracks didn't yield. The Juggernaut reached the point where it had to brake or certain catastrophe would ensue.

Just then, a bullet smashed through the windshield and ricocheted eerily within the cab. Everyone scrambled for cover as several more shots rang out. Shards of glass rained over their cowering heads. More shots peppered the train. One of them struck the engineer in the head, killing him instantly. The train hurtled uncontrolled toward the insurrectionists barricading the tracks.

The insurrectionists now recognized that the runaway locomotive wasn't going to stop. Shouts went up to abandon the blockade. The shouts turned to screams as terror spread like wildfire through the crowd. People leapt off both sides of the railway, but the embankments were soon clogged with frightened rebels tumbling over each other. The crowd was too compressed for everyone on the tracks to escape in such little time. The screaming doubled in intensity. They reverted to primitive barbarism to save themselves, kicking and clawing to move the mass of humanity blocking them. The tracks vibrated as the Juggernaut charged to within 100 yards of the crowd. The roar of the three powerful engines dwarfed the screaming of those scrambling toward safety. At fifty yards, the smell of fear intermingled with the smell of diesel fuel. At twenty yards, the looming profile of the locomotive blocked out the late afternoon sun, suddenly casting a foreboding shadow over the crowd. At ten yards, the cacophony of screaming subsided, partly because throats were choked by paroxysms of fear, and partly because the only hope remaining was silent prayer. But if any deities were listening, they chose not to intervene, so the Head Honcho's unstoppable Juggernaut, weighing 900 tons and traveling 65 miles per hour, slammed into a horde of helpless victims.

The coupler shroud crushed the first wave of humanity, plowing mangled bodies into the next rows of victims, as a macabre bow wave of broken corpses rose up and sluiced around the locomotive. Other bodies slid beneath the train and were carved into clumps of dead flesh by the scything wheels. The truly unlucky were dragged alongside the engine, their appendages mutilated into grotesque anatomical vestiges by the pumping connecting rods. Like a meteor ripping through the virtual emptiness of space, the Juggernaut sliced through the crowd with unaltered momentum and direction. The only evidence of a collision with living creatures was red viscera splattered on the cab's housing, as if it had just plowed through a patch of giant strawberries.

After the Juggernaut shredded the last row of insurrectionists, an off-shift engineer from the crew's quarters entered the cab and grabbed the controls. As he halted the rampaging train, he sent an emergency radio message to the nearest train station dispatcher and breathlessly reported the tragedy. He begged for medical aid to be sent immediately, because there was at least one casualty on the train and hundreds of dead and wounded on the tracks. Suddenly, he looked puzzled. "The dispatcher wants to know where we are!" he said to the people in the cab.

"Between Lexington and Concord", said Freeman.

The engineer relayed this location to the dispatcher. Meanwhile, the Head Honcho, his face bleeding from several cuts, frothed with rage. He pounded the train's instrument panel with balled fists. "Goddamn them! This is war! This is just the beginning!"

The Honcho's deranged ranting and the train's location triggered deja vu in Freeman. Suddenly, Cassandra's ghostly voice came quietly from nowhere and resounded in his mind, ". . . . History is always and everywhere, along with the men and women who lived it passionately. It surrounds us and compels us. It is lived and relived, in unending cycles. . . ." Even more haunting than Cassandra's voice was something Freeman had seen through the Juggernaut's window when the first gunshots zinged from the insurrectionists. He shook his head in disbelief, but the paranormal vision clutched his consciousness with increased vigor. He shivered, and his skin prickled with fear. It had to be a case of mistaken identity.

The Head Honcho was also deeply troubled. He returned to his private cabin to lick his physical and psychological wounds. The stark reality of being shot at terrified him. He opened another bottle of Old Bushmills and eagerly drained it, hoping to quell the fluttering fear in his heart and the strange sense of isolation in his soul. The darkness of his curtained cabin matched the darkness of his conscience.

The alcohol coursing through his veins numbed his sensibilities so much that he thought he saw someone move inside the cabin, even though he thought he was alone. Another pull on the bottle dimmed his awareness further, but he saw movement again. Dread gripped his heart. Only the damnable Coffee Account Dues Collector would invade his sanctuary like this. "Go away!", he commanded into the translucent darkness. "My coffee account is up to date." He took another tug on his bottle, fully expecting the shadowy figure to depart peacefully.

Unfortunately, the shadowy figure moved closer. "Your coffee account is not my concern", said a nasally voice in the darkness. "I'm a Hatter, not a brewer."

The Honcho's head fell into his hands. The last thing he needed was a visit by the Mad Hatter, who could dispense more tortured dialogue and nonsensical reasoning than even politicians. "Shit! I thought you were the Coffee Account Dues Collector."

"A common error." The Mad Hatter stepped out of the darkness and sat down. He was wearing a tall black top hat with a price tag still attached and a bow tie with red polka dots clasping a heavily starched white collar. A red waistcoat covered a red and white checkered shirt, which matched his red and white checkered pants. The pants were much too short, exposing pencil thin legs clad in tasteless yellow socks with red stripes. His stringy hair dangled shabbily out from under his hat. His much too prominent nose shadowed his grey, thin lips, which blended into his skin's lusterless pallor. "How are you today?" he asked cheerfully.

"Just great", said the Honcho sardonically.

"No you're not", contradicted the Mad Hatter. "You're going to be beheaded."

"What for?"

"It's really none of your business. I'm quite certain of that."

"How can it be none of my business? It's my head!"

"Oh very well. I'll tell you what for", said the Hatter, who was actually quite anxious to tell the Head Honcho what for. "You see, none of us have forgiven you for killing the Dormouse."

"I didn't kill him! Bureaucratic inertia did. Besides, what's so important about a lousy dormouse? I just ran over hundreds of people with a train."

"Tell it to the judge", said the Hatter. "Actually, you shouldn't tell the judge about killing hundreds of people with a train. You might lose more than just your head."

"Who's the judge?"

"The Red Queen is always the judge." The Hatter pulled two envelopes out of his waistcoat. "One is the summons for your trial. The other is an invitation to play croquet. You have to pick." He dangled the envelopes tauntingly in front of the Honcho.

The Honcho grabbed the envelope in the Hatter's left hand. He tore it open and anxiously read the contents. It was the summons for the trial.

"Don't be too disappointed", said the Mad Hatter. "The other one was a summons for the trial, too. I was just kidding about the croquet invitation."

"You bastard!" growled the Honcho.

"No need to flatter me. I've already agreed to be your defense counsel." The Hatter unleashed a smile reeking of licentious mischief.

"What do you know about the law?" asked the Honcho skeptically.

"Nothing at all."

"Then how can you be my lawyer?"

"It doesn't matter who your lawyer is, because I'm quite sure that you're guilty."

"How can I be guilty? I haven't even been tried yet!" The Honcho felt the familiar surge of frustrated disorientation that invariably resulted from conversations with the Mad Hatter.

"Everyone tried by the Red Queen is automatically guilty. The trial is just for sentencing, which is also unnecessary, since the sentence is always a beheading, which brings us right back to the beginning of this conversation. You've just wasted a great deal of my time", concluded the Hatter, as he pulled a watch from his waistcoat to check what day of the month it was.

"You're mad!"

"Of course I'm mad", agreed the Mad Hatter. "I'm mad. You're mad. We're all mad."

"How do you know that I'm mad?"

"How many other people have conversations with me?"

The Honcho moaned as his head fell back into his hands.

"What do you do for a living?" asked the Mad Hatter to lighten the conversation.

"I'm a U.S. Senator."

"Very curious. Very curious indeed. What does this occupation involve?"

"People get up to speak and say nothing to an audience that doesn't listen, and then everybody disagrees vehemently."

"We call that a Caucus Race in Wonderland", said the Mad Hatter. "The race contestants line up in random positions around a circular track and run madly with no apparent objective. After a while, everyone abruptly stops, whereupon they all argue about who won. It's a mad spectacle. Our greatest fear is that the Red Queen might someday pattern Wonderland's government after the Caucus Races. Wouldn't that be a disaster!"

"It certainly would", acknowledged the Senator, who intuitively understood the mechanics of a caucus race. "It would be even more disastrous if the Red Queen designated some of the caucus racers Democrats and the rest Republicans, who would then govern by running in circles, by constantly arguing over undefined objectives, and by endlessly debating which of them is likely to reach these undefined objectives fastest."

"I've think you've got it! It's unfortunate that you're going to be beheaded, because you would have done quite nicely as a politician in Wonderland."

"Where do I go from here?" asked the Honcho despondently.

"Where do you want to get?"

"I don't care", he sighed with alcohol-laden breath.

"Then it doesn't matter which way you go", replied the Hatter serenely. "What else can I do for you?"

"Can anything save me from a beheading?"

"Hmmmm." The Hatter pensively rubbed his chin. "Why don't you try this?" Out of a seemingly bottomless waistcoat pocket he pulled a glass bottle with a dangling label that said, "drink me".

"What good will that do?" The Honcho suspected it was the infamous treacle that the Hatter never had but always offered.

"It will make you only ten inches tall by shutting you up like a telescope".

"So then I won't be beheaded?"

"I really couldn't say", conceded the Hatter. "But it might be more difficult for the executioner. Maybe he'd just lop off part of your shrunken head."

The Honcho shivered and pushed the bottle away. "Isn't there anything else?"

"Perhaps", said the Hatter, pulling out of his bottomless waistcoat pocket a glass box containing a small cake with the words "eat me" written in icing. "Try this."

"What good will that do?"

"It will make you ten feet tall by opening you up like a telescope."

"So then I won't be beheaded?"

"I really couldn't say. But, the awful thud of your enlarged head plopping into the basket might disgust the Red Queen enough to abolish beheadings. After yours, of course."

"That's nonsense!"

"Of course it's nonsense", agreed the Hatter. "Everything in Wonderland is nonsense, just like everything on your side of the looking glass."

Tears welled in the Honcho's eyes. "Isn't there anything you can do for me?"

"No. However, I brought along an associate who is well versed in wizardry. Perhaps she can help you." The Hatter waved his sinewy arm with a flourish to announce the presence of a heretofore-unseen companion. "I give you Dorothy", he said grandly.

The Honcho was stunned that someone else was in the room. "Dorothy who?"

Just then, a creamy-skinned, sloe-eyed teenage girl stepped out of a shadow. She was wearing a blue checkered knee length jumper over a white blouse, with sky blue ribbons in her auburn pigtailed hair, sky blue anklets, and glittering ruby slippers. Hooked on her arm was a wicker picnic basket. This bizarre apparition dumbfounded him. He turned to the Hatter for an explanation, but the cretin had vanished.

The pigtailed apparition curtsied clumsily. "Pleased to meet you, Mr. Honcho sir", she spoke through pouty red lips. "I'm Dorothy Gale, and I'm from Kansas."

The Honcho's head dropped back into his hands as he waged mortal combat with his inebriated imagination.

Dorothy continued the conversation politely. "The Mad Hatter said you needed help. What troubles you? Cyclones? Wicked Witches? Straw men with no brains?"

The Honcho lifted his head slightly. "I'm troubled by millions of straw men who have no brains. I work with government bureaucrats."

"My goodness!" exclaimed Dorothy. "Why, that sounds very scary indeed. I've been chased by wicked witches, nabbed by flying monkeys, sucked up by a twister, and had apples thrown at me by angry trees, but I've never had to deal with anything so frightening as millions of government bureaucrats! I can see now why the Mad Hatter thought you needed help."

The Honcho chuckled at her naive eagerness to help. It seemed preposterous that a cherubic girl of so few years could have any wisdom to share with him. "I suppose you're going to tell me the Great and Powerful Wizard of Oz will fix everything."

"Oh, of course not!" said Dorothy with endearing earnestness. "Glinda, the Good Witch of the North, taught me a much different lesson. If you're willing, I'll tell you my story. Perhaps you could learn from it what I did."

The Honcho decided to humor the waif from Kansas, if only because her apparition was more charming than the Mad Hatter's. "Tell me your tale, young lady", he said grudgingly.

Dorothy sat on the couch and straightened her jumper. In a pubescent voice she said, "I was feeling very sorry for myself one day on Uncle Henry's farm, so I wondered what life would be like somewhere else. I figured that there must be a place far, far away, where there wasn't any trouble, where all my wishes and dreams would come true, a place beyond the moon and the stars, a truly magical and mystical place that you couldn't get to by boat or by train. I was looking for fulfillment somewhere over the rainbow, because I was unwilling to deal with my life as it was.

"Fate granted my wish in a painful way. I got caught in a twister after talking with a con man in a traveling sideshow that pretended to know all, see all, and offer all. During the storm, a flying shutter struck me. When I came to, the cyclone had lifted our house and dropped it somewhere over the rainbow, just like I wanted, in a magical place called Oz.

"I met many mysterious people there. There were Good Witches, Bad Witches, Munchkins, and other strange creatures. Everyone in Munchkin City was very gracious to me for crushing the Wicked Witch of the East with my house, but I missed Auntie Em and Uncle Henry terribly and I didn't know how to get back to Kansas. The Good Witch Glinda told me to follow the yellow brick road to the magnificent Emerald City, where the Great and Powerful Oz would grant all of my wishes. To protect me along the way, she gave me the dead witch's ruby slippers, which had lots of powerful magic. So, once again I was off on a lark to find fulfillment in some faraway magical place, thinking my problems could only be solved by some mystical power.

"On the way to Oz, I met three very dear friends who also desperately wanted help from the mighty Wizard. The Scarecrow needed a brain, since he believed his head was stuffed with nothing but straw. The Tin Man needed a heart, since he believed his metallic chest couldn't love. The Lion needed courage, since he believed he was a frightened coward inside a ferocious animal's body. They lusted after the deified

Wizard's magical power too, so we set off together to get our wishes granted.

"After a hazardous journey, we arrived at the dazzling Emerald City. Unfortunately, when we asked to see the Wizard, we were told that no one ever sees him. This should have been our first clue that something was amiss with our faithful quest, but we persevered. When we finally saw the Wizard, he frightened us terribly. He refused to grant our wishes unless we did the dangerous deed of bringing back the broomstick of the Wicked Witch of the West.

"This seemed impossible. The mighty Wizard probably hoped the quest to get the broomstick would be the end of us, thereby preserving the aura of his omnipotence. But, amazingly, we found within ourselves the cleverness, courage, and love to overcome not only the Witch, but also our own fears.

"When we returned to the Emerald City with the Wicked Witch's broomstick, we asked again for our wishes to be granted. The Wizard huffed and puffed, clearly perplexed by the success of our adventure. In the meantime, my dog Toto scurried over to a corner of the mighty cathedral where the Great and Powerful Oz presided. Toto pulled back a curtain to reveal a most amazing sight, which triggered an extraordinary epiphany.

"Because of Toto's curiosity, we discovered that the Great and Powerful Oz was just a fearsome mechanical contraption manipulated by a clever con man. There was no omnipotent Wizard to grant our wishes. Our dreams of mystical magic and mythical wizardry were just self-delusions. The Emerald City was an empty monument to a charade that had duped the citizens of Oz ever since the con man had mysteriously arrived in a hot air balloon.

"But our quest wasn't for naught. We discovered that we held the power to grant our wishes within ourselves. We didn't need a distant, omnipotent wizard to make us whole. We didn't need magic or spells or enchantment. We had more power and magic deep inside than existed in the entire mythical Emerald City. We just had to believe in it. Oh sure, the defrocked Wizard gave a diploma to the Scarecrow, but it was a mere parchment. The Scarecrow discovered his own intelligence by figuring out how to save me from the Wicked Witch. The Wizard gave the Lion a medal as proof of his courage, but it was a mere piece of iron. The Lion discovered his own bravery and heroism battling the guards at the Witch's castle. The Wizard gave the Tin Man a testimonial verifying his love for his friends, but it was just a string of hollow words. The Tin Man discovered his own heart by caring deeply enough to risk his rusty hide to save me.

"As for me, I learned that my wish to be somewhere over the rainbow, and my quest to find the Great and Powerful Wizard of Oz, were just mistaken diversions to find meaning outside of myself, when the real meaning I needed to discover was there within me all along." Dorothy sighed wistfully, then hooked her arm through her wicker basket handle and stood up. "If you please, I must go now."

"Wait!" shouted the Honcho loudly enough to startle her. "It's not clear what your tale means. Where should I go from here?"

Dorothy turned to face the great and powerful Head Honcho. Her dark eyes radiated an intense passion that strangely belied her otherwise timid adolescence. "Forgive me for what I am about to say", she said in a frail voice that paradoxically commanded attention. "Unlike my Auntie Em, who refused to tell Elvira Gulch exactly what she thought of her, I haven't learned my manners yet. You should go to hell!"

The Honcho was rocked on his heels by this fragile young girl in pigtails, much like the belligerent Lion had been stunned when Dorothy slapped its snout. Normally, the Honcho would have responded to such impudence with a volcanic tirade, but he was numbed by alcohol and intoxicated by her tender innocence. "What. . . . what do you mean?"

"My goodness!" exclaimed Dorothy. "Why, surely you must know what I mean. You work with lots of clever charlatans who pretend to be great and powerful wizards. Millions of people have been drawn to your version of the mythical Emerald City, attracted like flies to the beacon of your sideshow magic. You promise to grant their wishes and make their dreams come true, but all you can really do is lure them over the rainbow into an unfamiliar land where the only potential outcome for their quest is disappointment. You and your fellow wizards purposefully divert them from the real quest they should be embarked on, which is to find themselves within themselves. The best thing you can do for these people is to admit it's all a big con. Tell them to discover their own intelligence, courage, and love by themselves. Dispel the myths. Defrock yourself and the other Professor Marvel clones. Give back the money you've swindled. Then you and the other conniving wizards in Washington who maintain illusions and amass fortunes should climb into hot air balloons and drift away forever."

Suddenly, a scruffy dog wriggled out of Dorothy's basket, jumped onto the floor, and scurried toward the Honcho with a loud yelp. Before his numbed brain could warn his legs, the dog sank its teeth into his ankle. The Honcho yelped. The dog yelped louder. The Honcho roared in pain. Finally, the dog released its bite and scampered off into the darkness.

"Toto! Toto, come back!" shouted Dorothy, chasing after her wayward pet. Her checkered dress billowed above her pumping knees as she evaporated into the darkness at the rear of the caboose. To the Honcho's amazement, she seemed to run straight through the wall. Her voice, still calling out for Toto, slowly trailed off. But before fading to black, the illusion bid him an unfriendly adieu. "You're a bad man, Mr. Honcho. A very bad man indeed!"

After the casualties were cleared from the tracks, the Juggernaut headed home. The Honcho downed a pot of coffee to counteract his drunkenness. Unfortunately, this left him to ponder in the harsh light of sobriety the haunting images of the Mad Hatter and Dorothy Gale. Because of the bloody mayhem that his runaway campaign train had caused, he was afraid that the beheading threatened by the Mad Hatter and the directions to hell from Dorothy were possible futures looming directly ahead for him. Even more troubling was the realization that the Insurrectionist was gaining the upper hand. The shots fired by the angry crowd of protesters still echoed loudly in his mind, like thunderclap harbingers of the escalating struggle with his anonymous nemesis.

Suddenly, he had a premonition of Armageddon. It wasn't the Armageddon of nuclear war nor the biblical Armageddon prophesied in Revelations. There was no trumpeting of angels or the arrival of a portentous star called Wormwood foreshadowing a final confrontation between the seven headed dragons of Mephistopheles and Yahweh. Instead, he saw an hourglass in which only a few grains of sand remained unsifted. When those few remaining granules siphoned to the bottom, an enormous human conflict would occur with overwhelming finality, dwarfing the minor skirmishes that preceded this ultimate collision between Good and Bad, or more precisely, between Master and Slave.

Frightened by these visions, the Honcho called Freeman into his cabin to develop a plan to mitigate the disastrous political fallout that was sure to follow the catastrophe on the tracks. Unfortunately, when the senator asked him if he knew where his Insurrection Czar had been during the confrontation with the rebels on the tracks, he didn't respond, not because he didn't know, but rather because he thought he did. This knowledge clouded his understanding of an increasingly bizarre universe. The answer to the Honcho's question was the haunting vision that he had seen from the Juggernaut. Standing on the tracks, as stalwart and determined as any leader that any incipient revolution ever had, was a man who looked exactly like Thomas Jefferson, the Honcho's enigmatic Insurrection Czar. But this man wasn't quelling the uprising or hunting down the Insurrectionist. He was passing out guns and ammunition to the rebels.

Freeman was stunned by this vision. He chose not to mention it to the Head Honcho, who was now mumbling nonsensically about Armageddon. As Freeman quietly rose to leave, his legs moved with unexpected ease. He felt a surge of hope that his ball and chain had somehow disappeared. When he looked down though, the unwelcome contraption was still there.

However, the band around his ankle was looser, so he did something rare for him. He smiled, even though the Juggernaut was plunging headlong into the foggy depths of Washington, where dawn had not yet conquered the stifling silence of night, and where dark shadows were cast by a cityscape of blackened buildings that looked like tombstones rising out of the eerie mist of a graveyard, bearing epitaphs no one had the temerity to read.

Chapter Nine: "Honchogate"

"I am not a crook!"
—Richard M. Nixon

A scowl formed under the Honcho's bushy eyebrows and his flabby jowls wagged to and fro. "I'm not guilty!" he asserted.

"Be more specific", said Freeman. "What aren't you guilty of?"

"Everything. I don't give a damn what the Red Queen says."

Freeman cringed. His boss was straying again across the line separating sanity from madness. "Everything is a lot not to be guilty of", he said.

"Excuse me", the Honcho said to Freeman, But Sir!, Buxomus, and Sammy Giancarlo, who were there for an emergency meeting. With practiced proficiency, he pressed one of two buttons on his mahogany desk. "I'm taping my conversations", he announced. "That button activates an elaborate recording system operated by one of Sammy's best plumbers, Alexander Margarinefield. Watch what you say."

"What's the other button for?" asked Freeman.

"It activates an equally elaborate erasing system. Handy little devil".

"Won't the erased gaps in the tapes be suspicious?"

"Who gives a fuck?" barked the Honcho, as he pressed the erase button to delete the expletive he had just recorded. "The Soviets taught us that documenting history is the art of predicting the past. Erasing bits of recorded conversations is just another variation on the theme."

Buxomus raised a petite hand to get the Honcho's attention. "Why am I taking shorthand dictation if you're recording these conversations?"

"It would be unfair to lay you off just because you've been obsoleted by technology", said the Honcho. "Besides, we get to ogle your panties whenever you cross your legs."

"Oh!" she exclaimed with an embarrassed squeal.

"But Sir!" said But Sir!. "Why do you have to tape your conversations at all?"

"Because I work among cutthroat politicians. I want factual evidence to show who the real shysters are, even if I have to erase and splice tapes."

"How will you convince the world you're not guilty of your own sordid misdeeds if you record tapes with incriminating gaps?" interjected Freeman.

"What sordid misdeeds?" asked the Head Honcho with artfully feigned indignation.

"You ran over hundreds of protesters with a train", said Freeman, as the Honcho activated the erase button. "You almost blew up the planet in a drunken reverie. Your best friend is named Old Bushmills. You've slept with half of the sluts in Washington, some of whom were never seen again. Your secretary's only function is to excite your libido. You've siphoned millions of dollars from doting lobbyists. You lie to your constituents. Your mysterious golfing buddies all have Italian surnames. You started a war in Vhaicam with no justification. And, the Safari Golfer claims you cheat on your golf scores."

The Honcho lifted his finger from the erase button. "I don't cheat on my golf scores!" he asserted toward a hidden microphone. "The Golfer is a liar! But don't tell him I said that. He's God, you know."

"He already knows."

"He already knows I said that?" The Honcho nervously recalled that gods are typically omniscient, omnipotent, and omnivorous. He hit the erase button again to be sure.

"No, the Golfer already knows he's a liar", clarified Freeman.

"Careful!" said the Honcho. "He has the power to plunk you inside the belly of a whale."

"I'm already in the belly of a whale", said Freeman, scanning his surroundings. "But, we digress. Who's claiming you're guilty of everything you're not guilty of?"

The Honcho scowled. "It's Bottomless Esophagus again. That anonymous bastard told the media I was personally responsible for the Juggernaut tragedy and a shitload of other abuses and crimes. Worse yet, my opponent's entire party has jumped on the bandwagon to publicly humiliate me before the election. Their mud slinging is so brutal, cold hearted, slanderous, ruthless, and cruel that if I weren't the target, I'd admire their attack."

"We'll send you a cake with a file in it while you're in Leavenworth", said Freeman.

The Honcho glared at him. "There's no need for that. I've still got plenty of dirty tricks up Sammy's sleeve. Right Sammy?"

"Right, Boss", said Sammy, who was a man of few words and fewer scruples.

"As we speak, Sammy's boys are rifling through files at the headquarters of my opponent's political party to gather incriminating evidence to use against them. They're also bugging the offices, so we can learn their secrets, infiltrate their operations, and win this election the old-fashioned way."

"But Sir!" exclaimed But Sir!. "Isn't breaking into their headquarters illegal?"

"Vice is necessary in politics if virtue is to have any chance", said the Honcho.

"What if their Italian golfing buddies are more resourceful than yours?" wondered Freeman.

"That's unlikely", said the Honcho. "But I've cut the deck many ways, just in case. For instance, I've drafted letters of resignation for my staff, which will be kept on file in case I need scapegoats. Sign one on the way out today. Also, my Political Action Committees can flood the media with public assertions of my innocence. The media is in my back pocket, and my PAC's have enough money to fabricate whatever truths are necessary to defend my integrity. They're advertising's version of Orwell's Ministry of Truth, which rewrote every book, falsified every record, repainted every picture, and altered every date, in order to recreate the past as needed.

"Furthermore, my lawyers can lay down smoke screens of legal technicalities and motions that will take the U.S. court system generations to unravel, if they ever finish with Clinton's smoke screens. If worse comes to worst, I can resign my office, in exchange for an unconditional pardon from whatever puppet is appointed to replace me.

"If none of these strategies cover my ass, I'm linked into the international escape network called The Spider, which was created by the German SS at the end of World War II to spirit away the upper echelon of the Third Reich to safe houses in South America. There's a luxurious dacha in Paraguay ready for me to move in. It hasn't been used since Martin Bormann died."

Freeman whistled in admiration. He now understood why politicians never go to jail, no matter how heinous their transgressions. "What does the Safari Golfer think of this mess?"

"He's elated", said the Honcho. "He says he can emulate Christ and gain eternal fame by dying for my sins, but only if he perfects rising from the dead."

"But Sir!" exclaimed But Sir!. "Why are you investing so much effort to cover your trail and lay down smoke screens? Wouldn't your constituents be better served if you put forth thoughtful arguments justifying your re-election?"

The Honcho smiled condescendingly. "That's unnecessary. Even weak arguments are good when one has an arsenal of propaganda weapons to launch an attack of disinformation, mud slinging, and subterfuge. And we have the foot soldiers to do it. Right Sammy?"

"Right, Boss", droned the unflappable Sicilian. "But I need time to spring dem from da slammer and pull dem from deir day jobs with da Teamsters Union. I wanna use only experienced men, lika dose who were in Dallas in '63."

"Yell if you need help", offered the Honcho. "The CIA owe me some favors, since I pushed their black budget through Congress. They've got enough disposable cash now to infiltrate every government in the world. Including ours, I suppose."

"I've worked with dem CIA boys before", said Sammy. "Dey owe me some favors, too."

"Sammy knows how to run an organization", the Honcho said. "He's mastered the principles of blind allegiance, flagrant nepotism, and brutal purges. Just ask Jimmy Hoffa, if you can find him."

Unfortunately, Sammy Giancarlo's organization wasn't as effective as advertised. His conscripted plumbers were inept cat burglars. All five of his henchmen who broke into the opposition party's headquarters on June 17th were nabbed with their clumsy fingers immersed deep into confidential files. Their arrest threw an enormous monkey wrench into the Head Honcho's political ambitions.

The Honcho's Committee to Re-Elect the Presiding Senator feared that the five arrested operatives would implicate high level governmental officials, so these over-zealous members of CREEPS, including officials of the FBI, the CIA, the Justice Department, and the Attorney General, compromised public trust and immersed themselves in a stomach-churning display of democracy gone terribly awry. They mounted a surreptitious campaign to cover up crimes, obstruct justice, and deceive the world, in order to protect the Head Honcho and his cohorts.

This deception was ill fated from the start. Someone in the Honcho's inner circle leaked information to the media. Consequently, key government officials that had conspired to obstruct the American judicial and electoral processes were arrested, tried, and convicted. Thus, the U.S. Attorney General was sent to one of the prisons he was paid to oversee, which wasn't as sad of a commentary about the state of American government as the resignation of the Vice President for income tax evasion the year before, which wasn't as sad as the coup d'etat pulled off by the Cosa Nostra and the CIA when they assassinated an Irish Catholic President for cracking down on organized crime, botching the Bay of Pigs invasion, and downsizing the intelligence agencies.

After serving minimal jail sentences and paying nominal fines, these convicted government officials, who had protected their leader with Prussian loyalty, either became born again Christians or became inordinately wealthy selling rights to books, appearing on talk shows, and plying the dinner speech circuit. Meanwhile, the unfortunate security guard that originally discovered the break-in was laid off and later arrested for shoplifting while trying to put food on his family's table.

But the key question remained unanswered. Was the Head Honcho, the most powerful man in America, in on the conspiracy? The suspense was heightened by revelations of tape recorded conversations that might answer this riddle. A special prosecutor was appointed to ferret out the truth. Hearings were held by a Senate sub-committee, which was an interesting test of the Honor Among Thieves principle. Since the Honcho was the nation's most visible member of that fraternal gathering, it was widely believed that he was safe from prosecution.

Unfortunately, not even the Senate could protect one of its own in this case. Public pressure, fueled by continued revelations from Bottomless Esophagus and zealous reporters, forced the special prosecutor to go after the Honcho's tapes, which he refused to turn over, partly because of the Political Immunity Clause, and partly because he was still editing them. As pressure mounted to turn over the tapes, he finally did the honorable thing. He fired the special prosecutor. This move confused the public, who didn't understand how someone could fire their own prosecutor.

Since the Senate was making embarrassingly little headway prosecuting one of its own, the quest for the tapes was escalated to the U.S. Sublime Court. This was a pivotal case for the Sublime Court, which had just recently promoted itself from Supreme when it began ignoring the Constitution and the separation of powers, much like when the English House of Lords in the 17th Century counted the vote of a very fat member as ten votes. The Sublime Court now passed any verdict it damn well pleased. It legislated laws, enacted regulations, determined funding levels, and assumed powers previously reserved for Congress, the executive branch, and state and local governments. It not only was constructing a living constitution, it was recreating reality. The Sublime Court was competing with the Safari Golfer to become the Prime Orchestrator of the universe.

The Sublime Court ordered all 64 of the Honcho's tapes to be turned over to the Senate sub-committee. In the majority opinion, the Chief Justice wrote, "Tape recording conversations is an invasion of privacy, and therefore a violation of the fourth amendment. If the government becomes a lawbreaker, it breeds contempt for the law; it invites every man to become a law unto himself; it invites anarchy." This was a reasonable opinion, although the Sublime Court had already become a law unto itself, exhibited contempt for the Constitution, and laid the foundation for its own judicial anarchy.

The Head Honcho ignored the Sublime Court, citing the Political Immunity Clause. He also claimed that the Sublime Court's ruling was a clear case of the pot calling the kettle black, which must certainly be a civil rights violation. The Honcho's intransigence, the Sublime Court's ambition, and the waffling of Congress all converged to push the American political system to the brink of internecine civil war. The media treated these visceral events like a political soap opera. The daily drama of intrigue, blackmail, cover-ups, obstruction of justice, hush money, unindicted co-conspirators and secret tapes had to have a name, so the ink-stained wretches dug deep into the evolving American lexicon for such affairs and dubbed this one "Honchogate".

As this sinister drama unfolded in public view, Freeman became more cynical. What might once have been harmless political shenanigans now appeared to be craven disdain for law and the republic. Trusting public officials was becoming anathema to Americans. For Freeman, it was now impossible. He once believed that the American constitutional architecture could withstand assaults such as Honchogate, but something had gone horribly wrong. He harbored a growing suspicion that he was not merely surrounded by a government full of criminals, he was surrounded by a criminal government.

Disillusioned, he strolled down Constitution Avenue on a humid afternoon for his usual lunchtime walk among the throngs of legislators, bureaucrats, lawyers, lobbyists, protesters, and tourists. He plopped himself forlornly on the steps of the Lincoln Memorial and hung his head. With the white marble effigy of the Great Emancipator looming behind him, he declared under his breath, "Perhaps the Insurrectionist is right. Maybe it's time to revolt against our own government."

"There's no time like the present", came an unsolicited reply to his nearly silent declaration. "What country can protect its liberties if its rulers are not warned from time to time that the people preserve the spirit of resistance?"

Freeman's head jerked upward and his heart skipped a beat. Silently and eerily, Thomas Jefferson had materialized out of the shuffling crowd. He sat serenely on the steps of the Lincoln Memorial, just inches from Freeman, who had sensed no movement when his friend arrived. The only sensation he experienced was a wave of cold air sweeping over his body, momentarily chasing away the oppressive summer swelter. But there Jefferson was, in his familiar bicorne hat, red waistcoat, and black breeches tucked neatly into polished leather boots. His attire was incongruous, but it was everyone else who seemed out of place.

"We should be vigilant against elected officials remaining in office for life", continued Jefferson. "If we don't exercise our electoral prerogatives faithfully and often, then we will fall prey to tyranny. There's no other way for vacancies of political office to be obtained. Those by death are few, and those by resignation are virtually none."

"What are you suggesting?"

"To use your vernacular, we should occasionally throw the bums out. All of them. Nothing purifies the air as surely and completely as a violent, thundering tempest."

"Aren't you afraid to say that in public?"

"Nay", replied Jefferson. "We don't have to bow submissively to authority and speak reverently to our representatives. Our Constitution affirms that we the people are the sovereigns. State and federal officials are only our agents. We who have the final word can speak angrily. Every American should stand tall and measure himself with the vigor in which he challenges his wayward leaders. If your forefathers had lacked such courage and fortitude in the face of King George's tyranny, we would still be an oppressed colony of the British Crown."

"That's easy to say, but I work for a bastard who abuses his authority and treats the electoral process as a plaything, and there isn't much anyone can do about it."

"That is serious indeed", said Jefferson with a worried frown. "Interferences with elections by government officers should be cause for decisive retribution. If removal from office through election becomes nothing, because it has been smothered by the enormous influence, patronage, and illicit activity of the government itself, then democracy will be merely a cruel charade. The Honchogate affair and the farce in Florida during the 2000 presidential election are two of many examples. Government is defective in its primary purpose if it does not inflict due punishment on such criminal behavior."

Jefferson put a firm hand on Freeman's sagging shoulder and then continued. "But, it's too soon to despair, my friend. It's part of the American character to surmount every desperate difficulty. It is only when we are distracted from public affairs that our executives, congressmen, and judges become wolves eager to devour us while our attention is diverted. It's occasionally necessary to recapture America's attention and organize a posse to hunt down and slay the wolves. The wisdom of our sages and the blood of our heroes compel us to do this. Such a moment is upon us now."

"People won't hear that message", said Freeman. "Ismism permits public discussion of only those things that come under the choking umbrella of Political Correctness. Ousting all incumbent politicians is certainly outside that umbrella."

Jefferson snorted. "It disgusts me that our conversations must be as secret as if we were conspiring to destroy the Constitution, when, quite to the contrary, we are conspiring to resurrect it. I am for freedom of the press, and against all attempts to silence by force our criticisms against the conduct of our governmental agents."

"The press is a hopeless, illusory ally", said Freeman. "It's caught in the gravitational pull of Ismism and does the bidding of the entrenched liberal bureaucracy. Besides, not enough people read the papers to form a grass roots uprising."

Jefferson's eyes blazed. "If a nation expects to be both ignorant and free, it expects what never was and never will be! The best way to prevent the perversion of power into tyranny is to educate people about all of tyranny's disguises, and to inspire them to defeat it. Americans will eventually expose their corrupt politicians, either through an enlightened press or through the work of rebels spreading the word from door to door and from lip to lip with revolutionary fervor. It happened in 1776, and it can happen again. Truth is a sufficient catalyst for information to spread. It is only error that must rely on power."

"The Head Honcho has as much power as any king or dictator," said Freeman.

"Indeed", agreed Jefferson. "500 despots in Congress are likely to be more oppressive than one dictator. It's inconsistent with the principles of civil liberty, and contrary to the natural rights of all citizens, that a body of men should have authority to enlarge their own powers without restraint. Man didn't enter into society to have fewer rights than before, but to have those rights better secured. That's why separate branches of government were created, to balance and offset each other. When Congress takes a single step beyond its specific Constitutional boundaries, it seizes a limitless, undefined field of power. Personally, I can't conceive how rational beings can find happiness exercising power over others. Power is not alluring to pure minds. However, recognizing that there wouldn't be an eternal supply of pure minds stepping forth for election, the Judiciary was set up as an opposing branch, which wouldn't be subject to the temptations and contaminations of the electoral process."

Freeman gazed long and hard at his companion, who had removed his bicorne hat as a concession to the afternoon mugginess. "If there is such a thing as balance of power, how was the Sublime court able to promote itself from the merely Supreme?"

"In our Constitution, judges were to be the most harmless members of the government. Unfortunately, they became the most dangerous. The difficulty of their removal made them irresponsible in office. Their decisions, seeming to concern individual suitors only, passed silent and unheeded by the public. These decisions, nevertheless, became law by precedent, gradually sapping the foundations of the Constitution, before anyone noticed that this invisible and helpless worm had been busily consuming the nation's substance.

"The federal Judiciary works like gravity night and day", continued Jefferson, "gaining a little today and a little tomorrow, advancing like a thief with noiseless step over the field of jurisdiction, until all power is usurped from the states and consolidated into one government in Washington. To this I am unalterably opposed. It will neuter the checks provided by one government on another, and will become as venal and oppressive as the government from which we originally revolted. It will be, as in all centralized governments, where every man is either a hammer or an anvil. Our country is too large to have all of its affairs directed from Washington. Public servants at such a distance, out from under the eyes of their constituents, can't administer all the details necessary for good government. Distance also renders detection impossible to citizens, thus inviting the public agents to corruption, plunder, and waste."

"So why don't Congress and the Judiciary stop each other from usurping the Constitution?" asked Freeman.

"You may as well ask why vultures and coyotes don't attack each other when they're feeding on carrion. They're too absorbed with their own rapacious efforts to devour all that's in front of them to notice another scavenger. Also, Congressmen have to periodically get reelected to retain power, so they lack the courage to make legislative decisions on difficult issues, since taking sides would alienate some voters. They prefer passing fuzzy, spineless, vaguely worded laws, of no substance but expansive in scope, that dance around the issues, leaving the enacted legislation open to broad interpretation. These clouds of squid-like legislative ink pander to everyone and offend no one. Voters consider these amorphous laws harmless in the first instance, and meaningless in the second.

"This gives judges an enormous opportunity to interpret legislative intent. At the behest of special interest factions armed with supporting casts of lawyers big enough to film Ben Hur, they can make unpopular decisions, because they have lifetime tenure and aren't subject to periodic voter approval. This triggers a war game of lawyers and lobbyists, one group playing offense and the other group playing defense, with the judges as the final arbiters of this undemocratic battle. Thus, judges create a launching pad for their own personal agendas by constructing what is virtually a new constitution with decisions that interpret the undefined laws enacted by the spineless Congress. Litigation has become our basic form of governance, masked by a charade of democracy. We're becoming a dictatorship of judges! An elective and judicial despotism isn't what we fought and died for!" Seething passion raged in every feature of his face.

"Won't politicians with good intentions restrain the bad ones?" asked Freeman.

Jefferson spat on the marble steps. "In questions of power, do not speak of confidence in man or of good intentions! It is noble to trust everyone until they prove unworthy, but it is far wiser to keep them from mischief with the chains of the Constitution. How many times do we have to learn this lesson? It took mankind thousands of years to understand it once, and now in just two hundred years, we have forgotten the lesson altogether. We should bury our heads in shame, because the sin of civilized forgetfulness is far greater than that of primitive ignorance."

"Why are you so pessimistic about human nature?"

"Every government on earth has some trace of human weakness, some germ of corruption and degeneracy, which cunning will soon discover and wickedness expand. All institutions are susceptible to abuse in evil hands. We shouldn't assume that the powers we permit our leaders would never be abused, just because we aren't disposed to abuse them. Even if nuns ran the government, corruption would soon set in. The usual cabal of lobbyists, special interests, lawyers, cutthroats, and criminals would descend on them like jackals, creating a seething cauldron of mongering, bribery, and veiled extortion that the nuns would acquiesce to, if only to survive.

"Rather than wait with baited breath for saints to run our governments, we should ensure that the accumulation of power isn't possible, so that it doesn't matter whether our officials are sinners or saints. Once corruption and tyranny have planted their tentacled roots, democracy won't be sufficient to extricate them. There is no easy or painless way to cleanse governments of compromised legislators, executives, judges, and bureaucrats. No reasoning or argument will rehabilitate them; you might as well reason and argue with the marble columns encircling them. I told my compatriots back in Philadelphia that there would come a time when corruption in this country, as in the country from which we separated, will have seized the heads of our newly constructed government. Human nature is the same everywhere, and will be influenced by the same causes. Sadly, I was prophetic. Corruption has set in, and now I have unfinished business that won't allow me to rest until I've completed it." In a rare display of fatigue, Jefferson hung his head and massaged his temples.

"You're a mysterious person", Freeman said uneasily. "You come and go like a ghost. You speak of events none of us are familiar with. You quote dead people. You talk differently, and your clothes are bizarre. Your ideas clash with prevailing opinions. And you practically flew through the air to tackle the Head Honcho in the Bavarian Forest. What's all that about?"

"My friend, don't get absorbed in a frenzy of mysticism", Jefferson replied. "When I meet with a proposition beyond finite comprehension, I abandon it as I do a weight which human strength cannot lift. And, I prefer swallowing one mystery, rather than two. It requires only one effort to admit the incomprehensibility of matter endowed with thought, and two to believe, first of an existence called spirit, of which we have no evidence, and then secondly, how that spirit, which has neither extension nor solidity, can put matter into motion.

"But", continued Jefferson, "history is always and everywhere, along with the men and women who lived it passionately. There are those who lived with such passion, who began epochal creations not satisfactorily completed during their temporal existence, that their impact on history and the evolution of humanity carries their essences forward in what may seem like spiritual form until their nascent creation reaches maturity. I am a manifestation of such eternal restlessness. I've been consigned to an historical purgatory by a breathtaking political experiment gone maddeningly awry."

Freeman struggled to understand Jefferson's coy response. As he wallowed sluggishly in confusion, his mind resurrected the disturbing apparition that haunted him on the Juggernaut. "Were you passing out guns and ammunition to the rebels attacking the Juggernaut between Lexington and Concord?" he asked bluntly.

Jefferson stared at him coldly. "That isn't important. When future historians assess the apocalyptic conflict about to occur on earth, they will little note whether I was passing out weapons during a budding revolution. My fame was etched forever on the indelible tablets of history when I authored the declaration in Philadelphia to serve as the rallying cry for those who believe that man's proper state is to be neither oppressor nor oppressed, but simply free. That declaration will inspire the victorious army during the coming final showdown between master and slave, between monarch and subject, between baron and serf, and between priest and postulant.

"As human civilization evolves, it is no longer meaningful to argue whether a pharaoh, an emperor, a priest, a king, a chief, a dictator, a comrade, or a senator will hold the key to mankind's chains. It is time to shed the chains altogether. Likewise, it is no longer important to argue whether we will kneel in submission to the god of the Christians, the Muslims, the Buddhists, the Hindus, or the Jews. It is time to rise above cosmic mysticism. And, it is no longer important to argue whether we will bind ourselves to Ismism, Communism, Monarchism, Socialism, Feudalism, or Democracy. It is time to burst our bondage to these secular mythologies.

"Worry not about me. It's far more imperative that you examine your own soul and choose which side you will march with during the coming Second American Revolution. You can't escape the choice. Neutrality isn't an option. Extremism in defense of liberty is no vice, and moderation in the pursuit of justice is no virtue, to use the words Goldwater borrowed from Cicero, my alter ego in purgatory."

Though he was looking into Jefferson's blazing eyes, he was seeing Cassandra's radiant face instead. She had prophesied a life of great import for him, which was utterly ridiculous, since he was a menial government apparatchik. Triggered by the words that Jefferson brandished like a glinting sword, Freeman's memory replayed Cassandra's haunting prophecy:

". . . The forces of Good and Evil will confront Freeman directly. He will experience the worst hatred and abuse that mankind is capable of. He will see war, oppression, murder, fraud, slavery, and greed. He will remain confused for a long time. But then one day he will undergo a personal epiphany and discover his purpose in life. He will then expose the insidious schemes and deceptions of other men and dispel myths and conspiracies, leading us out of bondage to our gods and kings. But, this will not come without doubt, trial, and suffering beyond human imagination. And, there will be a man full of essential goodness and wisdom to help him. . . ."

The magnitude of Cassandra's prophesy and the weight of Jefferson's call to arms dizzied him. He looked down at the unholy ball and chain bequeathed to him by Cassandra as a reminder of his captivity to apathy and conformity. He couldn't yet summon the courage to be anything but a clump of seaweed clinging to the surging tides of history. "I . . . I'm not ready to choose anything yet", he confessed sheepishly. "You speak of a Second American Revolution, and of great conflicts looming on the horizon. I can't imagine such dire things happening here."

Jefferson laughed boisterously. "Please, look behind you."

Freeman turned and saw lots of tourists and a large statue of Abraham Lincoln. "So?"

"That statue depicts a man who presided over a cataclysmic conflict right here. America was torn apart by civil war once already over the transcendent issue of human freedom. The Great Emancipator frozen in marble behind you clung tenaciously to the concept of a people without manacles on their ankles and of a nation committed to preserving life and liberty. He knew that a country couldn't be half slave and half free forever, and neither can we.

"In the grand context of history, Lincoln lived not that long ago. The Second American Revolution can happen here, just as the Civil War and the First American Revolution did. It is far better to engage in one cataclysmic showdown now than to gradually surrender our humanity under the weight of a thousand niggling skirmishes. Postponing the showdown will only make the eventual battle more devastating. As Churchill observed about rising Nazism, 'Two years ago, it was possible to stand up to the dictators, three years ago it was easy, and four years ago a mere dispatch might have rectified the position. But, where shall we be a year hence?'".

Freeman shook his head skeptically. "Revolution seems so unlikely. I just don't feel it in my blood."

"To say that revolution isn't in your blood is poppycock!" Jefferson growled through clenched teeth. "Your Irish ancestors were revolutionaries of the highest order. They knew well the same British boot heels that tread on the American colonies, and they resented imperialistic tyranny just as ferociously as we did. Daniel O'Connell, Charles Stewart Parnell, Michael Collins, Wolfe Tone, and Bernadette Devlin are to the Irish as George Washington, Patrick Henry, and John Hancock are to Americans. Look deep into your soul, John Freeman, for within it burns an inextinguishable Celtic fire. Inside every Irishman is a rebel yearning to burst his chains."

His friend's glazed eyes told Jefferson that more advice would be wasted, so he arose and bade him farewell. Freeman, reflecting deeply on the intense conversation, didn't notice Jefferson's departure until there was no sign of him anywhere. Freeman scanned the area for the enigmatic Insurrection Czar, but it was fruitless. Once again, he had evaporated into the spooky haze shrouding Washington.

Freeman's head was heavy with thoughts of great import. Jefferson's words had given him an idea, albeit a farfetched one. He ambled back to the Honcho's empty office in the Senatorial Office Building. The Honcho wasn't there, because Congress had adjourned early after passing Joint Resolution 343 designating March 12th as Girl Scouts Day. This sapped the strength of legislators, so they passed a motion to take the rest of the week off. Coincidentally, pleasant weather that could best be appreciated on a golf course was moving in.

Unfortunately, even though Girl Scouts Day was now resolved, other situations remained dangerously unattended. Vhaicam was particularly troublesome. Not only was America running out of eligible youths to funnel into the human bologna grinder, Vhaicam's population had exploded to a staggering 236 million, despite the torrent of casualties from the Honcho's strategy to kill them at both ends.

The Honcho's staff had recently been researching techniques used by other governments to control population. For instance, But Sir!'s research revealed that the Chinese government used ultrasound machines to determine the gender of embryonic children. If the fetus was female, it was summarily aborted. This not only limited today's population, the subsequent paucity of wombs inhibited the mating opportunities of future generations.

Freeman's research revealed that the Russian government's most effective population control measure was pioneered by Stalin, whose NKVD simply lined people up and shot them in the back. At first, Russians who witnessed these mass executions were troubled. However, they eventually realized that this was a natural function of governments and learned to accept it on the same terms as thunderstorms, blizzards, and earthquakes. Enough political prisoners were machine-gunned in Butovo, Livashovo, and Kommunarka to populate 36 small nations. The timeless faith of the Russians in the government of their motherland blinded them morally to the atrocity.

Freeman arrived at the vacated Senatorial Office Building and slipped unnoticed into the Honcho's office. Jeopardizing his career, he opened drawers, looked behind pictures, peeked under the carpet, snooped in closets, and shuffled through stacks of paper. He found condoms, packets of cocaine, soiled panties, 64 unlabeled cassette tapes, tickets to Paraguay, a black address book listing hundreds of Italians and prominent criminal attorneys, a 45-caliber Smith and Wesson with the serial number ground off, and an enormous stash of cash. He mused that Reagan was wrong when he jested that crime wouldn't pay if the government ran it.

Unfortunately, his impromptu scavenger hunt had come up dry thus far, so he peeked and snooped faster. He carelessly burrowed into stacks of documents and emptied cluttered drawers. And then he found it. He laid the object reverently on the Honcho's desk and blew off a sheen of dust. He felt a rising sense of trepidation. Beads of nervous sweat sprouted on his taut forehead as he opened the "Book of Liberal Policies, Marxist Economics, and Other Occult Phenomena". He found the Marxist Economics section, and then the Time Travel sub-section.

His thoughts drifted back to his conversation with Jefferson, whose curt challenge to rediscover his rebellious Irish heritage struck a chord in his frigid soul. The names Parnell, O'Connell, Collins, Tone, and Devlin resurrected intense memories of his father regaling him decades ago about the heroic exploits of these brave Gaelic revolutionaries. Young Freeman loved these stories, not because of any latent revolutionary fervor, but because they were the only moments when real passion erupted from his taciturn father. Mental images crackled to life with startling clarity of his father with veins hardened in his neck, his eyes animated by zealous Celtic kindredship, his voice cracking from adrenaline-fired anger, salty tears streaming down whisker-stubbed cheeks, his crimson face stoked by a boiling furnace of conviction. He remembered feeling irreplaceably close to his father as he basked in his emotional energy.

Freeman didn't understand the political, religious, and racial hatred that drove the British government to exterminate the Irish, but he was always curious about the life of his great great grandfather, who had been deported from Ireland to America at the age of 14, cast adrift in a foreign land by a monstrous holocaust in his birthplace, without family or friend, penniless, and with his only possession a savage desire to survive.

Young Freeman often wondered how a youth could endure such tragic separation from his family, his people, and his land, and survive in a strange place that offered nothing but a chance to scratch out a meager living. He developed a sympathetic fraternal kinship with this abandoned ancestral waif that he knew only through his father's apocryphal tales. His progenitor's fate was the favorite part of his father's nightly discourses on his cultural heritage. He had often wished he could put himself in that unfortunate youth's place, to experience his pain and terror and loneliness, and to understand why his fellow humans put him through such hellish trauma. He sensed that something apocalyptically instructive could be learned by reliving the adolescent life of his great great grandfather.

Up till now, he considered this wish a whim that no power on earth could fulfill. But, Jefferson's harsh instructions to find the bodhran drumbeat of Irish rebellion in his stultified heart inspired him. With the mythically powerful "Book of Liberal Policies, Marxist Economics, and Other Occult

Phenomena" at his illicit disposal, he prepared to leap through time and space to become that 14-year old ancestor who was the source of his youthful commiserations and who could perhaps ignite an adult epiphany.

The Book required a quotation from a dreamy fairy tale to enable time travel, which was no problem for Freeman, since his father had implanted in his young mind a treasury of Irish folklore through countless recitations. To begin his journey backward through time and into the depths of his soul, he selected from his mental archives an old Irish verse called "Beside the Fire", because a fire was precisely what he hoped to start in his torpid heart.

He cradled the bible of left wing magic carefully in his arms. Taking a deep and suddenly uncertain breath, he closed his eyes and recited:

Where glows the Irish hearth with peat
There lives a subtle spell,
The faint blue smoke, the gentle heat,
The moorland odours tell

The cottage lights that lure you in
From rainy western skies;
And by the friendly glow within
Of simple talk and wise,

And tales of magic, love or arms
From days when princes met
To listen to the lay that charms
The Connacht peasant yet.

There honour shines through passions dire,
There beauty blends with mirth,
Wild hearts, ye never did aspire
Wholly for things of earth!

*Cold, cold this thousand years—yet still
On many a time-stained page
Your pride, your truth, your dauntless will,
Burn on from age to age.*

*And still around the fires of peat
Live on the ancient days;
There still do living lips repeat
The old and deathless lays.*

*And when the wavering wreaths ascend
Blue in the evening air,
The soul of Ireland seems to bend
Above her children there. . . .*

    His body went limp and his world faded to black. Suddenly, he was overwhelmed by a tornadic vortex of light that sucked his weightless body irresistibly into a yawing whirlpool of time. This continuous funnel of smooth light coiling mysteriously into the past dragged him into a disconnected existence of scrambled temporal linearity. Quantum mechanics in disarray created a condition where potential futures intermingled with infinite pasts and unlimited presents, so that any future could become any past, and vice versa.

    Freeman was sucked into the past like a speck of dust in a huge cosmic vacuum. The spinning lights became blurred streaks trailing behind his accelerating mass. Suddenly, chronological gravity braked his body. The luminous vortex narrowed, and he feared he was going to be crushed by the steadily diminishing funnel. Amazingly, he passed completely through the compressed end of the vortex like a watermelon seed being spit out of a child's mouth. Amid a final explosion of kaleidoscopic light, he was plopped indelicately on the soggy turf of County West Meath, Ireland. The year he somehow knew was 1846. More importantly, he somehow knew he was Padraic Freeman, his great great grandfather. The transmogrification was complete.

Padraic was 14 years old and desperately hungry, not from a single postponed meal, but from years of deprivation and famine. Tattered remnants of clothes hung on his emaciated frame. His thoroughly disheveled reddish-blond hair befitted a youth that knew more of the forest than of a bath and a comb. His feet were bare and callused. The comfortably suffocating cloak of Catholic dogma encased his soul, so he knew that if nothing good ever happened in this world, which seemed distinctly possible, he would still have eternal happiness in heaven. Alas, this happiness could only be obtained by dying.

The boy gingerly arose from the ground. He'd been mysteriously knocked prostrate by a blinding light that flashed out of nowhere. He shook his jangled head a few times. He concluded that he was unharmed by the strange encounter, other than his ears were ringing and he had a bizarre feeling that he was no longer alone, even inside his own body. This made no sense to him, so he included it with the other things of this world that made no sense. The accumulation of these nonsensical observations was becoming a disturbingly heavy burden.

Padraic shuffled aimlessly down the narrow dirt road that ran from the small village of Ballynacargy to the tenant farms where he lived. Anger consumed him on this grey Sunday afternoon. He slashed with his oaken shillelagh at the whin that grew dense along the road, pretending that the yellow flowering bushes were the animated demons that haunted his soul. With a vicious whack he truncated the imaginary body of the English landlord who kept him and his father in the field cultivating alfalfa fourteen hours every day to feed the cattle the landlord exported to England for people who knew the blessings of a decent meal but not of a clear conscience. In return for the cattle, the British sent undertakers to Ireland. With another whack at the tangled bushes, he crippled an imaginary cow. Padraic was jealous of the beast's robust diet as he and the rest of Ireland withered from starvation. Another blow of his shillelagh felled the sheriff, who had arrested Father O'Brien last week for celebrating the outlawed Catholic mass on a rock altar in a secluded grotto, with his congregation kneeling contritely in the hillside heather, concealed by a morning mist. For this dubious offense, an executioner hung Father O'Brien, sliced open his carcass, ripped out his heart and bowels, and cut off his head for display on a pike in the village square.

Another unfortunate bush succumbed as Padraic's angry imagination skewered the pompous teacher from England who tried to force-feed him the English language and fealty to the British Crown. A break in the hedge revealed the wooden schoolhouse with the thatched roof where this despised teacher vainly tried to convert unsophisticated Irish Catholic children into proper Protestant British subjects. Padraic didn't go to school there any more. His mother got him excused from attending, ostensibly because he was needed in the fields, but truly because tears welled in her eyes whenever she heard him practice the detested English tongue.

The Statute of Kilkenny had made it high treason to wear Irish clothes, speak the Irish language in public, or practice Irish customs. In spite of the statute, Padraic attended a Hedge School after dusk each day, where students hid behind the hedges lining rural roads and secretly learned their outlawed culture from a volunteer schoolmaster, who was often a priest. Furtively, they learned their Gaelic language, their Irish history, and their Catholic principles. They also learned Latin, Greek, math, and the sciences. These starving, half-naked waifs who studied in Irish glens were among the most educated youths in Europe, if only because they were fed knowledge instead of stew, mutton, and potatoes.

If caught in these hedge schools, the Penal Laws imposed by the English Parliament specified death for the volunteer schoolmaster and deportation for the school children. The Penal Laws were designed to reduce the Catholics to extreme ignorance, to separate them from their land, and in effect, to eliminate them from the face of the earth. Irish Catholics were forbidden to exercise their religion, enter a trade or profession, live inside a town, own a horse, purchase land, vote, carry arms, or educate their children. The French jurist Montesquieu would later write that the Penal Laws were "conceived by demons, written in blood, and registered in Hell."

Padraic spat in the direction of the schoolhouse. This was a ritual he had learned from his father, who frequently launched globules of phlegm toward the many symbols of English imperialism dotting Ireland. Padraic wiped spittle from his chin and continued his purposeless stroll. A herd of sheep approached, led by an English horseman. The sheep were on the way to Mullingar, where they would be poled down the Royal Canal to Dublin, ferried to Liverpool, and eventually become fodder for English woolen mills and butcher shops. The Englishman noticed Padraic only enough to nudge him with his horse out of the way of the more important wool-clad Irish denizens going to market.

Padraic wisely stepped off the road onto an unused path that led to a bridge over a river that didn't exist. He chuckled at the folly of this bridge, if only to avoid thinking about the humiliation of scurrying away from the British horseman. The bridge was built as part of an insulting public works project directed by the Saxons to help unemployed Irish. The useless structure was purposely built to traverse nothing and go nowhere, because the British didn't want these public works competing with British companies who were building bridges that were actually useful. This nonsense was replicated elsewhere, in the form of railroads with no destination, grain with no markets, and piers far removed from water. These pointless public works required thousands of government bureaucrats, inspectors, and clerks to administer them, all British citizens paid handsome salaries from Irish taxes extracted forcibly from peasants who were already destitute. Those who couldn't pay their taxes were evicted from their homes, which forced them to enroll in the public works programs, which thus expanded the scope of the public works, which increased the need for British bureaucrats and Irish taxes, which caused more Irish to be evicted from their homes, ad infinitum.

After the sheep passed, Padraic returned to the main road. Around a bend he saw Maeve Dougherty walking toward him. Maeve used to be his friend, but now she was no one's friend. She had abandoned her humanity, leaving behind a hollow shell of an emotionally comatose bipedal mammal. His heart ached as a surrogate for the feelings that she silently suppressed. He longed to talk to her, to run with her, and to tease her, as he had done when they were growing up together. But he knew that if he tried, Maeve would run away from him. Her body looked like a skeleton inside a rag that used to be a dress. He grimaced at the sight of her gaunt face as she drew near. He quivered as he remembered seeing her eat weeds in the woods yesterday. This image was not, however, as disturbing as that of starving Irishmen eating their own dead, which was rumored to be happening down in Offaly County.

Maeve ate weeds because she was orphaned. Her father had been drawn and quartered by the British army after joining the brief rebellion that flared up when rumors swirled that the French were going to invade Ireland and drive out the British. The premature uprising was squashed, and the Gaels who challenged the Crown's omnipotence were executed. A day later, two soldiers raped Maeve's mother. They left her to die from a vicious beating as punishment for aiding an enemy of the Crown, which was her deceased husband. Maeve was forced to watch the brutal soldiers defile her mother. They pinned Maeve's arms and gagged her mouth as the woman slowly died. Shouting for help would have been useless, because in 1846 Ireland, the only criminals were the Irish. Orphaned and starving, Maeve got no help from her British overlords, who didn't count her as a human. She passed by Padraic without recognition, and the sound of her lifeless footsteps faded behind him.

The village cemetery, which was where most of Ballynacargy called home, loomed directly ahead. The dead found peace there, and it was the last piece of Ireland that the living could call their own. Their schools were alien places, their churches outlawed, and their farmland stolen by foreign invaders. The cemetery was also the only place where families could be whole, because everyone in Ballynacargy had a parent or a child interred there. In the past fifty years, more Irishmen had died than were now alive. Ireland had become a massive green graveyard.

Padraic entered the moss-covered cemetery. It was surrounded by a rock wall that was deteriorating like the spirit of the Irish. He trod gingerly around makeshift tombstones that were decrepit and unsightly, since a proper death was a luxury beyond the means of people who couldn't even afford a proper living. Many of the epitaphs on the grave markers were now illegible, but the villagers didn't need to read them to know the fate of their fallen kin. Before the King of England and the Archbishop of Canterbury sent their legions to rid the Irish soil of Catholics and Gaels, people in Ballynacargy died from old age and accident. But with the Saxon attempt to confiscate the land and the soul of the Emerald Isle, people died prematurely and brutally in a religious and cultural genocide orchestrated by secular and divine tyrants in London.

Padraic reverently tiptoed past vine-covered tombstones under towering beech trees, mentally noting the apocalyptic stories told by the grave markers. A friend had succumbed to bubonic plague, which tore through the village last year. An uncle had been dragged from Tullamore to Kilbeggan by horses after being caught with a rosary, which his murderers used to hang his nearly lifeless carcass with. But at least in death, he no longer had to face the ignominy of soldiers coming to his home each Saturday morning with bugles blaring and bayonets fixed to exact their undeclared "taxes", confiscating money, clothing, furniture, and food. Father Duggan, for the crime of providing Communion to wounded Irish rebels, had his hands and feet broken with hammers and burned off from his arms and legs, and then finally had his heart torn from his chest and fed to dogs. Daniel O'Hennessey was beheaded for wearing green, after first being beaten and whipped. But, at least he had the honor of a grave, pitiful as it was.

Other deceased Irish weren't so fortunate. To make way for British landlords to confiscate their property, an entire village of Irish people was driven like stampeded cattle over the cliffs of Moher, cascading like a human waterfall seven hundred feet to perish on the rocks and surf below. Another village was cleared by driving the natives into a brushy grotto that was set afire, incinerating the evictees and leaving nothing but ashes intermingled with dirt as evidence that they ever existed. Other Irish wandered the land, their faces etched with uncomprehending scowls and their eyes growing dim and increasingly hopeless, until they succumbed to starvation, falling into roadside ditches to be devoured by rats and wolves. Those who survived were arrested as vagrants, and then impressed into the British navy. The only safe Irish lived in County Clare, where their land was so barren there wasn't enough wood to hang them, enough water to drown them, or enough earth to bury them.

Many mothers gave their paltry food to their children and starved to death. Death was probably better for them anyway, since not even motherhood was sufficient protection from the sanguine bands of soldiers who were systematically exterminating the Irish. Mothers of known rebels were hung by their hair, often with their children swinging grotesquely beside them. Small stones commemorated a whole generation of children who had died from typhus, cholera, encephalitis, starvation, or abandonment. Death was probably better for them too, because British soldiers had made a sport of tossing Irish babies into the air and catching them with their bayonets, ostensibly to prevent them from growing into adult insurrectionists.

Famine was a common denominator for many of the corpses buried in Ballynacargy's cemetery. But the potato blight alone wasn't responsible for so many starvation deaths. There were plenty of other crops flourishing in Irish fields. Unfortunately, these crops were owned by English landlords, and were destined for the cows, sheep, and dinner tables of Britishers across the Irish Sea. Native tenant farmers cultivated potatoes in the small, nearly barren fields they rented from landlords. When the potato crop failed, the British felt no mercy for their conquered tenants. To Saxon Protestants, death by starvation was a fitting reward for the misguided Celtic worshippers of the Pope. As Irish carcasses dropped from hunger, the British feasted on Irish beef.

Padraic spent much time in the cemetery. It was the only place in this world that he could talk with his brother and sister, who carried on their end of the conversation from the other side of death. Maggie, two years younger than Padraic and the apple of her doting brother's eye, died from the plague last spring. James, who was two years older and who always protected Padraic from bullies, avenged the death of

Maeve's mother. He stole one of the landlord's muskets, hunted down the two soldiers who had murdered her, and shot them both. But, the redcoated bully was more than his match. The British militia caught him before he could make it to Derrynane to escape on a clipper to the continent, where he planned to join other expatriates in France. His mutilated remains were dumped outside the door of Padraic's thatched hut, with a note promising a similar fate for any other Catholic that dared to challenge the Crown or the Archbishop. Padraic secretly buried the body in this cemetery. He didn't want his mother to see her son like that.

No official inquiry was made into his death, which would've been ruled accidental anyway, because it wasn't a crime to murder an Irishman. According to the British religion, it was no more of a sin to kill an Irishman than to kill a rabid dog, so it was open hunting season. Parliament authorized British agents to behead any Irishman without trial for the simple crime of not wearing the Kingdom's red colors. Ireland's own Parliament ordinarily would have repealed such an insidious law. Unfortunately, Britain instituted Poyning's Law, which forbade the Irish Parliament from enacting any legislation without permission of the British Parliament.

Today, as Padraic stood between the graves of his fallen siblings, he told Maggie and James that he was worried about mom. A note she had received from the landlord caused her to cry for hours. Her wracking sobs haunted his sleepless thoughts last night. His father, with hollow eyes and graven pallor, was unable to ease her inconsolable grief. This morning, the sheriff visited their home and argued bitterly with his parents, apparently in regard to the note. Padraic couldn't discern their veiled discussion, but he sensed that a crisis was imminent, especially when his mother invoked the spirits of Irish saints Brigid and Ciaran. It was then that he decided to leave his tension-filled hut for town. He stopped at the cemetery to commiserate with Maggie and James on his return trip home.

Padraic could feel Maggie's tender fingers gently wiping tears from his cheek, though he knew it was his own hand making the motion. And he could feel James' consoling hand on his trembling shoulder, though he knew it was just a spiritual recollection of brotherly contact repeated hundreds of times in days gone by. Strangely, standing alone among the dead of Ballynacargy, Padraic felt intense companionship. He basked in the warm love pouring out from his brother and sister from an eternal fount he couldn't comprehend. He thanked them with softly spoken words that settled on their graves like a comforting blanket. He told Maggie everything would be all right, that mom would find the strength to overcome her grief. And he thanked James once again for the ultimate sacrifice he had made to fight the Redcoated Bully.

Padraic hopped the stone wall entombing the cemetery and resumed his stroll on the dirt road. His step was livelier now, despite the light mist settling over the island like the humid breath of the sea god Neptune. The road was unnaturally deserted for a Sunday afternoon, especially since the Catholic friary was just ahead. In days of old, this road would have been crowded with churchgoers, rested from their labors and warmed by their congregation. But today, the stone-walled friary, with it's thatched roof, wooden steeple, boxed pews, and carillon that used to ring across the surrounding countryside, was abandoned. Father Brian's fiery sermons excoriating the evils of demon whiskey wouldn't echo loudly inside the stony church. Young Kathleen O'Flaherty's delicate flute playing plaintive carols and hymns wouldn't be heard. The intoxicating Latin canon rolling off melodic Gaelic tongues was silenced.

Catholicism was officially banned in Ireland, even though 90 percent of the Irish were baptized into that faith. By order of King Henry, Irish churches and monasteries were pillaged, their shrines desecrated, their sacred relics disinterred and destroyed, and their clergy evicted from convents and seminaries. A price was fixed on the heads of Irish Catholic priests equal to the price fixed on a wolf's head. The law required Catholics to give weekly tithes to the new Protestant clergy, even if they didn't attend services. This resulted in enormous salaries for Anglican pastors whose only congregation were their own families.

Ireland was overrun by external conquerors bearing the standards of two religions. Protestantism, of divine origin, was led by the Archbishop of Canterbury in England. Imperialistic Monarchism, of secular origin, was led by the King and Queen, the British Parliament, and the Saxon people worshipping at the altar of the Empire upon which the sun never set. The adherents of these two mythologies joined forces to convert the heathen Irish to Protestantism and to absorb their land into the Empire.

The Irish didn't know which was the viler of the two religions that oppressed them. When ordered to worship at the Church of England, did that mean they should prostrate themselves to the God of Protestantism or the King of the Empire? In truth, it didn't really matter. The secular and divine mythologies were intertwined, because mysticism begets political power, and political power breeds mysticism. The Irish didn't understand why these mythologies were invading, but they did clearly understand that the result would be the utter destruction of their race.

Padraic pondered this awful state of affairs during countless strolls past the abandoned friary on Sunday afternoons. He was at that peculiar stage in life, between childhood and adulthood, where he was too old to blindly accept the traditions of his forebears and too young to know the futility of questioning them. He was a simple adolescent who made simple observations. One observation was that his fellow

Irishmen were dying all around him. Another observation was that adults do things collectively they wouldn't do as individuals. It wasn't separate individuals coming here to steal Ireland and exterminate the Irish. It was convoys of British soldiers, congresses of British politicians, and congregations of Protestant evangelists. A final observation was that the essence binding these gangs together and emboldening their murderous actions was mysticism. The people who killed his brother James did so at the behest of their Archbishop and their King. From Padraic's innocent perspective, this faithful worship was not only an unnecessary human construction and an illusory fabrication of obeisance, it was inherently deadly.

These musings confused Padraic and disturbed his soul. It was one thing to disdain the vile British horde, and to spit upon their graven image of God. But, if it was the servility of the English people to their mythologies that created this woeful situation for the Irish, what woes did the servility of the Irish to their own mythologies cause for themselves? This led him to the blasphemous notion that the Irish mythology of Catholicism and the dogma of their ancient Brehon Laws were just as much to blame for the horrible bloodshed as was the British mythology of Protestantism and the dogma of the Empire. The only tangible outcome of this endless contest over whose secular and divine gods were supreme was that millions of people were now interred in earthen graves. These victims were being slowly devoured in body by fungus and worms, just as when alive they had been devoured in spirit by myths and allegiances. For him, the question was gradually shifting from which god Man should worship, to whether Man should worship at all. The zealousness and false piety of his fellow humans had overwhelmed their consciences, leaving them unable to choose between right and wrong. He couldn't even call these murderous adherents of faith hypocrites, since their behavior was consistent with the dogma that consumed them.

This distressing adolescent turbulence shook the foundations of the heritage and traditions still tugging mightily at Padraic's heart. His parents remained devout, unquestioning Catholics. If they learned of the blasphemous notions fermenting in his mind, their hearts would seize up with paroxysms of shock. He loved his father and mother desperately. They had given him life, and their unconditional love nurtured him through these terrible times. He also loved the traditions of Ireland, and Catholic rituals still beguiled him with their comfort and eternal stability. But, his soul harbored a suspicion that evil came in many disguises, including subservient worship of his parents' mythology. This was an enormous metaphysical conflict for one so young.

While the rest of Ireland feared that their gods had abandoned them, Padraic wrestled with the even more unsettling proposition that Ireland should abandon its gods. It wasn't the division between their religions driving Protestants and Catholics to kill each other, it was the mere existence of these religions. If the world could abandon the secular and divine gods that were at the root of all organized conflicts, then perhaps peace on Earth was a possible dream. If such a thing had happened just two years earlier, then James and Maggie would be walking gaily alongside him now, instead of lying under Ireland's loamy turf, serving as the main course for microbes in Earth's food chain.

Padraic was now ascending the massive hill overlooking Ballynacargy. His heart beat faster, partly from the effort of climbing, but more so from his memory of the gathering that occurred on this hill just two weeks ago. During this Monster Meeting, one of a series sweeping the island, Padraic saw a fleeting glimpse of his dream. It stirred his soul like nothing else. A hero named Daniel O'Connell was nurturing a ground swell of revolution in Ireland.

Four hundred thousand Irishmen came to this hill a fortnight ago from Roscommon, Longford, Offaly, Leitrim, Kildare, and Carlow to hear the renowned orator O'Connell speak. The only bigger gathering in Europe's history happened on Ireland's sacred Tara Hill outside of Dublin. One million Gaels came from throughout the island to hear O'Connell declare that freedom from England's Church and Empire was a possible dream. The exhilaration was indescribable as O'Connell stood on the highest point of Tara, the ancestral seat of Irish sovereignty, roaring that independence was the rightful quest of the Celtic nation, boldly defying the red-coated British militia that was powerless to act against such enormous Irish solidarity.

Just as America had its immortal written Declaration of Independence from British rule, now Ireland had Daniel O'Connell standing on blessed Tara with a spoken declaration against British oppression. O'Connell on Tara Hill, with a million Irish gathered around! Ireland's greatest bards and poets couldn't have conjured a more compelling scene. Padraic's heart leapt at this vision, because the same O'Connell had stood on this hill he was climbing now in Ballynacargy, delivering the very same immortal words to four hundred thousand Irish.

Padraic was among the teeming throngs that day in Ballynacargy, sitting on his father's powerful shoulders, straining to glimpse his hero sounding the rallying cry for dissolving the treacherous subservience to Great Britain. O'Connell's ringing oratory renewed their hope that had been nearly extinguished by three centuries of imperial subjugation. Emaciated from starvation, ravaged with disease, chilled from nakedness, and terrorized by the agents of the King and the Archbishop, the Irish nonetheless surged up the hill with irrepressible fervor, hearing words that their hearts barely dared to imagine possible, from the man that was the Voice of Ireland.

Padraic would never forget how O'Connell, who as a boy in Cahirciveen gleefully watched American men o' war battle British warships off the Kerry headlands, spoke as though the souls of his kindred spirits in America had somehow merged with his. As boldly as John Paul Jones sailed into Belfast Bay in broad daylight to sink stunned British merchantmen, he declared with Jeffersonian eloquence:

> "The time has come to break our manacles on the heads of our enemies, and to wrap around the necks of our oppressors the balls and chains that have entangled our legs. The atrocious British attempts to extinguish liberty make me young and vigorous again. Their occupation of our soil has made us weep tears of blood over fallen compatriots, over stolen property, over outlawed faith, over proscripted language, and over banned dress and culture.
>
> "What are we to do? Tamely surrender our land, our spirit, and our very lives? No! The centuries have recorded the Saxon and Protestant brutality, but our indomitable spirit has not been conquered. We must look to the West for the inspiration to ignite our fanaticism! The revolution shaking down the thunder across the sea is our answer. The Americans have removed the bushel shrouding freedom's light, and have shown the world that it is not only proper for man to rise up against his oppressors, but also that it is possible! The tempest that tore through America and ripped through France is now to be heard on our own shores. Through the darkening clouds engulfing our proud island we can hear the boom of distant thunder and discern the flashes of the coming lightning.
>
> "Let our enemies stand against us if they dare.

> *Where is the coward who would not die for such a land as Ireland? Where is the slave so lowly that, suddenly discovering he can burst his chains, would choose to keep them manacled about his ankles and wrists? I am not that slave!*
>
> *"We might soon have the choice to live as slaves or to die as free men. If that choice comes, I declare that it will be my dead body they will trample, if that be the fate of Ireland. Daniel O'Connell will not live as a slave!!!"*

Four hundred thousand Irishmen responded with a raucous cheer that rolled across the Irish Sea. Emotional energy plowed like a giant riptide through a crowd that would have been prouder to wear chains than be decorated with the Star of England. Ireland clearly had a leader, a purpose, and a vision now. If O'Connell had said the word on that glorious day, four hundred thousand tattered Irishmen would have somehow summoned the strength to ride night and day to Dun Loaghaire, swim the Irish Sea, charge across the English landscape, and storm London like rabid pit bulls to avenge three brutal centuries of attempted genocide.

But it wasn't yet time. O'Connell had more Monster Meetings to hold throughout Ireland to coordinate a unified insurrection. He urged the fervent throngs to preserve their energy and wait for the opportune moment to rise up. To keep the embers of revolution smoldering in their hearts, he read a poem written by Fanny Parnell to close the meeting:

> *Now, are you men, or are you cattle, ye tillers of the soil?*
>
> *Would you be free, or evermore the rich man's cattle toil?*
>
> *The shadow on the dial hangs that points the fatal hour—*

INSURRECTION RESURRECTION

Now hold your own, or branded slaves, forever cringe and cower.

The serpent's curse upon you lies—ye writhe within the dust,
Ye fill your mouths with beggars' swill, ye grovel for a crust;
Your lords have set their blood-stained heels upon your shameful heads,
Yet they are kind—they leave you still their ditches for your beds!

Oh, by the God who made us all—the seignior and the serf—
Rise up and swear this day to hold your own green Irish turf;
Rise up and plant your feet as men where now you crawl as slaves,
And make your harvest fields your camps, or make of them your graves.

Three hundred years your crops have sprung, by murdered corpses fed;
Your butchered sires, your famished sires, your ghastly compost spread;
Their bones have fertilized your fields, their blood has fallen like rain;
They died that ye might eat and live—God! have they died in vain?

The hour has struck. Fate holds the dice, we stand with bated breath;
Now who shall have your harvests fair—'tis Life that plays with Death;
Now who shall have our Motherland? 'tis Right that plays with Might;

The peasant's arms were weak, indeed, in such unequal fight!

On that sunny day, Padraic's spirit soared like eagles riding a canyon thermal. The world suddenly held out potential for his adolescent yearnings. Life now had meaning, beyond being just a desolate way station on a journey to the grave. Childishly, Padraic imagined he and O'Connell walking shoulder to shoulder, leading legions of Irish militia, planting the Irish Republican banner proudly in the green turf wherever they boldly marched. As his imagination hyperacted, he daydreamed that he and O'Connell were kindred spirits, cut from the same mold and destined for the same glory as liberators of Ireland.

As Padraic descended the hill overlooking Ballynacargy, he chuckled with embarrassment at his delusions of grandeur two weeks ago. How could he ever have imagined himself standing tall like the giant O'Connell, who would surely laugh till he cried if he heard that some starving waif pretensed to join him in the pantheon of libertarian heroes. Padraic's childish dreams evaporated as he slowly came to grips with reality.

The dreams of the whole Irish nation evaporated when O'Connell was arrested three days ago, by orders of the King. While organizing the climactic Monster meeting on the plains of Clontarf, where Brian Boru had cast a wave of Viking invaders into the ocean a millennium ago, O'Connell was seized by Redcoats and charged with insurrection. Ireland collapsed into greater despair than ever before as British soldiers punished the impudent Celts. Deportations increased dramatically and unexplained deaths jammed overcrowded cemeteries.

Padraic hurried down the narrow path leading to his tiny mud-walled home, since anyone caught outdoors after sunset was subject to deportation. He trudged up to the door, but didn't enter. He listened intently to see if the emotional rancor that had driven him away earlier had subsided. Unfortunately, he heard passionate argument, punctuated by his mother's wailing and his father's uncharacteristic cursing. Forlornly, he sat on a rock to wait until peace descended upon his troubled home.

While his bare feet toyed with weeds sprouting from the mossy turf, he heard much of the conversation unfolding inside the house. He began to understand what had been tormenting his parents for two days. The wave of deportations sweeping the country, in retribution for O'Connell's abortive insurrection, had descended upon Ballynacargy. Some unfortunate villager was slated to be forcibly exiled overseas. Mother wasn't resigned to letting it happen. Father tried to console her by rationalizing both the benefit and the inevitability of it.

Padraic gathered, from the depth of his mother's emotions, that the deportee was very dear to her. He heard her decry the brutality of the long journey on the deadly coffin ships, and the terror of a frightened immigrant landing on foreign soil with no acquaintance within four thousand miles and with nothing but a pervasive hatred for the perpetrators of this awful thing.

Padraic himself began to mourn when the conversation revealed that the unfortunate soul destined for deportation was an adolescent. His mother described the woeful trauma that a youngster would experience in heartless separation from family, village, and country. She told of the gruesome voyage, where one thousand deportees were jammed into the bowels of a ship fit for only a hundred cattle. Water was sparse, and food even more so. There was no privacy and no sanitation provisions. Daylight was rarely seen. Vomiting from seasickness added to the germ-laden effluence washing through the hold with bilge from the sea. Disease abounded, and death was frequent. So many corpses were summarily tossed overboard that coffin ship pilots could track their progress toward America, Argentina, and Australia simply by following the trail of Irish skeletons that haunted the world's oceanbeds.

Padraic's stomach churned with revulsion. For a fleeting moment, he wished he could trade places with the unfortunate deportee, but he knew he wasn't brave enough. He also knew that his mother's grief would be magnified tenfold if the last of her children not yet murdered by the British was to be taken from her, even as a voluntary self-sacrifice. He opted for the security of his rock perch as the sun slowly sank below the western horizon.

Moments later, two visitors strode down the narrow path to his house. They passed him without noticing his existence, but he noticed them in a way that he had never noticed anyone before or since. Seeing the sheriff and the landlord allied together, rapping forcefully on the door of his home, sent a charge of electricity down his spine that made every hair on his body stand on end. Their black coats, their lips pursed with grim resolve, and their strident knocking convinced Padraic that serious business was afoot. Morbidly, he imagined the two dour men as Grim Reapers incarnated.

When his mother opened the door, she unleashed an unholy scream that pierced the core of his being with a subliminal warning he didn't understand. She turned and ran from the doorway, her screaming unabated. Padraic was now completely disoriented and afraid. His heart beat faster and his palms began to sweat. His father appeared in the doorway looking haggard and defeated. The beaten man stared intently at the Grim Reapers for a long, silent moment, as if trying to make them disappear with what remained of his will. Sweat covered Padraic's entire body. His breathing was rapid and shallow. Adrenaline pumped through his veins as his body subconsciously recognized the imminent danger that his staggered mind didn't yet comprehend.

Comprehension came quickly enough. When his father's staring couldn't make the Grim Reapers vanish, the gaunt patriarch turned his head and looked at him. "Padraic", he said with a weak, cracking voice, "Come here." His father said nothing else, but his beseeching look that passionately begged forgiveness told Padraic all he needed to know. He now understood why his mother grieved so. He now understood why his father looked more vanquished than any man deserved. He now understood who was being deported to America. He was.

He didn't move. His world stopped momentarily, because he willed it to stop. He wanted to freeze this scene for posterity, because whatever was left of his childhood had now been purloined. This was his last look at the world through youthful eyes. From now on, his view of the world would be glazed with cynicism and hatred, and he would forevermore interpret life with a heart singed by brutish callousness.

His father summoned him again. Padraic rose mechanically from the rock, still in shock. As he walked, he dully heard his father explaining why this unfortunate situation was unavoidable. ". . . . there is not enough food for us all to eat. . . . America has food enough to feed the world. . . . the landlord doesn't want the starvation of another youth on his conscience. . . . there is opportunity to lead a real life in America, and the landlord will pay your passage. . . . we haven't paid our rent for seven months. . . . it's better to go it alone overseas than to join Maggie and James beyond the pale. . . . we can't go with you, because we have no money. . . . we must stay here to repay our debts to the landlord."

The words meant nothing to Padraic. He didn't need an explanation. He needed his mother. He suddenly dashed into the house past his surprised father and the two Grim Reapers. He flung himself onto his mother, who was crumpled in a heap on a wooden chair. She had just enough forewarning to open her arms and envelop him, on this last day of his childhood and her last day of his acquaintance. He buried his face between her neck and shoulders. The salty residue of her tears evoked a torrent of his own tears. They sobbed in unison, with great wracking spasms, trying to cleanse their souls of pain. He cocooned inside her suffocating hug. The soft warmth of her bare skin on his face became etched permanently in his memory. He kissed her cheek tenderly, an affection she returned several times over. Her pungent breath, heavy with the scent of intense crying, wafted across his nostrils, etching another indelible memory. Placing his head on her bosom, he heard her pounding heart thumping out an eternal message comprehensible only by mother and child. He absorbed these sensory souvenirs as secret little treasures to be cherished for the rest of his alienated life. They would be his only proof that he ever lived in a place called Ballynacargy, in a land called Ireland, raised by parents he would never see again.

The landlord, the sheriff, and his father entered the house. The two impatient Grim Reapers explained with little sincerity that maudlin displays of emotion only made it harder to get on with the inevitable, as ordained by the King and the Archbishop. His father, trying to salvage his family's dignity, instructed his wife to release Padraic. She did this, but the withering look she gave her husband made it clear her estimation of him would never be the same. He pleaded with her for understanding. "Whoever stays in this godforsaken emerald prison will surely die! The boy will live if he goes!" The words had no effect. She interpreted them as betrayal and surrender. No reasoned arguments could ever sway a mother to abandon her child.

Padraic watched this exchange between his parents with morbid fascination. His predicament had become surreal, as if he was an observer in this drama, rather than a participant who should be running or punching wildly at the Grim Reapers or collapsing to the floor. But, he did none of these. His father put a hand uncomfortably on his shoulder as a farewell gesture. Padraic just looked at him with an empty expression. This part of his life was already just a memory. As the Grim Reapers led him away, he heard his mother scream frantically. Then he heard a scuffle as his father physically restrained her from chasing after him. Then he heard no more, because powerful barriers had formed within moments around his heart and soul. He didn't look back. He couldn't look back.

Two days later, after a long coach ride through Tullamore, Tipperary and Mallow, Padraic stood on a wharf in Cork among a motley group of other Irish lads waiting to board the same ship and to endure the same fate. The looming clipper Albert Gallatin blocked their view of the Atlantic Ocean. Sea gulls squawked above them, waves slapped against the stone wharves beneath them, porters busily moved their wares in all directions, and sailors on the Albert Gallatin shouted commands and obscenities as they prepared for the thirty day journey to New York.

Stevedores pushed the orphaned Irish boys toward the clipper's ramp like cargo to be loaded into the hold and battened down. As the boys were shoved and cajoled, the shields around Padraic's heart let down for just a moment. Suddenly, he bolted from the ragged queue and leapt to the grass below the wharf. Two stevedores immediately chased him, fearing that they would be severely punished if some of their cargo escaped. Padraic ran as fast as his emaciated body permitted, keeping steadily ahead of his pursuers. On the wharf, the other boys cheered heartily for their daring cohort, vicariously reveling in his brazen defiance of the Union Jack.

Suddenly, Padraic plunged to the ground and pawed at the turf frantically. Within seconds, the stevedores nabbed him and gruffly berated him as they dragged him back to the wharf. Despite being pummeled, harangued, and kicked, Padraic said nothing and resisted little. The small crowd of onlookers, disappointed by a tame ending to an otherwise bold escape attempt, began to dissipate. They concluded that Padraic was just another crazy farm urchin. The other orphans clapped him on the back and offered lackluster praise for his bravado, but they too were disappointed by his strangely aborted flight. They were herded onto the ship without further incident.

But as the Albert Gallatin slid from the wharf into the murky waters of Cork Harbor, Padraic stood at the railing and smiled for the first time in several years, his eyes glistening like the silvery sheen of the River Shannon. As Ireland slowly faded from his life, he calmly took stock of his assets. Despite the best efforts of all the King's troops and all the Bishop's priests to completely disenfranchise and alienate him, he was leaving Ireland with three things of inestimable value.

The first of his three treasures was the never-to-be-forgotten memories of his family and of his life on the most beautiful and yet the most cruel place on earth. His young mind had encapsulated the images of his mother's tear-stained face, the carefree voices of Maggie and James, the smell of peat burning in the hearth, and the brilliant yellow whin blooming along the roads of Ballynacargy.

The second of his three treasures was the fire of rebellion that roared in his soul. The King and the Archbishop had dealt him staggering losses. Maggie and James were dead, Maeve was emotionally stolen from him, he was forcibly separated from his parents, he was exiled from his country, and as a final humiliation, his name was anglicized to Patrick. But, these injuries and injustices merely fueled his burgeoning zeal for rebellion. He was enroute to America, where rebellion against the tyranny of church and state was not only a possible dream, but already a reality. He saw in America mankind's first opportunity to throw off the chains of servitude to the strange class of humans who clutched at power over the rest. He didn't naively believe the stories of gold-paved streets in America. He did, however, believe that America offered something greater than gold, which was the freedom to live a life unfettered from the oppression of gods and kings.

The last of his three treasures, which he held gingerly in his palm, was acquired during his brief dash from the wharf back in Cork. This treasure was outlawed by the British, because it was symbolic of Irish solidarity and resistance. It was a simple thing, but possessing it was punishable by death. To Patrick, its value far outweighed the danger. Possessing it made him feel like a man with a reason for living. To an Irishman, the color green is synonymous with being Irish and being free, and in his hand he held the greenest green that Ireland could produce. He carefully unfolded his fingers to admire it. His heart pumped heavily as he absorbed its emerald beauty. He knew that if he could preserve this treasure in his hand and the fire of rebellion burning in his soul, the world would be all right after all.

He smiled and closed his fingers around the shamrock that he had plucked by the wharf. He couldn't wait to get to America. There were canals to be dug, railroads to be laid, farmland to be tilled, iron and coal to be mined, and freedom to nurture. America was a new world for him and his progeny to shape.

Coincidentally, the other person silently occupying Patrick Freeman's body couldn't wait to get to America either, although to a much different era. This other person was anxious to tell a certain acquaintance that he now understood why talk of insurrection was always on his friend's tongue. The fire of rebellion was flickering to life in John Freeman's soul.

Chapter Ten:
"The Insurrection Act"

> "It is unwise to introduce a gun at the beginning of a play unless you are planning to use it by the end."
>
> —Chekhov

Freeman could accomplish nothing more by coexisting with Patrick, so he was hurtling back through the tangled web of time to his rightful place in modern America. Suddenly, an explosion of light and sound overwhelmed him. When the furious display of pyrotechnics and percussion subsided, he became aware that he was laying on someone. Unpredictable quantum mechanics had ironically deposited him squarely on top of the Head Honcho, who was bellowing at him.

Amazingly, Freeman's crashing descent from nowhere wasn't the strangest occurrence of the day for the Honcho. Earlier, a mysterious tornadic force had trashed his office. Drawers were rifled, files dumped, pictures ripped from walls, his tickets to Paraguay scattered, his desk upended, and his personal library ransacked. He angrily pushed himself up, sending Freeman sprawling across the floor. "Where in hell have you been?"

"In 1846 Ireland", replied Freeman, checking for bruises. "I borrowed your 'Book of Liberal Policies, Marxist Economics, and Other Occult Phenomena'".

The Honcho now had a prime suspect for his office demolition. "Did you do this?" he growled.

"Of course not", lied Freeman. "Maybe it was the same guys who blew up the National Archives trying to kill the Dormouse".

The Honcho sank down into his leather chair. "Shit! What if those bastards killed the March Hare when they trashed my office? The Red Queen will have another reason to lop off my head." His forehead crashed heavily on his desk. "Let's change the subject. Tell me about your time travel to Ireland."

"It was horrible! The British slaughtered the Irish like they weren't even human."

"I didn't realize abortions were so common back then", said the Honcho. "I'm impressed with British willingness to dispose of unwanted life."

"Don't be so quick to admire them. The fiendish bastards stole vast amounts of land from the native Irish."

"Child's play", countered the Head Honcho, who wasn't going to be outdone by 19th century tyrants. "The U.S. Government owns 95% of Alaska, and 50% of the land west of the Mississippi. And nobody can top how we dispossessed the Native Americans."

"The King and the Archbishop forcibly replaced Ireland's Catholicism with their own secular and divine mythologies", said Freeman.

The Honcho yawned disdainfully. "Our government implanted Ismism in everyone's souls to not only squelch other religions, but to squelch thinking itself, which has been the goal of mysticism since the beginning. The Safari Golfer makes the Archbishop of Canterbury look like a cherubic acolyte."

Freeman wasn't ready to concede the supremacy of the American government's inhumanity to man. "The British sent Irishmen to foreign lands in deadly coffin ships."

"Big deal! We send our boys to foreign lands in troop transports with one way tickets."

"The British impressed the Irish into their navy and army", said Freeman.

"We not only draft Americans into our military, we built the Bimidji Barrier to keep them from escaping our human bologna grinder."

"The British put a price on the heads of Catholic priests", said Freeman.

"Hell, any sonofabitch can put a price on an adult's head. But it takes a special breed of human to put a price on the head of a defenseless unborn baby, which we do every hour with state funded abortions."

"The British replaced outlawed Irish schools with their own state supported schools", persisted Freeman, "thereby replacing Irish ideology and culture with theirs."

"We set up government funded schools to crowd out private schools and replace their ideology with the State's Political Correctness."

"The British placated unemployed Irish with meaningless public works projects, like building bridges that traversed nothing and constructing roads that went nowhere."

"Batting practice!", scoffed the Honcho. "We pay farmers to grow nothing. We subsidize tobacco production, and then warn people not to smoke the finished product. We pay bureaucrats to create regulations, and then we pay them again to protect us from those regulations. As a coup de grace, we fund a justice department in a political system that structurally precludes justice."

"Armed British tax collectors invaded Irish homes and confiscated their possessions to pay for dubious British services."

"You haven't experienced terror until the ravenous IRS sharks have sunk their teeth into you."

"The inhabitants of entire Irish villages were burned alive by British soldiers."

"In Vietnam, we sprayed Agent Orange on the foliage concealing the combatants, many of whom wished that they were burned alive instead."

"Ireland was infested with British civil servants being paid prodigious salaries to accomplish objectives that were unmeasurable, never defined, and often contradictory."

The Honcho didn't respond. His sudden silence confused Freeman, until it dawned on him that he himself was a highly paid civil servant who did little or nothing to improve American quality of life. His job was a sufficient rebuttal to his own argument. The Honcho broke the silence. "Ismism says that all debates are meaningless, because people who have more guns, myths, or lawyers than you have already decided what's right and wrong. Therefore, I won this debate even before it started, because no one commands more guns, myths, or lawyers than I."

"I'm a slave to your superior station in life", Freeman facetiously conceded to his master.

"Don't look so disappointed", said the Honcho. "Is slavery too high a price to pay for freedom?"

"It's an obscene price that makes no sense at all."

"So what? According to the Golfer, you're merely an insignificant speck compared to the universal human oneness of Ismism."

"My universe extends no further than the limits of my own mind and senses", Freeman countered. "Therefore, even though I'm of no significance to the universal human oneness, I'm of inestimable significance to me." He was surprised by his own eloquence. It was the only thing he'd said in the last twenty years that he didn't believe to be bullshit before the words escaped his lips.

"Don't be so proud just because you mumbled a few words of bullshit", said the Honcho. "Things have gone to hell, and I'm holding you personally responsible."

"How could I be responsible?" cried Freeman. "I've been in a different country and century!"

"It doesn't matter. You're responsible the same way that suburban middle class workers are responsible for the poverty of inner city indigents. We're all in this together, at least until I flee to Paraguay."

Freeman understood. Just like plankton in the ocean and chlorophyll in plants are the sources of the planet's food chain, the middle class worker is the foundation of the American social food chain. His spouse eats him. His kids eat him. The poor eat him. The bureaucrats eat him. The armies eat him. Even the rich are clever enough to eat him. At the end of every human social food chain is some poor Joe doing an honest day's work.

Fortunately, the Honcho interrupted his fixation on this disturbing food chain by ranting about a litany of bureaucratic foibles that occurred while he was in Ireland. The Vhaicam situation was a public relations disaster. Despite the prolifically deadly American military machine, Vhaicam's population was now four times that of China. The Honcho's campaign promise to feed and cloth the two billion good Vhaicamese in the South, and to maim and kill the two billion bad Vhaicamese in the North, created a two-headed "guns and butter" monster. Feeding the procreative South Vhaicamese consumed 50% of the American Gross National Product. Killing the stubborn North Vhaicamese consumed the other 50% of the American GNP. This left nothing of the American GNP for Americans.

Matters got even worse when thousands of Vhaicamese boat people arrived in New York harbor seeking asylum. They were tired of totalitarian communism, starvation, and meddling by strange foreign powers, so they sailed against impossible odds to be part of the American dream. "Tell them to go back home", the Honcho dispassionately instructed But Sir!, who had reported the arrival of the motley flotilla. "Those rabbit-eared bastards are more useful to me over there, where I can feed or kill them, depending on which ism they worship. Feeding some of them gets me huge emotional support from the voters, and killing the rest gets me huge patriotic support. If the refugees stay here, the voters will just be pissed about another slew of immigrants sponging off the dole."

Unfortunately, the Vhaicamese had an amazing aptitude for building boats and filling them with innumerable offspring. To counter this, the Honcho dictated that Vhaicamese couples have exactly zero children. In this variant of China's Birth Planning Policy, if a child was born, the mother had to either kill it or commit suicide. Having less than zero children was also forbidden because it made no sense, which was a prerogative the U.S. government hoped to monopolize. The Vhaicamese accepted this harsh Birth Planning Policy because the Honcho convinced them the prosperity of their future generations depended entirely on them having no children.

Back in America, another crisis began when the Department of Energy required energy producers to stop generating power until they proved they weren't harming reticulated salamander habitats, even though no one had ever actually seen a reticulated salamander, except for the Greenpeace lab technician who claimed he saw one on his way to a seminar about resurrecting pterodactyls. Human catastrophe was averted when the Honcho recommended using Bureaucracy Power, a limitless energy supply that required no mining or drilling, and therefore didn't threaten the mythological reticulated salamander.

He got this idea from the National Archives explosion that led to the Dormouse's death and shredded millions of government documents. No one ever missed those shredded documents, so the Honcho concluded that the zillions of documents stored in government vaults, file cabinets, and warehouses must also be useless. He commissioned a ten million dollar study by the Energy Department, which discovered that paper burns. The DOE also discovered that microfilm, red tape, manila folders, and cardboard file boxes burn. They calculated that burning the government's supply of unnecessary documents could fulfill all of America's energy requirements until long after the sun burned out. Bureaucracy Power was born, saving the economy and the reticulated salamander.

Unfortunately, an overzealous do-gooder named Rolf Raider protested against this new Bureaucracy Power. Rolf was a tireless consumer advocate dedicated to enhancing life by regulating to death the businesses that produce everything useful. The rules and regulations that he had assiduously created over three decades were being destroyed as America burned government documents. These documents included Rolf's two most cherished studies, one that concluded fluorocarbons from aerosol sprays were consuming the ozone layer and would inevitably turn us all into irradiated lumps of clay, and another that concluded automobile emissions were expanding the ozone layer and would unleash a scorching greenhouse effect that would turn us all into dehydrated lumps of clay. The complete contradiction between the studies didn't disturb Rolf Raider one iota, since he was quite happy to know we were going to be reduced to lumps of clay either way. This joyous realization was the zenith of his career.

Rolf Raider visited the Honcho to beg him to save his cherished rules and regulations from the furnaces. Unfortunately, the Honcho wasn't going to easily abandon Bureaucracy Power, so he challenged Rolf to justify saving his rules and regulations.

"Their value is limitless," began the consumer advocate, "especially if we enact the regulations still on the drawing board. We can give every citizen eternal life by eliminating all potential accidents. We can even eliminate the need for living, thereby saving us all lots of trouble."

"What will that cost?" asked the Senator.

"For a mere $182 per person, we can eliminate the bicycle, which is a leading cause of injury. For $16,000 per person, we can eliminate all steps, stairs, and ladders. And for $36,000 per person, we can eliminate the automobile. I have detailed costs for eliminating every potential threat."

The Honcho yawned and looked at his watch. "After you eliminate those things, what will that leave Americans?"

"With nothing to do and a humongous national debt."

This caught the Honcho's attention. "I like it! But won't most people be unhappy with nothing to do and a humongous national debt?"

"Absolutely! That's why I want to eliminate the need for living altogether."

"How would we do that?"

"Convince everyone that there is an eternal afterlife in which supreme beings fulfill every desire and we are incomprehensibly happy. Then everyone will realize that continuing to live on earth with nothing to do and a humongous national debt is rather pointless."

"That's not a new idea."

"It's not?" said the crestfallen consumer advocate, whose life's ambition was just crushed.

"Nope. Lots of other Isms promise eternal paradise if their adherents abandon their temporal concerns and subsume themselves in the myths. For instance, Catholicism substitutes humongous guilt complexes for humongous national debts, although the emotional effect is the same. But, don't look so despondent. The Safari Golfer is unveiling his version at the next Ismism Synod in Jerusalem. He'll need help rolling it out to the masses."

This boosted Rolf's morale. "Did I tell you my plans for eliminating heart disease?"

"No, do tell", said the Honcho, with acute boredom.

"We'll cut everyone's heart out."

"Isn't that dangerous?"

"To the contrary. Two million people died from heart ailments last year, which my plan will completely eliminate."

"But how will people survive without their hearts?"

Rolf Raider smiled impishly. "They won't need them after I've banned everything that's fun." After Rolf slithered out of the office, the Honcho concluded that he should proceed with Bureaucracy Power. He had learned during the Major Indian Hostage Crisis not to overreact to pressure from radicals.

The Major Indian Hostage Crisis began as the Minor Indian Hostage Crisis when militant Native Americans took some clerks hostage in the Capitol Building and demanded that the entire U.S. be returned to them, because it was forcibly taken from their ancestors. The Honcho convinced his fellow congressmen to ignore their demands. In a ringing speech, he vowed that America would resist their unlawful aggression and their barbaric demands to the bitter end.

Unfortunately, when the Indians heard his brazen words, they killed the captive clerks. Then, they boldly escalated the Minor Indian Hostage Crisis into the Major Indian Hostage Crisis by kidnapping Buxomus Blondus and reiterating their demands for the return of America. The Honcho reacted with courage typical of politicians. He did a complete about-face and implored his fellow congressmen to return the country to the Indians in exchange for the safe release of his voluptuous secretary.

Congress objected that the country wasn't theirs to give away. They abandoned this argument, however, when they realized that they'd been behaving as if the country was theirs to give away for years. So, they forged a compromise that wouldn't erode their tax base yet would satisfy the Indians' demands. Rather than surrender the U.S., they gave the Indians a large plot of land known as Europe.

So began the Great Indian Invasion of Europe. Indians streamed onto the continent wearing white hats and mounted on silver steeds, colonizing the Old World by offering the indigenous Europeans useless trinkets in exchange for vast tracts of prime French, English, and Spanish real estate. Recalcitrant Europeans who refused to surrender their land were forced onto reservations, where they were compelled to relearn their history from the perspective of the Red Men, who ignored all events prior to their invasion of Europe. The Indians negotiated peace treaties with the European tribes, and then violated them, because that's all they knew about treaties. They also brought diseases that native immune systems couldn't withstand, killing half of the indigenous population. In short, the Indians brought civilization to Europe.

In the meantime, prodded by a fiendish Democratic Party strategy to fractionalize the country for political advantage, all Americans joined activist groups for men, women, gays, straights, poor, old, young, veterans, conscientious objectors, atheists, born-again Christians, pro-lifers, pro-choicers, environmentalists, industrialists, taxpayers, welfare recipients, married, divorced, handicapped, black, white, yellow, red, criminals, victims, substance abusers, abolitionists, management, labor, tenants, landlords, homeless, homeowners, and numerous others.

Things were okay until these groups discovered "rights". Each militant faction translated its narrow focus into a corresponding "right", which became a claim on government resources, which became a claim on American taxpayers. Every group held mass rallies in support of their particular "right" in front of the White House, under the mistaken impression that those in power actually gave a damn about "rights", outside the context of the votes at stake.

It soon dawned on the factions that their "rights" were contradictory. For every group supporting an issue, there was another group against it. This was a corollary of Newtonian physics, in which every action has an equal and opposite reaction. At this point, leaders of the factions should have cooperated to develop a rational framework for society in which all interests could be given fair and impartial treatment. Instead, the leaders mobilized their factions and, on the count of three, 270 million Americans began history's largest Fistfight on the White House lawn. Rather than trample each other's "rights" in congress and in court, they simply trampled each other. This huge donnybrook saved lots of legal fees, which spurred the lawyers' activist group to join the Fistfight to protect their inalienable right to absorb the wealth of their fellow Americans in a manner unrelated to common sense.

The brouhaha on the White House lawn was intolerable to the President, because it kept him awake at night. His reaction was fearsome and swift. He hired sociologists to evaluate the problem. Sociologists are adept at inventing and analyzing collections of people, such as power groups, pressure groups, political groups, ethnic groups, and cultural groups. Their analysis of the conflict on the lawn had just begun when they started a Fistfight among themselves. Each had a different opinion of which activist group really had the pre-eminent "rights" to be protected.

While these academians punched faces and crashed chairs over craniums, the President fumed. He was in his second term and couldn't run for elected office again, so he had lost interest in American group dynamics, and no longer thought of people in terms of ethereal voting blocks. He suddenly realized that lumping people into insular groups with narrow identities and exclusive mythologies invited eternal conflict that would inevitably get sucked into Washington's vortex as the White House, Congress, and the Sublime Court refereed. When people think and behave as mythological groups rather than as individuals, human peace is impossible.

With this new perspective, the President hopped onto a table to get the attention of the sociologists wrestling around him like monkeys in a barrel. An uneasy silence fell over the bedraggled combatants. He spoke from his heart for the first time in many years:

> *"Stop this nonsense! No individual can be accurately represented or defined by a fictional group. Oh sure, an individual may join collections of other individuals. He may think of himself as part of these abstract, theoretical groupings. But, he is not them. He still has dreams, characteristics, and desires that simply do not fit the paradigm constructed for these groups by sociologists and political schemers. Groupings of individuals may conform to aesthetically pleasing bell shaped curves, but these abstractions say nothing about the hearts and souls of the people lined up as points on the curve. Sociologists construct straw men and shadow beings. They don't know what I'm really thinking or what I really want out of my brief and precious existence on earth. Their statistics ignore me, as they ignore every other real person. The archetypes constructed by sociologists violate the snowflake rule, because none of us are alike.*
>
> *"Open your eyes! We're all tyrannized when you sociologists encourage your artificial groups to militantly*

pursue 'rights' that can't exist, because these 'groups' really don't exist. The only meaningful rights are the rights of individuals. Any claim by a group to a 'right' is really a coercive and therefore immoral claim against other individuals. Go forth and disband the groups, slay the mythologies, and disavow the dogmas. Tell everyone fighting on my lawn to go home and live their own lives in peace, or else The Fistfight will never end."

The sociologists sheepishly slithered out to the White House Lawn, got the attention of the Fistfight participants, and made an official pronouncement. "The Groups we defined for you don't exist. The Group Rights we told you to pursue are illusory. Stop fighting and go home." Unfortunately, the 270 million combative Americans didn't consider the Fistfight completely over yet. They eyed one another conspiratorially, and then they charged the sociologists and pummeled them to death with hardcover copies of their doctoral theses. Then they went home.

After the Fistfight disbanded, a profound calm settled over Washington. Nothing moved at all. This wasn't unusual for the seat of American government, which has enough bureaucrats, directors, and managers, enough rules, regulations, and laws, enough conflicting goals, agendas, and strategies, to squelch the life out of any productive initiative that briefly flickers into being. The sheer size of the federal bureaucracy prevents its right hand from knowing what its right hand is doing, much less what its left hand is up to. The torpid metabolism of a large bureaucracy prevents it from progressing through its life cycle to actually die a natural death, which is why Reagan observed that government programs are the nearest things to eternal life. This is reinforced by the government's general policy to tax anything that moves and subsidize anything that stops moving, which creates an inertial bias toward nothing happening at all.

But the calm that now gripped Washington was unusually pervasive. Not only was nothing getting done, nobody was doing anything either. Normally, government workers busily spun their wheels while accomplishing nothing of benefit to taxpayers. But when workers were observed doing absolutely nothing, even skipping breaks and lunch hours for lack of energy to go to the cafeteria, it became clear something was seriously amiss.

Experts from the Center for Disease Control in Atlanta were called in to assess the situation. They quickly diagnosed that the entire Washington bureaucracy was infected with FAIDS. Federally Acquired Initiative Deficiency Syndrome disables the part of the pituitary gland that triggers the "move" and "think" signals. FAIDS is enormously contagious and almost impossible to cure. Victims of the disease don't even know they have it, because their brain never gets the signal to think about their condition. It's difficult to eradicate FAIDS from a bureaucracy, because the managers who would otherwise rehabilitate or fire their crippled employees also get infected.

On the brighter side, FAIDS-stricken employees became a lucrative tourist attraction. Madame Toussaud, curator of the famous London wax museum, moved her operation to Washington to use the frozen bureaucrats as live exhibits. They were cheaper than artfully crafted waxen effigies, yet were just as motionless. Visitors flocked to stare in wonder at the inanimate government workers that Madame Toussaud carefully staged each day. The human mannequins didn't even flinch at quitting time, so severe was the FAIDS epidemic.

Freeman's yawning convinced the Honcho to conclude his recounting of the events that happened during his time travel to Ireland. "Don't forget, you insolent sonofabitch. I'm holding you personally responsible for everything that's gone wrong with my re-election, including the latest poll results. None of my supporters are going to vote for me."

Freeman smirked. "Let's hope for a big turnout from the undecideds."

"You won't be so smug when it's time to head for Paraguay. I'm giving away your plane ticket. The Golfer doesn't want you along anyway. He doesn't trust you."

"Why not?" asked Freeman.

"He says you're too honest to be trusted."

"That doesn't make sense!"

"Who said it made sense? The salient point is that I'm taking Buxomus instead of you."

"Part of your negative image is that everyone believes you're having sex with her."

"That's malicious innuendo started by my opponent!"

"It's not innuendo. You screw the poor girl every day."

"You see? It's that frankness that the Golfer hates about you", sneered the Honcho. "You're not cut out for politics or religion. Besides, who really cares if I screw the bitch? A little sex on the side is a hallowed political tradition. FDR had a mistress, yet they still felt sorry for him in his wheel chair. Eisenhower's concubine slept in his tent during WWII, yet they still called him a hero. JFK was a notorious skirt chaser, yet they still put flowers on his grave. Clinton diddled half the sluts in Arkansas and Washington, yet they still reelected him. Hell, I think I'll call a press conference to clear the air on this issue."

"What will you say?"

"I'll tell them I have nothing to say about it."

"That doesn't make sense."

"Who said it made sense? My goal is to clear the air, not to be logical."

"What's the latest on the Honchogate investigation?" asked Freeman, changing the topic to something that did make sense.

The Honcho moaned. "They're accusing me of every wrongdoing under the sun, including embezzlement, loan sharking, tax evasion, bribery, and sodomy. They're also incriminating me in the Wedtech scandal, ABSCAM, the Ill Wind case, the junk bond fiasco, the Savings and Loan disaster, Irangate, Iraqgate, Whitewater, Travelgate, Tailhook, and lots of other misadventures they haven't named yet."

"Someone who knows you well must be behind this."

"Bottomless Esophagus is behind it", said the Honcho. "Worse still, I suspect he and the Insurrectionist are the same person."

"Why?"

"It's my seventh sense. A wave of insurrections accompanied the flurry of revelations by Bottomless Esophagus. Something cataclysmic is about to happen. Just like unusual seismographic activity precedes a volcanic eruption, I'm getting daily reports of citizens arming themselves, doing paramilitary training, evading taxes, assaulting government officials, voting against incumbents, writing letters condemning the federal government, dodging the draft, organizing demonstrations, and other seditious acts. The Insurrectionist is clearly instigating it all."

"Maybe it's time to use the tickets to Paraguay."

"Bullshit!" swore the Honcho. "I still have weapons in my arsenal, including one all professional politicians use when things go to hell."

"You're going to resign?"

The Honcho eyed him suspiciously. "No, I'm going to suspend some constitutional rights."

"Won't that just incite more insurrection?"

"Sure it will. But at least I'll have the authority to throw the seditious bastards in jail."

"Very clever", said Freeman. "How do you suspend constitutional rights?"

"The conflict in Vhaicam gives us the excuse of wartime emergency to resurrect the Sedition Act of 1918, which was originally enacted to ensure loyalty during World War I. With a few minor modifications, it will suit our purposes. It exemplifies the unadulterated goal of all governments, which is self-preservation at any cost to individual liberty. Us politicians have to scratch and claw to preserve our existence, just like other organisms fight to preserve their lives." He handed Freeman a sheet of paper with crudely scrawled prose. "Let me know what you think of my draft of the new Insurrection Act."

Freeman read it, struggling periodically to decode the Honcho's lurching scrawls:

> "Whoever, when America is engaged in war, shall willfully interfere with the operation of U.S. military forces or with the re-election of certain incumbent senators, or obstruct the sale of war bonds or tickets to political fund raisers, or incite insubordination, disloyalty, mutiny, or refusal of duty in the U.S. military or in the re-election committees of certain incumbent senators, or shall willfully obstruct the enlistment service, or willfully utter, write, or publish any disloyal, scurrilous, or abusive language about the U.S. government, the U.S. Constitution, U.S. military forces, the U.S. flag, or certain incumbent senators, and whoever shall willfully advocate doing any of the acts enumerated herein shall be punished by a fine of one million dollars, to be paid to the campaign funds of certain incumbent senators, or by imprisonment for twenty years, or both."

Freeman whistled appreciatively. "This will certainly give you extraordinary power to prosecute the Insurrectionist and his followers."

"It's a stroke of dictatorial genius! But, it's useless unless I find the Insurrectionist. Suspending civil liberties while the target of my oppression eludes me is like sex without orgasm. When I eventually find that homosexual communist sonofabitch, I'll throw the most celebrated lynching party since McCarthy's. That seditious bastard will feel the omnipotent wrath of the federal government. I'll have that rebel drawn and quartered, publicly flagellated, and scourged on national television. His torture will make Christ's death march up the Via Dolorrosa look like a Sunday stroll. I'll castrate him, I'll disembowel him, I'll carve out his heart, I'll . . ."

Freeman slipped out of the Honcho's office as a torrent of threats spewed from the giant man's blubbery lips. The Honcho was a lunatic with enormous power, and anyone who crossed him would now be cruelly persecuted. As a youth, Freeman feared that the neighborhood bullies who tormented him would someday assume positions of power as adults, from which they would harass him on a more formidable and inescapable scale. The Honcho's threatening behavior resurrected this youthful terror, because the deranged senator was a national leader more lawless and cruel than Freeman's warped nightmares had conjured. Up till now, the specter of an Adolph Hitler grabbing the reins of power was an academic abstraction in a history book. But today, Freeman realized that this abstraction had merged with the reality of the prepubescent bullies that assaulted him years ago, and was now manifested in a heinous American political thug.

Freeman hustled to the Lincoln Memorial to find Jefferson so he could warn him of the Honcho's dire threats. He breathlessly searched the crowded monument where he had last seen his eccentric friend, hoping against hope that he was there. He carelessly bumped into passersby in his frantic search. He pushed aside irritated tourists, ignoring their scornful glares. He circled the monument a dozen times, finding only bothered strangers in the faces of the tall gentlemen he encountered. In his haste, he tripped on a step and tumbled brutally to a concrete landing. He lay on his stomach moaning, partly because of the pain that engulfed his body, and partly because he failed to warn the only person he cared about.

Someone tapped his shoulder. He looked up to see Jefferson extending a reassuring hand for him to grab. He wondered at the strange combination of otherworldly coldness and soul stirring warmth that passed from Jefferson's hand to his own. Impulsively, he hugged Jefferson, much like he wished he had hugged his father years ago. Jefferson briefly returned the embrace, then stepped back with a look of concern. "What distresses you, my friend?"

"The sonofabitch I work for is going to annihilate whoever is foiling his ambitions."

Jefferson grinned. "What's he up to now?"

"The bastard has resurrected the Sedition Act of 1918 as a pretext for hunting down the Insurrectionist, who he believes has single-handedly ruined him."

Jefferson guffawed. "How very grand! I've encountered this nonsense before. Such acts are a crutch for politicians who have lost the support of their constituents and who must now rely upon force rather than principle and law. Sedition laws protect leaders who have assumed powers that the people never put into their hands. Rather than kowtow to these absurd laws, we should defy and even remove those leaders, who should be nothing more than our representatives. If government legislates itself immunity to criticism and corrective action, the only proper response is bold resistance. Power concedes nothing without a demand."

"How can you laugh in the shadow of a tyrant who has sworn to annihilate all who oppose him?" Freeman asked with astonishment.

"I am not given to false bravado", said Jefferson. "I know very well the nature of the beast that assails us today. It's the same noxious beast that has assailed humankind for millennia. Faced with such a monstrosity, it is imperative to take strength from being right, and to refuse to surrender to that which is wrong. The Head Honcho has no moral or constitutional basis for his Insurrection Act, nor for most of the laws and regulations he and his fellow brigands have legislated over the years. Acquiescence under insult and attack will not preclude war, which Neville Chamberlain made so obvious prior to World War II. I declare to you, to America, and to all of history, that I will never acquiesce. I will not rest until all men are free from the oppression of kings and mystics."

Freeman shivered. "Are you hinting a violent confrontation is inevitable?"

"Those who make peaceful revolution impossible make violent revolution inevitable. Americans have been exceedingly tolerant as this enormous experiment in republicanism has unfolded. But the experiment has edged, day by day, year by year, decade by decade, away from it's original premise, and now threatens the American people with a governmental leviathan no less imposing and intrusive than all previous examples put forth by history. That Americans have not yet responded violently to this political mutation is a tribute to their restrained willingness to let mankind's noblest experiment run its course.

"However", continued Jefferson, "Don't assume that Americans won't react violently. Churchill, when describing America's apparent acquiescence to the growing Russian menace, said, 'It cannot be in the interest of the Russians to go on irritating America. There are no people in the world who are so slow to develop hostile feelings as the Americans, and there are no people who, once estranged, are more difficult to win back. The American eagle sits on his perch, a large, strong bird with a formidable beak and claws. There he sits, motionless, and Mr. Gromyko is sent day after day to prod him with a sharp, pointed stick—now his neck, now under his wing, now his tail feathers. All the time, the eagle keeps quite still. But it would be a great mistake to suppose that nothing is going on inside the eagle's breast.' Likewise, it will be fatal for the Head Honcho to suppose that nothing is going on inside the minds and hearts of the silent Americans he continues to oppress.

"I trust that my fellow Americans do not desire another violent revolution", concluded Jefferson. "But, such an uprising may be only one or two sparks away. How many more Vietnam Wars, Watergates, tax increases, Waco incidents, Bill Clinton impeachments, Al Gore post-election fiascoes, and sundry other effronteries to the silent Americans will it take before the prairie fire of rebellion is ignited?"

"Why will violence be necessary?" asked Freeman. "Can't we just vote the bums out?"

"Aye, that has been the facet of our experiment most admired by the rest of the world. When we find our leaders defective, we assemble with all the coolness of philosophers and redress things through the suffrage, while many other nations resort to arms to remove their wayward leaders. But there comes a time when the erosion of liberty has become so egregious and the tendrils of bad government so entrenched that the democratic process becomes a useless charade, having no more effect on our political cancer than a witch doctor has on leukemia. It is right and proper for us to respect our democratic forms, but even in the best government, those entrusted with power will some day pervert it into tyranny. It is then that vigilant people must enforce the precepts of their written constitution and thoroughly flush the system of the accumulated tumors. And if a violent cure is required, then so be it."

Freeman shivered again. "The Honcho will arrest anyone who makes inflammatory statements, no matter how erudite their words or persuasive their arguments. I've come to warn you that he's vowed to capture the Insurrectionist."

"Why come to warn me, if it's the Insurrectionist he's after?" Jefferson asked coyly.

"He'll snuff out more than just the Insurrectionist during this witch hunt. Everyone who breathes treasonous words is in danger, and you say many inflammatory things."

Jefferson shrugged. "Treason, when real, merits the highest punishment. But most rulers do not distinguish between acts against the government, which are rare, and acts against the oppressions of the government, which are frequent. The latter are virtues, yet have furnished more victims to the executioner than the former. Unsuccessful strugglers against tyranny have been the chief martyrs of treason laws in all countries. Martyrdom doesn't frighten me. Every man has to die once.

"Cicero had similar disdain for laws that suppressed natural rights. Two thousand years ago, in the shadow of the tyrant Julius Caesar, he wrote, 'Many pestilential statutes no more deserve to be called laws than the rules a band of robbers pass in their assembly. If ignorant men prescribe deadly poisons instead of healing drugs, these cannot possibly be called physicians' prescriptions; neither in a nation can a statute be called a law if it is a ruinous regulation. Law is the distinction between things just and unjust. Laws should inflict punishment upon the wicked but protect the good.' Unfortunately, the vast majority of laws punish the good and protect the wicked. Knowing the spirit of this country, this will not be borne sheepishly by our people, who will choose between reformation and revolution, rather than acquiesce. Before the canker becomes inveterate, before its venom in the body politic gets beyond control, remedy should be applied. We can't allow history to some day note that our nation let more of the public liberty be swallowed by its own elected government than by the English monarchy it revolted against."

Freeman's ball and chain grated against the concrete as he shuffled his feet uncomfortably. "Why do people let liberty erode like this?"

Jefferson glanced at the iron contraption binding Freeman and smiled. "My friend, have you learned nothing from the ardor of toting Cassandra's gift? Do you not yet understand why you are burdened so?"

Freeman looked sheepishly at his metallic albatross. He truthfully hadn't considered why Cassandra chose this particular punishment for him, nor did he understand how Jefferson knew about its origin. The ball and chain was an integral part of his existence, a peculiar version of the biblical original sin, a penance for a crime not specifically committed by him but by mankind in general. "I don't understand", he confessed meekly.

"Perhaps it would be instructive if I shared with you an Aesop's fable called *The Horse, the Hunter, and the Stag*:

> *'A quarrel arose between the Horse and the Stag, so the Horse came to the Hunter to ask for help in taking revenge on the Stag. The Hunter agreed, but said: 'If you desire to conquer the Stag, you must permit me to place this piece of iron between your jaws, so that I may guide you with these reins, and allow this saddle to be placed upon your back so that I may keep steady upon you as we chase the enemy.' The Horse agreed to the conditions, and the Hunter soon saddled and bridled him. Then, with the aid of the Hunter, the Horse soon overcame the Stag, and said to the Hunter, 'Now, get off, and remove these things from my mouth and back.' 'Not so fast, friend', said the Hunter. 'I have now got you under bit and spur, and prefer to keep you as you are.'"*

A nascent epiphany dawned on Freeman. He was a victim of his own making, an instrument of his own bondage. He recalled Rousseau's observation that people are born free, yet are everywhere in chains. He had always assumed that some sinister, uncontrollable force in the universe was conspiring to enslave people against their will. It never occurred to him that people had willingly taken on their shackles, shouldered their yokes, and hefted their saddles, because of fear, infatuation with charismatic healers, addiction to beguiling myths, or the delirium of peer pressure. The Horse submitted himself to the bridle, not because the Hunter was more powerful, but simply because the undiscerning beast was entranced with the chimera of salvation through enslavement. The Horse struck a devil's bargain, unwittingly trading liberty in return for services rendered by a seemingly well-intentioned benefactor. This realization shook Freeman to his core. He recalled the chilling vision of Mephistopheles' Road to Hell, which was paved in jeweled splendor by humanity's compendium of Good Intentions gone awry.

While he digested these unnerving thoughts, Jefferson continued. "The mass of mankind wasn't born with saddles on their backs, nor a favored few booted and spurred to ride them by the grace of their secular or divine gods. But, saddled we have become. Americans today pay 45% of their incomes to governmental agencies, which is more than the average taxpayer spends on food, shelter, and clothing combined. Feudal serfs only paid 25% to their baronial masters.

"It's a repulsive contradiction to believe that murder is wrong but stealing man's productive effort through taxation is right. Murder and taxation are merely different degrees of the same immorality. Both assume that some humans can claim eminent domain over other people's lives. Therefore, do not be surprised when those who tax you for your own good someday propose to kill you for the collective good. There is no guarantee that the Hunter who bridled the Horse will not also see fit to slay the Horse if such becomes expedient. Thirty million Russians Stalin murdered are tragic examples.

"Just as medieval doctors sapped blood with leeches in the name of healing, American bureaucrats tax productive effort, under the pretext of enhancing life with government programs. Have we learned nothing over the centuries? Why are we so willing to put bridles in our jaws and saddles on our backs? Why do we condemn a poor man for stealing food, yet praise a bureaucrat for taxing productive citizens to benefit that same poor man? The only difference is that if the poor man steals, a bureaucrat goes unemployed. The bureaucrat buys votes by promising stolen tax dollars to the downtrodden, whom he would incarcerate if they had the audacity to pick his own pocket in a dark alleyway."

"Your words surprise me", Freeman interjected. "I thought you favored the welfare system."

Jefferson was stunned. "To the contrary! I believe that we have too many parasites living on the labor of the industrious, and among these parasites are the bureaucrats who pander to the indigent. It is an idle dream to believe in alchemy which turns everything into gold, redeeming man from the original sentence of his Maker, 'In the sweat of his brow shall he eat his bread.' The manna of the welfare system does not fall from heaven, but is harvested from increasingly angry workers who know well the meaning of the sweating brow. We who love this American experiment did not mean that our people should be burdened with oppressive taxes to provide sinecures for the idle or the wicked. To take from one whose industry has acquired much, in order to spare others who have not exercised equal industry and skill, is to violate arbitrarily the first principle of association, which is to guarantee to every one free exercise of his industry, and the fruits acquired by it. You know my feelings on this, so why do you conjecture I support the welfare system?"

Freeman pulled a slip of paper from his pocket and handed it to Jefferson. Jefferson studied it briefly before his face contorted into a raging crimson caricature. His lips pursed into angry thin lines. His breathing was rapid and irregular. The slip of paper that enraged him was an ordinary food stamp coupon. Printed on this standard issue of the welfare bureaucracy, next to an engraving of the liberty bell and in front of a picture of Independence Hall, was a portrait of Thomas Jefferson.

Jefferson spat out words drenched in acid. "These bastards worship the picture, but have forgotten the words and denigrate the morality! This two-dimensional image is an insult, because the very significance of the man's actual life, his undying devotion to liberty, is woefully ignored! It's nothing but a hollow caricature of a man consigned by this mutated political system to be a bizarre anti-ghost, whose body remains immortalized, but whose spirit has been cast to the winds like ashes, to be wasted on barren ground of slavish bureaucracy, as seeds that will never again bear fruit!"

"The Thomas Jefferson pictured on this food stamp coupon died 170 years ago. Why are you so offended?" Freeman asked coyly.

Jefferson glared at him. He countered the irritating coyness with an enigma. "Great men and great ideas are unbounded by time and mortality. History is always and everywhere, as are the people who lived it passionately. The picture on the food stamp offends me because I worship liberty as much as those who gave their lives so completely for it. Welfare is merely the government giving away with one benevolent hand what it must first take away with the other more sinister hand. It is loathsome to think that we submissively pay taxes to this sinister hand with as much certainty as death, without ever questioning why. To see the portrait of a man who wrote the Declaration of American Independence, which defined human greatness, now depicted on a food stamp coupon, which defines human degradation and dependence, should anger every true American."

"Aren't we obliged to help the unfortunate?" Freeman asked.

"Nothing contributes more to future happiness than a habit of industry and activity. Of all the cankers of human happiness none corrodes with so silent yet so baneful an influence as indolence. When body and mind are unemployed, our being becomes a burden, and every object about us becomes loathsome. The welfare system institutionalizes a subsidiary class of citizens who become diseased through such idleness, and who therefore become incapable of attaining their own happiness.

"Reality has never warranted that every man's life would last seventy years. We all face the problem of survival in an inimical world. The need for food does not justify slavery. The need for shelter does not make able men the chattel of less able men. The demand, 'feed me, because I am incapable of feeding myself' is the demand, 'serve me, slave.' No one can rightfully demand a part of another's effort. The right to life is a social protection of your life and the fruits of your efforts from expropriation by other men. The right to life is not, and cannot be, protection from Nature's harsh reality.

"The popular cry is we must help the poor and destitute. It's easy for compassionate bureaucrats to be Christ-like without the burden of taking up a cross. If you wish to help someone, in the name of human liberty, do it with your own time and money. Free men in a free country will not stop you. All else is involuntary servitude, regardless of how good the intentions.

He removed his hat and declared, "I hope it's now clear to you that I oppose the welfare system, no matter whose portrait is on what piece of paper."

Freeman looked down at the portrait on the food stamp coupon, and then back at Jefferson. The resemblance between the two was unholy. A chilling observation struck him. Perhaps it was because of the glare of the midday sun, but as he stared at Jefferson's face, he swore he could discern objects in the background showing through the seemingly translucent silhouette. He shook his head vigorously. He closed his eyes for a minute to let the disturbing image fade. Unfortunately, when he opened them, Jefferson had vanished abruptly, leaving behind only a faint aura of crackling electricity. A brief puff of coldness washed across Freeman's face like a draft slipping through an unseen door.

When Freeman returned to his office, Buxomus handed him an urgent message from the Head Honcho. Without reading it, he ceremoniously tossed it into a wastebasket. She handed him another piece of paper and said impishly, "Here's the real message. I knew you'd trash the fake one."

He opened the note, which demanded that he see the Honcho immediately, because he had an idea that he wanted Freeman to either agree was brilliant or to take responsibility for if it turned sour.

The Head Honcho was in familiar deployment, with two empty bottles of Old Bushmills standing as loyal sentinels on his desk next to soiled panties embroidered with the initials "BB". He had pen in hand and four sails set to the wind, which Freeman knew to be a dangerous combination. Alcohol didn't mix well with many things, such as driving a car, but the worst of these mixtures was alcohol and the drafting of congressional legislation, which has a tendency to destroy American civilization.

"Easy on the Old Bushmills", Freeman said. "The Mad Hatter visits you when you're drunk."

"That spindly-legged bastard has already been here today", said the Honcho jovially, pulling a fresh bottle from the liquor cabinet. "At first, I was afraid of him, but then we hit it off quite well. It turns out that he's a regular guy. The Honcho took a prodigious drink, then shakily extended the bottle to Freeman. "Have some. Maybe the Hatter will visit you, too."

"No thanks", said Freeman emphatically. "What did the Hatter say?"

The Honcho leaned back in his leather chair and described his latest encounter. Just before the visitation, he had sunk into deep despair after hearing of more insurrection activities across the country. The obvious failure of his Insurrection Act drove him to his liquor cabinet. After draining one bottle, the Hatter made his unwelcome entrance into the Honcho's inebriated sub-conscious.

"It's amazing how prodigiously someone without a head can drink", observed the Hatter, without offering any other salutation.

The Honcho instinctively reached for his head. Reassured that his cranium was still attached, he snarled, "You're full of shit, you double-talking bastard!"

"He speaks without a head, too!" exclaimed the Hatter. "This is indeed a spectacle. I'd offer you a cup of treacle, my headless friend, but consuming it would be quite futile."

"What in hell are you talking about?" shouted the Honcho much too loudly. "I've got a head on my shoulders, as sure as Ismism is the state religion and the Safari Golfer is the Supreme Being. Here, watch this." The drunken senator pounded his head viciously against his desk, creating nauseating thuds that only a real head could make. "There", he concluded proudly. "I'll have that treacle now." He wiped his brow with the soiled panties to sop up blood seeping from several wounds.

The Hatter shook his head disdainfully. "On our side of the Looking Glass, people who maim themselves are considered to have lost their heads. Also, since you were sentenced to be beheaded by the Red Queen for the

Dormouse's death, I'm doubly convinced that you have no head, because when the Red Queen says 'Off with your head!' your head invariably comes off. As for the treacle, I don't have any, so there's no use pretending you have a head to drink it with."

"What do you want from me?" the Honcho implored.

"Nothing", replied the Hatter obsequiously. "Why do you ask?"

"Then why are you here to torture me like this?"

"I'm here because my mother, who was a haberdasher, and my father, who was a seamstress, mated and gave birth, although I don't suppose they did it just to torture you, which is a rather self-centered presumption. Actually, I have no idea why they did it. My mother was rather homely, and my father wasn't well endowed, as you might suspect about a male seamstress. I'm surprised they both weren't celibate. Haven't we had this conversation before?"

"You're mad!" the Honcho spat out.

"At least I admit it", said the Mad Hatter haughtily. "Whereas you pretend to have a head by speaking foolishness."

Tears intermixed with the blood streamed down the Honcho's cheeks. "Please! Just tell me why you're here and get this over with."

The Hatter harrumphed. "Okay, but on our side of the Looking Glass, we do not rudely rush conversations to their conclusion prematurely. Actually, none of our conversations come to a meaningful conclusion in Wonderland, so it's all beside the point, which I'm sure you understand, since you're a politician. Anyway, I'll tell you a little secret." He looked around the room furtively and moved closer to the Honcho, as if to whisper something terribly clandestine. Instead, he shouted into the Honcho's ear, "I'm here because you've drunk yourself into a stupor again, you headless lummox!!"

The Honcho pawed his ravaged ear angrily. "Your visits are the worst moments of my life!"

"Then why do you drink so much?" asked the Hatter, feeling a twinge of sympathy for the wretched man who kept conjuring him up.

"That damnable Insurrectionist has ruined my re-election prospects, and all my schemes to capture him have failed. The only friends I have left are all named Old Bushmills."

Amazingly, the Mad Hatter grabbed a bottle of Old Bushmills, parked his feet on the Honcho's desk, and took a hearty swig. "Your situation isn't hopeless, even without a head. You're better off without your head anyway, because it was much too large. It reminded me of the Mock Turtle's shell after we had him for dinner."

"You ate the Mock Turtle?"

The Mad Hatter spit out whiskey and saliva in disgust. "Of course not! He merely engorged himself when he dined with us. Tell me, do you eat your friends for dinner?" The Hatter rubbed his chin for a moment, and then answered his own question. "I suppose that you do, in a manner of speaking."

"What hope do I have?" The Honcho immediately regretted his pensive interest in the Hatter's omnidirectional words.

"Quite frankly, your only hope is that everyone is stupid enough to listen to you, rather than to the Insurrectionist."

"That's hardly reassuring."

"Swallow your pride, lummox. Democracy isn't a contest of wisdom and character. Get back to the basics of American politics. You'll get re-elected, even if your head re-appears."

"Back to the basics?" the Honcho repeated quizzically. "Do you mean graft and corruption?"

"No, more basic than that."

"Unkeepable promises and mindless mud-slinging?"

"Close, but no cigar. Get to the core of the matter!"

"Flag waving and baby kissing?"

The Hatter waved his hand to dismiss the Honcho's errant musings. "No wonder the Insurrectionist is kicking your ass. You've forgotten the essence of political power."

"Out with it, you bow-legged cretin, before I give up drinking and banish you forever!"

The Hatter ignored this impotent threat. "Political power is a function of two things. First, you use mythology to confuse people into thinking it's proper to chain themselves to a master. Second, in order to convince them that you're the right master to be chained to, you bribe them shamelessly with riches from the royal treasury." The Hatter looked at his watch and suddenly jumped up from the chair. "Oh my! It's 6:00! The Red Queen will be angry that I missed her tea time."

"You said it's always 6:00 in Wonderland!"

"It is, it is. That's why it's so unforgivable to miss my appointment." The Hatter turned to go.

"Wait!" shouted the Honcho at the pot-bellied illusion who was already melting into the eternal continuum of dementia. "Thanks for the advice. I think you're a . . . a regular guy. I hope we can get along from now on."

The Hatter waved farewell and evaporated into the contrary world of Wonderland. When the Head Honcho finished his tale, Freeman asked, "How can anyone who appears and disappears, speaks in mind-twisting riddles, and thinks it's always 6:00 be a regular guy?"

"We all have idiosyncrasies", said the Honcho in a menacing tone. "If you don't agree with me, I'll fire you."

"You can't fire me! I'm a civil servant. No matter how useless or insubordinate I am, I have tenure for life." Freeman knew precedent was on his side. Just last week, a civil servant, who was being counseled for poor performance, punched his boss, shredded official documents, shit in the office coffee pot, and threatened to blow up the building. During a subsequent disciplinary hearing, the recalcitrant employee graciously declined to press charges against his boss and settled out of court for a promotion and a salary increase. As a final insult to sanity, the labor union representing this wayward civil servant demanded a formal apology from his impudent superior for expecting performance and respect.

"Then I'll just have my Italian golfing buddies kill you", said the Honcho nonchalantly.

"You won't kill me. Who would you blame when the brilliant ideas you haven't told me about yet turn sour?"

The Honcho glared at Freeman until he thought of a way to kill him without him actually dying. "Any more insubordination, and I'll have the IRS audit your last 17 tax returns. Now, back to business. The Mad Hatter gave me some ideas to resurrect my campaign. I'll order the Safari Golfer to use Ismism to confuse Americans into thinking they need to be ruled. Then, I'll expand the welfare system to include 10% more recipients and 190% more administrators. That bribe from the Royal. . . . er, Federal Treasury will buy me lots of votes. Great ideas, huh?"

Freeman quietly pondered the likely carnage from 17 consecutive IRS audits. "Fabulous, sir!", he finally concluded. "But, the welfare idea has some pitfalls. Expanding it will drag down the economy. If you tax productive effort, you get less productive effort, and if you subsidize inactivity, you get more inactivity. That's not only a rule of economics, it's human nature…"

The Honcho interrupted with a desultory hand wave. "Who gives a shit? The effects won't emerge until after the election, and even then I can blame the recession on the Jews or cyclical capitalism. Besides, as long as I'm getting rich, the rest of the economy can go to hell. What's another pitfall?"

"If there really are hungry Americans, why don't we just give them the billions of pounds of butter, cheese, and non-fat dry milk that our own government stores in Kansas caves?"

"We're saving it for emergencies."

"What's more of an emergency than starving Americans?"

"Lots of things. If the Russians have another poor harvest, we'll need to export our surpluses to them. Or, if dairy prices drop, we'll have to stash even more cheese, butter, and dry milk into Kansas caves to inflate prices, so that farmers will keep contributing to my campaign. Any other concerns?"

"The welfare system has become a sham. Food stamps are now used as a second currency in blighted neighborhoods to buy guns, drugs, and luxuries on the black market."

The Honcho waved both arms frantically to end the discussion. "Jesus Christ, quit hacking through the underbrush of life and look at the big picture. If I lose the election, you might lose your job. Leave the details to the devil. Tomorrow I'll introduce a bill doubling the size of the welfare system. In the meantime, we need to find the Safari Golfer. Where is he?"

"He's in Rome, sir", interjected But Sir!, who had just entered the office.

"What's he doing there? Comparing notes on mysticism with the Pope?"

"Not exactly, sir", said But Sir!. "He is the Pope".

"Don't you have to be saintly, celibate, and poor to be Pope?" the Honcho asked incredulously.

"You're a poor student of history if you believe that", said Freeman.

"Sir, remember his plan to convert Christians to the secular mythology of Ismism? He accomplished it easily. Then after the previous Pope mysteriously died, white smoke puffed out of the Vatican chimney, and the next thing you know, the Safari Golfer is waving from a balcony to adoring throngs in St. Peter's Square."

"What papal name did he take?" asked Freeman.

"Pope Safari Golfer I", said But Sir! reverently.

"What kind of religious name is that?" asked the Honcho.

"It's the most devout name possible for a human, according to him", said But Sir!. "Remember, he's the only man or god who can hit a two iron."

"I'll be damned!" exclaimed the Honcho. "Book us a flight to Rome."

"First class?"

"I won't stoop to flying first class! Commercial airlines are for ordinary people like taxpayers. We're going to fly compliments of the Air Force." The Honcho was referring to the practice of Congressmen flying on Air Force jets to avoid the hassles of commercial air flight and potential contamination from the masses. Military escorts accompany the congressmen throughout their overseas trips and handle their luggage. When they arrive in a foreign country, they're met by officials of the local U.S. Embassy, chauffeured to their destination, and handed a wad of local currency.

"But Sir!" objected But Sir!. "With the beating you're taking in the polls, shouldn't you do something symbolizing your affinity with ordinary folks?"

"No", replied the Honcho summarily. "But I will take Buxomus along. Have her bring her pink frilly panties and her French bikini. We're stopping over in Hawaii to recuperate from the long flight. Make sure the Air Force Base is ready for our arrival and warms up the ocean for me. I'll be pissed if it's less than 78 degrees."

"But Sir!" protested But Sir!. "Hawaii isn't on the way to Rome!"

"Bullshit! The earth is round. We can get to Rome from any direction. And make sure the plane is stocked with Old Bushmills."

"But Sir!" squealed But Sir!. "Won't your ostentatious travel upset the taxpayers?"

"Why? It's all paid for by the Octagon."

But Sir! trudged off to make travel arrangements. Meanwhile, after everyone vacated his office, a frightening realization hit the Honcho like a baseball bat on the bridge of the nose. He was going to Rome! The thought of returning to where Marcus Brutus had stabbed him in the neck two thousand years ago made his blood churn. A foreboding chill raced up his spine. He massaged the scar where the assassin had punctured his leathery skin and grimly recalled his narrow escape back to modern America. Fortunately, the liquor cabinet was full of his favorite whiskey. He spent the night downing shots and building courage, until he reached penultimate self-confidence and passed out. In the process, enough brain cells were damaged to eradicate his fear of Rome.

The Honcho's entourage stepped off an Air Force plane four days later into the balmy Italian air. On the way to their hotel near the Vatican, they toured the Roman Forum, the Circus Maximus, and the Coliseum. These ancient venues seemed oddly familiar to the Honcho, but he couldn't recall their significance because of his alcohol-impaired brain cells. However, one monument resurrected a hazy memory of a previous life, much like those fuzzy deja vu flashes that make reincarnation seem probable. It was dedicated to Cicero, the great Roman advocate of liberty, who died on the spot demarcated by the unassuming monument after Marc Antony, the successor to Julius Caesar, ordered him put to death. Cicero calmly waited there for his slayers to lop off his head.

Standing by the monument, the Honcho sensed that even though Cicero's body was murdered, his spirit wandered the universe, much like Julius Caesar's essence had somehow passed through the millennia into the Honcho's own being, or vice versa. Peculiarly, Cicero reminded him, in physical appearance and in philosophy, of his Insurrection Czar, Thomas Jefferson. This thought unnerved him, so he cajoled the group back to the hotel, where a fresh supply of Old Bushmills awaited to slay his mental dragons.

The next day, they went to meet with Pope Safari Golfer I. When their military chauffeur turned into a vista leading into St. Peter's Square, they saw hundreds of thousands of people swaying to the hypnotic ministrations of a tiny figure up on a distant balcony. The Pope was wearing a white cap and a white ceremonial robe. His arms were outstretched to the raptured throngs, as if embracing them in a communal transfer of mystical energy.

Audio speakers atop a giant obelisk in the sacred square oozed bland New Age music that washed over the crowd with as much meaning as a politically correct slogan. The smell of marijuana hung thick in the air. Ismism followers smoked ganja as a sacramental adjunct of their faith, to facilitate the temporary suspension of sound judgment necessary for absorbing the confusing philosophy. The sacrament also filled the Vatican coffers, since the Golfer skimmed most of the profits from the sale of the weed. These enormous profits made the secular religion of Ismism nearly as wealthy as the religion that previously controlled the Vatican.

It took them an hour to move through St. Peter's Square to their rendezvous with the Pope. When they were finally led into his private chambers, the Golfer greeted his old friends. "Who are you?" he demanded sternly.

"Quit fuckin' around", the Honcho said. "You know who the hell we are. We helped make you who you are today. And you're going to help make us what we want to be. That's the natural order of things. Power breeds mysticism, and mysticism begets power. It's the yin and yang of the political universe."

"Calm down", said the Golfer. "To hell with you if you can't take a joke."

"Careful what you say", cautioned Freeman. "You may actually have inherited the power to send us to hell from the last pope."

"Good point", said the Golfer. "One thing I didn't inherit is a lot of foxy babes. The last pope didn't even have a harem. Pretty bizarre, if you ask me. His acolytes look nervous as sheep."

"How did you pull this scam off?" asked Freeman.

"The lotus petals of my existential dichotomy unfolded to reveal a universe of diverse potential that crystallized, as a result of celestial and heavenly orientations, into the enigma which you now perceive to be our common reality."

They were awed by the Golfer's profundity, although no one understood what he said. "What the fuck does that mean?" Freeman asked bluntly.

"Loosely translated, it means that shit happens, so here I am."

"Really, how did you get here?"

"While studying eastern religions and drinking beer, I discovered the essence of being", the Pope professed solemnly. "Dharma, artha, and kharma are the keys."

"Aren't they the Three Musketeers?" asked But Sir!.

The Golfer frowned impatiently. "Dharma is the eternal law of life. It teaches that everybody has a place in the food chain of existence. Some are meant to lead, others are meant to follow. Artha is the materialistic aspect of being. It teaches that wealth is not inherently bad, as long as it is properly distributed according to the prescriptions of dharma. Kharma is the aesthetic aspect of being. It teaches that sensual pleasure gives meaning to dharma and artha."

"Neat shit", said Freeman insincerely. "But how did that religious mumbo-jumbo get you here?"

"I'll translate it into your vernacular, my son", said the Golfer in a priestly voice. "Some men are meant to be masters, and the rest slaves. If you're the master, you get all of the money. Once you have all of the money, you get to screw the pretty women and drink the wine. That's dharma, artha, and kharma. Being Pope is my ordained station in life. I now have access to the untold riches of the Catholic Church. And as soon as I can corral a harem and locate the wine cellar, I will experience pleasure beyond my wildest dreams."

"Got it", said Freeman.

"I didn't come here to listen to this drivel", interjected the Honcho impatiently. "I've got big problems, and I need help."

"Wait a minute." The Golfer put a stiff white collar around his neck, placed a benevolent hand on the Honcho's imposing forehead, and said, "Confess your troubles, my son, including the sordid details." A smile washed over his face. "This makes me feel so powerful!"

"Bless him, Father, for he has sinned", said Freeman on behalf of the Head Honcho.

"Do you do funerals?" asked the Honcho, addressing the Golfer but staring at Freeman.

"Not yet, but I'm an expert at circumcision." He looked at Freeman, who squirmed uncomfortably.

"Get on with it", pleaded the Honcho. "My world is in shambles. The Insurrectionist is igniting rebellions from coast to coast. The polls have me less popular than Saddam Hussein. The war in Vhaicam has killed a whole generation of registered voters. F.U.N. is consuming half of the American GNP feeding the 11 billion Vhaicamese. The war I started to control their population is consuming the rest. The Red Queen has beheaded me, according to the Mad Hatter. I murdered hundreds of people with the Juggernaut. The tabloids say I'm having a scandalous affair with my secretary. The Honchogate fiasco is in all the papers, and they're even accusing me of sleeping with Michael Jackson. Don't they know I'm too old for him?"

Spasmodic waves of distress shook him. He was clearly losing his sanity. Immediate intervention was required, and the only one who could save him from complete dementia was Pope Safari Golfer I. "Come back tomorrow, when I'm not so busy", said the Golfer gruffly.

"God damn you! I mean. . . . I guess you should damn yourself, since you're God, now. Christ, this is so confusing! I didn't come to Rome just to be rejected again!" The Honcho began to wail pathetically.

Moved to pity, the Golfer dipped his hand into holy water and sprinkled it on the Honcho's shaking body. "There, that should do it. Go forth in peace and love to proclaim the Word of Ismism!"

The Honcho angrily wiped his face. "I don't need holy water or any other pagan sorcery! I need good advice, and I need it now!"

"Go forth unto Washington, admit nothing, and deny everything", suggested the Golfer. "Then it's your word against theirs."

"I tried that", scoffed the Honcho. "And I'm still fucked. I have zero credibility with the voters and the media right now. They believe everything my opponents say."

"Hmmmm . . . try demanding proof of your crimes. Force your detractors to put up or shut up."

"That would fuck me even more. They actually have proof."

"But what exactly do they have proof of? Most Americans have been numbed into apathy because of the sheer volume of political scandals. So, even if your detractors reveal reams of damning evidence, they will extract nothing but a collective yawn, unless you've been found in bed with a dead woman or a live boy."

"I can't try that approach, then."

"My self!", exclaimed God disguised as the Safari Golfer. He did a vigorous sign of the cross. "Well, don't despair. You still have a captive army of people to control the election."

"It's getting harder for my Italian golfing buddies to tamper with elections, if that's what you mean."

"No, that's not what I mean", said Pope Safari Golfer I. "The federal government is the largest employer in history. Put the squeeze on the millions of bureaucrats feeding at the federal troth. Hit up the administrators, social workers, defense workers, contractors, consultants, developers, lobbyists, regulators, inspectors, and political science majors whose livelihoods depend on Uncle Sam. If you lose this election, the goose that lays their golden eggs perishes too. Then they'll have to get real jobs, which should scare them shitless into funding your campaign and voting for you. Sure, they may disapprove of your corruption, but it'll all be forgotten in the privacy of the voting booth when unemployment threatens those GS15's making 70 grand a year. If the Insurrectionist wins out, these people will hit the bricks right behind you. You're all in it together, just like the folks on the Titanic."

The Honcho's desperate face lit with a glimmer of hope. "Great idea! The government leeches would outnumber the taxpayers, who rarely show up to vote. It would be almost as fun as gang rape. Maybe we should distribute condoms to the bureaucrats and Vaseline to the taxpayers."

"Absolutely!", confirmed the Golfer. "If you get re-elected with this strategy, all you'd have to fear is another revolution, during which the rebels will kill you."

The gleam in the Honcho's eyes faded into reddened splotches. "Shit, who am I kidding?", he moaned. "It's no longer a question of voting for one leader or another. The commoners have simply lost their respect for power and authority. I miss the time when serfs were serfs, kings were kings, and everyone politely stayed in their place. I envy guys like Louis XIV, who could declare 'L'etat, c'est moi', and those who didn't agree were guillotined. Maybe this isn't the time or place for politicians like me to thrive."

"You are indeed fucked, especially if the Insurrectionist's growing band of revolutionaries takes things out of the hands of the sheepish voters." The Golfer stood, did a sign of the cross, and declared, "Go in peace to love and serve Ismism. Remember, tax evasion and avoidance of the tithe are both mortal sins, according to the new catechism we're publishing, so make good use of the collection basket on your way out."

The Honcho couldn't tell whether the Golfer was his friend or enemy. He came here for help, but instead the Confessor warned him that something apocalyptic was about to happen. With a heavy heart and a clouded soul, he left the Vatican and climbed into a waiting Air Force limousine. He was counting heavily on a two-week stopover in Tahiti to cheer him up. He had reliable information from military intelligence that most of the native girls in the South Pacific were virgins.

Freeman surreptitiously remained behind in the Vatican. Visiting the Pope had piqued his curiosity. He slid unnoticed into the Pontiff's private chambers where he found the Golfer ogling a Playboy magazine. "I'm aghast!", he exclaimed to the unsuspecting secular cleric, who hadn't noticed his intrusion. "Don't you have to forsake such pleasures when you put on the collar?"

The Golfer jumped at the sound of Freeman's voice. He dropped the dog-eared magazine onto his desk, leaving the pages to haphazardly display a ravishing young lady's naked physique. "This is for business, not pleasure. I'm auditioning candidates for my harem."

"Your harem isn't for personal pleasure?"

"Absolutely not!", lied the Pope. "According to notes left behind by the previous Pope, sex isn't for pleasure, it's for propagating the faith. With a huge harem, I can propagate the faith exponentially, which will help future offertory collections. But, enough civility. Why are you in my chambers uninvited?"

"Is there really a God?" Freeman asked bluntly. He fidgeted nervously, fearing the pontiff actually knew and would banish his comfortably confused apathy. He also fidgeted to generate body heat, because the air had suddenly grown cold and damp, as if the door to an old stone cellar had been opened.

"Why ask me?" sniffed the Pope disdainfully. "I'm a priest, not a philosopher. My job is to interpret the word of God, not to doubt it."

"And two plus two equals five", boomed a confident voice from a dark corner. The Safari Golfer and Freeman whirled toward the disembodied voice. To their astonishment, Thomas Jefferson stepped out from a shadow.

Jefferson's bizarre materialization dumbfounded the Golfer. "Pardon me?"

"Two plus two equals five", repeated Jefferson. "I believe that."

"That's ridiculous!"

"Prove it", challenged Jefferson.

The Golfer rummaged in his desk. "Okay, here are some matches. I'll put two here and two there. Now, if I slide one pile next to the other, how many total matches are there?"

"My faith compels me to believe that there are five", Jefferson asserted.

"Then show us the fifth match!"

"It's there. You just can't see it, because you aren't properly conditioned spiritually. You must discard your own perception of reality and rely on mine instead."

"Can you prove the fifth match is there, or must we helplessly believe your silly assertion, with no corroborating evidence?"

Jefferson's eyes twinkled. "Can you prove it isn't there?"

"But that's insane!", Pope Safari Golfer I declared. "How can I prove that things that aren't there really aren't there? That futile dialectic obligation would end any rational debate and make the Mad Hatter happy as a lark. The burden of proof is on you."

"Okay, let's change the subject slightly. I contend your God doesn't exist."

"Prove it!", said the Golfer.

Jefferson smiled. "According to your own rules, it's your burden to prove God's existence, not mine to prove his non-existence."

"Okay then", conceded the Golfer reluctantly. "Who created the universe, if not God? It had to get here somehow."

"Who created this creator of the universe? By extension of the same logic, the creator had to get here somehow."

"The creator didn't require creation. This is a special exception to my logic," bluffed the Golfer.

"I can more easily argue that the universe didn't require creation. One incredulity is easier to swallow than two. Why add the complication of a creator who doesn't require creation, especially when there is no evidence of this notion?"

"How do you explain the miracle of life?", challenged the Golfer. "There had to be a god to make humans in his own image."

"It is far more likely that we invented god in our own imperfect image as our feeble intellects evolved, than that some invisible being concocted us out of nothing on the sixth day. There is abundant evidence of biological and spiritual evolution, and none of divine intervention."

"How do you explain the beauty of flowers and rainbows, if god didn't create them?"

"How do you explain war, earthquakes, and Head Honchos, in a universe created by a god capable of making flowers and rainbows?", said Jefferson. "If your god created everything, then he also created evil, for which he ought to be despised, not worshipped."

"What purpose do our lives have if there is no afterlife with god?"

"What purpose do they have if there is an afterlife with god? The notion is too extravagantly redundant to be reasonable, and there is no evidence of heaven or hell, but for the quality of life and the psychological states we create for ourselves here on earth."

"The purpose of our lives", preached the Pope, "Is to earn an eternity with God."

"If your god put us on earth merely to run us through a metaphysical obstacle course or a moral maze like pavlovian rats, then I want nothing to do with him. If such a god exists, I will never bow to him and sacrifice the rationality that he presumably endowed me with."

"Aha! Your rebelliousness clearly demonstrates the need for a god to restrain people and to induce good behavior. Without religion, we would have moral anarchy."

"Religion has no monopoly on morality."

"But why would anyone do good, if not for love of Jesus or fear of an omnipotent god?"

"You cannot do good out of fear", asserted Jefferson. "Morality ends where the wrath of god begins. And there is certainly more love in the universe than that of Jesus to motivate one to do good. The love of mother for child is an example."

"But there's no way to know good without God to define it."

"Those who think that are the building blocks with which tyrants fashion their oppressions. If your idea of good is defined externally and imposed on you unwillingly, then you are a tool. And if the external definition of good is mystical, then you are a tool with infinitely malleable applications. Every tyrant uses secular or divine mysticism to support his rule. There is no difference between the Egyptian god-kings or the Marxian species being, between the divine right of kings or Hitler's Aryan race, between tribal rituals or Ismism's common good. All are different manifestations of unverifiable mysticism defining good and bad, benefiting those doing the defining and damaging the rest.

"If you can't define good without religion", continued Jefferson, "then you are condemned to intellectual slavery, with the shackles applied by your own mind. What tyrants fear most is people discovering what good is without ever opening a religious or political text. Good is what a thinking person values. Values are personally chosen building blocks that enable a fulfilling life to flourish. Personal choice requires freedom. Freedom and mysticism, whether secular or divine, cannot coexist. They are mutually exclusive. One requires constant thought, and the other requires constant suspension of thought. This translates into the political world very directly and elementally. Political power is founded on the unthinking slavery of mysticism, since freely thinking minds will never submit to the tyranny of some humans wielding power over others. One sentence can summarize man's social experience thus far: Ignorance breeds mysticism, and mysticism breeds power. Repeat this sentence a thousand times. It's everything you need to know about religion and politics."

"So, there is no God?", Freeman summarily asked Jefferson.

"You must answer that yourself. Allowing others to answer for you is the first step on the road to slavery. Fix reason firmly in her seat, and call to her tribunal every fact. Question with boldness the existence of god, because if there be one, he must more approve of rationality than of blindfolded fear. If God cannot be explained in rational terms, then he cannot be understood in any meaningful sense. I don't intend to make a religion out of denying god's existence, merely to add atheism to mankind's pantheon of Isms. Reality is what reality is, no matter what we believe. My intent is solely to inculcate a love of reason and intellect. I have sworn eternal hostility against every form of tyranny over the mind of man."

"You're a blasphemer!", shouted the Safari Golfer.

"Because I refuse to surrender my mind and submit to your mysticism?"

"No!", screamed the Golfer. "Because you dare to contradict the written Word of God!"

"Which god? Which words? Written by whom? If every memory of the bible and the works of Newton were lost, Newton's works would be replicated within a generation, but the bible would remain forever forgotten. We have evolved beyond the need for such mythology, which reduces our perception of the universe to the level of black magic, mysterious to everyone and understandable by no one. Being incomprehensible it therefore becomes omnipotent in the hands of oppressors."

This verbal onslaught staggered Pope Safari Golfer I. His face was bloodless and gaunt as he searched for words to throw against Jefferson. "You must have faith", was all he could muster. "You can never have enough faith."

"I agree that we're suffering from a crisis of faith", replied Jefferson. "However, the crisis is that we have too much faith, not too little. We have faith in everything but ourselves. Faith is a powerful yet dangerous agent. It can inspire us to move mountains, just as it can delude us into believing that if we jump off a cliff and flap our wings hard enough, we will fly. The road to hell is jammed with people who had faith in all kinds of secular and divine mysticism."

The Safari Golfer slumped on his desk, drained by the debate. Freeman turned to Jefferson to congratulate him. Unfortunately, the intruder had vanished in the blink of an eye. Freeman resisted the urge to search for his mysterious companion, because he somehow knew it would be futile.

He exited the Vatican into the countless Ismism fanatics in St. Peter's Square who were still under the Safari Golfer's spell. He felt thoroughly alone amid this sea of humanity. He wasn't one of them. He had never been one of them. Unfortunately, he didn't know who he really was. He still dragged his heavy ball and chain behind him, along with similar metaphysical baggage in his soul. However, because of the lessons learned by osmosis through his ancestor Padraic and through Jefferson's timeless words, he now harbored deep hope of learning how to unbind his chains. He saw the potential for a rebirth of his essential humanity. He sensed salvation for his spirit in the abandonment of mysticism. And he felt a new and virulent hatred for the Head Honcho.

Chapter Eleven: "Revolution Redux"

"In the beginning, all the world was America"
—John Locke

The Honcho was in excruciating pain when he returned to Washington after two weeks in Tahiti. He had screwed every tantalizing native girl that strayed too close to his cabana, most of whom were not actually virgins and one of whom infected him with the dreaded South Pacific clap. "They're going to kill me", he moaned aloud while massaging his burning crotch.

"You should wear a condom", said Freeman. "Getting an island girl pregnant would be extremely dangerous because their fathers are head hunters. If they knew you were the 'Head Honcho', they'd surely decapitate you."

"Shit, I wasn't even thinking about them! I was thinking about the Insurrectionist and his band of rebels. They're out to kill me, too. Even the Safari Golfer thinks so." The Honcho moaned louder. He was still tormented by the Pope's ominous parting prophecy.

"Condoms won't help you with the Insurrectionist. Is it time for the tickets to Paraguay?"

The senator inflated his prodigious chest. "Hell no! I'm not running off to Paraguay with my tail between my legs!"

"What are you going to do?"

His arrogant posture degenerated into a slouch. "I'm going to run off with my tail between my legs to a different spot in history. 'The 'Book of Liberal Policies, Marxist Economics, and Other Occult Phenomena' will send me to a time and place safer for a tyrant."

"Didn't you learn any lessons from your excursion to ancient Rome?"

"The Caesar thing was a fluke", snapped the Honcho.

"You'll encounter a Cicero, a Daniel O'Connell, or an Insurrectionist no matter what time or place you run to. It's the natural order of things, much like matter and anti-matter. You'll also encounter a Marcus Brutus wherever you run to," Freeman observed ominously.

"That wasn't a fair fight! The sonofabitch stabbed me in the back!"

"A fair fight has never been one of your principles", fumed Freeman. "Where were you when the federal government exposed unsuspecting civil servants to nuclear test detonations to study the effects of radiation?"

"Some other senator's committee did that. Mine studied the effects of LSD and chemical weapons on prison inmates and the mentally retarded, so I'm innocent. Let's get back to business. I'm going to a time and place where rulers are rulers, peons are peons, and everybody accepts the difference."

"Can the Book take you to a different planet?"

"Of course", sniffed the Honcho haughtily. "This book can increase wealth simply by increasing taxes. The difficulty of interplanetary travel pales in comparison. But, space travel won't be necessary for me to find my nirvana. I can simply go back to medieval Europe and become a feudal baron, with my own castle, fiefdom, and serfs."

"Why would that be nirvana?"

"The only thing wrong with our bureaucratic feudalism in Washington is that Americans are uncooperative vassals. Medieval European vassals were much more submissive. They even believed in kings and queens."

"You should do a temporary flashback, just in case things go badly."

"Can the book do that?", the Honcho asked eagerly.

"Sure. It can send you backward in history for a specified trial period of time. If something dire happens, your return home is as certain as the Great Society was to eliminate poverty."

"Count me in!" The Honcho executed the temporary flashback instructions in the Time Travel chapter and was transported backward in time to a Medieval castle perched atop a forested hill overlooking what would someday become Germany. He had been magically transmogrified into a royal baron, replete with exquisite clothing, a vast assemblage of doting vassals, and a castle with great towers, alabaster figurines, and walls of polished marble. He found himself sitting on a gleaming throne holding a golden scepter.

A submissive vassal who looked amazingly like But Sir! approached him. "Sire, a serious matter requires your attention. An angry band of fiefs murdered the Royal Tax Collector. We need another agent to gather revenue for the barony. The Royal Lifestyle, the Royal Orgies, the Royal Wars, and the Royal Graft, Greed, and Corruption are draining the Royal Treasury."

"The IRS has a million tax collectors!", the Baron blurted. "Just order another one to empty the serfs' pockets."

"But Sire!", exclaimed the But Sir! look-alike, "It's not that simple."

A familiar rage broiled in the Baron's innards. "What's so fornicating complicated?"

But Sire! cringed. "First, I've never heard of the IRS. Second, we're mired in the Dark Ages, so we aren't civilized enough to use millions of people to empty our pockets. We had only one tax collector, who is now dead."

The Honcho moaned. Forgetting what had been invented yet was a pitfall of time travel. He searched his memory for the tax collecting methods used in Medieval Europe. Surely, they must have already discovered the beauty of taking from the rich and giving to the poor, in order to buy political support from the masses. Then it hit him: Robin Hood! Surely, Robin Hood was a familiar name, and his philosophy a familiar ploy, even to these unsophisticated political Neanderthals. The Baron triumphantly declared aloud, "Bring me Robin Hood to serve as the Royal Tax Collector!"

"But Sire!", exclaimed But Sire!. "That's impossible!"

The Honcho clenched his massive fists. "How can it be impossible? I'm the royal tyrant!"

"Robin Hood is just a mythical character whose legend has been passed down via folklore", explained But Sire! patiently.

"Are mythical characters exempt from conscription into my service?"

"Sire, it appears so."

"Pray tell, why?"

"Because . . . mythical characters don't exist, sire", explained But Sire! carefully.

"Find out which of these mythical characters profess not to exist, and I'll have them boiled in oil! Be quick about it, knave!" he snarled through clenched teeth.

"Sire, I know the answer already", squeaked But Sire! nervously. "They all profess not to exist."

"My God!", exclaimed the baron. "This is worse than I thought. If the mythical characters turn against me, it won't be long before everyone is swept up in the riptide of insurrection!" Beads of sweat bubbled on his huge forehead. "I need names, knave! If we can capture one of these mythical characters, my agents can infiltrate and destroy this infant conspiracy."

But Sire! was learning how to deal with his demented leader. "That's easy, sire. Robin Hood is one of the conspiratorial mythical characters."

"Holy Grail shit!", shouted the Honcho. "I almost hired that insurrectionist bastard as my Royal Tax Collector! Capture Robin Hood, squire, and don't return until you do!"

Thus, But Sire! was tasked to apprehend someone who didn't exist. Fortunately, he had a friend named John the Mischiever, who was a seditious knave that looked exactly like Freeman. But Sire! went to him for advice. "I'm in a quandary", he said miserably. "The baron ordered me to capture the mythical Robin Hood."

"You're really fornicated!" said John the Mischiever. "Not only is he mythical, he doesn't even exist! I'm glad I'm not in your tights. I'll bet the baron is boiling a cauldron of oil for you as we speak."

"You arsehole!", swore But Sire! "I need advice, not sarcasm."

John the Mischiever rubbed his chin pensively, looking alternately confused and bemused. Then he shouted, "Eureka!"

"What? What?" implored But Sire! impatiently.

"We'll bring Robin Hood into existence magically. Here's how it'll work. The Royal Treasurer will print cartloads of paper money, backed only by the baron's bluff that they might be worth something. This will give the baron immense purchasing power. It will also cause inflation, which will push wealthy people into higher tax brackets, so that the baron can collect even more taxes from them. This inflation magic will accomplish everything that the mythical Robin Hood is famous for. The baron will steal from the rich and give some of the stolen wealth to the poor to buy their support and keep them quiet. If you can show the baron the effects of this unseen inflationary Robin Hood, he won't care that you didn't physically apprehend him."

"You're a genius!" exclaimed But Sire!. "But are there any pitfalls to this scheme? Every scam you conjure up has dangerous side effects."

"There is one minor risk", confessed John the Mischiever. "Inflation will push everyone into higher tax brackets, including the serfs, who might get pissed off enough to revolt against the baron, storm his castle, and hang the rogue and his ministers from a tree."

"How do we prevent that minor risk from happening?" asked But Sire! acerbically.

"Start a war", said John the Mischiever nonchalantly.

"I don't get it."

"You dolt! Even the court jesters understand this one. The Baron can use the fabricated war as a pretext to rally the serfs behind his rule and his Ism. War will also justify higher taxes, a bigger baronial bureaucracy, and an expanded defense department. When the war is over, the surviving serfs will be grateful they weren't killed, so they'll forget about the higher taxes, the bigger bureaucracy, and the bloated defense complex."

But Sire!'s splendid report thrilled the Baron. Not only was Robin Hood doing great work for the barony, his altruistic philosophy laid the foundation for a military adventure. However, he feared the Archbishop might not approve, so he sent But Sire! to get the religious figurehead's blessing.

When But Sire! arrived, the Archbishop was distracted by a new sport he was inventing, which he obliquely called "golf". He fanatically struck at a small spheroid with sticks that he periodically threw in puerile disgust. But Sire! earned the Archbishop's gratitude and support for the war by suggesting that digging a hole in the ground to serve as a target for the little white ball might spice up the game.

But Sire! reported back to the Baron that the Archbishop supported going to war, with a few caveats. First, the Archbishop wanted lots of soldiers killed, so that he could sermonize about how wonderful the kingdom of heaven is compared to the dangerous real world. Second, he wanted his share of the new taxes in the form of increased tithes. Third, when the soldiers were done fighting the Baron's war, he wanted them to retake the Holy Land from the Saracens. After all, they were fighting for his ism as much as the baron's.

The Honcho eagerly agreed to these stipulations, because the ghastly carnage of war beckoned like a temptress. It was exhilarating to know that anonymous people would die defending his rule and his ism. It didn't bother him that they sacrificed themselves out of ignorance, fear, or conditioned worship of the political and religious order of things. He picked a neighboring barony at random from a map and declared war on its unfortunate inhabitants, using a nearly forgotten territorial dispute as a pretext. As the war escalated, the serfs forgot about the inflationary ravages of the invisible Robin Hood, and the Baron achieved daily orgasm with the reports of battlefield casualties.

Then, in a rare but illuminating moment in man's history, the naked soul of the species was briefly unmasked of mythology and isms. In the heat of a particularly gruesome conflict, the flag bearers of each barony got carried away by the emotion of slashing swords and skewering lances and charged each other. They collided and fought, and their banners became tangled and indistinguishable from one another. This confused jumbling of the baronial flags stunned the combatants of both factions, as if a sorcerer's spell was abruptly broken. Warfare unexpectedly ceased. Swords hung idly in the hands of bewildered soldiers. Mesmerized jousters looked at their lances without recognition. They looked like dancers after the band suddenly stopped playing in the middle of a heretofore irresistible tune that had choreographed their steps since time immemorial.

With no flags to kill for and therefore no isms to die for, the soldiers now saw each other as fellow individuals involved in a common struggle for survival and fulfillment on an inimical planet suspended in a mystifying cosmos. Battlefield enemies intermingled, conversed, and gradually came to know each other. They soon discovered that through trade, cooperation, and friendship, they could achieve an existence far superior to the one that previously guaranteed them only a hero's mortal bon voyage if they sacrificed their lives dutifully to some omnipotent purveyor of myths. Once the flags were destroyed and the isms deconditioned, they no longer had a reason to kill each other.

The Baron was crimson with rage when he heard of this astounding pacifism. How dare the ungracious serfs abandon their duties and commingle with the enemy? Their ordained reason for living was to die for the barony and the bishopric. There was territory to be won, riches to be plundered, souls to be herded to heaven, and royal and priestly lifestyles to be maintained. Demonstrations of anarchy and agnosticism couldn't be tolerated! The Honcho knew that the Baron had to quell this nascent insurrection immediately. If such disobedience were tolerated in this millennium, successive centuries of evolving liberty would make life as a modern senator impossible for him.

The two combating barons hastily dispatched fresh squadrons of flag bearers to the stymied battlefield. The pacified serfs were startled from their reverie by the flag-bearing reinforcements galloping toward them. Old passions suddenly flamed anew. Loyalty to barons welled up again in the souls of the soldiers. Sense of duty once again gripped them as the sorcerer's spell seized their hearts. The cosmic bandleader struck up his tune in mid-measure, as if the dance had never been interrupted. While the baronial flags fluttered proudly, swords were unsheathed, lances were hefted, and hatred ruled the day once more. A charge was sounded. Human carnage ensued. This time, the flag bearers refrained from despoiling their holy banners. They stood silhouetted on the ridge, like religious icons atop temples, watching paternalistically as vassal slaughtered vassal. When the sun finally set on the bloody plain littered with carcasses, only Death emerged victorious.

Unfortunately, the Head Honcho couldn't bask in the glory of Death's victory. The cosmic clock pacing his temporary intrusion into Medieval Europe triggered the magic of the "Book of Liberal Policies, Marxist Economics, and Other Occult Phenomena" to whisk him back to 20th century Washington.

"Welcome back", obliged Freeman, who was still there in his office.

"I wasted my time", groused the Honcho. "Tyrants got no respect in the Middle Ages, either."

"What happened?"

"The serfs killed my only tax collector. And even if they hadn't, I couldn't have emptied their pockets with only one agent. But that wasn't the worst part. In the middle of a pitched battle, my soldiers laid down their weapons and embraced the enemy. Those imbeciles couldn't even die for their ism properly! I won't be part of a culture where the peons think their lives have meaning outside of what I and my divine brethren plant in their feeble brains."

"What now?" asked Freeman half-heartedly. "The Caesar thing didn't work out. Neither did the medieval thing. If you stay here, the Insurrectionist will continue to haunt you. You have to exist somewhere and sometime."

The senator morosely grabbed a bottle of Old Bushmills. "What would you do if you were in my shoes, smart ass?"

"Is suicide one of my options?"

"If you don't answer respectfully, suicide won't be necessary."

"Then my next choice would be to go back to the year 1775 and become King George III of Great Britain."

"Why?" the Honcho asked suspiciously, wondering if the Mad Hatter was behind this somehow.

"I'm surprised you didn't think of it yourself", lied Freeman, who knew that the Honcho never thought up his own ideas. "King George reigned over an empire so broad that the sun never set on it. Also, my experience in 19th century Ireland suggests that the repressive British Empire is your kind of work environment. Most importantly, if you insert yourself into 1775 as King George, you could prevent the American Revolution and change the course of history. It would be far easier for you to monopolize power today if America hadn't been emancipated from Monarchism."

The Honcho guzzled whiskey as he pondered this beguiling suggestion. He suspected it would backfire, but going back into the past to influence the future tantalized him. Perhaps he could even distort the fragile fabric of time to completely preclude the Insurrectionist's existence! This serendipitous thought slayed his indecision. He set down the bottle of Old Bushmills. "I'm going for it!" he announced boldly.

He eagerly opened the "Book" to the time travel chapter and quoted aloud a dreamy fairy tale. Before he finished the final stanza, he was once again absorbed magically into the churning vortex of time. This warp in the fabric of the cosmos gradually transmogrified him into King George III of Great Britain. He was transported through four-dimensional space to London, England, while the cosmic clock was adjusted back to January 12th, 1775.

The Honcho became aware that he was in Windsor Castle. Dressed in royal raiment, he was surrounded by attendants and regal splendor that only the leader of an empire could command. He was seated in an ostentatious drawing room by a table sporting chess pieces exquisitely carved from Indian elephant tusk. He was playing chess with a man he somehow knew to be Dr. Benjamin Franklin, an ambassador from the American colonies.

The chess match was a lopsided affair. When the Honcho inserted himself into the scene, Franklin was executing his final victorious maneuver. He physically removed the King's king piece from the board, which was an egregious violation of European etiquette. The Queen, seated at George's side, bleated shrilly, "In Europe, we do not remove kings so!"

"In America, we do", replied Franklin calmly. He winked mischievously at the Queen, who didn't catch his meaning.

The King angrily shoved the game table, spilling the chess pieces noisily onto the marble floor. He hated losing, particularly to Franklin, who was in London for a final attempt at negotiating a peaceful settlement of the multiplying conflicts between the American colonies and the British Empire. His anger was exacerbated by his wife's pontificating voice whenever he lost, which was rather frequent, since he was endowed with such ordinary mental capabilities that it was his good fortune accession to the throne was hereditary.

The Head Honcho, finally noticing the homely Queen, was crestfallen that he had left behind Buxomus Blondus for her. King George had obviously married for royal convenience rather than animal passion. Ruing the fate of his libido, the Honcho took a mental note to influence his physical host to pursue celibacy.

An attendant announced another visitor. Dr. Franklin arose to greet the guest, who was there by his invitation. After exchanging brief pleasantries, he offered an introduction to the King. "Your majesty", he said with a bow and a flourish, "I give you. . . ."

"Freeman!" the King abruptly blurted. This bizarre exclamation confused everyone. Even King George had no idea why he shouted the name "Freeman". The Head Honcho, however, knew exactly why. The visitor was a dead ringer for the 20th century Freeman that he was excruciatingly familiar with, although the twin wore 18th century attire.

Franklin attributed the strange outburst to the King's periodic dementia. Whispers in the castle halls suggested that the King wasn't always entirely lucid, although no one dared to accuse him of madness. Franklin noted to himself that the inbreeding common to royalty was another reason to abandon monarchism altogether. He attempted again to introduce his guest. "Your majesty, I give you Thomas Paine."

"Forgive me, Mr. Paine", said the King. "I don't know why I called you Freeman."

The visitor bowed cordially. "T'is no trouble at all. If truth be told, I had a strange compulsion to call your majesty 'Head Honcho'". The King smiled tentatively at this apparent condescension.

"Mr. Paine is a former officer of the British Excise Service, your majesty", explained Franklin. "He will be emigrating to the American colonies with me when I return home."

The King was uncomfortable again. He vaguely recalled an excise officer named Paine who generated a small uproar by publishing a critique of the royal bureaucracy. "Tell me, Mr. Paine, why are you emigrating to the colonies?"

Paine was indeed the excise officer the King remembered. His job was to collect taxes on liquor and tobacco to help underwrite Great Britain's enormous royal bureaucracy, of which he was an outspoken critic. In London he had met Franklin, who enraptured him with avid descriptions of the rebellions proliferating in the American colonies. Franklin often described in vivid terms, for all who would listen in London, the enormous rising tide of insurrection in America, which British leaders weren't taking seriously. What began as a tax revolt after the Seven Years War was growing into the penultimate challenge to British monarchism and to all political and religious suppression of Man's rights.

Britain dismissed the rumblings in America as the mischief of scattered bands of uneducated ragamuffins who were no match for the Empire's storied institutions and omnipotent military. America was viewed mainly as a source of colonial income, particularly after the Seven Years War drained the Royal treasury with the costly victory over the French. Heavy taxes were imposed on the colonies, ostensibly because they had been protected from the French by the British military. The colonists argued that they had no quarrel with the French, and gained nothing from the British acquisition of Florida and Canada as spoils in the war. The Sugar Act of 1764, The Stamp Act of 1765, the Townshend Acts of 1767, and the tea tax exemplified the British leeching of the colonies.

Outspoken Americans, such as Patrick Henry and George Mason, objected vociferously to the Acts, arguing that the distant British had no right to tax the colonists, who derived no benefit from the revenue and who had no representation in Parliament. Mason's "Fairfax County Resolves" and "The Virginia Declaration of Rights" fueled widespread hatred of British Parliament. Tax resistance caught fire, led by the Sons of Liberty, who held parades and mass meetings to inflame the colonists. They also harassed tax collectors and burned their reviled stamps in the streets of New York and Philadelphia. In Boston, tax officials were hung in effigy on a selected tree, which thereafter became known as the Liberty Tree. Passionate oratories erupted from the Raleigh Tavern. Mobs rioted and attacked customs officers. The colonies were becoming a powder keg.

Hatred of high taxes evolved into hatred of British imposition into American lives. Mercantile controls subordinated American enterprises to government-sponsored monopolies, such as the East India Company, so that the colonies were nothing more than captive sources of raw materials and captive markets for finished products. Manufacturers of beaver hats, woolen goods, and iron articles were forced out of business in the north, and large plantations in the south fell deeply in debt to British firms because they were forced to sell their cotton, tobacco, and hides to England at artificially low prices and to buy English manufactures at artificially high prices. The little trade that was permitted had to be conveyed to Europe on merchant marine ships owned by British middlemen, who skimmed off huge vigorish.

An influx of paper money into the colonies ignited inflation and stock speculation. American legislatures that agitated against these imperialistic practices had their charters annulled, triggering feverish anger against taxation without representation. America argued that British Parliament had no more right to pass laws for Massachusetts, than the Massachusetts Legislature had to pass laws for Britain. The British responded with the Declaratory Act, which asserted Parliament's right to impose laws on the colonies "in all cases whatsoever".

British Admiralty Courts, who received a commission for unilaterally set fines, replaced trial by jury. Many trials of colonists were held in Britain, where an adequate defense was impossible, given the cost and impracticability of transporting witnesses overseas. The British searched American ships, warehouses, and homes for smuggled goods without warning or warrants. The colonies were overrun by British civil servants that intruded into every aspect of production and every question of property.

British troops were garrisoned in the colonies, often in the homes of unwilling Americans, authorized by the Quartering Act and financed with colonial taxes. Eventually, colonists were impressed into British military service against their will, and even forced to bear arms against their fellow colonists. The British incited Indian savages to lay siege to frontier settlements, which became another pretext for quartering British troops in the colonies as protection. Using such Mafia-like tactics, the King and Parliament tightened their control over America.

Predictably, armed conflict erupted, beginning with the Boston Massacre, which started when a rambunctious youth heckled a British soldier. Unfortunately, the soldier lost his composure and struck the youth in the head with his rifle butt. The youth staggered down the streets of Boston decrying the soldier's brutality. A crowd formed. Someone rang the church bell to sound an alarm. The crowd followed the boy to the British Customs House, where they found the villainous soldier, who called for reinforcements. Undaunted, the crowd threw stones and dared the soldiers to open fire. A projectile struck a soldier in the head. He fired into the advancing crowd, killing a colonist named Crispus Attucks. Hearing gunfire, other paranoid soldiers leveled their weapons and launched a volley into the crowd. The horrified Bostonians broke ranks and scattered for shelter, leaving on the ground three dead and eight severely wounded.

Word of the slaughter spread like wildfire. Prominent citizens used the brutal episode to fan the flames of revolt. Paul Revere authored a cartoon labeled "The Bloody Massacre", graphically depicting Redcoats firing a hail of bullets into a peaceful crowd. In fiery prose, the cartoon described the barbaric carnage. The thousands of printed copies depicting unarmed citizens dropping into bloodstained snow wildly incited the colonists. Samuel Adams, a prominent political leader in Massachusetts, vowed to never let the British forget their ignominious and cowardly act. The subsequent sensational trial, in which five British soldiers were acquitted of murder, stirred up even more rebellious fervor.

Tensions grew elsewhere in the colonies. In Rhode Island, the British schooner Gaspee constantly patrolled the waters around Providence. It was extremely unpopular, because it had curtailed the flow of contraband goods. But, on one auspicious evening, it ran aground on the shallows off Point Namquit. Word quickly spread that the despised ship was stranded and vulnerable. A rabid crowd of conspirators gathered at Sabin's tavern, where they amassed weapons and planned an attack on the disabled warship. The colonists rowed out to the wallowing Gaspee, evacuated the British sailors, and ignited a spectacular blaze. Pyrotechnic sparks leapt into the black sky above Rhode Island, a rousing symbol of revolt against British occupation.

The British manhunt for the rebels who destroyed the Gaspee was unsuccessful, so they retaliated by paying the salaries of each colonial Governor from the Royal Treasury, rather than from the colonial treasuries. This extortion effectively made the governors beholden to British Parliament. In response, Samuel Adams declared that it was time for the colonists to choose to live as free men or as slaves.

Back in Massachusetts, another confrontation occurred. Americans had long resented the British East India Company being their sole purveyor of tea. They were even more furious over the import tax added to the monopolized price, so they boycotted tea altogether. The East India Company persisted in shipping tea to the colonies, but Americans turned back the ships without allowing them to unload their cargo, in order to avoid the tax. When three more British merchant ships arrived in Boston Harbor loaded with tea, Samuel Adams called hundreds of colonists to the Old South Meeting House and convinced them to stop the vessels from unloading. Meanwhile, the British-paid governor instructed the merchants to leave the port, but not until the colonists paid the tea tax, even if the cargo wasn't unloaded. This audacity incensed the patriots. After rancorous debate at the Old South Meeting House, a "tea party" was planned.

Shouting "to Griffin's Wharf!", colonists disguised as Mohawk Indians stormed from the meetinghouse to the docks. They boarded the ships and dumped the tea into murky Boston Harbor. This violent refusal by the colonists to pay taxes shocked the British government. Parliament vowed to hang hundreds of rebels as an example for insurrectionists everywhere. One particularly furious Parliamentarian, sensing the enormity of the precedent for civil disobedience, declared "we should blow the town of Boston about the ears of its inhabitants." Instead, Parliament ordered the navy to blockade Boston until the colonists paid the tax on every submerged leaf of tea.

Boston was immensely dependent on harbor traffic, so the blockade was cruelly effective. Food and other commodities became scarce, and the affluent town was reduced to beggary in weeks. The American reaction to this was swift and ominous. Neighboring states circumvented the blockade by transporting sheep from Connecticut, corn from Virginia, rice from South Carolina, flour from Pennsylvania, and fish from many coastal towns. The Massachusetts Assembly sent swift riders to call other state legislatures into united action. Virginian George Washington admonished the other states not to sit on their hands while the Empire reduced their brothers to utter slavery.

The First Continental Congress gathered in Carpenter's Hall in Philadelphia the following summer. Delegates were uneasy about escalating the conflict with England, but a fiery speech by delegate Patrick Henry, who declared with searing conviction, "I am not a Virginian, but an American!" catalyzed them into a united body. The spirit of a new nation was born.

But King George and his parliament weren't yet sensitized to this new, menacing American identity, despite Franklin's best efforts in London to warn the British that a serious confrontation was looming. Thus, when the King asked Thomas Paine why he was emigrating to the colonies, he was blissfully ignorant of the attraction that the rebellious American spirit held for those who despised the oppressive British government. So when Paine passionately replied, "Even though my body was born in Britain, my soul was born in America", the King continued to wallow in denial.

The Head Honcho's spirit, however, wasn't as complacent as his corporeal host. He had intruded into this slice of history to prevent the American Revolution. Unfortunately, he was having difficulty influencing the King's speech and behavior, because the Time Travel transmogrification had gone slightly askew. He watched helplessly as King George stumbled into history's greatest showdown, as if viewing his own dream as a detached entity.

Oblivious to the Honcho's seething frustration, the King returned his attention to Franklin. "Why all of the hullabaloo in the American colonies about no taxation without representation? My own subjects here in Britain don't have that luxury. What deludes your ragamuffin rebels into asserting such astounding claims? Don't they realize they're violating God's divine wish that they be indentured to me? They are my subjects, and they should behave like subjects!"

Franklin answered with a tale about an American backwoodsman who had been conscripted by the British during the Seven Years War. The buckskin-clad American was reluctant to fight the French, with whom he had no personal quarrel. "You call yourself a loyal subject to the crown?" scolded a British officer, who assumed that no man could ignore humankind's historical propensity for subjugation. The recalcitrant American, known only as Hawkeye, had no such inclination. "Don't call myself subject to much at all", he calmly replied. Franklin accentuated this punch line by observing, "America is full of Hawkeyes who believe that kings are servants, not proprietors, of the people. Open your mind, sire, to expanded thought. Let not the name of George the

Third be a blot on the pages of history. Loosen the reigns on the American colonies, before terrible events unfold."

"The American colonies are mine by Divine Right!" George III whined. "Your melodramatic tales don't frighten me. The colonists will heel to my command, just like all other subjects since time began. There's nothing special about those uncouth renegades. What is Carpenter's Hall compared to Buckingham Palace?" Inside the King's cranium, the Honcho's spiritual essence resoundingly cheered, "The fight is on!"

Franklin solemnly pulled a parchment from his greatcoat and handed it to the King. "This letter expresses the sentiments of all Americans. It's addressed to you, from a Virginian named Thomas Jefferson, although who wrote it is of little consequence. Read it and heed it."

As the King unfolded the parchment, the Head Honcho reeled from the shock of hearing Jefferson's name through George's ears. "How can this be?" he wondered to himself. "Is he the ancestor of my Insurrection Czar?" While he wrestled with this disconcerting enigma, the King read the letter.

It began with a long description of how Britain had abused the American colonies. King George hastily scanned these complaints, as though they were natural and harmless observations of the way things ought to be, rather than angry objections to unholy imperialism. But, the closing words of the obscure American author sent a chill down his slackened spine:

> ". . . . *The God that gave us life, gave us liberty at the same time. The hand of force may destroy, but cannot disjoin them. Every man, and every body of men on earth, possess the right of self-government. They receive it with their being from the hand of nature. This sire, is our determined resolution, and all that is left for us is*

to awaken and snap the Lilliputian cords which entangle us.

"In Great Britain, it's said that their constitution relies on the House of Commons for honesty, and the Lords for wisdom; which would be a natural reliance, if honesty were bought with money, and if wisdom were hereditary. They are hired to lie, and from them no truth can ever be extracted but by reversing everything they say. With money they will get men, and with men, they will get money. Taxation follows from this credo, and in its train, wretchedness and oppression. If we allow ourselves to be taxed in our necessaries and our comforts, in our labors and our amusements, for your callings and your creeds, then we have hired ourselves out for the chains to be riveted to our necks. We in America have made our election between liberty and slavery. We will not submit to your taxation or your laws.

"Your officers cover our land and reach into every article of produce and property, and thence to every thought, of all Americans. To this intrusion of government into the crevices of our lives, we can no longer acquiesce. While the evils encompassing the life of man are sufficiently numerous that it isn't prudent to add to them by destroying one another, and while peace is better than war, Europeans have habitually confounded force with right, so if force be the language you understand, then force shall be the language we speak.

"Word from London suggests you perceive our effort to be an insignificant rebellion propagated by just a few, and that the mere specter of the awesome might of the empire is sufficient to quell any potential uprisings. In fairness to your majesty, let it be known that our resolve is unshakable. We prefer freedom with *danger than slavery with ease, and we despise all timid men who prefer the calm of despotism to the boisterous sea of liberty. We understand that the tree of liberty must be refreshed from time to time with the blood of both patriots and tyrants. A little rebellion now and then is as necessary in the political world as storms are in the physical. From the blood of such rebellions is fertilized the fruit of freedom.*

"We consider it a universal truth that governments exist for men, and not vice versa. If we must bear arms in defense of this, we declare to your majesty and to the world at large that we will bear them with perseverance, and exert our utmost energies to preserve that liberty which was committed to us in sacred deposit from the beginning of time. We do not delude ourselves into thinking that we can be transported from despotism to liberty in a feather bed.

"We do not desire separation from the Crown for the mere sake of separation, nor do we desire revolution for the sake of revolution. But our rights are inviolate, and we stand prepared to leap over the awful chasm that lies between here and there, knowing all the while that a chasm cannot be traversed in two bounds, and therefore the one bound should be powerful enough to accomplish the task.

"We also believe that, once started, a chain of revolutions will encircle the globe, and that Britain itself won't be exempt. You have loaded the inhabitants of Great Britain with debts equal to the whole value of their island, selling it to creditors who lend money to be lavished on priests, plunder, and perpetual war. With the weight of your taxes, the shackles on commerce by monopolies and on industry by guilds, the censorship of conscience, thought, speech, and the press by venal judges, the enormous expense of the

Queen, the princes, and the court, and the luxury, indolence, and immorality of the clergy, surely, under such massive misrule and oppression, the people of Britain might justly press for a thorough reformation, and might even dismount their rough-shod riders.

"Do not delude yourself into thinking that the sheer might of the empire will prevent insurrections, because no degree of power in government hands can do so. In Turkey, where the sole nod of the despot means death, insurrections happen every day. And pay no heed to your sycophantic ministers, who daily inform you that yours is the most perfect government ever established on earth. They are blind, mistaken, and corrupt themselves. And so, we entreaty you to reconsider the brutality with which you wield your power over the American colonies, and ask you one last time, peacefully, to let us be. History awaits your answer, and is amply prepared to render its verdict on your choice. Humanity stands poised on the threshold of a bold new vision of restrained power and neutered mysticism. Your answer to our plea will not deter us from crossing that threshold; it will simply determine whether we cross it peacefully or violently."

The King's corpulent, manicured hands trembled uncontrollably. His confused mind, which was barely equal to the task of governing under sedate circumstances, was ill prepared for such portentous conflict. Worse still, his brain was haunted by another presence whispering ethereal words that didn't quite enter into direct consciousness, begging him to crush the nascent American quest for liberty with all the power of his church and his state. He stood transfixed between Jefferson's written wisdom and the Head Honcho's totalitarian urgings, and he yearned to quietly shrink from the enormous metaphysical storm raging around him. As he struggled with this mental maelstrom, he tried to stall the Americans who watched him expectantly. "Things cannot be all that bad", he mouthed emotionlessly. "Surely we can accommodate each other's. . . . requirements."

Franklin started to respond, but Thomas Paine placed a forceful arm across his chest and stepped forward to address the King himself. The King felt another twitch in his curdled brain from the Honcho's reflexive reaction to a Freeman look-alike stepping forward to argue with him. Paine's jutting jaw and blazing eyes drove home his strident words. "There will be no accommodation! For thousands of years, mankind has accommodated the likes of you, and the result, always and everywhere, has been slavery. With the world's biggest military to enforce her tyranny, Britain has declared that she has a right not only to tax, but to bind the Americans in all cases whatsoever. If that is not slavery, then there is not such a thing as slavery on earth.

"Cowardice, submission, and accommodation thus far have given the Americans a ravaged country, unsafe habitations, corruption everywhere, slavery without hope, homes turned into barracks and bawdy houses for your soldiers, and a future race to provide for whose fathers they shall doubt of. Let history look on this picture and weep over it!

"The Declaratory Act contained the full grown seeds of the most despotic government in the world. It placed Americans in the lowest state of vassalage, demanding unconditional submission in everything! A congress of men wielding such power over a people, from such distance, with so little accountability, will inevitably make that people mere beasts of burden for their enrichment.

"There are two classes of people . . . those who pay taxes, and those who live upon the taxes. When taxation is carried to excess, as is happening in America, it disunites these two classes. Parliament, an evil and indolent congress of men, is the most prolific taxation machine ever invented. It has created a leviathan of a government, an overblown monster spewing forth spurious jobs and deadly wars. The taxation required to support you as King is sufficient to feed, house, and clothe entire villages!

"Your greedy ministers thrust their hands into every crevice of American industry, grasping at the spoils of those who produce. This enormous expense and intrusiveness has provoked men to think that governments are evil incarnate. They engage in wars abroad and oppress and usurp at home. Their sole capability is to exhaust the property and resources of the productive world. Governments lavish these stolen resources upon kings, courts, parliaments, congressmen, ministers, and a host of other impostors and prostitutes, such that even the poor must support the fraud that oppresses them.

"It doesn't matter what form the government takes, for when one government goes out, another comes in, and still the same vices, extravagances, and corruptions occur. Who the ministers are is insignificant, because the defect lies in the system, which defines some as vassals and some as masters. When extraordinary power is allotted to any politicians in a government, they attract every kind of corruption. Give to any men access to millions each year, along with the power of disposing the resources and managing the expenses of an entire nation, and the liberties of that nation will no longer be secure. As the old saying goes, 'Make me a king today, and I shall be a robber tomorrow.'

"Government parasites living in luxurious indolence on taxes not only saps our lives, it also leads to our extinction. War is the common harvest of those who suckle on public money. War is the art of conquering at home, because it's a pretense for increasing government revenue. Taxes aren't raised to carry on wars; wars are raised to carry on taxes. One fourth of mankind's labor is annually consumed by barbarous war and defense, promulgated by governments. We are thus compelled to not only finance the indolence of our oppressors, but also to die for them as well, after our labors have sufficiently stocked the war machine. No war in the entire history of the world was started by innocent citizens pursuing the honest objects of their individual lives, except for the one about to erupt in America.

"Don't look so startled at the mention of a violent insurrection in America. You still wallow in the mysticism that it's only God's prerogative to anoint kings and governments, for causes known only to Him and his earthly interpreters. The Archbishop tells us that it's not our business to overturn the government, that our role instead is to worship the king and pray for his ministers. Fortunately for the world, this mythology didn't cross the Atlantic Ocean. The Americans understand that kings aren't taken away by miracles, and that changes in government require only enough guns and courage.

"Alas, mankind has long made large sacrifices to ancient superstition. But it's now clear to us that priests and tyrants are co-conspirators against liberty. We now understand that the mystery clouding the justification for kings and governments was only to cover the incredibility of it all. The age of political and religious superstition is passing away. All national institutions of churches, whether Jewish, Christian, or Muslim, are merely human invention, set up to terrify and enslave mankind by subjugating reason, enabling some men to monopolize power and profit.

"I don't believe in the creed of the Jewish Church, the Roman Church, the Islamic Church, the Protestant Church, nor any other church. We can all see the absurdity of worshipping Aaron's molten calf, and we laugh at the folly of the Egyptians who put a pebble on a throne and acknowledged it as their king, but yet we are still blinded from the absurdity of worshipping our popes, our kings, and our parliaments, all of equally earthly constitution, and all likely to do us more harm than if we worshipped pebbles or calves instead. Future generations will burst into laughter when they examine our pious fairy tales.

"It is only by blinding man into believing that government is some wonderful mysterious thing that the ignorant are quieted and excessive taxation is foisted upon the world. When priests and kings set up religions and governments repugnant to human comprehension, they invented a word that served as a barrier to all questions and speculation. This word is 'mystery', and it has been used throughout history to ensconce priests and kings into dominant positions. Truth never envelops itself in mystery, because mystery is a fog of human invention. Ignorance and mystery are mirror images of the same thing.

"We have reached the juncture in human evolution where it's necessary to declare that we no longer fear god, that we no longer look with awe to kings, nor with affection to parliaments, nor with duty to magistrates, nor with reverence to priests, nor with respect to nobility by birth. We must now inquire into the reason why we have a distinction between kings and subjects, and how came a race of men into the world so exalted above the rest as to become nearly a separate and privileged species.

"We must separate church from state, and see if the state can stand on its own. I think we should find, could we take off the dark covering of antiquity, that the first kings were simply the principal ruffian of some restless gang, whose savage manners or pre-eminence in conjuring and mysticism obtained for him the title of chief among plunderers. As time unfolded, we were confronted with a plethora of oppressors staking a claim upon us. Between the monarchy, the parliament, the church, the feudal despotism operating locally, and the bureaucratic despotism operating everywhere, oppressors have overrun us, for reasons unknown to us. Kings on their own deathbeds dispose of their crowns by will, and consign their subjects, like beasts of the field, to whatever successor they appoint. This is so monstrous as hardly to be believed, as are the rest of the mysterious powers binding us.

"Monarchy, aristocracy, and democracy are but creatures of imagination, and a thousand such creatures may be contrived, all of them with the same result. Democracy is the most beguiling and confusing of these imaginations. Because a government is elective does not make it less despotic, if the persons elected possess afterward unlimited powers and are subject to no effective restraint. They merely become candidates for despotism, and one is as bad as another. Swamps breed serpents, and governments breed oppressors. History's annals abound in such hideous wickedness, such horrible cruelties propagated by governments and churches, that only by reading of them can we form any idea of the baseness of which human nature is capable. The pictures that we behold of kings and priests and their ministers are so horrifying that humanity turns away from them with a shudder.

"Louis XIV said, 'If I were to comply with the will of my people, I would no longer be king.' No more universal truth was ever spoken. For myself, I would suffer the misery of devils rather than make a whore of my soul by swearing allegiance to a sottish, stupid, stubborn, worthless, and brutish tyrant. I cannot condone crowning a man's head to make him king. Like the Americans, I would instead glorify the rights of individual men. Every man wishes to pursue his occupation and to enjoy the fruits of his labor and the produce of his property in peace, safety, and with the least possible expense. When these things are accomplished, all the reasons why government ought to be established are answered. We shall then find, if we let the American vision manifest itself, that kings and parliaments are dispensable.

"Universal peace, civilization, and commerce can only be accomplished by a complete revolution in the world's system of governments. Do not underestimate Mankind's ability to accomplish this. We are maturing with each passing century. We are beginning to see with other eyes, to hear with other ears, and to think other thoughts. And what we are seeing, hearing, and thinking is that it is of no significance to enthrone one king or another, or to elect one parliamentarian or another, but to have nothing to do with them all. Everything that is right pleads for separation from our governors. The blood of the slain and the weeping voice of nature cries, 'T'is time to part!'

"There is an old tale about the canton of Berne, Switzerland, in which it was customary, from time immemorial, to keep a bear at the public expense. The people were taught to believe that if they had not a bear, they would all be undone. It happened some years ago that the bear became ill, and died too suddenly to be replaced immediately by another bear. During this interregnum, people discovered that the corn grew, the vintage flourished, the sun and moon rose and set, and everything went on the same as before. Taking courage from these observations, they resolved not to keep any more bears, which are very voracious and expensive animals, and likely to eat you if you aren't careful to declaw them.

"The stage is set for the world to abandon its royal bears and golden calves. What were called revolutions in the past were little more than a change of persons or of insignificant particulars of governance. These revolutions rose and fell without measurably altering posterity. But the incipient revolution in America is a universal rejection of the whole order of things that have oppressed mankind forever. Our generation will appear to the future as the Adam of a new world. Governments will fall around the globe, especially where citizens can read and have access to guns.

"Will you now accuse me of insurrection? If, to expose the fraud and imposition of government, to lessen the oppression of taxes, to extirpate the horrid practice of war, to promote commerce, to break the chain of political and religious superstition, and to raise the degraded common man to his proper rank in the order of things, if these things be insurrection, let the name of insurrectionist be engraved on my tomb! I fear not your priests or your ministers or your armies!

"We have the power to begin the world over again. John Locke said, 'In the beginning, all the world was America.' The cause of America is the cause of all mankind, of those who ever lived or ever will live. The sun never shined on a vision of greater measure. T'is not the affair of a city or a state or a country, but of all the continents of the world. T'is not the concern of a day or a year or an age, because all of posterity is involved in this contest, and will be affected to the end of time. We need no longer wait for the right time, because the right time hath found us.

"Your request for accommodation is impossibly late! The Rubicon is passed. There is no turning away from it. If I ask an American if he wants a king, he asks me if I take him for an idiot. You are now an object more of contempt than of hatred, and the Americans jeer at you more as an ass than they dread you as a lion. For them, the debate is over. Arms, as the last resort, will now decide the contest. Your actions leave no choice, so the Americans accept the challenge."

When Paine finished, the drawing room fell deathly still. Benjamin Franklin was stunned that his companion, who was born and bred in Britain, was so deeply committed to the American cause that he had issued a declaration of war on their behalf. This was clearly inappropriate, but he admired the man's passion and daring. Franklin hoped that the King would realize Paine had no authority to issue such a declaration, and would react with restraint, since Franklin had come here to negotiate a peaceful resolution, not to initiate armed conflict. He feared, however, that the King would simply order the astonished sentinels to lead Paine to a dungeon to await execution, having uttered his last words.

The Head Honcho was infuriated by his inability to respond to the insolent man who had just challenged the King's legitimacy, which was tantamount to questioning the Honcho's reason for being. His fury was further compounded by Paine's haunting resemblance to Freeman, and his inflammatory words seemed like they were directed at the Honcho's essence lurking inside the King. He felt the rebel's eyes, which were to him the eyes of Freeman, boring right through the King into his own heart and soul. He was particularly incensed by Paine/Freeman's statement that he would suffer the misery of devils rather than make a whore of his soul by swearing allegiance to a sottish, stubborn, stupid, worthless and brutish tyrant. He had always suspected that Freeman's allegiance to him was feigned, or at least simply a matter of apathy, and these words seemingly confirmed his suspicion. With a burning rage for retaliation, he frantically urged his bodily host to order Paine/Freeman's immediate execution and to declare war on the insolent insurgents across the ocean, in order to defend the honor of all governments and rulers against Paine's degrading accusations. This was clearly the critical moment to purge the American Revolution from the future course of history.

The King was excruciatingly silent, despite the Honcho's desperate cajoling. He was ill-prepared for the tense conflict swirling around him. He had achieved his office by birth, not by ability, and nature had not bestowed upon him the gift of leadership. Something inside his brain begged him to lash out at these disrespectful men, to eloquently negate Paine's heresies and assert his right to rule the world. As tortured moments slowly ticked away, he felt the oppressive pressure like a sack of lead beads on his shoulders. He began to hallucinate. In a dark corner of the drawing room, he saw an eerie green demon with scorching red eyes and an evil, rumbling laugh that seemed to originate in hell. He attributed this mirage to the onset of madness, which he yearned to succumb to. But, dignity compelled him to act like a king instead of a maniac, although sometimes not even he could tell the difference.

"You bastards will regret this insolence to your dying day!" he suddenly barked to Paine and Franklin. "You can't ignore millennia of precedence by denying my divine right to rule. You can't burn my ships, toss my tea into the ocean, and attack my tax collectors with impunity. You can't escape the might of the British Empire. After you misfit anarchists are escorted out, I will instruct General Thomas Gage to commence military action against the American colonies. A state of war is hereby declared!"

The eerie green demon lurking in the corner receded back into the nether world of eternal suffering, leaving humanity to worship the awesome specter of his handiwork. Once again, Mephistopheles had orchestrated another cataclysmic war to draw into the portals of hell scads of innocent humans, simply because the British had surrendered control of their lives to their leaders, whose souls were owned by the Evil Incarnate.

General Gage commenced hostilities quickly. On April 18th, 1775, he marched with 700 infantrymen toward Lexington, Massachusetts to seize weapons cached there by the rebels and to arrest their leaders, John Hancock and Samuel Adams. He lost the element of surprise, however, when Paul Revere, a silversmith acting as a scout for the Sons of Liberty, spied the attacking soldiers crossing the Charles River. Revere hurried to the North Church, where he hung two lanterns in the tower as a pre-arranged signal that the British were coming by water, rather than by the land bridge connecting Boston to the mainland. He and two other riders then dashed madly through the darkened towns around Boston, mobilizing local militias by shouting "The British are coming!" Hancock and Adams were awakened and hustled to safety.

The rebels formed a band of 77 minutemen in Lexington Green, led by Captain John Parker, to confront Gage's forces, led by Major John Pitcairn. When the two squadrons converged, Pitcairn ordered the rebels to lay down their guns and disperse. Parker's men refused, drawing courage from the ominous, incessant beat of William Diamond's drum. Parker yelled to his fellow rebels, "Don't fire unless fired upon, but if they want a war, let it begin here!" Infuriated by this intransigence, Pitcairn shouted "Damn you! Lay down your arms!"

Tension mounted. Frightened townspeople gawked from the doorways of the town hall and Buckman Tavern, uneasily eyeing the unfolding drama. Suddenly, shots rang out on both sides, and the first casualties of the war dropped to the ground. Among these was Jonathan Harrington, who crawled 100 yards across Lexington Green to die in a pool of blood at the feet of his horrified wife and his shocked eight-year old son, whose glimpse of the start of the war was lost in the image of his father's lifeless body. The blood of unpretentious men seeking only to be free of kings, ministers, and tax collectors thus christened the American Revolution.

Lexington Green exploded in a hail of bullets, mostly from the muzzles of the superior British forces. Pitcairn pushed the rebels all the way to Concord. Enraged by the slaughter on Lexington Green, four thousand colonists counterattacked the British at the North Bridge, drove them back to Boston, and inflicted heavy casualties. That night, as the surviving British troops lamented their brush with annihilation, hundreds of rebel campfires twinkled against the surrounding black hills like stars suspended in the sky. The American nation and its rebel fighting machine were coming alive.

British reinforcements streamed into Boston Harbor while America formed an official army. To lead it, John Adams nominated "a gentleman whose skill as an officer, whose great talents, and whose universal character would command the respect of America." Seconding this nomination, Thomas Jefferson said, "This man is determined that our experiment in liberty should have a fair trial, and has said that he would lose the last drop of his blood in support of it. He knows that government is force and that it is a dangerous servant and a fearful master. This man's memory will be adored as long as liberty has votaries. His name will in future ages assume its just station among the most celebrated worthies of the world."

Forty-three-year-old George Washington, a tall, tenacious and calm leader, accepted this nomination as Commander-in-Chief of the Continental Army. His love of soldiering would eventually inspire the rebels through desperate months of cold, starvation, inadequate weapons, and waves of casualties. The whistle of bullets charmed him, and this attitude pervaded his troops.

Before Washington could reinforce Boston, the British launched a severe naval bombardment against the American positions surrounding the city. Thousands of Redcoats assaulted the two nearest hills, inspired by their leader, General Burgoyne, who chastised, "What! Ten thousand peasants keep five thousand king's troops shut up! Well, let us get in and we'll soon find elbow room". However, when they charged up Bunker's Hill and Breed's Hill, murderous volleys of musket fire from the entrenched rebels decimated them.

The rebels had strategically held their fire, following Israel Putnam's command "Don't fire until you see the whites of their eyes", partly to conserve scarce ammunition, and partly to lure the British into lethal range. Twice waves of unprotected Redcoats stormed up the hills, and twice the deadly accurate sniping of the backwoods rebels slaughtered them.

Desperate for a victory of any kind after their ignominious retreat from Concord, the British charged a third time. This final surge crested the hill because the Americans had run out of ammunition. A small rebel contingent remained on the hill, facing certain death by bullet and bayonet, as the rest of the colonists escaped down a narrow peninsula.

When the smoke cleared and the mayhem subsided, the British had won the two hills, but there was little joy in their camp. They knew in their hearts that if they won another victory like this one, there would be no one left to carry the good news back to the King. The Americans, on the other hand, despite having lost their position, were elated. One rebel declared, "I wish we could sell them another hill at the same price."

Thomas Paine, after emigrating to America, served as an aide for General Nathaniel Greene, which enabled him to keep his finger on the pulse of the war and the surging and waning American morale. In order to fuel the spirit for insurrection, he published an incendiary pamphlet entitled "Common Sense", which sold 500,000 copies. Its strident call for separation from England caught America's imagination. He described the King, not as the fairy tale royalty they were conditioned to believe in, but rather as the Royal Brute, a wicked dragon who had supreme control over his ministers and the empire. Paine made it clear that they were choosing between slavery and independence. Since he was British and had worked in the King's government, his words rung true with Americans and convinced them of the rightness and importance of their cause.

Paine then published a series of papers entitled "The American Crisis" to bolster the nation's sagging morale. The most famous of these began with the immortal words, "These are the times that try men's souls. The summer soldier and the sunshine patriot will, in this crisis, shrink from the service of his country; but he that stands it now, deserves the love and thanks of every man and woman. Tyranny, like hell, is not easily conquered, yet we have this consolation with us, that the harder the conflict, the more glorious the triumph. All history awaits the battle's outcome." Paine convinced the Americans that their new country was the only stronghold of liberty on earth, and that they must prepare an asylum for all mankind against the kings and priests tormenting the world.

The King, however, wasn't ready to concede such a refuge. Under the command of General Howe, 130 British ships sailed into New York harbor, carrying 30,000 troops and enormous stocks of ammunition and artillery. Many of these troops were Hessians, German mercenaries hired by the King because the British people had begun to withhold support for his war against the Americans. This domestic resistance was due in part to natural reluctance to kill fellow Englishman in the colonies and in part to a growing fear that if the King could dispose of the wayward colonists with violent ease, their own paltry liberty could be squelched as easily.

The ominous specter of an armada in New York harbor teeming with the King's hired butchers cemented American sentiments. Thomas Jefferson declared, "I am sorry to find a bloody campaign is decided upon. But, we hope General Howe will march on us and take another drubbing like Gage took in Boston. We must drub him soundly, so the sceptered tyrant will know we will not crouch under his hand and kiss the rod with which he scourges us." This bravado fed a growing lexicon of American courage to snub noses at the Crown's superior forces. In Nathan Hale's "I only regret that I have but one life to lose for my country", Patrick Henry's "Give me liberty or give me death", and John Paul Jones "I have just begun to fight!", American rebels set a standard for bravery in the face of the world's most powerful military machine.

This battlefield bravado was eclipsed by more enduring events unfolding in Philadelphia. Inspired by a resolution from the Virginia state legislature in June, which asserted that the united colonies were rightfully free and independent states, and that they should be absolved from all allegiance to the British crown, the Continental Congress initiated a formal break from their colonial masters. Seeking to put into words an appropriate declaration to the King and to the world justifying their insurrection against the Crown, Congress appointed John Adams, Benjamin Franklin, Roger Sherman, Robert Livingston, and Thomas Jefferson to draft such a document. This committee delegated the task directly to Jefferson, who had already demonstrated a keen ability for turning a stirring and memorable phrase. Justifying history's most important insurrection thereby fell onto the shoulders of one man.

It took the 33-year-old Jefferson eighteen days to draft the Declaration. He wrote in solitude, in a rented three-story house owned by a German immigrant named Graff, underneath a dim parlor lamp, conjuring words of genius that would define the American Revolution for all generations to come and for all peoples in the world. Later, he described his purpose as "not to find out new principles, or new arguments, never thought of before, not merely to say things which had never been said before; but to place before mankind the common sense of the subject, in terms so plain and firm as to command their assent."

Jefferson wanted to not only declare separation from the Empire, but also to lay the moral and philosophical foundation for a bold new vision of governance and to arouse men to burst the chains that ignorance and superstition had persuaded them to bind themselves with. His words gave life to a view of human society centered upon inalienable rights of individuals, separation of church and state, equality before the law, and empowerment of people to form and reform their own government. This constituted a revolution in political thought more stunning than the military revolution swirling outside his parlor.

On a humid July 1st, the Continental Congress convened to review Jefferson's draft and to address what John Adams called "the greatest question ever debated". They met in a large white paneled chamber with a sawdust strewn wooden floor inside the red brick Pennsylvania State House in the heart of Philadelphia. The temperature reached 82 degrees by 9:00 that morning. All eight windows were opened to ventilate a room made hot by nature's summer and by the intensity of America's metamorphosis. Ironically, in a cupola above their heads was a bell inscribed with words from Leviticus XXV.10: "Proclaim liberty throughout all the land unto all the inhabitants thereof."

After the first day, the emotional debate yielded only 9 assenting votes to declare independence from Great Britain, out of the 13 states represented. The presence of 30,000 murderous Hessians only 60 miles away in New York, combined with the unnerving realization that what they were contemplating was high treason in the eyes of the commanders of these soldiers, drove fear into some of the representatives sweltering in the State House. The shadow of the gallows and the headman's ax weakens even the bravest outlaw. These men, on a very personal and frightening level, weighed Death in the balance against the extraordinary value of the gift that they were creating.

On the second day of the debate, Benjamin Franklin encouraged the wavering delegates by shouting "we must all hang together, or assuredly we will all hang separately!" But, legend says that the tide truly turned when an elderly gentleman that no one recognized stepped forward and passionately recounted the afflictions brought upon them by their British oppressors. He closed his fiery remarks with the plea "they may turn every tree into a gallows, every hole into a grave, and yet the words of Jefferson's Declaration can never die. Sign that parchment, even if in the next moment the noose is around your neck, for it will be the textbook of freedom, the Bible of the rights of man forever."

Moved by this legendary oratory, twelve states ratified the motion, with only the New York delegation abstaining, so the monumental debate was considered decided. After the balloting, they searched the room for the anonymous man who had been the pivotal catalyst. He was nowhere to be found. The unidentified stranger had entered and left without notice, past the locked and guarded entrance.

On the third day, the delegates reviewed the wording of Jefferson's draft Declaration, occasionally striking and adding phraseology, but leaving it essentially intact. On July 4th, the delegates approved the modified text. John Hancock, President of the Congress, and Charles Thomson, Secretary of the Congress, signed the document, knowing full well that their signatures were damning evidence of treason, and that they may as well have signed their own death warrants. When the Declaration was sent to the printer to be copied, Franklin said, "Now I have the happiness to know that the half sun carved into General Washington's chair is a rising, not a setting sun."

On July 8th, while the Old State House Bell, later known as the Liberty Bell, clanged proudly above their heads proclaiming the prophesied liberty, the Declaration of American Independence was read to Philadelphians in the State House yard:

> *"A Declaration by the representatives of the United States of America in Congress assembled, July 4, 1776.*
>
> *"When, in the course of human events, it becomes necessary for one people to dissolve the political bands which have connected them with another, and to assume, among the powers of the earth, the separate and equal station to which the laws of nature and of nature's God entitle them, a decent respect to the opin-*

ions of mankind requires that they should declare the causes which impel them to the separation.

"We hold these truths to be self-evident, that all men are created equal; that they are endowed by their Creator with certain inalienable rights; that among these are life, liberty, and the pursuit of happiness. That, to secure these rights, governments are instituted among men, deriving their just powers from the consent of the governed; that, whenever any form of government becomes destructive of these ends, it is the right of the people to alter or abolish it, and to institute a new government, laying its foundation on such principles, and organizing its powers in such form, as to them shall seem most likely to effect their safety and happiness. Prudence, indeed, will dictate that governments long established should not be changed for light and transient causes; and, accordingly, all experience hath shown, that mankind are more disposed to suffer, while evils are sufferable, than to right them by abolishing the forms to which they are accustomed. But, when a long train of abuses and usurpations, pursuing invariably the same object, evinces a design to reduce them under absolute despotism, it is their right, it is their duty, to throw off such government, and to provide new guards for their future security. Such has been the patient sufferance of these colonies, and such is now the necessity which constrains them to alter their former systems of government. The history of the present King of Great Britain is a history of repeated injuries and usurpations, all having, in direct object, the establishment of an absolute tyranny over these states. To prove this, let facts be submitted to a candid world:

"He has refused his assent to laws the most wholesome and necessary for the public good.

"He has refused to pass other laws for the

accommodation of large districts of people, unless those people would relinquish the right of representation in the legislature; a right inestimable to them, and formidable to tyrants only.

"He has called together legislative bodies at places unusual, uncomfortable, and distant from the depository of their public records, for the sole purpose of fatiguing them into compliance with his measures.

"He has dissolved representative houses repeatedly, for opposing, with manly firmness, his invasions on the rights of the people.

"He has obstructed the administration of justice, by refusing his assent to laws for establishing judiciary powers.

"He has made judges dependent on his will alone, for the tenure of their offices, and the amount and payment of their salaries.

"He has erected a multitude of new offices, and sent hither swarms of officers to harass our people, and eat out their substance.

"He has kept among us, in time of peace, standing armies, without the consent of our legislatures.

"He has affected to render the military independent of, and superior to, the civil power.

"He has combined, with others, to subject us to a jurisdiction foreign to our constitution, and unacknowledged by our laws; giving his assent to their acts of pretended legislation: for quartering large bodies of armed troops among us; for protecting them by a mock trial, from punishment, for any murders which they should commit on the inhabitants of these states; for cutting off our trade with all parts of the world; for imposing taxes on us without our consent; for depriving us, in many cases, of the benefit of trial by jury; for transporting us beyond seas to be tried for pretended

offenses; for taking away our charters, abolishing our most valuable laws, and altering fundamentally the forms of our governments, for suspending our own legislatures, and declaring themselves invested with power to legislate for us in all cases whatsoever.

"He has abdicated government here, by declaring us out of his protection, and waging war on us.

"He has plundered our seas, ravaged our coasts, burnt our towns, and destroyed the lives of our people.

"He is, at this time, transporting large armies of foreign mercenaries to complete the works of death, desolation, and tyranny, already begun, with circumstances of cruelty and perfidy scarcely paralleled in the most barbarous ages, and totally unworthy of the head of a civilized nation.

"He has constrained our fellow citizens, taken captive on the high seas, to bear arms against their country, to become the executioners of their friends and brethren, or to fall themselves by their hands.

"He has excited domestic insurrections amongst us, and has endeavored to bring on the inhabitants of our frontiers, the merciless Indian savages, whose known rule of warfare is an undistinguished destruction of all ages, sexes, and conditions.

"In every stage of these oppressions, we have petitioned for redress, in the most humble terms; our repeated petitions have been answered only by repeated injury. A prince, whose character is thus marked by every act which may define a tyrant, is unfit to be the ruler of a free people.

"Nor have we been wanting in attention to our British brethren. We have warned them, from time to time, of attempts by their legislature to extend an unwarrantable jurisdiction over us. We have reminded them of the circumstances of our emigration and settle-

ment here. We have appealed to their native justice and magnanimity, and we have conjured them, by the ties of our common kindred, to disavow these usurpations, which would inevitably interrupt our connections and correspondence. They, too, have been deaf to the voice of justice and consanguinity. We must, therefore, acquiesce in the necessity which denounces our separation, and hold them, as we hold the rest of mankind, enemies in war, in peace, friends.

"We, therefore, the representatives of the United States of America, in general Congress assembled, appealing to the Supreme Judge of the world for the rectitude of our intentions, do, in the name, and by the authority of the good people of these colonies, solemnly publish and declare, that these united colonies are, and of right ought to be, free and independent states; that they are absolved from all allegiance to the British Crown, and that all political connection between them and the state of Great Britain is, and ought to be, totally dissolved; and that, as free and independent states, they have full power to levy war, conclude peace, contract alliances, establish commerce, and to do all other acts and things which independent states may of right do. And, for the support of this declaration, with a firm reliance on the protection of Divine Providence, we mutually pledge to each other our lives, our fortunes, and our sacred honour."

This pledge of lives, fortunes, and honor was severely tested by ensuing events. Nine of the 56 signatories of the Declaration fought and died in the continuing war. Five more were captured as traitors and tortured to death. Others lost their life savings, their businesses, and their property, ending their lives in rags and bankruptcy. Twelve had their homes ransacked and burned. Thomas Nelson permitted General

Washington to bomb his own home, after discovering that the British General Cornwallis was headquartered there. Benjamin Franklin became estranged from his son, who remained loyal to the Crown. John Hart lived in caves for a year to avoid capture, after he was driven from the bedside of his dying wife and his children fled for their lives. He died heartbroken shortly thereafter. Robert Morris, the wealthy financier of the early war efforts, spent three years in a debtor's prison.

But, for all of their hardship, these men of means and education bequeathed to humanity a legacy whose lasting value is impossible to measure. Their Declaration would stand for centuries as mankind's rallying cry for liberty, as a catalyst for humanity's general insurrection against enslavers, and as the moral justification for those who must fight their own government to attain freedom. A few signers of the Declaration lived to see their creation grow to maturity, including John Adams and Thomas Jefferson, who would both later become President, and who would both die simultaneously on July 4th, 1826, fifty years to the day after America was born.

News of America's Declaration of Independence rocketed around the country and the world. In New York, jubilant citizens pulled ropes around a two-ton statue of King George III mounted atop a horse. The monument toppled to the ground with a starkly symbolic crash, and was melted down into musket balls for killing the tyrant's Hessians. For the first time in history, citizens of a nation dismounted their leader without allowing another tyrant to assume his place in the saddle on their backs. The French Revolution soon followed the American Revolution, which became the model for other peoples assuming power unto themselves around the planet.

Britain waged war until 1783. However, its military cause was lost in 1781, when General Cornwallis surrendered at

Yorktown. Or perhaps their cause was lost as early as July 4th, 1776, since a taste of freedom is more powerful than mythology or demagoguery in inspiring people to enormous wartime feats of courage and determination. The inspirational American triumvirate of Patrick Henry, "The Tongue"; Thomas Jefferson, "The Pen"; and George Washington, "The Sword", checkmated the British.

Washington in particular drove the message home at Yorktown. While the French fleet cornered the British navy, Washington's troops marched into Virginia and laid siege to the Redcoats with withering artillery volleys. For ten days, America's 200 cannons rained death and unrelenting destruction on the demoralized foreign invaders. Eventually, a British officer waved a white flag to negotiate surrender. Cornwallis, too distraught to surrender personally, instructed his second-in-command to officially hand his sword to Washington.

The 7,000 remaining British troops, exhausted of ammunition and will, became prisoners of war. They marched forlornly in a line that stretched over a mile, led by a fife and drum corps that played a haunting English tune fittingly named "The World Turned Upside Down". On October 19, 1781, while British POW's wept at the incredibility of it all, America indeed turned the world, if not history itself, upside down.

The King, however, persisted with the war, despite opposition in his own Parliament and despite having only fragmented forces remaining in America. He feared that abdication to the American insurrection would trigger a domino effect throughout the rest of his empire. British citizens were angry because their leaders were unable to either win the war in America or to end it, an eerie foreshadowing of the American quagmire in Southeast Asia 200 years later. Eventually, the King's stubbornness succumbed to the inevitable. He signed the Treaty of Paris on January 20, 1783, officially recognizing the independence of the United States of America and ending the hostilities.

Shortly thereafter, Jefferson and Adams went to London to establish post-war relations with the British. In one of history's most uncomfortable face-to-face meetings, the author of the Declaration of American Independence met with King George III, who was the direct object of that document's political and philosophical vituperative. Jefferson later described this meeting by saying, "On our presentation to the King and Queen, it was impossible for anything to be more ungracious than their notice of Mr. Adams and myself. The disinclination which they betrayed in their conversation, the vagueness and evasions of their answers, confirmed my belief of their aversion to have anything to do with us."

The Head Honcho, still captive inside the squirming King, was shocked by what he saw through the King's eyes. His first glimpse of Jefferson, dressed in a white linen shirt with a red waistcoat, with heavily powdered orange-tinged hair, resolute jaw, and penetrating eyes, sent rolling waves of stunned recognition through his disembodied brain. The defiant insurrectionist from 18th century America was the same Thomas Jefferson he knew in modern America as his Insurrection Czar! They were identical in every detail!

The implications of this hammered his bodiless mind. It defied logic for a man who lived in the 1700's to also have lived in the 1900's. However, the Honcho himself was ensconced inside a man 200 years before his own birth, thanks to the incomprehensible powers of the "Book of Liberal Policies, Marxist Economics, and Other Occult Phenomena." So perhaps this Thomas Jefferson was indeed his Thomas Jefferson. But what did that mean? The modern Thomas Jefferson was his Insurrection Czar, yet the Thomas Jefferson standing proudly before him now was the world's most famous Insurrectionist!

His mind raced. If Jefferson was an insurrectionist in this life, wouldn't he be an insurrectionist in subsequent lives? The Honcho, after all, was always a tyrant in whatever life he inserted himself into. His mind raced faster. When the Honcho was Julius Caesar two millennia ago, Cicero also looked exactly like Thomas Jefferson, and Cicero was a rebellious enemy of Caesar. He reached a startling conclusion. His 20th century Insurrection Czar was the Insurrectionist! Thomas Jefferson was the mysterious man igniting rebellions and agitating the masses against his rule. He had escaped detection simply by lurking right under the Honcho's nose! What a tremendous irony to discover the identity of the man he'd hunted all of his political life 150 years before he himself was born!

The Honcho's elation took control over the King's mouth. "Jefferson, you homosexual communist sonofabitch!", exclaimed George III uncontrollably, to his own astonishment. "You're the Insurrectionist!"

Everyone was flabbergasted by the King's bizarre outburst. The Queen clucked at the word "homosexual". Adams was perplexed by the word "communist", which was gibberish to men who lived a century before Karl Marx. A sentry snickered at the uncouth reference to Jefferson's mother. Jefferson smiled wryly and replied, "Who commenced the insurrection in America is as indeterminate as who was the first of the three hundred Spartans to offer his name to Leonidas".

The King ignored Jefferson's coy rhetoric, hoping that everyone would quickly forget his inexplicable outburst. He was acutely afraid that his ministers would deem him mad and dethrone him. He suffered from a disease called porphyria, which intoxicates the nervous system, producing periodic bouts with delirium highlighted by conversations with invisible characters, much like the Head Honcho would later entertain with the Mad Hatter. History proved George's fear to be well founded. Parliament eventually deemed him insane and consigned him to Windsor Castle under the custody of his wife in 1820. However, today he was still the ruler of an enormous empire, so he was compelled to defend the honor of his throne. Aware that Jefferson and Adams hadn't bowed upon arrival, he said, "Don't you owe me the courtesy of a proper greeting?"

Jefferson replied coolly, "We owe gratitude to France, justice to England, good will to all, and subservience to none. We bow to no earthly kings."

"Doesn't my aristocracy merit some deference?"

"In America, the grounds for aristocracy are virtue and talent. You, to the contrary, were simply born into your station. There is not a crowned head in Europe whose talents or merits would entitle him to be elected a vestry man of any parish in America."

"But I'm the leader of the world's greatest empire!" declared the King, combining pout and protest in a single slobbering expression.

"The sun of Britain's glory is fast descending to her horizon", said Jefferson. "I would not be so proud to wrap myself in its banner. The wrongs committed by your Empire are unimaginably numerous and degrading to Man's dignity. Your rule is nothing but a poised bayonet constantly reminding every citizen of the stillness of the grave."

"There was a day when insolent bastards like you would be led to the gallows!"

"And there was a day when political martyrs would take poison, rather than allow their tormentors the satisfaction of leading them to the gallows. But, plunging a dagger in the tyrant's breast is a better remedy, which we in America are quite willing to administer."

"Why do you hate us Englishmen so?" snarled King George III.

"It isn't the English people we hate, who are as respectable as those of other nations. It is their government we despise. Governments are the catalyst for organized evil in nations, not individual citizens, whose only evil is generally that they do not recognize and eradicate government corruption quickly enough."

"Government by the people will never succeed. You will succumb to the temptation of royalty again."

Jefferson winced. "It's true that we already have a sect in America lusting after an English constitution of king, lords, and commons, and whose heads are itching for crowns, coronets, and miters. But the majority of our citizens are keenly aware that every king, with sufficient force, is always ready to make himself absolute. History gives us experience of other times and other nations, enabling us to know ambition under every disguise. In view of the throes and convulsions of the ancient world, in view of the agonized spasms of infuriated man seeking through blood and slaughter his long-lost liberty, and in view of our conquest of tyranny in America, we can never regress to the royal and priestly slavery of days gone by. Rather, we remain committed to bringing the kings, nobles, and priests to the scaffolds which they have deluged with the blood of others."

"But", persisted the King, "you must admit that every state has to have a supreme, absolute, uncontrolled authority, or else there will be anarchy."

"I admit no such thing!" declared Jefferson defiantly. "We have matured beyond that primitive notion. In days passed, we habitually believed that it was our duty to be subservient to the government and even to observe a bigoted intolerance for all religions and myths but hers. That unholy relationship between master and slave was a perpetual exercise of unremitting despotism on the one part, and degrading submission on the other. But a change is already perceptible in the world since the revolution in America. The master is abating, and the slave is rising from the dust. If, as we slaves rise up we fall into anarchy, that would certainly decide the unfortunate destiny of mankind, and confirm your view that man is incapable of self-government. However, it will be the distinctive mark of Americans that, in cases of commotion, they enlist under no man's banner and instead rally to the standard of the laws. We will then never fear anarchy or tyranny."

"The world won't follow behind you!" ranted King George. "Even your own people will lose their revolutionary fervor, and fall back under the spell of powerful men. Call them kings or presidents, but unscrupulous men will seize and corrupt America, just as they have every other nation in history."

"The flames kindled on July 4th, 1776, have become a bonfire inextinguishable by the feeble engines of despotism!" Jefferson said vehemently. "The preservation of this holy fire is our gift to the world. Like an Olympic torch, its sparks will spread the blaze of our spirit around the globe. We in America will be a barrier against the return of ignorance and barbarism. The hope of human liberty rests on us. Old Europe will have to lean on our shoulders and hobble along by our side, under the monkish trammels of priests and kings. When totalitarianism casts its dark shadow over the planet time and time again, the light and energy of the Americans will drive it back into the unfathomable abyss. I like these dreams of the future better than the history of the past, and I will dream onward."

"Indeed, you are a dreamer", chided the King. "Knowing tainted man as I do, your fledgling government of the people, by the people, and for the people will become nothing more than another form of tyranny. It only takes a few corrupt and ambitious men to pervert an entire nation, under the guise of some obsequious mythology." Silently and unseen, the Head Honcho nodded his intimate agreement.

"It's true that we in America are like the woodsman who has a wolf by the ears", replied Jefferson. "He can't hold the wolf forever, and the beast will devour him if he lets go. The natural thing for our species has been for liberty to yield and government to gain ground. War, corruption, betrayal, and inequality will find old outlets and new formulas. The shackles which we have attempted to remove during this revolution remain on us, though loosely hanging now. These shackles will likely become tighter and tighter as the years unfold, until at some future time in America, another revolutionary crisis will emerge, when our rights will either be fully restored or will expire completely, relegating my Declaration to a marbled museum as a tattered artifact.

"But, I still believe that our experiment in America stands a better chance of succeeding than any other in history. When I pledged my life and my sacred honor to achieve the American ideals, I meant it more than any man can fully understand. I will pursue my dream to all ends of the earth, and to all extremes of eternity. I won't rest until the totalitarian beast who has reveled so long in the blood and spoils of this planet is finally, like another Prometheus, chained to his rock, where the vulture of remorse for his crimes will prey on his vitals without consuming them. I vow to fight until I see the eighth wonder of the world, which is the dethronement of this Beast, who has destroyed millions of the human race, whose thirst for blood appears unquenchable, who has been the great oppressor of rights and liberty in all ages. I will never surrender in my mortal combat with this Beast!

"My freedom is worth whatever it costs. My rights are not negotiable. I am committed to a society of individual liberty, civil rights, free markets, and non-intervention in foreign affairs. I will inspire a general insurrection of people against their governments. I will champion freedom of thought and slay the connection between mysticism and political power. Our rights have no dependence on religious or metaphysical opinions, like they have no dependence on opinions in physics or geometry. My hour of peace will not come until the mystics and tyrants have been slain."

The King and the American entourage, unable to reconcile, went off in separate directions to finish out their lives. Jefferson became Governor of Virginia, Secretary of State, President of the United States, and founder of the University of Virginia. His skill as an architect, inventor, agriculturist, author, scientist, musician, and mathematician led to general recognition as one of the most gifted humans who ever lived. John F. Kennedy, while speaking at a White House dinner honoring a group of Nobel Prize winners in 1962, would declare, "This is the most extraordinary collection of talent and of human knowledge that has ever been gathered together at the White House for dinner, with the possible exception of when Thomas Jefferson dined alone."

King George later succumbed to madness, shaking hands with bushes and conversing with clouds. But before the straight jacket was applied, the other entity lurking inside him reached an epiphany. The Head Honcho had finally found the Insurrectionist that had tormented him for years, so there was nothing further to be gained by remaining inside a despot who was plummeting into dementia. He had journeyed backward to this era to prevent the American Revolution and secure subsequent centuries in America as safe havens for power mongers like himself. Having failed in this mission, his only hope to secure a safe haven was to return to the 20th Century, where he could invoke the Insurrection Act and arrest Jefferson for treason against the United States.

Thomas Paine, whose passionate writings stoked the American Revolution, returned to England to ignite a similar fire there. Unfortunately, the English government ordered his writings banned and him arrested. He escaped to France before he could be captured, but the British tried him in absentia. He was found guilty of sedition for advocating the abolition of the monarchy in his book "The Rights of Man". The government fanned anti-Paine fervor, burning his effigy and heaping vituperative on him. He would later write, "It's extraordinary that a book written by an individual unconnected with any sect or political party could completely frighten a whole government, which proves that either the book has irresistible powers, or the government has major defects, or both."

Paine continued to attack power and superstition throughout his life. The religious establishment in England excoriated him after he published "Age of Reason", a scathing attack on organized religion. For the egregious act of thinking freely and rationally, he was branded a "loathsome reptile, a demi-human archbeast, an object of disgust, and of absolute abhorrence." Just as the Jews chose Barrabas over Christ, Satan would have been more highly regarded than Paine.

Failing to incite insurrection in Britain, Paine returned to New York. He died there in 1809 in anonymity, having been absent from the American political scene for too many years. He was remembered more for his strident heresies against organized religion than for his powerful revolutionary prose that catalyzed the American Revolution. Thus, the man who wrote "Common Sense", which sold an astounding 500,000 copies in 1776, which was translated into nearly every language on earth, and which was one of the most politically influential works ever penned, died a forgotten pauper. Lucifer surely appreciated the perverse irony.

Those few who remembered him fondly, such as Thomas Jefferson, convinced the State of New York to grant him a parcel of land in New Rochelle, in gratitude for his contribution to the American cause. Paine's physical remains were laid to rest there in a sparsely attended ceremony. Robert Ingersoll later observed, "Paine's crime was to deny the authority of bibles and creeds, and for this the world shut the door in his face, and emptied its slops upon him from the windows."

Ten years later, William Cobbett, an English political journalist who admired Paine's fiery works, journeyed to New York to exhume his remains and bring them to England for a funeral worthy of his great contributions to the causes of political liberty and freedom of thought. Unfortunately, in a bizarre and unexplained episode while crossing the Atlantic, Paine's skeleton was lost at sea. Cobbett, rebutting religious critics who severely criticized his attempt to transport the remains, said, "The hypocrites were in alarm, lest the bones of Paine somehow injure the cause of religion".

Before death, Paine had written, "O ye that love mankind and dare oppose the tyrant, stand forth! Every spot of the Old World is overrun with oppression. Receive the fugitive, and prepare in time an asylum for mankind". The sea had received the fugitive's body, but could the ocean depths lasso the spirit of a man who fervently believed that "in order to be free, it is sufficient for a man to simply will it"? As Dubois put it, "There is no force greater than that of a man determined to rise. The human soul cannot be permanently chained."

Another wayward spirit wandered eternity seeking relief from a timeless struggle. Cassandra, tortured by Mankind's incessant disbelief of her prophecies, used clever trickery to circumvent the curse imposed on her by Apollo three millennia ago. In a desperate attempt to nurture the tenuous freedom budding on earth, she manifested herself as a wizened old man on that torrid July day in 1776 in the Philadelphia State House. It was she that turned the tide of the revolutionary debate with her legendary exhortation to the delegates of the Continental Congress to sign the Declaration of Independence, in spite of the fearsome shadow of the King's gallows. Two thousand years earlier, it was she who exhorted Marcus Brutus to plunge his dagger into Julius Caesar. And two hundred years hence, she was carefully nurturing in a man named Freeman a growing awareness of his own rebellious spirit, which was eerily similar to Thomas Paine's wayward spirit. After all, history is always and everywhere, along with the men and women who lived it passionately.

Chapter Twelve: "The Man Who Died Twice"

> "There is nothing so powerful as an idea whose time has come."
>
> —Victor Hugo

The Head Honcho returned to the 20th Century amid prodigious puffs of smoke and kaleidoscopic lights that were metaphors for the sideshow magic of his political career. An unidentified visitor in his office greeted him with a gruff cough inside a billowing cloud of smoke pouring out of the 18th Century. The Honcho, disoriented from traveling across centuries in just milliseconds, had no interest in dealing with the unwelcome intruder. "Hit the fucking road!" he shouted into the murky smoke bank. "I'm in no mood for socializing. I don't even crave sex."

"Why should I hit the road?" asked the visitor from deep inside the smoke. "It's never harmed me. Now, if you asked me to strike the Mock Turtle, that would be very different altogether. Except, of course, the Mock Turtle hasn't done anything to me either, and also makes very good soup. Tomato soup, that is, in case you...."

"Oh God, it's you", moaned the Honcho, recognizing the Mad Hatter's nasally voice.

"That's very flattering", replied the Hatter graciously, emerging from the smoke. "But the Safari Golfer is God on your side of the looking glass. I'm just a humble hatter with a clever knack for madness, which helps make sense out of your world. Where've you been, you big galoot?"

The Honcho knew it was futile to ignore the reality of the imaginary cretin tormenting him. "I was in the 18th century, inside King George III."

The Hatter recoiled. "You didn't have sex with his wife, did you? Fornicating with a toad would be more erotic, if she's anything like the Red Queen."

"I didn't screw her!" lied the Honcho, who couldn't shake the hideous detail of the Queen's manatee-like body. "What do you want from me?"

"Halibuts can fly", said the Hatter matter-of-factly.

The Honcho stared in abject confusion at the pot-bellied hallucination who had discovered another way to torture him with convoluted words that were not only mad, they didn't make sense, either. "Why did you say that?"

"Why wouldn't I? Are you saying halibuts can't fly?"

"Not at all!" said the Honcho, who as a politician was afraid to take a position on the issue. "It's just an absurd thing to say!"

"Perhaps it is", teased the Hatter. "On the other hand, there you sit, a fat slobbering leech with your teeth sunk into the jugular of humanity. I think that's absurd!"

"I don't slobber!" bellowed the Honcho, as drool oozed inadvertently from his corpulent lips.

"Of course you don't", the Hatter empathized insincerely.

He subtly slid a pewter ashtray under the Honcho's slimy chin. "It's a good thing I showed up here."

"Why?" shot back the Senator nervously.

"They're out to get you."

"Who's they?" The Honcho suddenly realized that the Hatter had appeared for the first time without him being inebriated. He grabbed a bottle of Old Bushmills from his liquor cabinet.

"They is everybody. Have you forgotten the catastrophes you're mired in? There's the F.U.N. fiasco in Vhaicam, which now has a population of sixteen billion, give or take a few zeros. Your printing presses can't produce enough bogus money to support them. The non-war you started there has killed everyone between the ages of 15 and 46 who hasn't fled. CREEPS botched the Honchogate cover-up, so you're being hounded for subverting the American electoral process. The media hasn't forgotten your drunken attempt to blow up the planet at the Bavarian Forest. A special prosecutor investigating the hundreds of people killed by the Juggernaut will soon arrest you for manslaughter. And the supermarket tabloids published lurid pictures of you and Buxomus."

The Honcho drooled some more. "Can I see them?"

"You idiot! Your world is collapsing, and yet you persist with your puerile perversions!"

"You obviously haven't seen Buxomus with her clothes off."

"No, but I've had many unpleasant opportunities to look into your naked soul through the bottom of an Old Bushmills", the Hatter retorted. "If I were you, I'd spend more time worrying about the Insurrectionist than lusting after mindless bimbos."

The Honcho glared defiantly. "I'm not worried about the Insurrectionist! I'm going to personally escort that sonofabitch to the gallows."

The Hatter looked at the Honcho as if seeing him for the first time. "My, my, such bold words", he muttered. "But wouldn't an execution be more likely if you actually knew who the Insurrectionist was?"

The Honcho leaned toward the mirage he normally shrank away from. "I know who the Insurrectionist is", he whispered conspiratorially.

The Hatter raised an eyebrow. "What did I miss?"

"The key to the whole puzzle! The Insurrectionist is my Insurrection Czar. He's the same Thomas Jefferson who revolted against King George. They're identical in every detail. If Jefferson was an insurrectionist in the 18th century, then surely he's one in the 20th century, just like I'm a tyrant in every period of history I manifest myself in. My case against him is ironclad!"

"You're a lunatic!" the Hatter squealed between convulsions of laughter. "What jury will allow you to invoke evidence and witnesses from the 18th century?"

"I'll invite the Safari Golfer to be the jury. He'll listen to me."

The Hatter strummed his fingers. "This isn't so far-fetched after all. Can I be the judge?"

"Why not?" said the Honcho magnanimously. "I'm going to be the prosecutor."

"How very grand! I never trusted this Jefferson fellow. He was always much too honest."

"That doesn't make any sense", the Honcho chided.

"Which is precisely why you want me as the judge for Jefferson's trial. If things were allowed to make sense, you'd be the one on trial."

"I suppose I should be grateful", said the Honcho pensively. "Shall I appoint my Italian golfing buddy, Sammy Giancarlo, to be the Bailiff?"

"Grand idea! I would have expected nothing less", said the Mad Hatter. "Unless, of course, you came up with a worse idea, in which case I wouldn't have expected anything more."

"What the fuck does that mean?"

"Whatever you want it to. As an Ismism devotee, you should know that. Logic, truth, and facts will just cause everyone to start making sense. Then you'll have a disaster on your hands." The Hatter paused momentarily and then said nervously, "I hope there aren't any facts in this case. If there are, I'll have to disqualify myself as judge."

"Actually, there is one fact", the Honcho confessed.

The Hatter tapped his slender fingers on the Honcho's desk. "What might that be?"

"Thomas Jefferson is guilty as hell."

"That's not a fact. The rules of American jurisprudence compel us to presume that the defendant is innocent until we discover he can't afford as many lawyers as we can. On the other hand, as a congressman, you have access to all the money in the country, so perhaps Jefferson's guilt is already a fact. But, let's not jump to hasty conclusions, because I expect this trial to be great fun. When will you arrest the guilty sonofabitch?"

"Today!" shouted the Honcho. "I don't want to waste another goddamn minute."

The Hatter fell out of his chair. "You shocked the bejesus out of me!", he snapped as he pulled his frail body up from the floor. "I've never heard a U.S. Senator say he didn't want to waste another minute before."

"It happens all the time when we're voting to raise taxes."

"Perhaps so", acknowledged the Hatter. "What's your pretext for arresting Jefferson?"

"I'll have Pope Safari Golfer wrangle a confession out of him."

An expression of terror swallowed the Hatter's face. "Is there no limit to your cruelty? It's one thing to extract a confession with the brutal means of mortal men like the Russian

KGB, the American CIA, and the National Inquirer. But using the threat of eternal damnation in a hell beyond description as a cudgel to force a confession out of a sinning infidel is cruelty elevated to the sublime. I thought your goal was to kill Jefferson, not to amputate his humanity with the blunt-edged scalpel of your mysticism while he's still alive."

"Don't be so squeamish. As Lenin said, 'the purpose of terrorism is to terrorize'. We'll borrow the Catholic ritual of confession as a terrorist tactic to enforce conformance to Ismism's dogma. Jefferson must be cudgeled into confessing because the U.S. Government is too damned important."

"Important to whom?" asked the Hatter, who used to automatically be the maddest person in any conversation.

"To me!" snarled the Senator. His fleshy jaw was locked and his beady eyes blazed with passion. With that, the Hatter retreated into the secret place inside the Honcho's mind reserved for imaginary characters, affirmative action quotas, and other demented neural fabrications.

Pope Safari Golfer lured Jefferson into confessing with a cryptic invitation to resume their debate about the existence of God. Jefferson, always eager to discuss topics of great import, bit the hook. The invitation directed him to the Catholic cathedral downtown.

Inside the imposing gothic structure, Jefferson scanned the cavernous dusk for his intellectual adversary. He guessed that the Golfer was in the center of a large screaming crowd. Some of the screamers were nubile teenage virgins wanting to join his harem in Rome. Others were afflicted souls seeking to be healed by the wondrous cleric. The rest were screaming simply because everybody else was, much like how many modern Americans formulate political opinions.

Jefferson wormed his way through the frothing crowd. He didn't find the wispy Golfer among them. Instead, he found a traditional Catholic confessional with three doors. The doors on the right and left were for repentant sinners to unburden their souls by confessing their transgressions to a manipulative mystic who likely needed just as much unburdening. Jefferson entered the door on the right, guessing that the Golfer was in the center booth that priests usually occupy. He was unaware of the sophisticated eavesdropping devices planted there by CIA agents.

In the feeble illumination of a small red light, Jefferson saw a padded kneeler intended for supplicating sinners. Refusing to demean himself by kneeling to a mystic, he squatted on his haunches and aligned his face with the portal to the priest's booth. He waited patiently for the promised debate with the founder of Ismism.

The small portal was pulled open from the other side. The Safari Golfer, whose delicate features were silhouetted by a dim aura of light, broke the silence. "I'm impressed, Jefferson. You're not afraid of this monument to emotional terrorism. Usually, people kneeling there are wracked with guilt and fear as they wait for a psychologically and philosophically unqualified mystic to tell them they are forgiven and have been spared eternal damnation for one more month, but only if they recite enough Hail Mary's and put enough money in the collection basket."

"Likewise, you impress me", replied Jefferson. "You recognize that this religious institution is a cruel charade. So why do you persist in propagating the cruel charade you call Ismism?"

The Golfer smiled, because Jefferson's riposte gave him an opportunity to leap directly into the real purpose of their encounter. "We all propagate charades. You, for instance, pretend to be the Insurrection Czar, whose mission is to capture the Insurrectionist. I believe, however, that the Insurrectionist is actually you." He cringed, fearing that his blunt accusation would cause Jefferson to angrily end the encounter without confessing anything.

"I am indeed the Insurrectionist", Jefferson declared without hesitation.

The Golfer was so flabbergasted by Jefferson's forthright admission that he wondered what kind of trap was being sprung on whom. "Do you also admit to committing all of the treasonous crimes that the media has associated with the Insurrectionist?"

"I performed those acts, but I don't admit to treason. I admit instead to undying passion for individual liberty and unyielding hatred for men who torture the human race with mystical constructions that inevitably become padlocks on our souls, ankle chains on our freedom, and liens on our hard-earned wealth."

"Noble sentiments indeed", mocked the Safari Golfer. "But events will soon prove they are nothing more than words. This world belongs to me, not to you. Ever since Man became intellectually aware, the mystics have held sway. He who controls the mythology rules the world. And he who rules the world propagates the mythology. You will never destroy the symbiosis between mysticism and power as long as people are unwilling to think with unconditioned independence. The best that you can hope for is to die spectacularly pursuing your hopeless cause, along with all the other quixotic visionaries."

"I dread that you're right, and passionately hope that you're wrong", said Jefferson. "I have committed my eternal soul to winning this battle. I have sworn upon all that is sacred to eradicate mysticism from the minds of men, to unlock the political chains that have bound him since time began. But this is all just talk. Arrest me, as you and the Head Honcho have conspired. Let the subsequent trial decide the fate of us all."

The Golfer stared in astonishment. "How did you know we were going to do that?"

"I've expected this encounter ever since I wrote the Declaration of Independence in 1776. No matter how perfect and potent that declaration was, it could never have served as the final victory in a struggle that has been waged continuously across untold millennia. Mankind had too much to learn then, and still does. But we are making progress, in fits and starts. Two centuries have gone by, so it is time to engage in the conflict once more. It's time to ignite the passions of revolution for another attempt at universal emancipation from those who believe that individual men are just pawns in a cosmic chess match orchestrated by the Mystical Priest and the Powerful King. I knew you were going to arrest me, simply because the time has come for it to happen."

Americans were astounded when news of Jefferson's arrest broke across the news services and the Internet. The Head Honcho's official statement identified him as the Insurrectionist and charged him with violation of the Insurrection Act, treason against America, terrorism, defamation of the state religion Ismism, hate crimes, and Political Incorrectness. The Honcho claimed substantial evidence had been amassed against the suspect, including a CIA-taped confession to the Safari Golfer.

The dizzying media hype preceding the trial exceeded that of the O.J. Simpson murder and even Clinton's impeachment for L'affaire Lewinsky, which was a tribute to the maturation of the general American intellect, since Jefferson hadn't killed his wife, seduced a young intern, castrated an estranged lover, or fallen in love with an underage lolita named Amy. This was a drama of compelling philosophical polarities, rather than the usual titillating drivel and comically inane pabulum of contemporary journalism.

After the media achieved orgasm with hyperbolic foreplay, the day of Jefferson's trial finally arrived. To avoid the crush of public attention and the inevitable swarm of paparazzi, the venue of the trial was moved from Washington to the Bavarian Forest. Here, the tight security measures that ensured the secrecy of the Brotherhood would prevent an invasion of fifth estate voyeurs. As a concession to his own egocentric need to record for posterity his adversary's ignominious defeat, the Honcho permitted one video camera to tape the trial.

Dressed in the Forest's ceremonial purple and gold toga, the Honcho felt invincible. He walked confidently into the makeshift courtroom that had been set up in a large chalet. Judge Mad Hatter sat behind the bench wearing an oversized black robe that exaggerated his emaciation and a black top hat with a dangling price tag. The Safari Golfer sat in the jury box with 11 empty chairs. Freeman was the only spectator in attendance, at the insistence of the Head Honcho, who suspected that his public relations liaison was a latent sympathizer of Jefferson. He wanted Freeman to see what happens to those who defy the almighty power of the federal government, as if Waco and Ruby Ridge weren't convincing enough.

Sammy Giancarlo entered the courtroom towing a handcuffed Thomas Jefferson, whom he positioned next to the Head Honcho in front of the Mad Hatter's bench. He solemnly pronounced, "The defendant is in court and the juror is present, your Honor." Nobody moved for several uncomfortable moments. They were all playing unfamiliar judicial roles and didn't know what to do next. Finally, the Safari Golfer broke the suffocating stillness. "Shouldn't the guilty sonofabitch have a lawyer?"

The Hatter hammered his gavel. "Whether or not to provide counsel for the defendant was decided before the question arose," he riddled with a laconic smile wrapped around his pallid face. "My decision is thus: One is too many, and two is not enough."

This proclamation was disarmingly simple, since only the numbers one and two were involved, but the indecipherable equation confused everyone nonetheless. "What the fuck does that mean?" the Honcho asked the wily judge.

Before the Hatter could declare the Honcho in contempt of his own court, Jefferson interjected an interpretation. "The Judge means that two, three, or even a hundred lawyers would be insufficient to properly defend me in a court where law has no objective validity. On the other hand, one lawyer would be too many, because having counsel at my disposal allows the remote risk that his predetermined guilty verdict would be upended. Therefore, one lawyer is too many, and two is not enough."

The Hatter angrily rapped his gavel again. "Off with his head!" he screamed to the stunned bailiff. "He's making sense!"

Sammy grabbed Jefferson by the arm to lead him to wherever heads were lopped off, but then the Hatter gleefully pulled a pencil-thin arm from behind his back and shouted, "I had my fingers crossed! Let the guilty sonofabitch keep his head for a while so he can flounder in agony like a fly that's been de-winged by a wicked child. The bailiff will now swear the jury."

"You're a sonofabitch", Sammy said to the Golfer, uncertainly.

"Excellent", beamed the Hatter. "Prosecutor, what is this convict guilty of?"

The Head Honcho, looking like Julius Caesar in his purple toga, ceremoniously unfurled a papyrus scroll. Caesar was spitefully confronting Cicero for the last time, just as King George was confronting the American rebels, just as the Head Honcho was confronting his Insurrectionist. A timeless gantlet was being tossed down. "Your honor, in this case of the People versus Thomas Jefferson, the defendant is hereby charged with violation of the Insurrection Act, treason against America, terrorism, defamation of the state religion Ismism, hate crimes, and Political Incorrectness. I offer as evidence People's Exhibit 'A', which is his taped confession to the Golfer, and People's Exhibit 'B', which is his signature on the Declaration of Independence."

The Mad Hatter whistled in amazement. "You should be ashamed of yourself, traitor. By the way, Mr. Prosecutor, you forgot one charge."

"What did I miss?"

"Foolishness. The sonofabitch believes that he can derail the Juggernaut and swallow the Leviathan. How do you plead?" the judge asked the defendant.

Jefferson smiled sardonically. "First, this isn't the People versus Thomas Jefferson. Acknowledge our confrontation for what it really is: the State versus Thomas Jefferson. And the State is nothing but you three parasites—the Mystic, the Power Monger, and the Irrational—allied into an insatiable Man-eating political machine whose only relationship to the People is that of the whale to plankton. Second, if I made a plea, it would merely validate the farce that is about to ensue. If a plea is procedurally necessary, make one on my behalf."

The Head Honcho salivated over this unexpected opportunity. "Let the record show that a plea of 'guilty' has been entered on the defendant's behalf."

The Mad Hatter turned to Jefferson. "Even though your plea is 'guilty', don't spoil our fun by giving up yet. We'd like you to put up a spirited defense, at least until teatime. Then we'll lop off your head. Will you call any witnesses? Not that it matters, you understand."

Jefferson stared through the demented judge as if the double-talking cretin was invisible. "I'll testify on my own behalf." He pulled away from Sammy Giancarlo and ascended the witness stand.

Holding out the "Book of Liberal Policies, Marxist Economics, and Other Occult Phenomena", the Hatter said with a seditious grin, "Raise your right hand and put your left hand on the bible of Ismism. Do you swear to tell lies and half-truths, and nothing but lies and half-truths?"

Jefferson ignored the Hatter's instructions and swatted the book of mysticism onto the floor. He spat out words drenched with passion. "Reality is the only bible I will swear on, and reason is the only means I will use to interpret it. To do anything less would invalidate my mind and negate the purpose of existence."

The Hatter frothed at the mouth and banged his gavel repeatedly, as if trying to squelch Jefferson's insolent words with the sharp blows. "This is hearsay, not testimony! "You're in contempt of my court!".

"Objection!", interrupted Jefferson. "I'm not in contempt of your court. I'm in contempt of you. I'm in contempt of anyone who purveys madness and irrationality. It gives root to mysticism, which grows like mental crabgrass to suffocate objective thought, paving the way for tyrants to seize the day. Irrationality breeds mysticism, and mysticism begets power. And then power nurtures both."

The Mad Hatter suddenly slumped into a dead faint from an apoplectic seizure. Having dispensed with this irritation, Jefferson faced the Head Honcho squarely to begin his defense. "You call me a traitor? What system of morality have I betrayed? Whom have I offended? Whom have I oppressed or killed? What on earth am I a traitor to?"

Without waiting for a response, he continued. "This trial will show that the first object of my heart is America, in which I have invested my life, my fortune, and my eternal spirit. I fathered this nation. I risked my life to nurture it, and my soul has watched over it through the decades as it flourished and then began to whither. I have never betrayed my precious creation. I've walked every step of the way with every true American. I was always there to transfuse love of liberty into them during some of history's darkest moments.

"I was there inside every American's heart when Adolf Hitler and his Axis minions, who had conquered more land and people than Napoleon, Ghenghis Khan, and Julius Caesar, were sinking the planet into a totalitarian abyss. The world cowered in the shadow of a tyrant whose vision of life was silent printing presses, concentration camps, burning churches, and falling bombs. No bigger struggle was ever recorded than World War II, and no other nation than America could have conquered the pure evil of it.

"I wept the same frightened tears that mothers and wives wept on June 6th, 1944, when Eisenhower sent a half million courageous American men onto D-Day beaches code named Omaha, Utah, Sword, Gold, and Juno in history's largest invasion. Humanity held its breath that day, knowing the enormous consequences of the roiling conflict on those sandy strips of French soil turned into churning valleys of death. The sole hope of the planet rested on the Americans.

"The American-led triumph of freedom over totalitarianism was foreshadowed decades earlier by shot-putter Martin Sheridan, who was the flag-bearer for the American contingent in the London Olympics. It was customary for foreigners to dip their flags in deference to the host country's ruler. But, when Sheridan passed the King of England in the stadium, he held the American flag even higher and snarled, "This flag dips to no earthly king!" This same defiant ritual was repeated by the American contingent when Hitler hosted the Berlin Olympics. This proud American defiance would later be all that stood between the Europeans and concentration camps.

"I stood with the exhausted workers on the Detroit assembly lines, as history's most productive peacetime economy was converted into the Arsenal of Democracy to rescue the free world during World War II. While the bloodiest battles were waged with mortal vigor in Europe and Asia, a subtle yet more telling battle was waged by the irrepressible might of American capitalism in our factories. Rosie the Riveter was as much a hero as General Patton. Every morning, she left her children at home, overcame the gripping fear in her heart for the unknown fate of her husband on a distant battlefield, and put her back into building the planes and tanks that would eventually destroy the Axis powers. Ford Motor's Willow Run plant produced one B-24 Liberator every hour. While the dark thunderclouds of dictatorship threatened to extinguish the light of liberty across the planet, it was the lights burning late into the night in American factories that ultimately drove the satanic darkness of government run amok back into hell where it belongs.

"This wasn't the only time America saved the world from its cancerous governments and isms. American troops tipped the balance in the World War I episode of the eternal conflict between liberty and totalitarianism. In one battle, the advancing Germans forced the French troops out of strategic Belleau Wood. The recently arrived U.S. 2nd Division was ordered to plug this dangerous gap. As the battle continued, a French colonel advised the Americans to retreat from another German thrust. Marine Colonel Wendell Neville replied with words that defined the unconquerable American spirit, 'Retreat hell! We just got here!' This brave stand earned them the nickname 'Devil Dogs' and turned the tide in a war that had been a stalemated bottomless pit of casualties.

"When Paris was later liberated by the Allies, American troops were showered with flowers and wild kisses by French citizens in a celebration held on the 4th of July. Aware of this irony, General Pershing, the head of the American Expeditionary Forces reviewing the parades on a balcony of the Crillon Hotel, declared, 'Lafayette, we are here!', in homage to the French general who helped America win its own independence 150 years earlier. As I stood with Pershing on that balcony, I wept tears of gratitude for every GI who ever fell into a grave to free the rest of us from mankind's self-inflicted political monsters.

"I was there in Lake Placid when our hockey team defeated the Russian juggernaut in the most emotional athletic event ever witnessed. Though it was simply a contest of sport against our cold war nemesis, the struggle waged on the ice that day was a metaphor for decades of ideological confrontation between the two superpowers. Broadcaster Al Michaels screamed 'Do you believe in miracles?' at the end of the match, as America deliriously celebrated the stunning upset.

"During the next decade, Ronald Reagan stared down the Russian Bear by building up a military, strategic, and technological superiority. The resolve of America to maintain its inviolate capability to defend against the aggression of the Soviet Empire shattered the paper tiger facade of communism. Unable to match the fabulous power of capitalism to produce and innovate, and the power of individual liberty to inspire an unconquerable spirit, the USSR collapsed under the strain.

"When I stood at the Brandenburg Gate as the Berlin Wall and the Iron Curtain came tumbling down, I silently answered the prophetic question asked in Lake Placid a decade before. 'Yes, I do believe in miracles', I replied across the eternal continuum of time. I rejoiced as giddy East Germans and West Germans intermingled while dismantling the Wall, having suddenly escaped from the onerous shadow of humanity's greatest monument to slavery. 'Yes, I do believe in miracles', I repeated tearfully, never more aware than in that emotional moment of the incredible miracles that the American vision of individual liberty had inspired since July 4th, 1776.

"I walked alongside Abraham Lincoln as he steered the nation through a gut-wrenching Civil War. He not only held the union together, he brought completeness to the vision of American liberty. Eradicating the scourge of slavery removed the glaring contradiction of our revolution and affirmed my initial draft of the Declaration of Independence. The Great Emancipator reminded us, with his immortal Gettysburg Address, that we all are created equal and that all men are free. As I stared with Lincoln out over the desolate Gettysburg battlefield, where passionate men had fallen in defense of that sacred covenant, I shook with tormented agony at the bloodshed needed to make evident the simplest truth of the human condition. All men indeed are born free, not only from each other, but from myths and governments.

"I stood shoulder to shoulder with Thomas Edison, Alexander Graham Bell, Henry Ford, Andrew Carnegie, John Rockefeller, Bill Gates, and all of the other titans of American enterprise and inventiveness who had the daring and ambition to lead mankind through the Industrial and Information revolutions. These giants bequeathed to future generations an unrivaled economic engine of contagious wealth creation that fostered a magnificent new phenomenon called the middle class.

"These giants stood on a foundation of individual liberty, private property, and free markets. In just two centuries, this country rocketed from a sparsely populated subsistence economy to nearly 300 million citizens drawn from all corners of the globe, enjoying an economic miracle dwarfing all other attempts at general prosperity. Not only did we dazzle the world with unprecedented material abundance, we demonstrated the sheer joy of living. American music, television, movies, and other creative expressions of our unfettered intellect wowed the world with a kaleidoscopic cultural display.

"By the mid-20th Century, our magnificent productivity and creativity sculpted a world that was essentially an American one. But unlike other empires, this American hegemony was not manifested by forced occupation of foreign territories. Instead, it was manifested by the sheer power of a vision whose time had come, by a determined people exemplifying the power of individual liberty and the potential of life freed from oppressive governments. We didn't send soldiers as the pillaging vanguard of American domination. Rather, we sent abroad an example of human felicity derived from freedom, with Radio Free Europe and the Voice of America as our ideological beacons piercing the desolate skies of totalitarianism.

"In view of all this, I stand here with unequivocal pride at what my philosophical precepts engendered on those hot July days in the old Philadelphia State House back in 1776. America was no longer just an ideal etched on the Declaration of Independence, it was a magnificent reality that rendered the empires of Greece, Rome, and Britain small, profane, and spiritless by comparison.

"Then there was that magic moment in 1969 when Neil Armstrong, an American from Wapakoneta, stepped noiselessly onto the dusty soil of another celestial body, giving life to the most enduring fantasy of our species. We flew through the cosmos and etched our American autograph for all time across the heavens. I watched this epic drama unfold on live television, as another product of our incomparable technology settled on the Moon's surface with only 20 seconds of fuel left, after a desperate, daring, and therefore consummately American search for a clear place to land.

"I'll never forget the surge of pride and relief coursing through my arteries as Armstrong's voice crackled across a quarter million miles of space, declaring to eternity, 'Houston, Tranquillity Base here. The Eagle has landed.' Yes, the American Eagle had landed. Then the hatch to the lunar module opened. Armstrong stepped down the ladder and fulfilled an impossible dream by planting his foot onto the moon. 'One small step for man, one giant leap for Mankind', were his timeless words, generously including everyone else in this American triumph.

"Armstrong planted the American flag into the Moon's virgin soil, not as an act of conquest, but as a statement of supreme purpose and genius that fittingly reached across 200 years and 250,000 miles into the restless spirits of those who had the courage and the vision to father the American nation. My own spirit soared higher than those intrepid astronauts. Tears streamed down my cheeks and strangers around me hugged each other out of the sheer joy of being an American. For a special moment in time, we were starkly aware of the staggering greatness humans were capable of.

"I trembled at the awesomeness of a seemingly impossible Earthrise glowing blue-green against the dark silhouetted rim of the moon. It wasn't just the awesomeness of our technology, our spirit, and our daring that moved me, it was the awesomeness of what this nation has meant to the world for two centuries. If America had never existed, what would the world be like today? My mind quickly abandons the despairing proposition

"A thousand years from now, people will look back on this achievement as the finest of our species. We matured from worshipping gods to being gods, from staring in wonder at lightning to creating our own magnificent lightning strike across the heavens. No longer bound by terrestrial limitations or by the ball and chain of our primitive mythologies, we achieved a fundamental spatial and spiritual liberation. The Egyptians created the Great Pyramids. The Chinese created the Great Wall. The Romans created their great networks of roads. But with this adventure to the moon, we Americans created something more enduring and magnificent than all the other world wonders combined.

"Since the moon exists in an airless void, Armstrong's footprints will remain undisturbed for a long, long time. It would be unforgivable if evidence of American greatness on the moon outlasted evidence here on Earth. This impending irony conjures despondence out of joy. Our dream is now crumbling around us as we descend into the hellhole of government run amok. Our greatness is evaporating into ignominy. Bill Clinton is replacing Abraham Lincoln as the epitome of our national character."

Jefferson spun to face the Head Honcho. Tears of passion ran down his cheeks. "Treason, when real, merits the highest punishment", he growled. "But most governments do not distinguish between acts against the government, and acts against the oppressions of the government. The latter are virtues, yet have furnished more victims to the executioner than the former. The unsuccessful strugglers against tyranny have been the chief martyrs of treason laws in all countries.

"Am I the Insurrectionist? Yes I am!" he snarled with unrepentant pride. "Have I refused to pay taxes? Yes I have! Have I evaded the draft and stopped voting? Yes I have! Have I published condemnations of the bureaucratic leeches in Washington that suck out our lifeblood? Yes I have! Have I exposed corruption at every level of government? Yes I have! Have I unearthed the decadent sham of our democracy by uncovering scandals like Watergate? Yes I have! Have I rallied against the needless deaths of my fellow countrymen in spurious wars? Yes I have! Have I armed myself and my compatriots to defend us from the enemy within? Yes I have! Have I planted the seeds of revolution against a government that is now more abusive than the one we revolted against two hundred years ago?" He paused, knowing full well that these were the final words of confession that his accusers wanted to hear. "Yes I have!"

"I am the Insurrectionist, and overthrowing this government is my mission. But I'm not a traitor. How can I be guilty of treason against the nation I founded with my Declaration of American Independence? That document was our philosophical foundation, our compact with limited government of the people, by the people, and for the people. As its author, I'm the spiritual father of this nation. If there is to be judgment today, it should be rendered by me, not you.

"America isn't a physical location. It's a state of mind, a philosophical attitude, a vision. The vision is being abandoned now, not because it lacked validity or because it failed to produce spectacular results, but simply because it was attempted in an intellectual environment where irrationalists, mystics, and power-mongers still reigned. You hold power in a physical place traditionally called America, but I am the American. I'm not a traitor to the concept of America. I'm simply your enemy."

The Mad Hatter recovered from his fainting spell. His grogginess wore off just when Jefferson confessed his conspiracy to revolt against the government holding power over the American people. He banged his gavel and half-heartedly declared, "The convict has admitted his guilt. Off with his head. This trial is over."

"This trial is not over!" shouted Jefferson to the astonished judge. "It hasn't begun yet! If this is to be a trial about the crime of treason, then we ought to turn the spotlight of judgment on the real traitors in this courtroom. Laws should protect life and property, yet this trial is being administered by cutthroats whose actions violate the lives and possessions of every citizen. This court cannot judge me to be a criminal, because this court itself is criminal. No government so defiant of individual rights and private property can have any recourse to the concept of justice. This government can't offer any meaningful distinction between a shoplifter and a tax protester, so how can it possibly distinguish a traitor from a liberator? The real traitors are those who have formed an unholy alliance of mysticism, insanity, and power in a corrupt government that tramples the individual rights it was created to protect. I will name these traitors and specify their crimes against America.

"The first traitor is you", he accused the Mad Hatter. "You're a traitor to the ideal of reason. Your madness and illogic encourage mankind's misguided submission to those who have no rational justification for putting chains around their necks. No truth can ever be extracted from what you say except by taking its opposite. You ignore facts and logic, so therefore you ignore reality. When your insanity prevails, people sacrifice their only real resource, their thinking minds. Without reason, we must entrust our lives to priests or governors, who mysteriously know things we mysteriously cannot. We are free to think or to evade that effort. But we are not free to escape the fact that reason is our means of survival. The question 'to be or not to be' is the question 'to think or not to think'. The unrestrained torrent of irrational killing in our world underscores this."

Jefferson boldly pointed at the Safari Golfer lounging in the jury box. "You too are a traitor against America and against mankind. When people stopped thinking, you plied your treasonous subterfuge of the American ideal. While all hands were below deck mending sails, splicing ropes, and minding their own business, you ran our ship into an enemy port like a rogue pilot. You took advantage of our intellectual weakness facilitated by the Mad Hatter's insanity and replaced our rational thoughts with mystical opiates. Out of nothingness you conjure gods and religions to which we become inexplicably chained.

"You deal out enchantment incomprehensible to the thinking mind. You are deified, because in your foggy conceptions, people find an impenetrable darkness inside which they fabricate untruths as delirious as yours. Your mystical mantras of the common good, political correctness, and amoral expediency became the secular religion Ismism, an absurd concoction of abominable will o' the wisps. Priests have always constructed bridges of mysticism over the moat of reason, enabling our enemies to slip across and put abusive kings and evil tyrants into our midst with our confused blessing.

"He who controls the mythology rules the world, and evil mythology purveyors have torpedoed our great country. Contrary to conspiracists, the world isn't ruled by the CIA, the Skull and Bones Society, the Council on Foreign Relations, the Tri-Lateral Commission, or the Bavarian Illuminati. It is ruled by people who have stolen our minds through mysticism, leaving us at the mercy of imperious men over whom we have no powers of punishment or removal.

"Mysticism, whether secular or divine, is the worst thing to ever happen to humanity. It is the root of all organized evil. The plows of the world turn over corpses every day that were fodder for man's myths and religions. You are a traitor for having violated the dearest and most fundamental of our constitutional protections, the separation of church and state. The religion you propagated is a secular one, yet it has infiltrated our state as completely as Catholicism infiltrated the monarchies of the Holy Roman Empire or as Islam infected the despots in the Middle East. Mysticism is unnatural and anti-human, killing millions of men, women, and children as it spread around our globe, leaving those remaining alive to muddle onward either as fools or as hypocrites.

"Once man surrenders reason to mysticism, he has no guard against monstrous absurdities. Like a rudderless ship, he's the sport of every wind. Faith takes the helm from the hand of reason, and the mind becomes a wreck. Faith is volitional ignorance, putting everything into the hands of politicians and priests. Faith keeps the intellects of foolish humans chained. He who believes nothing is closer to the truth than he who believes what is wrong through faith. Faith torments us with fables of which we have no evidence.

"Witch doctors, magicians, and priests of primitive societies wielded tremendous power. Early man sought to understand the mysteries of the universe, and it was our eternal misfortune that the priest stepped forward before the scientist to explain. Rational inquiry has ever since been beaten into conformity with faith and dogma. We naturally sought knowledge and mastery; what we got in return was mysticism and bondage. Priests were the original traitors to mankind, just as you are a traitor to America.

"As history unfolded, the palace grew out of the temple. Pharaoh was a divine monarch, a military and civil protagonist for the priest. Mankind's slavery to himself arose through this transformation. It is but a small step from slavery to a theocratic state to slavery to the secular 'common good' or 'species being'. Man as slave to god-kings evolved into man as slave to amorphous collections of other humans. Mythical views on the cosmos evolved into mythical views on social organization, leaving us with Mao, Castro, Stalin, Hitler, Lenin, and Johnson, all purveyors of social mysticisms that differed only in semantic particulars. They all force-fed us spurious values and half-truths that transcended all others, and then coercively or violently suppressed any contrary inclinations by rebellious heretics. Many of history's worst tragedies resulted from mass psychosis fed by worship of irrational, mystical, and therefore deranged isms.

"Ignorance begets faith, faith begets priests, priests beget kings, and kings beget chains. This is the food chain of power, of which you, the Safari Golfer, are an integral link. You throw pixie dust into our eyes, so we stumble blindly into the unfathomable abyss of dreams, phantasms, and gods. Your treason translates ignorance into bondage, using faith and mysticism to enslave the unthinking masses to the king and tyrant. When people fall prey to mysticism, they become powerless, because their intelligence is abdicated to a spurious authority lurking behind an ism. You are the reincarnation of Pope Innocent, who annulled the Magna Carta on behalf of King John and the barons at Runnymede. Your only fear is that people will rediscover that reason is the sole oracle of substance in the universe, and that it doesn't matter if charlatans profess there is one god, twenty gods, or no god.

"Your mysticism laid the foundation for the power of the Royal Tyrant, whom I will now accuse of being the most traitorous criminal of all." Jefferson stood eye-to-eye with the Head Honcho, who was bathed in nervous sweat. The pro forma lynching of the Insurrectionist had turned unexpectedly into an intellectual joust that confused and frightened him. No one ever had the courage to stare directly into his soul through his eyes except, he suddenly recalled, Marcus Brutus, just prior to plunging the dagger into the carcass of Julius Caesar.

Jefferson silently pierced the armor shrouding the Honcho's essential being. He hated the Senator. He hated everything the man and his ilk had ever stood for throughout history. He harnessed this consummate hatred to launch a moral assassination. "No man can chain his fellow man without eventually finding the other end looped around his own neck. Man wasn't born in bondage to anyone or anything here or in the heavens. He is an end in himself, and not the means to the end of society. We are each a sovereign universe, acting interdependently with other sovereign universes. But you have made your universe more sovereign than all others, and for that you are a traitor to everyone else.

"You are the most vile and despicable traitor America ever had because you stole our right to life and liberty. Each finite moment of life is infinitely precious. Our allotted specks of evaporating time are by nature insufficient to achieve all the joy and fulfillment we each yearn for. To claim any of these finite moments by force from another human is the ultimate moral abomination.

"You're a traitor because you've sown the seeds for the destruction of the greatest nation on earth. America is plummeting from a shining example of all that is magnificent about the human race to a tawdry example of all that is reprehensible. We have now gone completely through the classic cycle of every major civilization. We have moved through the typical phases of bondage, spiritual awakening, courage, action, liberty, abundance, selfishness, complacency, apathy, inaction, and now back to bondage.

"We have become a lazy nation of squabblers and shabby proclaimers of entitlement, when we were once a proud nation driven to accomplish. Our moral foundation has evaporated into mindless confrontation between single-issue special interest groups. Your band of traitors in Washington have herded us into a demoralizing debate about how to manufacture excuses and split up dwindling national resources, rather than fueling the engines of productive ambition. You've drawn us into a political quagmire, where all power and wealth are becoming concentrated in the federal government, and we are all becoming enslaved to it. We now pay more taxes than we spend on housing, food, and clothing combined. We are now either recipients of federal largesse or we are the victims from which the wealth behind the largesse is confiscated. You lurk within that unimaginably huge machinery of extortion and detrimental reliance, insidiously bankrupting the nation and crushing our spiritual backbone.

"You're a traitor because you've turned us into a nation of thieves. Our civic life has become a zero sums game, in which some piece of the pie must be stolen from someone else, in order for the game to properly proceed. To enforce some rights, other rights must be sacrificed, because you have obliterated the meaning of rights. For some people to gain wealth, it must be stolen through taxation from someone else, because you have forgotten the importance of production. Your government is consuming our wealth, in perverse spite of its reason for being, which was to safeguard our property, and ultimately, our lives. All we have left is to finish riveting the chains on each other's necks.

"You're a traitor because you've created a world where personal responsibility no longer matters. Your governmental intrusions have relieved citizens of the necessity for making choices, and therefore of the need to develop a rational set of values. The demanding environment of freedom has been sacrificed for the comfortable yet debilitating environment of entitlement and subjugation to a bureaucracy run amok. When you guarantee a man income through welfare, health through socialized medicine, a job through affirmative action, and markets protected from foreign competition, what need does he have for values? He can exist without them. Do you wonder then why he is hedonistic and apathetic? His choices don't consider the rigors of survival, for which he is no longer responsible. The expectation of paternal care from the government has undermined our national character. We will never return to a values-oriented society until individuals are held responsible for their own existence, and reason, ability, and productivity are honored. Meanwhile, disenfranchised urban youths, wallowing in your destructive moral view, will learn that there is no difference between a transfer of wealth through the welfare state and a transfer of wealth by robbing people directly, because there isn't.

"If one can claim the right to his own life, and then behave as if no one else has a similar right, it creates an atmosphere where all rights are arbitrary and therefore illusory. We either all have a right to our lives and property, or none of us do. Everyone squawks about rights, but they forget that people do not have an enforceable claim on others for anything more than being left alone.

"You're a traitor because you've turned our democratic process into a corrupt sham riddled with abuse and devoid of representation for the people. You trade our rights for votes, putting political expediency on an exalted pedestal and the voters in a constitutional dungeon. You're a whore for special interest groups, taking their filthy money in exchange for unwarranted access to the plundered riches and coercive might of the federal bureaucracy. You siphon money from the public till, you take kickbacks from power brokers, you put your cronies on the public payroll, you bribe potential enemies, and you lie incessantly to everyone while employing hirelings who do nothing but lie to you. You sacrifice your allegiance to what is right to the devil worship of party politics.

"You dine and travel in opulence, and then pay for your ostentatious hedonism with funds taxed from a struggling farmer in Nebraska. Despite your drunken and drugged escapades, you insult us by outlawing alcohol, drugs, and other presumed vices that adults indulge in of their own volition and consequence. You engage in sexual escapades so obscene that lurid accounts in the daily papers are turning them into pulp periodicals of sleazy voyeurism. You then have the audacity to censor our television and radio, setting yourself up as a laughably hypocritical judge of our morals and leaving us with nothing but the illusion of choice.

"You abuse your incumbency by diverting the nation's resources to get perpetually re-elected. You barter in Congress with your fellow traitors, supporting each other's pork laden bills, thereby casting our wealth down the yawing funnel of the frivolous and the spurious. You tax Peter to buy Paul's vote. When this doesn't ensure your re-election, you desecrate our constitution by perpetrating scandals like Watergate. As your power grows, fewer and fewer citizens vote out of revulsion for your contamination. As Mark Twain observed, the only inherently criminal class in America is Congress.

"Every government on earth has some germ of corruption and degeneracy, which cunning will discover and wickedness openly cultivate. For every roach you see, there are ten you don't, which illustrates one of the pervasive fallacies of big government. If the justification for big government is that individuals are flawed, then who in this big government will restrain and guide these individuals? More flawed individuals? Who will guard the guardians? The FBI or the CIA, who are as likely to kill us as to protect us? If man can't be trusted with governing himself, can he then be trusted with governing others? Or have we found angels in the form of senators and bureaucrats? Let history answer that question.

"You're a traitor because you're a purveyor of death. You are the worst mass murderer in the annals of crime. You sent 50,000 American youths to die in Vietnam, where they were ripped open by grenade fragments, charred by chemical defoliants, and devoured by maggots and buzzards. You subsidize the tobacco industry, which is the leading cause of death in America. You subsidize abortion, killing ten million defenseless babies, surmising life doesn't begin at conception just as Hitler surmised Jews aren't human beings. You test exotic weapons on military veterans, the indigent, and the insane, using these unsuspecting social captives as human guinea pigs. Your bans on drugs, guns, and sex created an organized crime tidal wave and a general breakdown in civil obedience, resulting in hundreds of corpses and thousands of victims every day. Your national health insurance is simply a means for the government to ration medical care and become the arbiter of who lives and who dies, creating another way to selectively kill us, under the guise of 'efficiency' and 'the greatest good for the greatest number'. You forced workers to contribute to social security their entire lives, and then blithely informed them the system will be insolvent when they retire. You finance organizations of terror like the CIA, unleashing cutthroats that assassinate our leaders and murder our dissidents. Your welfare state created a terrorist breeding ground of abdicated personal responsibility, giving birth to a generation of alienated and morally adrift hooligans who pillage our inner cities.

"You are as vile and morally contemptible as Hitler for cremating six million Jews, Stalin for starving 16 million peasants, and the British for decimating the population of Ireland. A grave is always your answer to the right to life question. Your genocidal ambition has filled cemeteries and garbage cans with millions of fetid corpses. And if you don't directly kill us, you confiscate nearly one half of our life's energy through taxation. You have the perverse hypocrisy to kiss babies, smile for campaign posters, and shake the hands of your next victims, while you continually contravene the only legitimate purpose of government, which is to protect life, from the first stirrings in the womb to the final groans on the deathbed.

"You're a traitor for trying to disarm us, because our weapons are all that stand between you and the totalitarianism you lust for. General Washington told us 'Firearms stand next in importance to the Constitution itself. They are the American people's liberty, teeth, and keystone under independence. From the hour the pilgrims landed to the present day, the rifle and pistol have proven equally indispensable to ensure peace, security, and happiness. The very atmosphere of firearms anywhere and everywhere restrains evil influence. When firearms go, all goes. We need them every hour. They deserve a place of honor with all that's good.' Washington understood that the 2nd Amendment is to you as a silver bullet is to a vampire. Without it, the Beast is unstoppable.

"Two hundred years ago, my colleague Daniel Webster warned that Congress, with its power to tax, would clutch the purse with one hand and wave the sword with the other. An elective despotism isn't the government we fought for, but it has descended upon us anyway, proving Webster correct. We banished the tyrant King George, but 500 despots in Congress rose in his stead, making us 500 times worse off. You criminals in Congress have declared war on mankind with injustice and slaughter. The time has come for mankind to declare war on you. Your treason has led us to this unavoidable crisis. We can continue as we are and die as a nation, or we can hoist the banner of revolution and save ourselves and our dream.

"Throughout history, the magician, the priest, the emperor, the king, and the politician have held our devotion and allegiance. Yet as the succession of wars, slaughter, and slavery have proven, none of these objects of devotion have emancipated us. The magician led us to madness, the priest disillusioned us, the emperor stole our wealth, the king led us into deadly war, and the politician made an ostentatious and useless beast of himself.

"Humankind has seen nothing but a succession of masters and institutions shackling it. Rousseau knew of your pervasive treason when he wrote, 'Man is born free, yet is everywhere in chains'. The time has come for us to escape from this desolate predicament and eradicate you and your ilk from the planet. It is time to burst our chains!

"You, not I, should be punished for treason. You put the chains on our ankles and sucked the lifeblood out of our veins, taking advantage of minds weakened by the Mad Hatter's irrationality and the Safari Golfer's faith. But, you won't be tried in this courtroom, because I am the accused. However, rather than grovel at your feet pleading my innocence and trying vainly to save myself, I will instead plea for all those who can still call themselves Americans to rise up and destroy the abusive travesty that the federal government has become. Like the old Indian Chief, who didn't go to war over every petty injury, but rather put a straw for each injury into his pouch, we have been patiently filling the pouch of American liberty with oppressions by our government. The pouch is now full, so we should be sending up smoke signals with ominous and unmistakable intent.

"Our government is tumbling off the precipice of politically correct fascism. The seeds for our ruin are sprouting very deep and very broad roots. We must be as aware of this dire threat as was Aesop's Swallow, who foresaw the hemp seeds being planted by the farmer as the harbinger of the cords and nets that would ensnare all the birds. We must destroy these seeds of evil now!

"After we destroy your criminal government, what shall we put in its place? I'll offer you a vision. It starts with the right to life, which is the foundation of all rights and all morality. There is nothing more precious than life, and nothing that can be so completely and uniquely possessed by each person. All else is derived from this sacred right.

"The purpose of life is to achieve happiness, which means to experience the joy of existence. Any other motive for living is destructive, because unhappiness is the only alternative. Happiness requires values as a foundation for the actions and choices that will lead to fulfillment. Nobody, not even God or Caesar, can determine these values for us, and nobody else can make the thousands upon thousands of choices consistent with our values to enable our happiness. If we aren't free to choose our values and to act consistently with them to achieve happiness, then we are essentially dead, even if we still have a pulse. Individual liberty is therefore a pre-requisite for happiness and a direct extension of the right to life.

"All men have the right to their own lives, not just a privileged few. The right to life is an all or nothing proposition for humanity. No man is born into this world as chattel of another man or of a social entity. We possess individual desires and ambitions, which are supreme in each of our own universes. If some men are allowed to forcibly violate other men's right to life, then all such rights will become untenable as society devolves into anarchic chaos or totalitarian lock down.

"The right to earn and keep private property is the only guarantee of a man's right to his own life, and it is founded in our natural right to what we acquire through our efforts, without violating the similar rights of other sensible beings. If a man doesn't own the fruit of his productive effort, then he doesn't own his life, because his ability to sustain it is owned and controlled by someone else, rendering the rest of his rights meaningless. Each man's physical and intellectual effort belongs to him alone. If he doesn't have the sole right to that which his life brings into being, then he is a slave in every sense of the word and is merely chattel to be bargained away in grand political initiatives to transfer wealth from those that produce to those that don't. Thus, the only moral justification for creating governments among men is to protect property and life, with property understood as that which life produces. If property rights are not protected, then life is not protected, and the social compact will disintegrate as bands of thieves pirate what other people produce. The glaring contradiction of our history is that the governments which should have been protecting us have been instead the greatest threats to our lives and the most audacious thieves of our productive efforts.

"Since individual liberty is a corollary of the right to life, voluntarism must be the fundamental mode of social and economic interaction. Anything else implies forcible coercion by some men over others, which is slavery and which violates the right to life. Every transaction and interaction among men must be voluntary, based on mutual consent and mutual benefit.

"A market system with free exchange of labor, capital, and goods is the only moral economic structure consistent with everyone's fundamental right to life. It's the only mechanism that guarantees societal ambitions will be subordinated to individual rights. It's the only system in which men can consensually trade their labor for other things of value. It's the only system in which accumulated capital can be made available consensually for others to use, in return for a profit. It's the only system in which the products of our efforts can be exchanged for other valuables with mutual consent. Thus, it's the only system in which men can cooperate on an enormous scale, while retaining their individual sovereignty. That it's also the most efficient way to organize economically is merely a serendipitous coincidence. The true beauty of the market system is not its magnificent productivity, but rather its moral requirement that all interactions and transactions be voluntary. Free men require free markets. Any other system for economic activity is, by definition, a form of slavery. It's as simple and inescapable as that.

"The sole justification for government is to protect life, civil liberty, and the property, equal or unequal, which results to every man from his own industry, or that of his fathers. Rights enforcement, property laws, police, and national defense are therefore legitimate functions of the state.

"The way to have good and safe government is not to create one centralized behemoth, but to divide it among many smaller local governments, distributing to each exactly the functions it is competent to execute. This puts each citizen closer to more of the governmental apparatus than if all things are directed from Washington, enabling them to oversee their appointed officials more effectively. If scoundrels make their way into government, they will be more easily detected, more readily eradicated, and less likely to surreptitiously accumulate irreversible power.

"Any attempt by politicians and judges to enact laws which violate the right to life and property is cause for their removal, first by procedural means, and if those fail, then by violence justified as self defense by citizens. Any step a government takes beyond its charter of protecting life and property must inherently be destructive of either life or property, even if good intentions are professed, and the ultimate result will be slavery, terror, and bloodshed.

"In summation, the moral compact of society is based on each man's right to his own life, and to that property which his life brings into existence. Governments are instituted solely to protect these rights. When governments abuse these rights, it is our birthright to revolt. We have a fundamental right to defend ourselves against our government. Without the 2nd Amendment, all of our other rights are superfluous. As Patrick Henry admonished, 'Suspect everyone who approaches the jewel of public liberty. Unfortunately, nothing will preserve it but downright force. Whenever you give up that force, you are ruined. The great object is that every man be armed.' We must retain the right to bear arms to protect ourselves from tyrannical government when society and law are unequal to the task. Our greatest security is to be found in organizing for defense with our brothers and neighbors in local militias.

"Does this vision have a name? Naming a philosophy is dangerous, because men are quick to suffocate the principles with dogma and suspend their worship of reason for worship of canons. When men look at their philosophies with sanctimonious reverence, faith gradually supersedes reason under their sleepy watch, until the dogma looks nothing like the original doctrine and enslaves them with something unrecognizable and horrible. This is how America ended up with politically correct Ismism, which means nothing and everything at the same time simply because we allow it to, having lost the ability to make proper judgments with reason as our guide.

"America religiously worshipped its founding isms, and then forgot the principles they were built on. These foundations have crumbled, but our dulled minds continue to worship capitalism, federalism, and republicanism, even though we don't understand their moral and philosophical precepts. We are enslaved by ignorant faith in them, because we have abdicated our responsibility to think.

"We don't need another ism put forth by me. We simply need common sense, which is a commitment to thinking. Thinking will yield more enlightenment in one day than any dogma or ism can in a lifetime. Our lives aren't meant to be subsumed into grandiose social movements, urged along by terminology and syllogisms beyond our ken. The time has come to abandon our isms, for they are the chains on our ankles and the nooses around our necks. Rousseau wondered why man is born free, but is everywhere in chains. It's because we surrendered reason in favor of faith, which is the first link in the chain of enslavement to kings and priests.

"We shouldn't worship our past, our Constitution, or even the Declaration I wrote, merely for their tradition. They served us well, but they are simply manifestations of the much larger human greatness of common sense, the catalytic engine for evaluating reality in a manner that is proper for individuals to grow and prosper. Never let the worship of common sense degenerate into an ism, with dogma, faith, and ritual. Simply recognize that the minds of individual men are sacred, that they must be utilized constantly, and that they must remain free and independent. All rational constructions of society will then be continuously regenerated.

"We should have revered common sense all along. Ironically, Thomas Paine used the title 'Common Sense' for his dramatic writings that fueled the intellectual and emotional fire of the original American Revolution. So, if you must name my philosophy, follow Paine's inspiration and call it Common Sense, or call it nothing it all. In our brief lives on this planet, the goal isn't to choose one ideology or faith over another, but to resist all such calls and to instead rationally exercise our individual minds to stand firm against all who oppose life, liberty, and the laws that protect both. We must pursue ideas because they are common sense to us, not because our priest or our king has decreed them. If we chain ourselves to an ideology, we will eventually discover that a man like the Head Honcho is holding the other end of that chain. Like Rousseau, we will be left with nothing but to wonder why.

"Terrible times are ahead. Happiness depends on freedom, and freedom demands courage. Your ancestors handed you a free country, and now you must fight to regain it. But you won't be alone in this struggle. Great people have given their lives in this battle already. They aren't known just by inscriptions on their graves; the whole earth and all of time are their memorials. History is always and everywhere, along with the men and women who lived it passionately. They will abide in your hearts and souls, if you let them. Their bodies may be buried in long-forgotten sepulchers, but their ideas live in eternal rage. Drawing from the vision and courage of those whose passion still rages among us, I believe, as Victor Hugo did, that there is nothing so powerful as an idea whose time has come. The time for the Second American Revolution has arrived.

"The spirit of 1776 isn't dead, it has only been slumbering. Americans are naturally reverent of common sense. Unfortunately, they've been played upon by mystics who duped them with artful maneuvers into forging chains for themselves. But time and truth will unmask the mystics and remind us that the freedom to revolt is one liberty that no power on earth can eliminate. It's the one thing impossible for Congress to outlaw. It is our birthright.

"Human history didn't start with this criminal government as its cornerstone, and human history won't falter without it. True Americans preceded this obscene leviathan, and true Americans will succeed it. Perhaps some fear we're too weak to cope with so formidable an adversary. But when will we be stronger? When we're totally disarmed and have federal agents in every home? People armed in the holy cause of liberty are invincible by any foe. To become a soldier in this battle, we need only to buy a gun, stop paying taxes to the federal government, and if violence becomes necessary, exercise care to injure only the culpable and not the innocent.

"You will find my closing declaration familiar. This modernized version is as appropriate today as when I wrote the original two centuries ago:

"A new Declaration of Independence by Patriots of the United States of America.

> "When, in the course of human events, it becomes necessary for a people to dissolve the political bands which have connected them with their government, a decent respect to mankind's opinions requires them to declare the causes compelling them to revolt.
>
> "We hold these truths to be self-evident: that all men are created equal; that they have inalienable rights to life, property, and the freedom to pursue happiness; and to secure these rights, governments are instituted among men, deriving their powers only from the consent of the governed; that whenever government becomes destructive of these ends, it is the right of the people to alter or to abolish it, and to institute new government in a manner likely to effect their safety and happiness. When a long train of governmental abuses and corruption occurs, it is their right and their

duty to revolt and to provide new guards for their future security. Such has been the patient suffering of American citizens. The history of the present federal government is one of repeated injuries and oppression, all with the intent of establishing absolute control over Americans.

"Therefore, we the people of the United States of America, acting according to the precepts of common sense, solemnly and publicly declare that we are rightfully free; that we are absolved from all allegiance to the current federal government; and that all political connections between ourselves and this corrupt government are rightfully and totally dissolved.

"In compliance with this Declaration, we hereby solemnly vow to boycott all elections and referendums put forth by this criminal government, to suspend all financial contributions to its treasury, and to reserve for ourselves the right to use violence in self defense from the armed agents of this now outlawed government. In support of this, we mutually pledge to each other our lives, our fortunes, and our sacred honor.

"Are you finished?", asked the Honcho sardonically. It seemed un-American to him that guilty sonsofbitches were permitted to say anything at all.

"He was finished before the trial even started", said the Hatter.

"You're absolutely right!" said the Honcho excitedly. "He confessed to being the Insurrectionist! He even threatened to overthrow my government right in front of us!"

"Well then", said the Hatter. "There's nothing left to do but finish going through the motions. Ladies and gentlemen of the jury . . . "

"Yo, Hatter", interrupted the Golfer. "There's just me here. Get on with the lynching party."

"My mistake. Supreme mystical leader of the universe, please consider all the testimony presented to you, and render your verdict according to the dictates of Ismism. And do hurry—it's tea time."

The Safari Golfer arose, strode purposefully to the bench, and handed his verdict to the Mad Hatter. "I filled it out before the trial, your honor."

The Hatter read the verdict silently. A cynical grin spread like contagion across his pallid face. "The verdict is 'guilty'", he beamed. "Does the defendant have anything to say on his behalf?"

"You should have paused before you perpetrated this act of suicide on yourselves, and of treason against the world", said Jefferson in a measured voice.

The Head Honcho laughed. "Give it up! Nobody was listening to your hopeless call for revolution."

"One man with courage makes a majority, to borrow the words of Andrew Jackson."

"Dead men have no courage. You are about to be executed for treason."

"I know my fate. However, I'm not alone in this room."

The Honcho looked around in confusion. Jefferson couldn't have been referring to the Golfer, the Hatter, or him. That left only Freeman, which seemed preposterous. Freeman had been his trusted public relations liaison ever since he could remember being suspicious of him. He was apathetic and lethargic and therefore an ideal aide. "You've lost your mind, Jefferson. Freeman is a political and moral eunuch devoid of courage and conviction. And he has that ridiculous ball and chain strapped to his ankle."

The Mad Hatter pounded his gavel. "Enough drivel! Does the defendant have any last words before sentencing?"

"Yes!" snapped Jefferson. "The first attempt to establish liberty has failed, and so may a second and a third. But as younger and wiser generations mature, common sense will become more and more intuitive, and a fourth, a fifth, or some subsequent attempt at complete emancipation will ultimately succeed. However, we must be prepared for rivers of blood to flow and years of desolation to pass over us. Yet, the object is worth this specter of Armageddon, for what more valuable inheritance can man leave to his posterity?

"I am utterly convinced that I shall look down some day on man's glorious attainment of liberty. As Albert Camus said, 'Great ideas come into the world as gently as doves. If we listen attentively, we shall hear, amid the uproar of empires and nations, a faint flutter of wings, the gentle stirring of life and hope. Some will say that this hope lies in a nation; others, in a man. I believe, rather, that it is awakened, revived, nourished by millions of solitary individuals whose deeds every day negate the crudest implications of history.'"

The Mad Hatter banged his gavel again. "How appallingly naïve. Off with his head!"

The Honcho was suddenly distracted by something profoundly evil wafting eerily in the dark void behind the Hatter. It was an iridescent demon with a greenish aura and two red piercing eyes like those of an enraged cat on a dark night. The Honcho shivered involuntarily. He was chilled to the core of his being. No matter how much death he was responsible for, no matter how habitual killing had become, today's impending murder was the most brutal and primal. His darkened heart still had enough humanity for him to know that when the bells tolled for Jefferson, they would toll not just for a man, but for mankind. Unfortunately, his soul was too dark to care. When the iridescent demon evaporated, the shell of pure evil suffocating the Honcho's barren soul thickened. A calendar hanging on the wall behind the departed apparition showed the date as 'July 4'. The irony didn't register with him.

Freeman also saw the iridescent green demon. He suspected that Lucifer was here to renew the lien on his soul, which left him confused rather than afraid. He felt as if Jefferson had been speaking directly to him today, delivering something powerful and essential that was looking for a place to lodge. Unfortunately, he wasn't yet ready for such a potent spiritual transfusion. He wrestled with this spiritual turmoil while the Head Honcho stared blankly at the calendar on the wall. The Mad Hatter banged his gavel angrily, shattering their introspective reveries. "This trial is boring as hell. Bailiff, take the prisoner to the Lopping Chamber!"

Dutifully, Sammy Giancarlo handcuffed Jefferson and pulled the doomed man toward a door, half believing that a Lopping Chamber actually existed on the other side. Jefferson looked beaten and exhausted. Freeman's heart plummeted to his toes. He felt utterly adrift. Suddenly, Jefferson whirled away from the bailiff's grasp and lunged toward Freeman. His eyes were lachrymose, yet more passionate and intimate than ever. Sympathetic tears welled in Freeman's eyes. He arose, placed a consoling hand on Jefferson's shoulder, and whispered through clenched teeth, "I'll kill that bastard for doing this to you!"

A melancholy smile slipped from Jefferson. "Do not do so on my account. I have ridden out countless storms on the boisterous ocean of political passion. This is the last storm I will weather, and that consoles me. I've looked to this day with the longing of a wave-worn mariner, who finally has land in view after counting the days and years of separation from it. My only regret is that I will be going away fearing that the sacrifice of the generation of 1776 to acquire individual liberty is being squandered by their unwise and unworthy descendants."

Freeman was shocked by the condemned man's courage. "Aren't you afraid of dying?"

"Death isn't as complete as we mortals fear", Jefferson said cryptically. "These cutthroats can execute me, but they can't kill me. They can lock me up and throw away the key, but I will still be everywhere. I am eternal, because the ideas of passionate people penetrate every barrier, including the vale of death. As Franklin Roosevelt said, 'No man and no force can abolish memory. No man and no force can put thought in a concentration camp forever. No man and no force can take from the world the ideas that embody man's eternal fight against tyranny.' I have done for my country, and for all mankind, all that I could do. I cherished the opportunity to lead the battle for liberty. I sincerely believe that I've left the world better than I found it. Now, I resign my soul to the deeper completeness of eternity. Look upon my life and my ideas as inspiration. My body may be buried and eaten by worms, but my infectious spirit will live on. Let my ideas and my inspiration make you think and be moved."

"I've been moved, but I fear I'm too weak to do anything about it", said Freeman.

"My good friend, do you realize that you left your ball and chain behind when you arose to face me?"

Freeman jerked his head downward. Amazingly, he had slipped the encumbrance that had been his constant companion. But, rather than feeling exhilaration, he felt overwhelmingly naked. Liberation was an alien, intimidating sensation. He wasn't quite ready for the magnificent disequilibrium of freedom that spiritual growth requires, so he perversely yearned to once again wear his ball and chain. Shamed, he retrieved the wayward contraption and tried to clasp it on his ankle. To his chagrin, it didn't fit. He wrestled with it, jiggled it, and cursed it, but he couldn't reattach it. Finally, summoning all of his strength, he forced his ankle back into its clutches. He was numbly secure in captivity once again.

Jefferson smiled at his friend's foolishness. "You tasted a moment of freedom, during which your ankle almost outgrew its shackles. Your soul shall soon experience the same effect. You just need a quest."

"A quest?" mumbled Freeman uncomprehendingly.

"The biggest tragedy of life is having no purpose. You need a quest, like that of Don Quixote. Remember his anthem?

> 'To dream the impossible dream
> to fight the unbeatable foe
> To bear with unbearable sorrow
> to run where the brave dare not go
> To right the unrightable wrong
> to love pure and chaste from afar
> To try when your arms are too weary
> to reach the unreachable star.'

"Reach for the unreachable star of America. The last hope of human liberty lies with those who will rise to my challenge. There's no other quest so important and so urgent. The Wolf is in our midst, devouring us silently and completely. Our situation is mortally dire, and for so dear a stake, you should stand ready to sacrifice everything. Your ancestors made this sacrifice in 1776, and fate offers you the same opportunity. As I depart this time and place, my sincerest wish is that the seeds of revolution I have planted and cultivated will now sprout and bear magnificent fruit. My heart tells me that we have never been riper for a complete emancipation of the human spirit, for shedding our bondage to baseless tradition, groundless myths, and political connivers.

"Grab the torch of liberty from my hands! Carry it aloft for the world as an eternal beacon, as a perpetual call to arms, as an insignia of the Second American Revolution! The Statue of Liberty in New York Harbor is such a beacon, but it is made of inanimate bronze. The torch that America needs now must be a living torch, the torch of a leader, a thinking and breathing spark for this final epic battle against the priests, kings, and politicians.

"I'm leaving now, but the ideal of America will never disappear, because it's as eternal as man himself. If we can cleanse our government now, this nation will grow and prosper until we become an association of people that is powerful and wise and happy beyond what has yet been imagined by men. We can become a rising nation again, spreading across a wide and fruitful land, traversing all the seas with the rich production of our industry, advancing rapidly to accomplishments beyond the reach of our mortal eyes. We can give birth again to Fords, Edisons, and Lincolns. We can be like gods once more."

"Americans don't want those gods anymore", interjected the Safari Golfer. "They're content worshipping me and my philosophy of Ismism."

"They're also content worshipping me and my totalitarianism", interjected the Head Honcho.

"You're all mad!" declared the Mad Hatter with studied finality. "Americans simply want to worship the illogic underlying your mysticism and your totalitarianism. Today's moral and political morass makes sense, in a mad sort of way. Your side of the looking glass and my side have merged into one. So, let's finish this before Alice falls down the rabbit hole and becomes ten feet tall again. Bailiff, take the prisoner to the Lopping Chamber. The Executioner will make him one head shorter."

Suddenly, Jefferson screamed a primal cry that seemed to surround the earth and echo against the walls of eternity. An enormous explosion rocked the makeshift courtroom. Smoke and dust choked the air. The Mad Hatter, the Safari Golfer, and the Head Honcho were thrown helter skelter by the mysterious detonation. Sammy Giancarlo, the bailiff, was killed instantly, his vital organs crushed by the concussive shock wave that originated from where Jefferson had been standing.

When Freeman recovered from paralysis of fear and surprise, he groped his way through the thinning smoke to where Jefferson had been. To his dismay, there was nothing left except his handcuffs, which lay broken on the floor, constraining nothing but smoky air.

He laughed, softly at first, then loudly and boldly. He laughed, because he had finally grasped Jefferson's unconquerable greatness. He laughed at the foolish men who thought it was possible to destroy a spirit that dwarfed the enormity of their insignificance. He laughed, because it was suddenly clear to him that Jefferson was what every American should be—rational, free, confident, determined, curious, and happy. But most of all, he laughed at the reprehensible stupidity of himself and the human race, which in stark contrast to Jefferson's greatness, seemed monumentally ridiculous and . . . purely mad!

Chapter Thirteen: "The Man Who Lived"

> "Nothing that was worthy in the past departs;
> no truth or goodness realized by man ever dies,
> or can die."
>
> —Thomas Carlyle

Hours later, Freeman succumbed to a much different madness that erupts when a soul admits self-deceit and failure. He was ashamed of himself and his life. He was emotionally crushed by the abrupt departure of Jefferson, who had become not only an intellectual and moral inspiration, but also, he realized now, like a father to him. He wandered aimlessly down Constitution Avenue in the darkness, disillusioned and brutally disoriented. His mind was caught in a bizarre loop, replaying like a broken record the words to a Thomas More poem read at his father's funeral years ago:

> *The harp that once thru Tara's halls*
> *the soul of music shed*
> *Now hangs as mute on Tara's walls*
> *as if that soul were fled.*

The melancholy poem drew him even deeper into alienated disassociation. He plodded forward, one forlorn step after another, with no purpose or direction. He started to hallucinate. The streetlights became kaleidoscopes rampaging through his brain in spectacular chromatic arrangements. Neon advertisements animated into grotesque contortions. Sexy models became gargoyles. Tranquil scenery became terrifying scapes of death and apocalyptic destruction. The streets coiled like snakes, threatening to strike at him. Buildings melted like liquid and transformed into bizarre jellyfish-like objects. Existence became a disconnected series of psychotic imagery.

Freeman stumbled into the dark, abandoned Senatorial Office Building. He sunk deeper into paranoia, as if living out a Hitchcock film, locked in a psychological closet with his worst fears. He was more terrified than Orwell's Winston, who had a cage full of gnawing rats strapped to his face. He was more frightened than the Poe character who was sealed up in a basement brick by brick, screaming in the black suffocating silence. He was tortured with the worst terror imaginable—purposelessness.

Staggering down the hallway in a mental fog, he opened the door to the Head Honcho's office suite. He recoiled in horror. Instead of desks and computers, he saw a Roman coliseum filled with rabid spectators urging two slave gladiators to hack each other's limbs off with gory swords. Julius Caesar stood regally above the carnage, rendering a thumbs up verdict on the slaughter. Blood streamed from his mouth like Dracula after a midnight repast.

Petrified, Freeman slammed the door shut. He groped his way down the hallway and opened the next door. His heart cramped in terror once more. Inside the room were giant incinerators belching black smoke and grey ash into an angry sky already heavy with ominous storm clouds. A little man with a comic mustache was screaming dogma at legions of saluting people in rapt attention. They were being fomented into socialized hysteria by an unspeakable evil, chaining their souls to Hitler's deranged mind. As flecks of ash, which were all that remained of their Jewish brethren, settled gently onto the heads and shoulders of the morally bankrupt crowd like a November snowfall, Freeman vomited, his spiritual disgust now a physical ailment.

He crawled to the next office. Deathly afraid but apocalyptically curious, he opened the door. Inside, Lyndon Johnson was pontificating about his humanitarian vision of the Great Society. Behind him, a movie screen projected images of the escalating war in Vietnam, in which the children of his Great Society were being killed and maimed. As the horrific tragedy of warfare scrolled across the screen, Johnson's flowery vision was overdubbed as a macabre and slightly disconnected narration. The gory video silently contradicted his words professing love for kids and compassion for humanity. In truth, he was nothing but a cynical, dishonest politician with blood of children on his hands, the very ones he promised to rescue with his War on Poverty.

Freeman crawled dutifully to the next suite, drawn by something profoundly evil yet irresistible. When he opened the door, a brilliant path winding off into a sinister darkness dazzled him. It was the Road of Good Intentions, inlaid with mesmerizing ruby nodules. In the middle of the Road were nine Sublime Court justices shredding the U.S. Constitution. Freshly polished ruby nodules radiated through the confetti of the tattered constitution piled at their feet, including one tantalizing ruby Good Intention labeled "Roe versus Wade". Freeman tried to slam this door shut, but a heap of slaughtered human fetuses blocked it. His stomach retched horrifically.

As his diaphragm spasmodically purged poisons that were really the metaphysical waste of his soul, he hypnotically crawled down this hallway of horrors and opened the next door. Inside was a scene that clawed open his chest and ripped out his heart. The Head Honcho was standing triumphantly with a bloody dagger in his powerful left hand. His luminescent green face with piercing red eyes had a scowl of raw hatred more potent than anyone could sanely comprehend. Thomas Jefferson lay mortally wounded at the feet of the devil-headed senator. His mutilated body had been slashed countless times by the totalitarian beast towering over him.

Enraged, Freeman plunged headlong into his own hallucination and slid across a pool of blood into Jefferson's body. But, he was too late to save his fallen friend. Jefferson was dead, leaving Freeman with nothing but clammy blood smeared on his hands. Repulsed, he frantically wiped them on his clothes, but the stains were indelible. He crawled back into the hallway on his belly, hoping desperately to escape the illusions that were digesting his brain.

Unfortunately, his mind disgorged another tormenting mirage. A gentle whisper wafted lightly like wispy smoke about his ears. Amid the din of his mental confusion, he heard a woman's lilting soprano. Her enchanting voice bore intriguing words he had heard before, but hadn't comprehended. "These doors are the gates to hell. . . . These doors are the gates to hell. . . . ", the voice repeated over and over. This time, he understood the meaning of Cassandra's words.

Freeman's agonizing hallucination transformed the hallway into a funeral scene. Jefferson's corpse sat on a catafalque in the great hall of the Capitol Building. His mahogany coffin was draped in black broadcloth, with four massive silver handles protruding in stark contrast. An ashen throng of patriots shuffled by to mourn the death of America's progenitor.

The coffin was carried down the Capitol steps by impassive Marine pallbearers and placed on a gilded horse-drawn hearse draped in the Stars and Stripes. The funeral procession headed toward the Jefferson Memorial for his burial. Only creaking carriage wheels and the clop-clopping of horses broke the silence. Empty black boots were perched backward in the stirrups of one riderless animal, as a symbol that Jefferson would never ride again.

A fife and drum corps beat a heavy, dirge-like cadence for the procession, as if trying to replace the nation's silenced heartbeat. Thousands of mourners filled every roof, window, doorway, and sidewalk along the route. The distant bells of St. Matthew's Cathedral began tolling. Plaintive, soul-wrenching peals rolled across the countryside, answered only by rhythmic hoof clops and drumbeats.

The mausoleum inside the Jefferson Memorial had been prepared for his second interment. The epitaph from his first passing read, "Here lies buried Thomas Jefferson, author of the Declaration of American Independence, of the Statute of Virginia for religious freedom, and father of the University of Virginia—Born April 2nd, 1743, died July 4th, 1826". Freshly appended words read, "I wish to be remembered as The Man Who Died Twice. My first death was a physical passing, a fate which all mortals encounter. My second death was a spiritual assassination by a country I fathered and dedicated my life to nurturing. America's soul now lies buried with me in this mausoleum, because my spiritual murder was also an act of national suicide."

Freeman moved slowly through his own hallucination to the mausoleum. Standing on his toes, reaching against the pull of his ball and chain, he touched the epitaph chiseled into the course stone. He fingered the letters forlornly, absorbing their cold finality. When he got to the word 'suicide', he lost his strength and collapsed. Barely conscious, he heard his departed father singing the melancholy Irish air "Eileen Aruin":

> *Who will console thee now,*
> *Sean of the Gael?*

Who lived in hope with thou
Sean of the Gael?
What lips will smile so gay,
laughing their fears away?
Who now to lead the fray,
Sean of the Gael?

The song faded to black, only to be replaced by the sound of a lone, plaintive bugle. An unseen muse was playing Taps as if her soul had fingers, her heart had lips, and the very essence of Man was being exhaled from her lungs. It was a slow, deliberate, and infinitely rueful lament that made Sinatra's magnificent rendition in "From Here to Eternity" seem mundane by comparison. Each morbid tone from the bugle ripped another gash in Freeman's wounded heart. He lost consciousness as the final wrenching note bade farewell to his hero.

When he awoke, he was curled in the fetal position, shivering like a lost child in a cold, dark forest. Somewhere very near, wolves were howling at the moon. His shivering intensified. He was drowning in emotional pain from a scathing self-assessment. One of the most brutal lessons in life, he now understood, is learning who you are. Years of youthful exuberance are spent wondering and planning and becoming who you will become. Everything in you and in the world seems malleable and correctable and possible. Then a threshold is silently crossed, and the soft clay of your soul hardens into granite. Your limitless future becomes a limited, uncomfortable present. You are then confronted with the painful discovery that you aren't who you were supposed to become, in the youthful eye of your idealistic mind. Freeman, like America, had reached this stage in life. He felt irretrievably lost.

Suddenly, he remembered the gift that Cassandra had given him on a fateful morning long ago. He fished a rumpled leaf of vegetation out of his pocket. She had given him this laurel leaf for precisely this moment, when the torment of hopelessness overwhelmed him and he was desperate for release from the bondage of his own mind. Utterly despondent, he pushed the laurel into his mouth and chewed. It was acrid and distasteful, and he gagged instinctively. But then, every discomfort in his body euphorically disappeared. He felt a gossamer lightness, as though gravity ceased operating. He succumbed to that deliciously satisfying eye-closing urge that precedes restful sleep. He sank completely into the magic of the incubation, finding a strange universe within himself that not even hypnosis could penetrate. This strange universe was his soul. Somewhere in it was the purpose of his life.

From deep inside this dream within a dream, Freeman saw a ship passing majestically beneath the shadow of the Statue of Liberty. It was the Albert Gallatin, carrying Irish immigrants into New York Harbor. There was a boy on the ship's deck. Tears glistened in the boy's eyes from an inner fire stoked by the statue's symbolism. Freeman recognized the youth as Padraic, his ancestor whom he became one with in 19th century Ireland. He felt the fire burning in young Padraic's soul. He had an intense, desperate, jealous need to understand that fire, to harness it for himself. He wanted that passionate reason to go on living. He willed himself to find its source.

The unseen oracle facilitating Freeman's incubation complied with his will. The dream within a dream flashed backward in time thirty more days to Cork, where the Albert Gallatin had just slid away from the wharf. The powerful incubation allowed him to once again be Padraic Freeman. He stood at the railing of the Albert Gallatin and smiled for the first time in several years, his eyes glistening like the silvery sheen of the River Shannon. As Ireland slowly withdrew from his life, he calmly took stock of his assets. Despite the best efforts of all the King's troops and all the Bishop's priests to completely disenfranchise and alienate him, he was leaving Ireland with three things of inestimable value.

The first of his three treasures was the never to be forgotten memories of his family and of his life on the most beautiful and yet the most cruel place on earth. His young mind had encapsulated the images of his mother's tear-stained face, the carefree voices of Maggie and James, the smell of peat burning in the hearth, and the brilliant yellow whin blooming along the roads of Ballynacargy.

The second of his three treasures was the fire of rebellion that roared in his soul. The King and the Archbishop had dealt him staggering losses. Maggie and James were dead, Maeve was emotionally stolen from him, he was forcibly separated from his parents, he was exiled from his country, and as a final humiliation, his name was anglicized to Patrick. But, these injuries and injustices merely fueled his burgeoning zeal for rebellion. He was enroute to America, where rebellion against the tyranny of church and state was not only a possible dream, but already a reality. He saw in America mankind's first opportunity to throw off the chains of servitude to the strange class of humans who clutched at power over the rest. He didn't naively believe the stories of gold-paved streets in America. He did, however, believe that America offered something greater than gold, which was the freedom to live a life unfettered from the oppression of gods and kings.

The last of his three treasures, which he held gingerly in his palm, was acquired during his brief dash from the wharf back in Cork. This treasure was outlawed by the British, because it was symbolic of Irish solidarity and resistance. It was a simple thing, but possessing it was punishable by death. To Patrick, its value far outweighed the danger. Possessing it made him feel like a man with a reason for living. To an Irishman, the color green is synonymous with being Irish and being free, and in his hand he held the greenest green that Ireland could produce. He carefully unfolded his fingers to admire it. His heart pumped heavily as he absorbed its emerald beauty. He knew that if could preserve this treasure in his hand and the fire of rebellion burning in his soul, the world would be all right after all.

He smiled and closed his fingers around the shamrock that he had plucked by the wharf. He couldn't wait to get to America. There were canals to be dug, railroads to be laid, farmland to be tilled, iron and coal to be mined, and freedom to nurture. America was a new world for him and his progeny to shape.

John Freeman, silently occupying Patrick's body, experienced a magnificent epiphany. He discovered the meaning of his life, not in a Washington office or in a cathedral pew, but deep inside his own soul. The answer was so simple. Patrick, who had been shorn of everything dear except his own passion for life and freedom, was the fountainhead for Freeman's realization that he himself was the meaning of his life. His desires and dreams were all the reason he needed to exist and be happy. He didn't need myths and dogma and kings and priests. These were his enemies. They enslaved him, forced him to deny his self, anchored him down with oppressive dehumanization. He was infinitely tired of being chained to them. Hatred for them swarmed every ounce of his being. He not only wanted to rid himself of them, but also to rid the world. John Freeman vowed to avenge Padraic by discarding his Anglicized name and living henceforth as Sean. Sean of the Gael.

Freeman's dream within a dream ratcheted backward in time a few more days. Padraic was ascending the massive hill overlooking Ballynacargy. His heart beat faster, partly from the effort of climbing, but more so from his memory of the gathering that occurred on this hill just two weeks ago. During this Monster Meeting, one of a series sweeping the island, Padraic saw a fleeting glimpse of his dream. It stirred his soul like nothing else. A hero named Daniel O'Connell was nurturing the groundswell of revolution in Ireland.

Four hundred thousand Irishmen came to this hill a fortnight ago to hear the renowned orator O'Connell speak. The only bigger gathering in Europe's history happened on Ireland's sacred Tara Hill outside of Dublin. One million Gaels came from throughout the island to hear O'Connell declare that freedom from England's Church and Empire was a possible dream. The exhilaration was indescribable as O'Connell stood on the highest point of Tara, the ancestral seat of Irish sovereignty, roaring that independence was the rightful quest of the Celtic nation, boldly defying the red-coated British militia that was powerless to act against such enormous Irish solidarity.

Just as America had its immortal written Declaration of Independence from British rule, now Ireland had Daniel O'Connell standing on blessed Tara with a spoken declaration against British oppression. O'Connell on Tara Hill, with a million Irish gathered around! Ireland's greatest bards and poets couldn't have conjured a more compelling scene. Padraic's heart leapt at this vision, because the same O'Connell had stood on this hill he was climbing now in Ballynacargy, delivering the very same immortal words to four hundred thousand Irish.

Padraic was among the teeming throngs that day in Ballynacargy, sitting on his father's powerful shoulders, straining to glimpse his hero sounding the rallying cry for dissolving the treacherous subservience to Great Britain. O'Connell's ringing oratory renewed their hope that had been nearly extinguished by three centuries of imperial subjugation. Emaciated from starvation, ravaged with disease, chilled from nakedness, and terrorized by the agents of the King and the Archbishop, the Irish nonetheless surged up the hill with irrepressible fervor, hearing words that their hearts barely dared to imagine possible, from the man that was the Voice of Ireland.

Padraic would never forget how O'Connell, who as a boy in Cahirciveen gleefully watched American men o' war battle British warships off the Kerry headlands, spoke as though the souls of his kindred spirits in America had somehow merged with his. As boldly as John Paul Jones sailed into Belfast Bay in broad daylight to sink stunned British merchantmen, he declared with Jeffersonian eloquence:

> *"The time has come to break our manacles on the heads of our enemies, and to wrap around the necks of our oppressors the balls and chains that have entangled our legs. The atrocious British attempts to extinguish liberty make me young and vigorous again. Their occupation of our soil has made us weep tears of blood over fallen compatriots, over stolen property, over outlawed faith, over proscripted language, and over banned dress and culture.*
>
> *"What are we to do? Tamely surrender our land, our spirit, and our very lives? No! The centuries have recorded the Saxon and Protestant brutality, but our indomitable spirit has not been conquered. We must look to the West for the inspiration to ignite our fanaticism! The revolution shaking down the thunder across the sea is our answer. The Americans have removed the bushel shrouding freedom's light, and have shown the world that it is not only proper for man to rise up against his oppressors, but also that it is possible! The tempest that tore through America and ripped through France is now to be heard on our own shores. Through the darkening clouds engulfing our proud island we can hear the boom of distant thunder and discern the flashes of the coming lightning.*
>
> *"Let our enemies stand against us if they dare.*

Where is the coward who would not die for such a land as Ireland? Where is the slave so lowly that, suddenly discovering he can burst his chains, would choose to keep them manacled about his ankles and wrists? I am not that slave!"

"We might soon have the choice to live as slaves or to die as free men. If that choice comes, I declare that it will be my dead body they will trample, if that be the fate of Ireland. Daniel O'Connell will not live as a slave!!!"

Freeman's dream within a dream faded to black. Suddenly, a loud voice stunned him out of deep sleep into complete awareness. He was startled to realize that the voice echoing in the empty halls of the Senatorial Office Building was his. "I am not a slave!!!", he screamed. "Sean Freeman will not live as a slave!!!"

A shimmering dawn splashing through a hallway window cast an eerie glow around Freeman. The morning sun's scintillating rays were as fresh as a newborn child entering the world, sparkling with the infinite promise of all things great and wonderful. A particularly brilliant aura glowing around his clenched right hand piqued his curiosity. He slowly opened his fingers. The light from the rising sun radiated gloriously onto the petals of an emerald green shamrock. He somehow knew it was the shamrock Padraic had picked during his dash from the wharf in Cork 150 years ago, before boarding the Albert Gallatin for America.

Freeman felt something strange yet invigorating course through his veins. This alien energizing force was courage, but he didn't know it by that name. To him, it was the shamrock of Padraic Freeman, a symbol of rebellion against tyranny. It was the patriotic spirit of Thomas Paine, settling into Sean Freeman's soul after a tortured hiatus in purgatory. It was the wisdom and fortitude of Cicero, who championed liberty in the midst of Caesar's blood lust. It was the fiery eloquence of Daniel O'Connell, who transformed the spoken word into an engine of revolution. It was the sheer anger of Marcus Brutus, who loved humanity enough to kill a tyrant. Most of all, it was the life force of Thomas Jefferson, who was his hero.

Suddenly, Freeman also felt heroic. He loved the feeling, and, for the first time, he loved himself. His body shook with purposeful passion. He felt an indescribable lightness of spirit, a remarkable feeling of freedom and release, as if the deadweight of existence had magically been lifted from him. He laughed. He danced. He wanted to fly. He felt like a seed that had finally pierced the topsoil and erupted into a flowering expression of creation's limitless potential.

With a start, he realized why he felt so light and free. The ball and chain was no longer bound to his ankle. The metallic clasp had simply melted away. As he stared at the unattached contraption, he chuckled at his folly. He had dragged that horrible burden around for so long, and yet it was amazingly easy to finally shed. Thinking freely and abandoning myths and dogma was all it took to neuter the power that others held over him. Mischievously, he grabbed the ball and chain, walked over to a statue of the Head Honcho adorning the hallway, and wrapped the demeaning tool of bondage around its neck. This was his first act of the quest Jefferson bequeathed to him. He was ready to take the torch of liberty from him.

Freeman left the Senatorial Office Building, wanting nothing more to do with it than destroy it. He needed help to do this, which he couldn't possibly find in Washington. As he ran for his car to flee the city, an incredible change in weather assaulted him. This July day began with a glorious dawn, but it was now engulfed in a bizarre Arctic blizzard. Large snowflakes whipped through the air, covering everything with a pristine white blanket. Freeman was mesmerized. It was as if the sordid city was being smothered by a force of nature greater than it.

A sheet of paper that the wintry gale blew past him broke his reverie. He instinctively grabbed it. It bore elegant handwriting that read, "The devil is powerless against a thinking man. I retrieved this for you." These words were scrawled across the contract through which he had traded his soul to the Devil for a few more years of apathetic earthly life. A large "void" was stamped across it. Further down were more handwritten words. "If the departed are able to care for things of this world, every action of your life will be under my regard." Freeman's spirits soared when he saw Thomas Jefferson's bold signature emblazoned on the voided contract, as if Mephistopheles had been beaten back by a pen stroke of the same immortal man who wrote the Declaration of American Independence.

Burning desire to escape Washington consumed Freeman like an infectious madness. He jumped into his car and careened through the early morning streets, oblivious to the treacherous conditions. He lurched onto the freeway, accelerating against the gravitational pull of the deadly swamp he was fleeing. There was no enslaving him any more. The deepening snow squelched Washington's powerful vortex, and the fire burning in his soul dwarfed its sucking, swirling deadliness. He did not look back, recalling the biblical admonition.

Suddenly, as soon as he pulled free of Washington, the snowstorm evaporated into the blazing sunshine of the real America. The spiritless non-America he used to know in the city remained suffocated by nature's snowy funeral shroud. As visionary passion pounded in his heart, he planned the next steps that would consume him. He needed to quit his immoral job as the Honcho's public relations liaison. He needed to get a videotape of Jefferson's trial and distribute it to the American people. He needed to contact Cassandra to tell her of his spiritual salvation. Most importantly, it was his turn to fight the eternal battle. He smiled, as could only a man who was completely free and alive with purpose, while his memory replayed a slice of history from two millennia ago:

> *". . . . a cosmic wrestling match was being furiously waged while the dagger, nominally in the hands of Brutus, was plunging toward a body nominally inhabited by Caesar. This match had been repeated many times throughout history, and would be repeated many times henceforth. While Cassandra screamed into the ears of Brutus to hurry his downward thrust, Mephistopheles frantically worked to rescue the soul of Caesar and the Head Honcho, who were one and the same. Cassandra screamed louder. Satan evoked every nuance of his black magic. Something had to give. . . . "*

The beginning. . . .